THE ROWEN
JC RYAN

By JC Ryan

Rossler Foundation Mysteries

The Tenth Cycle

Ninth Cycle Antarctica

Genetic Bullets

The Sword of Cyrus

The Skywalkers

The Phoenix Agenda

The Rowen

Termination

Vinci Books

vinci-books.com

Published by Vinci Books Ltd in 2025

1

Copyright © JC Ryan 2017

The author has asserted their moral right to be identified as the author of this work in accordance with the Copyright, Designs and Patents Act 1988.
This work is a work of fiction. Names, characters, places and incidents are the product of the author's imagination or are used fictitiously. Any resemblance to actual persons, living or dead, places and incidents is entirely coincidental.
All rights reserved. No part of this publication may be copied, reproduced, distributed, stored in any retrieval system, or transmitted in any form or by any means, including photocopying, recording, or other electronic or mechanical methods, nor used as a source for any form of machine learning including AI datasets, without the prior written permission of the publisher.
The publisher and the author have made every effort to obtain permissions for any third party material used in this book and to comply with copyright law. Any queries in this respect should be brought to the attention of the publisher and any omissions will be corrected in future editions.
A CIP catalogue record for this book is available from the British Library.
Paperback ISBN: 9781036700447

The EU GPSR authorised representative is Logos Europe, 9 rue Nicolas Poussion, 17000 La Rochelle, France
contact@logoseurope.eu

Rowen is a word from Middle English meaning, a second growth of hay in one season, also known as the aftermath.

Part I

THE AWAKENING

Part 1

THE AWAKENING

Chapter One

THE EARTH WAS SHIFTING

June 30, 1908, Podkamennaya Tunguska River in Siberia, Russian Empire

Shadows appeared in the complete darkness as faint light began to illuminate what was hidden in the blackness. Rows and rows of neatly lined up silver, egg-like pods reflected the dim light making it slightly stronger than it would have been otherwise. Each elongated pod rested horizontally on a sturdy stand and had a small panel on one side, some with glowing lights, and some without. On one of the pods the lights on the panel were bright and flashing, and with a quiet hiss, the transparent top of the pod began to move. It slid halfway down the eight-foot length of itself revealing the body of a man, dark hair, and a clean-shaven, chiseled face. The man moved, sitting up, revealing a well-muscled upper torso and arms, bearing the scars of many battles.

Emerging slowly from his pod, he blinked in the dim light, the skin of his bare chest prickling in the crisp air. He found himself in a large, cavernous room and felt uneasy.

Looking around, seeking the source of his disquiet, he eyed the other pods in the room as his memories flooded back.

Ligator! Where is Ligator?

As the commander, the awakening routine had been programmed to activate Ligator's pod and awaken him first; then it would be up to him to decide if he should awaken his second in command.

Where is Ligator?

He stared at the pod next to his and saw that it remained sealed, its control panel lights still dark.

Ligator's pod must have malfunctioned.

Another wave of anxiety hit him. The wake sequence was programmed to trigger only in two instances—when a new and advanced human society found them or when there was an imminent natural threat that could destroy them.

Which one is it; clever humans or a threat from nature?

I must get to the control room to see what has triggered the waking cycle.

He disconnected the tubes and wires connected to his body and climbed out of the pod. The pods were designed to sustain life while the body was in a deep, near-death sleep, for up to a hundred thousand years. Necessary sustenance and periodic stimulations to keep the muscles strong and moveable, ensured the person would awaken invigorated and alert.

He looked into Ligator's pod; there was only a small pile of what looked like dust and debris—no body. He took in a sharp breath.

Ligator is dead. I am in command now.

How long has it been? It must be less than a hundred thousand years but...

He shivered as he approached the lockers on the far

wall. He was looking forward to the warmth of coverings and the security of his weapon.

He opened the airtight locker where his personal items had been stored before entering the pod and dressed in a black shirt and black pants— the uniform of a soldier of the Eighth Cycle. He sat on the nearby bench to put on his boots and then returned to the locker for his weapon.

The small silver and black cylinder, about an inch in diameter, fitted easily and comfortably in his hand. It was a powerful weapon that accurately fired an invisible, deadly pulse, capable of incinerating a target, leaving only a heap of ash with no chance for re-animation. It was a close-quarters weapon—ideal in a facility like this. For now, there was no need to retrieve one of the long-range weapons.

Feeling warmer and more secure in clothes and with a weapon in hand, he headed for the control room after triggering the awakening cycle on a pod across from his. It was standard procedure to always have at least two officers in every operational detachment at all times.

Soltan is intelligent and capable. I'll promote him to second in command—he will serve me well.

By the time he left the pod room the lights had come to full illumination, allowing him to see clearly. He moved quickly but cautiously through the deserted hallways.

If someone has entered the facility, where would they be?

Pausing frequently to listen for voices or sounds of movement, he worked his way toward the central hub. The emptiness and absolute silence, almost hurting his ears, left him with an eerie, surreal feeling.

The closer he got to the central complex without detecting any sign of life, the tenser he became.

Where are they?
Are they hiding?

Why would they hide if they think this facility is deserted?

He slowed as he entered the large hub and then even more as he approached the corridor leading to the control center—every muscle in his body on alert, his weapon raised and ready to fire.

Warily, he stole down the corridor, stopping every other step to listen and check behind him. Finally, he reached the door to the control room and leaned against it, listening for noises in the room but hearing only silence. An apprehensive tingle started at the base of his spine and worked its way up his back, making the hair on the back of his neck prickle.

I don't like this.

Something is wrong here.

Gently he tested the square, palm-size gray pad next to the door. As designed, it responded to the pressure of his hand and he saw the door start to move. He took a step back and raised his weapon.

He checked the corridor again.

It's too quiet in here.

Stepping over the threshold, his eyes darted around the room—nothing. He moved forward. Nothing out of the ordinary caught his eyes, but then this wasn't his installation—he didn't know much about it. Every one of them, including the captured scientists and civilians, had been put into the deep sleep cycle shortly after attacking and overpowering the facility. There had been no time for them to familiarize themselves with the place.

One by one, he examined the multitude of panels, screens, switches, and lights.

Something is wrong. What is it?

He felt a tingling sensation under his feet—it grew

stronger, and suddenly he lost his balance as the floor moved under his feet.

The Earth is shifting!

Regaining his feet, he noticed a green light glowing on one of the panels on the wall to his left. Approaching to examine, it appeared to be a monitoring and control panel. There were four tall, rectangular displays side by side on the panel that appeared to be some kind of gage. Each display was divided into four equal vertical sections holding four similarly colored lights. Blue at the bottom followed by green, amber, and red at the top.

To the left of each gage, corresponding to the colored lights were labels with numbers. Next to blue was 0 – 1, green was 1 – 2, Amber 2 - 3 and red was labeled 3 – 4. A narrow line, probably made of metal, hovered horizontally over the colored lights and appeared to be made to move up and down the stack in response to some stimulus.

Below each rectangular display were a set of dials that he surmised were used for making adjustments to whatever the displays were monitoring.

On the first display, the one to the left, the light was green; on the others, the lights were blue. The line on the first gage hovered over the middle of the green section. His eyes darted to the other gages, similar to the one he just inspected. The needles on them were all hovering near the bottom of the displays in the lower portion of the blue sector.

The only one that's different is the green one; Why?

He paced the room, clueless, checking gauges and equipment. Returning to check the first gauge after every few paces, he noticed it continued a slow climb through the green sector toward the amber sector.

I'm a soldier, not a scientist. How am I supposed to know what to do?

There is some kind of threat lurking—that much I know.

"There are no other humans here. It must be another type of threat then," he mumbled.

He checked the green gauge again, noticing it had moved up again, almost touching the amber section now—that spurred him into action.

Returning to the pod room quickly, he checked the panel on Soltan's pod noting that the cycle was progressing without problems.

Although Viktor knew the deep sleep procedure was technically sophisticated, it was fairly simple to enact, even for a layperson. He recited the process mentally just to be sure he would recognize a problem if one arose.

A person entering the deep sleep was placed in a pod and hooked up to an intravenous drip that released an anesthetic to render the person unconscious before a very cold fluid with a high concentration of oxygen filled the pod, and the person began breathing it.

A drug was then administered to stop the heart, and the blood siphoned from the body and stored, in a frozen state, in a container inside the lining of the pod. Artificial blood, filled with nutrients that would keep the muscles strong and joints flexible, was put back into the body to slowly circulate throughout for as long as it remained in the deep sleep.

Finally, micro electrical stimulations, continuously sent to the brain through tiny electrodes that penetrated the skull at the temples, kept the brain unconscious but alive and ready to function when the person awoke.

When awakening someone out of the deep sleep, the process was reversed. The liquid inside the pod, the chemical inside the body, and the person's real blood would be warmed; the electrical stimulation would increase in strength, and when the liquid in the pod reached the specified core body temperature, the artificial blood would be removed and replaced with the person's real blood.

The liquid in the pod would drain out and be suctioned out of the lungs. Then the heart would be restarted through electrical and chemical stimulation while brain wave stimulation continued to increase.

Soltan would be awake soon—which was not soon enough, but he knew he could not interfere with the process. Not unless he wanted to turn Soltan into a pile of dust like the hapless Ligator.

I need another brain here to help me figure out what is happening.

But Soltan is a soldier, he probably understands as much as or less than I do.

He turned and approached a pod at the far end of the room, hesitated for a moment, and pressed the button to begin the awakening cycle. It would take time for the woman to regain consciousness and be able to leave the pod —all he could do was wait.

"Don't want any more dust heaps, especially not this scientist. We need her now." He muttered as he started pacing impatiently again.

How long have we been asleep?

What is happening outside?

Or perhaps I should first ask; what has happened outside while I was asleep?

This L'gundo scientist might have the answers to those questions.

Soltan, a tall, blond haired man whose physique easily matched his in comeliness and strength, emerged from his pod.

"Viktor," Soltan shouted from inside his pod, "good to see you!"

Viktor moved quickly to Soltan's pod when he heard it opening, "good to see you too my friend."

"Do you know how long we've been asleep? How long have you been awake? Where are the others? Where is Ligator?" Soltan fired off a barrage of questions.

Shaking his head, Viktor replied, "Ligator's pod malfunctioned, he is dead. I've only been awake a short while, so I don't know how much time has passed. You are the second to awake. There is a problem in the control room—the pressure is rising in something, at least that's what I think is happening. Do you know anything about the technology in this place?"

"No idea—I'm a soldier like you. I can fight, destroy, and kill—I don't know how to fix things. Do you have any ideas?" Soltan said as Viktor assisted him to climb out of the pod.

"I don't know anything about the equipment in this installation. I've started the awakening cycle on one of the L'gundo pods; the woman scientist we captured when we took control of this place. She should know what the readings mean and what actions to take."

While the awakening cycle on the woman's pod progressed, Soltan followed Viktor as he strolled among the one hundred pods, carefully checking the status on each of them. Viktor was pleased to find that only Ligator's and two others had malfunctioned.

When the familiar hiss announced that the awakening cycle for the L'gundo woman was complete, he drew his weapon and carefully moved toward it just as the cover came fully open.

He drew in a sudden breath as a dark-haired woman sat up exposing her stunning, bare upper body to his view. Viktor swallowed hard, barely noticing her beautiful lips and brown eyes as he focused on her perfectly shaped breasts, staring at the nipples, hardened from the cold. He felt his groin respond to the beauty and fitness of her young luscious-looking athletic body as she clambered out of the pod. She was a little on the shorter side of average height with well-muscled legs and hips, firm buttocks, and luring skin that looked too soft and smooth not to touch.

She turned to face him and, recognizing him she frowned, hatred and anger immediately washed over her face.

"You," She hissed through her teeth.

"Yes. Me." Viktor replied as he leveled his weapon at her. "There is a problem in the control room—the pressure is rising in something. I need your help."

"How long—"

"I don't know. I've only had time to check the equipment and wake you and Soltan up."

She gave the tall, dark haired man a withering look, hate radiating from her eyes. "You are the one called Viktor, are you not?" She hissed.

With a slight incline of his head he answered, "Yes, I am Viktor."

She exploded in rage. "You and your soldiers came in here and killed everyone, including my son. Then you reanimated us and put us into the deep sleep. Where is my son? And what makes you imagine I would want to help you?"

"The reason you will want to help me is simple—if you don't, we might all be dead soon, this time forever, and that includes your son."

"Where is my son? Where is the rest of my team?"

Viktor pointed to the pod next to hers, "Your son." He said and then waved his hand at the rest of the pods in the row, "The surviving members of your team. And we," he pointed to Soltan and himself, "are the only ones who have the code that can start their wake-up routine."

"Then start it," the woman snapped.

"Yes, of course, I will—" he paused for a few moments, smirking, "just as soon as you have resolved the technical problems, and not one moment before. Understood?"

She glowered at him. "Well, *Viktor*," she emphasized his name with hostility, "in that case—I am Telestra, and I suggest you let me put on some clothes, and we go have a look at the problem."

Two more worrying earth trembles shook the place while Telestra was busy reviewing the data retrieved from the control room.

Soltan had forced his way into the storage area, and one of the sealed food storage boxes. He brought back packages of preserved food. He and Viktor were sitting at the round, white, marble table in the control room eating from bowls that contained a green colored mushy looking substance.

Telestra joined them at the table. "What is that?" she asked indicating the green mush that was rapidly disappearing into their mouths.

"Vegetables," Soltan responded, "ugly, tasteless, and nourishing vegetables."

Without looking up from the food in front of him, Viktor added, "Between the chemical preservatives and the flash freeze-dry process it leaves everything tasteless. By the time they get through pulverizing it with the vitamin additives, you can't tell what you're eating. But it keeps you alive and..."

When he looked up from his bowl, Viktor noted

Telestra's worried expression, paused mid-sentence and asked, "What's going on?"

"This installation was built at this location because of the subterranean volcanic activity that occurs here. All the power for the facility comes from the hot gasses released by the magma from the mantle. Those gasses flow through the four natural fissures that occur here and our equipment harnesses the gas, controls the flow of it, and utilizes it to generate power to the facility. One of the flow regulator valve mechanisms has failed, and pressure is building up in the other fissures as a result."

"What does this mean?"

"It means that if that regulator isn't repaired, and very quickly, there will be a devastating explosion and this installation will be blown into pieces; very small, very hot pieces, as a new volcano is born."

Soltan stared at her—alarmed. "Can you repair it?"

"Definitely not by myself; the pressure is already dangerously high in fissure three and starting to rise in fissures two and four. I'm not sure if it can be stopped in time."

"What do you need?" Viktor asked.

"I need my colleagues; they know how to operate this equipment. Did you happen to leave any of them alive?" she asked sarcastically.

Viktor clenched his jaw and narrowed his eyes at her. "There are some."

"Then I suggest you wake them up so we can get to work." She had a slight grin when she added, "unless you want to be dead—forever."

Viktor stood up and moved as if to examine the gauges again. *If I wake up more of the L'gundo, will Soltan and I be able to keep control?* He weighed his options while pacing the room.

Telestra went back to the control panel and studied the gauges.

Soltan joined him and matched his steps. He whispered, "I think we'd better wake the L'gundo scientists."

"That goes without saying. The challenge is maintaining control over them after they have been awakened." Viktor spoke softly and slowly. "Go to the pod room and wake twenty of our soldiers. When the soldiers' wake-up cycle is halfway done, start the cycles on ten of the L'gundo scientists. Stay there and when our soldiers are awake, apprise them of the situation and give them their orders. But don't wake up her son—under any circumstances."

"On my way," Soltan acknowledged, turning to leave the control center.

Telestra wiped the sweat from her brow. It was already too hot in the fissure access area. She had been examining the malfunctioning mechanism and thought they were going to be lucky if they could save the installation. She had already concluded that they would probably be unable to stop the explosion. Her highest priority was to wake up her son and as many as possible of her team and then try to escape.

I need my son, and I need my team, and I need them now! She thought with frustration, but there was no hurrying the awakening process—doing so had ghastly consequences as they had learned while developing the process. She had seen the dusty remains in two of the pods on her way out of the pod room earlier.

She slowly walked the edges of the access area weighing her options—working on a plan. Wondering if she had considered everything—maybe she *could* stop the explosion.

But she wouldn't know that without having her team around her. The rock walls of the fissure access cavern were a stark contrast to the immaculate white walls of the rest of the facility. Here in this rough, dirty, cavern was the raw power that provided them with clean, comfortable living spaces and all the energy they needed to run the facility. Staring at the rock walls and knowing the fissures that were behind them made her marvel, not just at the force of the Earth itself, but the ingenuity of her ancestors who learned to harness the power of a forming volcano and tame it for their use.

These fissures are just the tip; they extend down for hundreds of miles to the mantle. Gas that was stored as a fluid, more than 1,800 miles below the earth's crust, was seeping through the mantle into the fissures. If not for my ancestors learning to control the flow of the gas, it would have grown to become a volcano, spewing toxic gasses and molten lava onto the surface of the planet.

As another tremor rolled through the Earth, it was a relief to hear the stumbling footsteps of her colleagues, herded by the soldiers. Her heart dropped when she noticed her son was not amongst them.

"Where is my son?" She asked fiercely.

"He's not a scientist." Viktor retorted. "He will be awakened only when you and your team have fixed this problem. Now get on with it."

Telestra's eyes were filled with fury as she fought against the impulse to jump on Viktor like a tigress and rip his throat out.

Her team, blinking and confused, gathered around her to hear what she had to say. There was no time to talk about anything else. Viktor stood nearby leaning against the rock wall, arms folded over his chest.

Slowly she got her emotions under control and started

talking to her team. "Here's the situation. Due to a shift in the fissure, most likely caused by the recent tremors, the flow regulator valves in Fissure One have been crushed in a closed position—blocking all flow."

The entire team looked alarmed, instantly recognizing it could not be repaired. They began talking nervously among themselves.

Soltan and some of the soldiers saw their anxiety and looked to Viktor for his reaction.

Viktor presented a calm front to his men, but he felt the muscles in his gut tightening. *If the L'gundo are this worried, it must be more critical than I thought.*

"Settle down everyone, settle down," Telestra commanded. "Fissure Three is amber, and Fissures Two and Four are green. I need you to organize yourselves into four teams." She gave them a few moments to organize themselves into the requested teams.

"Team one." Two people stepped forward. "Look at Fissure One and see if you can find a way to open those flow regulator valves." The two team members looked at each other in disbelief. The regulator was crushed—it could not be repaired. What was she thinking? They would have to look for alternatives.

"Team two." Three people stepped forward. "Work on releasing some of the pressure from Fissure Three." They looked at one another in dismay. This was a dangerous assignment and almost certainly meant death. Should the pressure reach critical levels while they were inside the fissure they wouldn't have time to… well, they just wouldn't have time for anything.

"Teams three and four," four people stepped forward in sets of two. "You work on Fissures Two and Four, coordinate with Team Two to try to divert some pressure from Fissure Three and funnel it through Fissures Two and Four. Dekka and I will go up to monitor and assist you from the control room."

She saw Dekka look at her sharply, but she didn't acknowledge him—she hoped none of Viktor's men noticed. Dekka wasn't a geological scientist; he was a biomechanical engineer who worked with nanotechnology. If there was an explosion, the control room might survive, and if it did, she would need his expertise.

Viktor snapped a look at her, suddenly alert, "No! All of you L'gundo will stay down here and work; none of you are going to be allowed in the control room."

Telestra rounded on him, "Excuse me? I thought you wanted help with this problem."

"You will all work from down here." Viktor snapped. He didn't like being challenged in front of his men.

"Do you or any of your soldiers know how to interpret the readings on our equipment and make the necessary adjustments as they are needed?" She snapped back.

"No. But you can monitor and make adjustments from here." *Soldier mentality—give them command, and it goes to their head.*

"Look, Viktor," she fairly spat the words at him. "That is *not* an option. The equipment can be adjusted from here, but the main controls, readouts, and programmed adjustments are in the control room—the two *have* to be worked in conjunction.

"You are going to *have* to allow at least the two of us into the control room—there should be four of us, but two is the bare minimum."

Viktor hesitated. He didn't want the L'gundo to have

access to the control room. He didn't know enough about it and wasn't sure what they might be able to do with what was accessible on the many panels. "You, Telestra, may work from the control room, but no one else."

"I assume you like the idea of a hot molten lava-lined casket then, because that's what this place is going to be for all of us."

"I think you are making more out of this than it really is to trick us and regain control of the installation."

"You are a fool!" she exploded in exasperation.

"Then explain the situation to me so that I can understand it."

"We don't have time for this!"

"We will make the time."

"Fine, send Dekka to the control room so he can get started, and I will explain this to you." *I just hope Dekka will be able to fake his way through it for a few minutes until I can convince this idiot.*

Viktor nodded his agreement. "Soltan, take a soldier with you and take Dekka to the control room. Monitor what he does and if he tries anything stupid—kill him, and I mean kill him forever."

Telestra and Dekka looked at each other in disbelief and shook their heads. Then Dekka turned and followed Soltan and another soldier as they left for the control room. "Good luck," Dekka mumbled, "you're going to need it."

"Teams, get moving!" Telestra said as she glowered at Viktor.

The teams scattered to the nearby lockers and under the watchful eyes of the soldiers, gathered their equipment, donned their protective suits and headed into the fissure accesses.

"Alright, Viktor, here's a quick science lesson for you,"

Telestra was furious, and she made no attempt to hide her disdain as she spoke measuredly. "This facility collects and disperses highly volatile gasses from the magma in the Earth's mantle. This is done by sealing off and controlling the gas released from the four natural fissure vents that are present here. The flow regulators are what control the flow of the gases and thus the pressure in each fissure.

"If the flow is not regulated properly to control the pressure it will cause a devastating explosion.

"There are four zones, or pressure levels, and a color associated with each one. In the normal operational zone, the pressure level is between zero and one and is colored blue. On occasion, more power is necessary, and the pressure is allowed to rise to level two, this is the warning zone and colored green.

"The danger zone, between level two and three, is colored amber. The only time the pressure reaches this level is when something has malfunctioned. If the pressure reaches level three, red, a blast is imminent.

"Right now, the pressure in Fissure Three is approaching level three, the red level. If you have paid any attention to what I've just told you; can you tell me what that means?"

Viktor didn't reply, he grabbed her arm, turned, and dragged her toward the control room.

Telestra watched in horror as the pressure in Fissure Three reached the mid-point of level three. She had no idea what was preventing the explosion, but she was now sure it was coming.

"Get them out of there!" she screamed. "Get them out

of there!" Her fear for her colleagues and friends working in the fissures was palpable.

"No. Keep working. You have to stop this!" Viktor yelled.

The argument had started a short time ago when Fissure Three had reached level three. Telestra and Dekka both knew they were fighting a losing battle and had tried to reason with Viktor but to no avail.

Dekka shouted, "There is no stopping this you idiot! The ground tremors have caused physical shifts in the fissure, there is no way of unlocking those flow regulator valves, and the relief systems are at maximum capacity."

Viktor grabbed Dekka by the front of his shirt with his left hand and clenched his other fist to punch Dekka in the face, but the sound of rumbling stopped him as the tremor rolled under their feet and through the rock walls, stronger than ever before.

"The explosion is about to happen! If you don't get them all out of there, they will die! Get them out and seal off the facility or we will all die!" Dekka yelled.

Viktor glanced over at the pressure gauges. Fissure Three's indicator was red—in the blast zone—Fissures Two and Four were both amber and nearing the red line.

"Evacuate!" He shouted. "Then seal off the facility."

Soltan repeated the command over the intercom. He, Viktor, Telestra, and Dekka watched on the video feed as the scientists and soldiers scampered out of the fissure access area.

Telestra gave a sigh of relief, but it was premature. Another tremor rumbled through the ground, and she saw the telltale signs near the opening of Fissure Three. A soft glow had appeared, and although she couldn't hear it, she could see on the faces of those remaining in the access area that they could hear the hiss and pop as the gases began to ignite.

"Run!" she screamed.

Chapter Two

A BRIGHT FLASH CAME FROM THE SKY

The forest is unusually quiet, lifeless. Petya thought as he shouldered his rifle and paused to listen for the sounds of animals. He heard nothing; no birdsong, no scuttling of small animals in the underbrush, not even a breeze stirring the leaves of the trees. *I haven't seen or heard any animals all morning—strange.*

Sunshine brightened his brown hair and warmed his thin face and arms. Petya was small for his age, but he was a skilled hunter, never failing to bring home food to help feed the family. Not many thirteen-year-olds were as dedicated to helping their families as he was; his parents took great pride in him.

He left the house in Moga Village early this June morning, to hunt for game near the Tunguska River. By sun-up, he had traveled nearly three miles.

Standing on a rocky ridge, he surveyed the area around him for any sign of wildlife. The forest was a dark summer-green, as it should be this time of year, the sky a beautiful blue—unblemished by clouds.

The Rowen

There should be a breeze and birds soaring on the currents. Where is everything?

Then the ground shifted under his feet. It was the third time this morning he had felt the tremors. This time it seemed stronger than before.

Perhaps the tremors are frightening the animals, and they have all gone into hiding.

As he picked his way across the ridge, an unfamiliar feeling of fear started to spread through him.

What's wrong with me?

There is nothing for me to fear out here!

He continued to move, stumbling as another, stronger, tremor rolled through the ground. A sudden impulse to run like a frightened animal filled him despite his earlier assurances to himself—he quickened his pace. The fear in him grew into terror; he broke into a run as if driven from the ridge by an invisible force.

Just as he reached the edge of the forest, a bright flash came from the sky turning everything red—the sky, the earth, rocks, and trees. He heard a rumbling sound in the distance that quickly grew in volume; the ground began to shake violently. The wind picked up, quickly growing to hurricane force as Petya staggered toward the shelter offered by the large trunk of a fallen tree.

Diving to the ground next to the trunk, he noticed a burning pillar of fire in the sky and felt the air grow warmer, becoming hot as it blew over his body. He heard several loud booms like huge cannons, followed by the deafening roar of thunder. The ground continued to shake forcefully, and the wind whipped around him. He saw trees blow over in the distance.

What is happening?

Petya scooted closer to the trunk and found a depression

into which he quickly slipped his thin body, with the huge old tree as a shelter over him. Feeling a little safer, he closed his eyes against the searing light and covered his ears to shield them from the frightening noise.

After what seemed like an eternity, the shaking ground quieted, the wind slowly began to die down, and the roaring subsided.

Just as he was crawling out from under the trunk he heard several more loud bangs, looked up, and saw blazing objects raining down from the sky landing around him. A small piece hit his arm, and he yelled out in pain as it burned through his skin. He quickly scrambled back under the tree trunk hoping it would continue to protect him.

Fires were burning in the distance causing a glow in the sky.

Will this never end?

Is this the end of our world as the prophets predicted?

Chapter Three

LET'S GET THIS DONE

Telestra blinked her eyes against the settling dust and tried to remember where she was. She was lying face down on a hard, white surface and it took her a moment to realize she was on the floor. She heard coughing somewhere to her left and someone groaning nearby.

Explosion. The gas ignited. I'm in the control room. Survivors! Deszik! My son! I have to get up!

She pushed against the floor and carefully came to a kneeling position. Her head spun as she gazed around the room which was lit by the soft glow of emergency lighting. Most of the equipment panels were dark; a few still flickered. She cringed as a piece of the ceiling gave way and crashed to the floor on the opposite side of the room.

Grabbing the countertop next to her tightly, she pulled herself to her feet and winced when she tried to put weight on her right ankle. *I must have twisted it when I fell. It doesn't feel broken, but it hurts.*

She saw Dekka trying to rise from the floor and limped over to help him. He was coughing and holding his left arm against his chest. It was bent at an odd angle and the tip of a bone protruded through the skin near his wrist.

"My arm is broken," he coughed.

"Yes, I see that. Here," she offered her hand, "let me help you up."

He accepted her hand, and after raising him from the floor, she righted a chair and helped him sat down.

"The others?" he asked, jerking his chin toward Viktor, Soltan, and the soldier.

Telestra went to examine them. As she bent over Viktor, his eyes flickered, and he groaned.

Where is his weapon? I need it before he is fully conscious!

She looked around him but couldn't find it. Just as she was about to give up, she spotted the weapon and reached for it.

"Don't bother." A voice commanded.

She looked up and froze. Soltan was pointing his weapon at her.

"Back away."

Viktor was stirring behind her.

"Help him up," Soltan commanded.

Telestra grudgingly assisted a disoriented Viktor to a chair; blood was dripping from his head. "He needs medical attention—we all do."

Indicating the unconscious soldier on the floor, half buried by a piece of equipment, Soltan ordered, "Check him."

With difficulty, she maneuvered around the fallen equipment. One look at the soldier's head told her all she needed to know. "The equipment must have hit him when it collapsed; he's dead."

"Did anyone else survive?" Dekka asked.

"I don't know," Telestra replied as she moved toward the

access room monitors. All of them were dark, except one that was giving off a blinking red glow. "It looks like the fissures have filled with lava that has flowed into the access room. If there are any survivors, they won't be in there."

She moved toward the door.

"Where do you think, you're going?" Soltan asked.

"To find my son."

"No. You will stay here and attend to Viktor."

"Try and stop me," she said, continuing toward the door.

He pointed his weapon at Dekka. "How about I kill him?"

She stopped. "That won't be necessary."

"How about we all go to the medical station, get what we need, and then see to the survivors," Dekka suggested in an attempt to defuse the tension.

Viktor, who had regained full awareness, mumbled. "Yes, that is what we will do."

With Viktor leaning heavily on Soltan, and Dekka assisting Telestra while protecting his injured arm, they made their way out of the control room and into the hallway. Parts of the ceiling were hanging, and other parts had tumbled down completely; in some areas, the collapsed walls revealed the rocky structure behind them. Rocks and debris partially blocked the hallway.

The emergency lighting was dim, in some places nonexistent; they had to pick their way carefully through the mess. Dekka stepped around a boulder and nearly fell to his death—a chasm had opened in the floor. They placed some of the fallen ceiling beams across it before continuing further.

When they reached the central area, they found it damaged beyond recognition. It would be a long time, if ever before people would be able to use it again.

They finally reached the medical station where Dekka started treating their wounds. First, he wrapped the malleable material of a portable mendar —a healing stimulator—around his arm to let it fuse the broken bone back together. Then he put a similar unit on Telestra's ankle, which would rapidly restore the injured muscle and tendons.

He used the V-scanner, a small handheld ultrasound imaging device, to check Viktor's head wound but found no severe damage. A few passes of the Sealer over the wound stopped the bleeding and sealed it. He handed Viktor a small cloth and pointed toward a counter.

"I set some disinfectant cleanser on the counter over there; you can use it to clean yourself up while I tend to the rest of us."

Viktor scowled at him and moved off toward the counter.

Except for a few minor scratches and some dust in his eyes, Soltan came through it unharmed.

"You can use the cleanser to treat your scratches. There's some eye wash that will help remove the dust from your eyes. The liquid bonds with the dust particles lubricating your eyes, soothes the itching, and then takes the particles with it as it leaves your eye."

Soltan nodded at Dekka and stepped over beside Viktor, who had turned around to keep watch on the two L'gundo scientists.

"Telestra, your ankle wasn't broken. The mendar should have healed the muscle and tendons by now," Dekka said as he removed the portable mendar from her leg.

Looking at Viktor, he said, "My arm will need a little while longer to heal completely, but I can take this with me, and we can leave if you're ready to look for other survivors."

"I want to find my son," Telestra said solemnly.

Viktor fixed his eyes on Telestra as he walked up to her. "We will look for your boy later. First, we will look for other survivors that might need medical attention."

"I will look for my son now—alone if necessary—now, not later," Telestra said with vehemence as she started for the door.

"You will do as I say!" Viktor roared, grabbing her by the arm.

"Get your hands off of me!"

"Telestra," Dekka interjected, "Deszik is in a pod. If the pod survived the explosion, he is safe—if it did not, he is beyond your help—beyond anyone's help."

She slumped against the wall, crying, "I just want to see my son, to know for sure he is safe."

Dekka squatted next to her and whispered, "The quicker we do as he says, the quicker we can go and look for your son."

She nodded, wiping her eyes and sighed, "Let's get this done."

The four of them returned to the hallway, working their way toward the fissure access area.

Chapter Four

SHE DIDN'T RESIST

Petya crawled slowly and painfully from his shelter under the log. He blinked as he stood to look around him. The trees were leaning at severe angles, small bushes had been uprooted, and all the grass appeared withered and dry as if it had been in a drought.

What happened?

The skin on the exposed side of his body was bright red as if sunburned, and small blisters appeared in places. They were painful, but he was curious to see what had happened and set off walking in the direction from which he thought the bright flash had come.

He traveled quite a distance seeing the devastation to the forest increase almost with every step. By the time he reached an area where all the trees had been blown to the ground and charred, he was feeling nauseous and had a headache. He took a few steps into the area of the fallen trees—there were thousands of them, and the ground was rocky where the wind had swept it nearly clean of soil. It was getting late in the day, and the sky was dark even though a strange glow illuminated the Earth as far as he could see. He felt dizzy and weak and realized he needed water and a place to rest for the night. An odd-looking object in the distance caught his eye. *It might provide shelter,* he thought, as he moved toward it.

It took him fifteen minutes to reach the smooth, dome-like structure. It appeared to be made of metal and had an opening that Petya stepped into. The hollow under the dome was smooth and slightly warm to the touch, the ground inside was flat.

This will be a good shelter for the night.

Petya lay down on the ground, using his pack as a pillow and fell asleep.

Telestra was in her bed, quietly staring at the ceiling. The rescue efforts, medical treatments, and finding the corridor to the pod cavern blocked had exhausted her physically and emotionally. She was so tired she didn't have the strength to cry.

Oh, Deszik, are you still alive, my son?

As they had explored the facility on their way to the fissure access area, they were dismayed at the enormity of damage to the place. Very little was left intact; hallways were blocked, cutting off entire areas of the installation. Floors had opened up in chasms, making passage challenging and treacherous, if not entirely impassable. Ceilings had caved in, equipment was damaged, and entire rooms had completely collapsed on themselves. Repairs would be difficult and time-consuming, if at all possible.

Halfway to the fissure access area, they found the first survivors. Two guards had been pinned under a collapsed wall. They were unconscious, but some liquid from the medical case Dekka carried, brought them around. Once the fallen wall had been removed, it was found that their injuries were minor scrapes and bruises, and they were able to help look for more survivors.

They found eleven more survivors; six soldiers and five scientists had made it out of the fissure access area before the heavy doors had sealed it off from the rest of the facility. Those nearest the door, two scientists and a soldier, were badly burned, and had many broken bones and internal injuries from falling rock. The other six suffered minor burns, a few broken bones, and many scrapes and bruises.

It took most of the day to stabilize and move the injured to a temporary infirmary that Viktor had ordered Telestra and Dekka to set up. Treatment of the severely burned had gone long into the night. When Dekka finally said it was safe to leave them to rest, Telestra had begged Viktor to allow her to look for her son. He had finally relented and accompanied her, along with two soldiers, but only to check to see if the pods survived the explosion—not to awaken her son.

It had been devastating to turn the corner in the corridor near the pod cavern entrance only to find that the entire ceiling had collapsed, filling the space, and blocking all access to the doors. She had sunk to the floor in dismay, and although Viktor had helped her to her feet and led her back to the temporary infirmary, there was no tenderness in his touch.

"Let me give you a sedative to help you relax." It was Dekka. He had come to check on her.

"No, I'll be fine."

"Telestra, you will need your strength tomorrow and in the days to come. Going without sleep will not help you."

"I'm fine." She insisted.

"Please, let me help you."

She began to sob. "I just want my son," she said through her tears as she rolled onto her side.

"I know," she heard Dekka murmur and felt the slight cool pressure of the injection as the medication entered her upper arm.

She didn't resist.

Chapter Five

WE WILL RULE THE WORLD

"Soltan, take Santosh with you and see if you can reach the surface. We need to find out what is happening on the outside," Viktor ordered.

Telestra awoke with a start as she heard Viktor's voice.

"On my way," Soltan replied.

Telestra sat up, looking around in confusion—it took several moments to get her bearings and remember where she was and what had happened. As soon as she remembered, she wanted to lie back down and forget about everything.

"How do you feel?" Dekka asked.

"Like I wish I were dead."

Dekka patted her shoulder. "It will get better."

"I wish I could believe that. I have a feeling it's going to get worse—a lot worse."

"I don't know how it could get any worse than this," he said. "Let's hope you're wrong."

She looked at him ruefully. "Let's hope."

"I could use your help checking our patients."

She stood up to join him. "Are they improving?"

"Come see."

As they moved between the patients, Telestra saw that only the three burn victims would require additional time to heal. The remaining eight were already conscious and eating some of the green mush that Soltan had found—*was it only yesterday?*

"We need access to the large Regen unit in the infirmary to treat these burn victims," Dekka said.

"We'll need to restore main power to that area to run the unit." Telestra paused and then continued in a whisper. "What is the situation with the B'ran?"

Dekka lowered his voice. "Viktor sent Soltan and one of the soldiers to try to find a way out and see if they can learn anything about what is happening on the surface. Some time ago he also sent two of the soldiers to examine the corridors to the infirmary and the pod cavern to see if it will be possible to gain entrance to either one."

"Well, at least that would be useful."

He nodded. "Access to the infirmary would definitely be helpful. I'm not too sure about the pod cavern. I've overheard him talking with Soltan, and it sounds as if they have more soldiers in those pods. We could find ourselves outnumbered again."

"I guess that is a chance we'll have to take," she shrugged, "my son is there, and I am still holding out hope he is alive. Maybe there will be more L'gundo… and maybe we will be able to wake them and overpower him and his men."

"That is a pleasant thought," Dekka smiled. "Let's not pin all our hopes on that though."

Just then, they heard footsteps approaching their area—two soldiers entered the room.

"Viktor," one of them reported, "we have examined both of the corridors as you requested. They can both be cleared with time; the easier one will be the access to the infirmary.

"Good. Take two more soldiers with you and start clearing it."

"Will do."

They chose two of their fellow soldiers that had just finished eating, waited while they dressed and then the four of them disappeared to clear the way to the infirmary.

"Well, Telestra, it seems your son will have to wait a while longer," Viktor smirked.

"Main power will have to be restored to the infirmary if you want to make full use of it," she said, turning her back on him to check on the two burned scientists, ignoring the burned soldier.

Viktor looked at the recovered scientists. "Which of you knows how to restore the power?"

The scientists looked to Telestra. She gave a slight nod.

"I can work on the power systems," Rauel spoke up.

Viktor turned to one of his soldiers, "you; take him up to the control room and watch him. Kill him if he offers any resistance or appears to attempt subterfuge."

Dekka looked at Viktor and shook his head.

Viktor grinned and sat down to await the return of his men. The lack of action frustrated him, but he refused to show it—he was careful to keep up an appearance of calm and control at all times.

It took quite a while, but the four soldiers cleared a path to the infirmary and then helped them move the three burn victims.

Telestra and Dekka carefully laid the last burn victim on a bed in the infirmary. Rauel had managed to re-establish partial main power, including to the infirmary. Dekka turned to check on the soldier in the Regen unit—Viktor insisted his soldier be treated first.

Just as they finished, Santosh returned and called Viktor aside. They were talking in quiet but excited voices; suddenly Viktor turned and left the room. "Keep your eyes on her," he said pointing to Telestra as he passed through the door.

Telestra and Dekka looked at each other. "I wonder what that's all about?" Dekka whispered.

"Whatever it is, I don't think it's good," she replied.

Within minutes, Soltan and Viktor returned with a bewildered, and terrified young boy between them.

Telestra took a sharp breath but refrained from saying anything.

"Who is that?" Dekka asked.

"We don't know. He doesn't speak our language. We found him at the entrance," Soltan said.

"Do you have a translator?" Viktor demanded.

"Yes, there is a program in the control center. If we can access it, we should be able to train it to understand each other," Telestra said.

"Let's go," Viktor ordered.

Telestra could see the boy was frightened of Viktor and his men. She smiled and slowly offered her hand, beckoning for him to follow her. He glanced around uneasily and then stepped closer to her and took her hand.

They traversed the ruined corridors to the control room where Rauel was still working to restore full power.

"If we can get him talking, the translator will analyze his speech patterns and syntax to provide a language translation for us," Telestra explained as she started the program.

"What's your name," Viktor asked abruptly causing the boy to step away from him in fear, closer to Telestra.

Viktor grabbed him by the arm, pulling him back to stand before him. "I asked you what your name is!" he said in a low, menacing tone.

The boy began to tremble but said nothing.

"You're frightening the boy," Dekka broke in. "I'll talk to him."

Viktor flushed with anger and shoved Dekka away, but Soltan stopped him.

"Let him try, Viktor, the boy is afraid of us."

Viktor let the boy's arm go and allowed Dekka to approach. He gently took the boy by the arm and led him to a chair, indicating that he should sit down.

Dekka sat in a chair across from him and looked to Telestra, who nodded confirmation that the translator program was on, and she was ready for him to proceed.

Patting himself on the chest, Dekka said "Dekka," then pointed to Telestra saying "Telestra."

The boy looked at the two of them but remained silent.

Dekka repeated the gestures and names and then pointed to the boy who still said nothing.

"Maybe he can't speak," Viktor said with an edge of frustration in his voice.

Dekka ignored Viktor and tried again; patting his chest and said, "I am Dekka." He looked at Telestra.

"I am Telestra," she spoke.

"What is your name?" Dekka asked, pointing at the boy.

There was a pause before the boy moved his hand to his chest and said, "Petya."

Dekka grinned broadly, "Well, it seems we have made a start!"

The strangers were speaking, but Petya didn't understand them, everything was strange; their clothes, this place, the machines, the lights. The tall one that appeared to be the leader frightened him, but he tried not to show it. The woman was beautiful and seemed kind, and the voice of the man before him sounded kind.

Petya gathered that the man's name was Dekka and the woman's, Telestra. *A pretty name.* Beyond that, he didn't understand anything.

When the one called Dekka spoke, it sounded to Petya like, "Wh erea rey ouf rom."

Petya shook his head "I don't understand you."

"Wh erea rey ouf rom." He repeated.

He shook his head. "I'm sorry, I don't understand you." He touched his chest and said. "My name is Petya. I'm from Moga Village. It's nearby—if you let me go, I can get home quickly. My parents will be worried about me. I won't tell anyone about you—I promise!"

Telestra, following the translator screen, asked, "Where a rey ou from?"

The boy looked at her, paused for a moment as he was playing her words over in his head and smiled.

"I – I – I'm from Moga Village."

"Morg Vilge?" Telestra asked.

"Mo—ga. Vill—age," Petya said. "I'm from Moga Village."

"Moga Village," Telestra repeated to make sure she pronounced it correct.

The boy smiled and nodded his head.

"Petya, from Moga Village." Dekka had moved over to the translator screen. "I am called Dekka, and this is my associate Telestra," he said. "These are Viktor, Soltan, and Rauel."

Petya looked around at all of them in surprise. "How can you learn my language so quickly—just a few minutes ago, I couldn't understand you?"

"We have a translator to help us." Telestra smiled as she pointed to the screen in front of her.

Looking around Petya asked, "Where am I? What is this place? Did you cause the fire in the sky?"

Telestra recognized immediately that the boy was from a less advanced culture and shook her head slightly at Dekka, indicating that he should reveal no more.

Telestra drew near and questioned, "We can answer all your questions later. First, tell us about yourself."

Petya nodded.

"Tell me about your life, Petya, what is it like?"

"I live in the village, not far from here, with my family and I hunt for food in the forest, I have two sisters and a brother, they are younger than I am."

"Are there many people in your village?"

"Not a lot, maybe a hundred or so."

"How do you travel between villages?"

"We walk mostly; those who have donkeys or horses sometimes ride."

"How do you communicate?"

Petya looked at her questioningly. "We talk; just like I'm talking to you now."

"But how do you talk to people in other villages?"

"Some people can write, and they send letters. I think some of the bigger villages and towns have a way to send words over wires but I don't know how they do it."

"I see," Telestra said. "Do you have aircraft—machines that fly in the air like birds?"

"I have heard of them but have never seen one."

"How many people are there in the world?"

Petya scoffed, "everyone knows there are millions of people in the world."

"Soltan," Viktor interrupted. "Take Dekka back to the infirmary, have one of the soldiers escort Telestra to the pod corridor, she can help them clear the hallway, and then return here to me and bring a soldier with you."

Telestra motioned for Petya to follow her.

"No," Viktor stated. "The boy stays here."

Petya looked to Telestra with fear in his eyes.

"He's no use to you," Telestra said.

"Leave him here I said," Viktor ordered.

She smiled at Petya, "it will be alright."

"You, Rule, or whatever your name is, where is the reanimation center?"

Soltan had only just stepped back into the control center with the soldier when Viktor grabbed him by the arm and steered him back out the door, ordering the soldier to guard Petya and Rauel.

"Viktor, what has happened?" he asked with alarm.

"This isn't our world or our time," Viktor replied excitedly as they strolled down the hall. "I asked the boy for the calendar time and he gave an answer that indicates this is the year 1908. I don't know what that means except that this is not even close to the world we left.

"We were put into deep-sleep in the year 26,000 of the Eighth Cycle—I have no idea what cycle this is.

"These people are just beginning to develop basic technology—they are primitive by our standards—most of them are probably uneducated, simplistic beings—easily exploited and controlled."

Soltan stopped suddenly. Viktor's mind was sharp and Soltan realized he was up to something. "What are you planning?" he asked with a slow, suspicious smile.

By the time Viktor finished telling him, Soltan wore an expression of wicked glee.

"Marvelous," he whispered almost to himself. "We will rule the world—"

Chapter Six

BIRTH OF THE RE'AN

In the days after Petya's arrival, Viktor drove the soldiers and scientists alike to clear the passageway to the pod cavern as quickly as possible. He ignored injuries, refused to let them rest, and provided little time to eat the green, foul-tasting mush that had become their only sustenance. He also had Rauel working feverishly to restore power to the entire facility.

Two of the soldiers had mysteriously disappeared at about the same time. Telestra and Dekka questioned Viktor and Soltan about the urgency to clear the hallway and the missing men, but received no answers. In their private discussions, Dekka pondered the possibilities and Telestra expressed her fear that nothing good would come from it.

A shout rang out from one of the soldiers. They'd reached the entrance of the pod cavern but could not trigger the door's opening mechanism.

One of the scientists hurried over to the access panel and triggered the mechanism manually. The door opened, and Viktor stepped through, followed closely by Soltan and Santosh.

"Deszik!" Telestra shrieked and ran toward the opening. Viktor stopped her as she forced her way through the door.

"Keep her out of here!" he shouted.

"I want to see my son!"

Soltan stepped to Viktor's side and whispered, "Perhaps it would be useful to let her verify her son is alive. If he is, we will have total control over her; if he is not, we can reprogram her."

Viktor turned to Telestra who, restrained by the arms by two of the soldiers, was struggling to free herself. He smoothed his finger across her cheek and down her jaw line and neck to her shoulder. "What is it worth to you to see your son, hmmm?"

Telestra froze and fixed Viktor with a hateful scowl. "You're despicable."

Viktor snorted, releasing her shoulder. "You have no idea how nice I can be."

"Soltan, Santosh, start the waking cycles on the pods of all the soldiers. Leave the L'gundo for now."

"I will take you to see your son Telestra, but we will not wake him."

"Thank you," Telestra whispered with tears in her eyes.

They made their way down the rows of pods to the one that Telestra knew held the body of her son. She closed her eyes before stepping beside it. *Please let it still be functional. Please let him still be alive.*

Slowly she opened her eyes and saw the face of her beloved son. "Deszik," she whispered, "Oh, Deszik; you're alive!" she cried as she leaned her body across the top of the pod.

A strong hand gripped her arm. "Okay. I've let you see

your son. Now tell me which of these pods contain scientists that are familiar with the reanimation process and equipment. I want only the ones that are capable of performing a re-animation."

"Why would you want that?"

"It doesn't matter why. Just answer my question; I think you know the consequences if you don't," he nodded significantly toward Deszik's pod.

She sighed. "Dekka is the lead reanimation scientist. His assistant was killed in your attack. Tellek and Baynor are under-assistants. They are in the two pods on the end," she indicated the row next to the far wall. "There were others, but Dekka will have to tell you who they are, I don't know."

"So, you lied to me when you told me that you needed Dekka in the control room before the explosion." He folded his arms over his chest. "Did you do that to cause the explosion?"

"No. The explosion was inevitable; there was no way to stop it since the flow regulator valves couldn't be opened. He is head of our medical unit, and I wanted to be sure he remained alive."

"I see that you are capable of, and skilled at, deception. I won't bother asking you what else you've lied about. However, understand that I have noted your deception and will take it into consideration when dealing with you in the future. Now, get out." He shoved her toward the cavern door, the soldier assigned to guard her followed. "Take her to the reanimation chamber. Don't let her talk to anyone."

"Soltan!" he shouted.

"Yes, Viktor," Soltan dashed to his side.

"Wake the scientists in those two pods," he pointed to the ones that Telestra had shown him. "Place two soldiers with them as guards. The woman says they are reanimation scientists, but I don't trust her, she has been lying to us."

Soltan nodded and started to move to the pods.

"Also, get the boy," Viktor ordered. "Bring him to me in the reanimation chamber and don't let him talk to anyone. Before you go, tell the guards to bring the scientists to the reanimation chamber when they awaken."

"On my way."

Viktor strode out of the cavern, pausing at the entrance to speak quietly with Santosh, and then he crossed the hall and stepped into the reanimation chamber.

He turned to a tall, stern-looking soldier. "Bring the L'gundo called Dekka in here."

The soldier nodded and hurried to do Viktor's bidding.

Viktor slowly paced the chamber while he waited, examining the equipment. When he heard footsteps in the hallway, he stopped and faced the entrance.

Telestra and the boy Petya stood before him, each with a guard at their side. He did not speak to them.

"What's this about?" Telestra wanted to know.

Viktor resumed his pacing without answering. Her eyes followed him around the room, but he ignored her.

Soon he heard more footsteps, and Dekka entered the room.

"Dekka; Telestra admitted she has been lying to me, that you are not a geoscientist at all, but rather the head of this facility's medical unit and the lead reanimation scientist."

Dekka looked to Telestra, who gave him a slight nod.

"Is this correct?" Viktor asked.

Hesitating for only a moment, Dekka answered, "yes, it's true."

"So, you have been part of the deception. With your

silence, you lied. I don't like liars. Fortunately for you, I have need of you, or I would kill you where you stand."

Viktor circled Dekka like a predator, allowing his words to sink in.

Dekka and Telestra looked at each other in quiet apprehension.

"Tell me, Dekka, what do these machines do?"

"This is the reanimation chamber; they make it possible to reanimate a person after death, provided that no more than half a day has passed."

"Idiot!" shouted Viktor. "I know what the reanimation process is, I am a Re'an. I want to know the purpose of each machine—what part it plays in the reanimation process."

Dekka cringed, "How much detail do you want?"

"Just tell me what each one is used for; you don't need to explain the technical details."

Moving to a floating table that adjusted to waist height as he approached, Dekka began describing the equipment in the room.

"The body is placed on this table. The brain is connected to the Itran—Identity Transfer Unit—and the person's memories, identity, full brain analysis and record of synaptic pathways are removed and stored here," he indicated another machine, "in the Synastor. This is done using the PHS—Proton Hydroxyl Scanner—adjusted to a setting that allows glucose and radio waves to cause the information in the brain to move through specially designed fibrodes into the Itran unit which then transfers the information to the Synastor." Dekka held up a few micro-thin thread-like wires.

"Those look like the strands of fiber in the fiber-optic cables that were once used to transfer information at faster-than-light speeds," Viktor commented. He was fascinated in spite of himself.

"Yes, they are very similar, but also quite different," Dekka, agreed.

"Once the identity transfer is complete we use whatever medical devices are appropriate to treat the cause of death, restoring the body to health. Then the identity can be returned."

"Or another identity can be placed in the body. Is that not correct?"

Dekka swallowed hard and looked at Telestra. "Yes, that also is correct."

"Continue."

"Part of what the Synastor does is repair damage and deterioration that may cause changes in memories, personality, abilities, and such that begins at the moment of death due to lack of oxygen to the brain. If we just brought the person back, they would most likely be severely brain damaged if the Identity transfer process were not used."

"I see. So, after you've repaired the physical damage, you put the memories back and reanimate the body?"

"No, not quite. In order to put the identity back in the body, a microchip has to be inserted in a specific place in the brain and then the body must be reanimated first. You can't put an identity into a body that has not been reanimated—the body must be able to breathe and circulate blood without mechanical support—the brain requires oxygen to function, and oxygen is carried by the blood."

"Hmmm." Viktor nodded as the guards brought in the two awakened reanimation scientists. He wandered around the room again stopping behind Telestra and the boy. "Is all of this equipment fully functional?"

"Yes, I believe so."

"Be sure of your answer, Dekka. Telestra and her son's lives depend on it."

"What are you going to do?" she asked nervously.

Viktor ignored her. "Well, Dekka? Is it all fully functional? Is there even one minor piece that is not functional?"

Dekka cleared his throat. "Yes, Viktor. I am sure. All of it is functional."

"Fully functional?"

"Yes."

"Good," and with a quick motion, Viktor grabbed Petya and twisted his head—they all heard a snap as the boy's neck broke.

Telestra screamed.

"What have you done? Why?" Dekka yelled in horror.

Viktor let the body drop to the floor. "I need another soldier."

Dekka shook his head. "I will not help you."

"Really?"

"Absolutely not. Never."

"Santosh!" Viktor called.

"Here!"

Dekka and Telestra turned toward the voice. To their horror, Santosh stood next to a newly awakened Deszik, holding a weapon to his head.

Telestra shook violently, and Dekka grabbed her before she collapsed to the floor.

"Have you changed your mind, Dekka?" Viktor asked with a grin.

"No. I won't do it."

"Dekka, please—my son." Telestra pleaded.

"Telestra, I cannot. This is beyond horrific. He murdered an innocent boy."

"We are all reanimates." She pleaded.

"No. He will only kill more people and turn them into soldiers as well. Is that what you want?"

"Dekka, this is my son. Please, save him," she begged.

"Well, Dekka? What's it going to be?" Viktor asked. "Last chance."

Dekka saw Santosh tighten his grip in preparation to fire the weapon pointed at Deszik's head. "Stop!" he yelled. "I'll do it."

"Good!" Viktor responded, waving in someone from the hallway. "Now that you've agreed to help me, you can start with these two—they've been dead longer," he smirked, "but they are still fresh enough to go through the procedure."

Telestra broke down in sobs as she watched the missing soldiers carry in two more people belonging to the outside world.

"These are from the boy's village—they were searching the forest for him. There are more villages nearby with many more people." Viktor looked pleased. "I am going to build an army of reanimated soldiers."

Telestra and Dekka gasped in unison. "No!"

"Ligator was right. This will be a new race—a race of reanimates. You are about to witness the birth of the Re'an. We will be the most powerful race ever to inhabit this planet. And we will live forever."

Chapter Seven

HE WAS MY LOVER

115 years later

The 8th Cycle Compound, Grand Canyon, Arizona

A lanky man stood silently on the rocky ledge of the alcove formed by the canyon walls, watching the helicopter rise from the canyon floor and move away into the night. The top of the man's head was bald, but blond hair dropped from the side of his head to his shoulders. His pale blue V-neck tunic and pants fit loosely and fluttered around him in the breeze. He squinted his blue eyes against the bright, strobing lights of the helicopter until they disappeared into the distance.

Turning, he moved carefully down the steep slope to the mound of rocks the men in the helicopter had piled over their dead companion, the one they called Robert. One by one he quickly removed the rocks, revealing the body beneath. He took a moment to gaze upon the tall, well-muscled body of Robert Cartwright. His brown curly hair was dirty with dust, and stiff with dried blood. *He is strong and fit. An excellent specimen.*

Gently but effortlessly, as if lifting a baby, he hoisted the body onto his shoulders, climbed the slope back to the ledge, and disappeared into the lift that would take him far underground to the installation buried in the depths of this remote canyon. Stepping off the lift into the featureless room, he approached the opposite wall. It had a slight sheen of brushed metal and was perfectly smooth; there were no flaws anywhere, nor any protrusions that would indicate an opening, and yet as he waved his palm over the wall at waist height, an opening appeared before him. The disguised sensor panel detected the chip in his hand that allowed him access to the secret, restricted lab of the facility.

Stepping through the entrance, he adjusted the weight of the body on his shoulders and entered a brightly lit white room. Everything was white; walls, ceiling, cabinets, shelves, counters—even the floor and sinks. White containers, their contents identified by white labels with a variety of colored lettering, were organized neatly on the shelves in the alcoves. Numerous hand-held instruments lay in their cradles on the counters, and several microscopes and other machines stood ready for use.

A desk and chair hovered at the far wall; several tables floated along the wall nearest him. He knew they all would adjust their position according to the height and need of the person using them.

"Ah, Korda, I see you have retrieved Robert's body," his mentor, Linkola, said as he entered the lab.

Linkola, a man of average height with a trim build, except for a slightly rounded belly, was more than a mentor to Korda—he was more like a father. Korda had been

Linkola's student and later became his assistant. Linkola's wavy reddish-brown hair had dulled some over time and had flecks of white in it, but he was still a handsome man and a phenomenal scientist.

"Yes, I have. I believe we have enough time to reanimate him if that is what we decide to do."

"Excellent! Let us see what we can do for him; shall we?" Linkola said pointing to the floating table.

Korda gently placed the body on the floating lab table as Linkola joined him to examine the head wound.

"The weapons these Eleventh Cycle people use are so primitive and destructive. I would have thought that over the past 72,000 years since our Eighth Cycle ended, the human race would have at least found better ways to resolve their differences other than killing each other," Korda lamented.

Linkola reflected for a few moments on the events since Joshua Rossler, nicknamed JR and the Australian born geologist, Robert Cartwright first entered the Command and Control Center in search of information from the Eighth Cycle. Their discovery and subsequent entry into the compound was what triggered his own, Korda and Siasha's awakening. He remembered how scared they were of the two strangers speaking a strange language. They were relieved when the two strangers left within a few hours. But the respite had been short-lived; within a few weeks the strangers were back and brought more of their people with them. Recording the strange language and feeding it through the language decoder program enabled them to understand what these odd people were saying and learn a little bit about them and their society.

"It worries me too," Linkola replied. "What I have witnessed of their behavior since our awakening gives me no confidence in them. If anything, they have descended into savagery over the seventy-two millennia."

"It's frightening to think that all of our scientific knowledge has vanished. There have been no advancements, and the world seems to be much worse than it was when we left." Korda said grimly.

"That might be so Korda, but I think we should not be too quick to form a final opinion. We have only seen a few of them so far; we can't base our beliefs on what we have observed in the behavior of that person John Brideaux," Linkola said. His thoughts turned briefly to the man whom they had seen pretend to be friends with Robert and his party and then betray them, killing Robert and shooting JR through the left hand and of the others in the lower right leg. He left them bleeding and tied up, to die in the facility.

"Well, I am just happy that they never became aware of our presence here. Can you imagine being in the hands of John Brideaux? It's agonizing to think what he is going to do with the Beast." Korda said.

Linkola nodded. "Judging by his behavior, I have no doubts that he has nothing but malicious intent."

"I don't know what the future holds for us," Korda replied, "but I'm not sure I want to meet the people of the Eleventh Cycle."

"We'll have to wait and see about that Korda, at the moment I agree with you. I don't have a desire to meet with them either," Linkola said as he lifted Robert's head slightly to get a better look at the back. "There's no exit wound here, so the projectile is still lodged in his brain. We will need to remove it first."

Korda nodded. "If his genetic makeup is such that we want him amongst us, at least we get to decide who he will be."

"Agreed," Linkola said as he pushed a button on the side of the table and took a step back to allow panels hidden underneath to slide out automatically and over Robert's body, enclosing him in a glass-like sarcophagus. "Please let Siasha know that you have returned—we will need her expertise as well."

Linkola adjusted a few settings on the diagnostic panel and pushed a button. Different colored lights came alive in the sarcophagus and slowly started moving up and down its length.

Korda watched for a moment as the Dima-Scanner, Diagnostic Imaging Scanner, began to move across the body, shooting protons through it—a detailed, ghost-like hologram of Robert appeared above the sarcophagus. Linkola would have the full body scan completed before he returned with Siasha if he didn't hurry. He nodded and left to find Siasha.

Moving through the familiar, deserted hallways, Korda felt an eeriness descend upon him. He was not accustomed to seeing them empty. Before the end, they had always been full of workers, colleagues who would greet him or smile as they passed each other.

He shivered as he remembered the fear that fell across their world when they realized someone had tampered with The Healer and it had escaped their control, turning against them, becoming 'The Beast' and killing all but the untouchables like himself, the reanimated.

He and Linkola had been the only two B'ran left at this installation. The others had been assigned to attack and seize control of the second installation on the other side of the planet.

It was quite by accident that they had discovered Siasha, a L'gundo woman who was held captive in the detention area.

And a fortunate accident it was for her; by the time they found her she was weak from starvation and dehydration. If he and Linkola had not removed her from that cell and put her into the deep-sleep cycle, she would have died and been gone forever.

When Korda and Siasha entered the lab, Linkola had just started the diagnostic sequence on the PHS, the Proton Hydroxyl Scanner. The holographic double of Robert hung in the air to one side. Linkola had completed the full body scan and had already injected the glucose into the body so he could focus his examination on the brain.

"Thank you for coming so quickly, Siasha," he said as he pressed a button on the panel. They heard a slight hum as it activated the radio waves that would change the magnetic properties of the protons in the hydroxyl groups so they would get a better picture of the brain.

They joined him at the console and stared at the PHS screen as a digitized display of Robert's brain took form.

"The Dima-Scanner shows his body to be quite healthy and in good physical shape. His heart is strong. Have a look while we wait for the PHS on his brain to finish. The genetic tests should complete momentarily as well."

They turned to the holographic image of Robert hovering in mid-air.

"Mhh, strong skeleton, healthy bone structure, not much deterioration," Korda muttered as he checked the readouts on the screen.

"Yes, and so is his cardiovascular system, arteries, and all his organs," Siasha added.

"The genetic tests just completed," Linkola said enthusiastically. Genetic makeup looks good..." suddenly he took a sharp, deep breath and then froze.

"What is it Linkola?" Korda asked. "What have you found?"

"He is a descendant of the X'ran people," Linkola whispered in awe.

Korda looked closer at Robert and then back at Linkola. "Are you sure? It is believed they were all killed off during the third cataclysm."

"Who are the X'ran?" Siasha inquired.

"They were a brave and intelligent people. Some believe all the 'ran class people descended from them. They were extraordinarily strong, brilliant, and innovative, but they were also fierce warriors—even warmongers. From all accounts, they disappeared without a trace, as Korda mentioned, during the third cataclysm when the world was almost destroyed by the asteroids. That was about seventy-thousand years ago."

Linkola sighed. "I was hoping we could reanimate him and use him, but I don't want to take the chance. The X'ran were too vicious."

"Wait, Linkola. Not so hasty." Korda interjected. "Remember we decide who and what he is going to be, we only need his body to be strong and healthy; we control his mind—well, at least the memory we give him."

Siasha nodded her agreement. "It's *that* memory, which is going to determine who he will be. Besides we need more people; not only that, we need people who will be able to protect us from the B'ran."

"You forget that although Korda and I are L'gundo sympathizers, we are still B'ran. We don't know if any other B'ran exist anymore. For all we know they are non-existent now. If they were awakened, don't you think they would have turned up here by now?" Linkola countered.

"We don't know what is happening in the outside world Linkola, we can only hope the B'ran soldiers have been destroyed, but we won't know until we can get to the L'gundo facility where their soldiers were sent and see for ourselves." Siasha countered.

"I agree with her," said Korda. "We should not ignore the possibility that the B'ran could still be out there—it would be better to be prepared."

Linkola slowly nodded. "As much as I hate the idea of resurrecting a violent human being, I have to agree you might be right. So, who will he be?"

"I think we need a military person; someone who knows the strengths and weaknesses of this facility, and how it operates; someone who can think strategically and is capable of situational analysis and action," Siasha said.

"A military person!" Korda exclaimed. "Have you lost your mind? They are the ones who unleashed The Beast that killed everyone! We can't trust them!"

"Easy, Korda," Linkola soothed, "Not all the soldiers were bad. Some of them still had minds of their own."

"Only the Commanders and a few of the officers. Are you asking me to believe that a soldier of that rank would betray the B'ran as a L'gundo sympathizer?"

"If only we knew of one," Linkola said.

"I do," Siasha said softly. "He was my contact since I first joined the Liberty Movement."

"Who?" Linkola asked.

"Tawndo." Siasha said without hesitation.

Linkola looked stupefied. "Tawndo? As in Second-In-Command of the strongest military force on the planet during the Eighth Cycle, Tawndo?"

"Yes," Siasha replied. "I knew him very well, he was my contact and... also my... friend. He told me everything about the B'ran."

She paused and lowered her eyes. Korda and Linkola saw she had not told them everything. They remained quiet, and looked at her inquisitively, waiting for her to continue.

Then in a low whisper, she said, "He was my lover, we had a child—a son."

Chapter Eight

FORMERLY KNOWN AS ROBERT CARTWRIGHT

"The projectile penetrated the head at this point," Siasha pointed to a red circle between the eyes of the hologram. At a touch of a button on the panel, the head of the hologram divided into two halves along the trajectory of the damage.

Tracing the path of the bullet with a red line on one half of the display she indicated the areas of damage. "It traveled along this route and became lodged here," Siasha indicated an area near the back of the head where the red line ended. "The damage to the areas the projectile passed through is extensive but repairable."

Had Robert been able to see what they were looking at, he would have been alarmed to see that John Brideaux's bullet had passed through and, by Eleventh Cycle medical terminology, destroyed his sinus cavity, prefrontal cortex, hypothalamus, thalamus, corpus callosum, and lodged in the parietal Lobe.

"Very well," Linkola said. "Let's get started."

Siasha glanced at the hovering instrument tray. Eiser,

extensor tip, separator, grips, microchip, micro-sealer, and sealer were all in place—they were ready.

"Alright. I will handle the opening, damage repair, and closing. You will complete the implant process and revival," she instructed.

"Very good. Korda is an able assistant and will help as needed."

"Set up the IV and hand me the Eiser, please."

Korda handed the surgical tool to Siasha and watched with fascination as she used its ultra-fine beam to cut through the bone of Robert's forehead and expose the tissue beneath.

Linkola inserted a needle into a vein in Roberts left arm. "IV ready."

"I need the extensor tip now, please," Siasha requested.

Korda quickly handed it over; Siasha attached it to the Eiser with an efficient snap and inserted it into the wound. The extensor tip, thin as a needle, would electronically detect the damaged cells and use its primary directed heat beam to cut them away and vaporize them. A secondary stimulator beam would stimulate cell growth in the area cleared of damaged cells. When the process was complete, there would be no difference between the new cells and the original cells. It would be as if the damage never happened.

Siasha worked quickly but carefully, and in no time, announced, "The repairs are complete." She picked up the Sealer and held it over the wound, stimulating the cells of the skin to regenerate and cover the wound, sealing it up.

"I'll open the skull for the implantation and then turn the surgery over to you Linkola."

"Very good," he acknowledged.

Siasha completed sealing the wound on the forehead and moved to the top left side of Robert's head and made an incision, removing a circular section of the skull bone. Then she stepped aside.

As Linkola took Siasha's place beside the table, it automatically adjusted to the proper height for him to work. Korda handed him the separator tool when he asked for it, then he gently parted a few folds of tissues beneath the incision and worked his way deep into the central sulcus of the brain.

He set the 'lock' feature on the separator and, holding it in one hand, reached with small tweezer-like grips to pick up the miniature chip that he had placed on the instrument tray.

Slowly and carefully Linkola placed the tiny chip near the bottom of the central sulcus. "Inject the nanites," he ordered and watched as Siasha connected a small tube to the IV catheter and depressed the plunger.

"Nanites injected and on the way," she reported, knowing that they would quickly repair and restore all damage to the organs and cells caused by the decay that commenced from the moment of death.

"Micro-sealer," he said and immediately received the tool from Korda, who placed it in his hand in exactly the correct position for use.

Aiming the beam at the edges of the chip, he sealed it to the surrounding tissue to keep it in place. Then, handing the micro-sealer back to Korda, he pushed a button on the panel and watched as various lights began flashing in colors of amber and blue. When he didn't see any red lights, he knew the chip was functioning properly and was running through the set-up process.

"Alright," he said as he released the lock on the separator and gently let the tissue resume its natural place. "By the time you finish closing up, Siasha, the chip will be fully functional, and we will be ready to start with the reanimation process."

Siasha stepped forward, picked up the Sealer, held it over the wound, and began fusing the skull bone together. It then stimulated the cells of the skin to regenerate and seal up the wound. "That's it," She announced placing the Sealer back onto the tray. "Revive him, and this will be a successful reanimation."

"Excellent! Well done Siasha!" Korda congratulated her.

Linkola had been monitoring the microchip and the progress of the nanites, watching as one by one each indicator light turned green. By the time she finished, the nanites had completed making repairs to the existing synapses and pathways through the brain, making it function again, and completed the repairs and restoration to the rest of the body.

"The chip is ready for new programming. Let's get him reanimated and get Tawndo loaded," Linkola said. "Stand back, and I will start his heart."

"Korda, let's help him out with some oxygen."

Korda stepped to the head of the operating table and adjusted the dials on the panel. They all heard the soft hiss as the oxygen began to flow.

Siasha stepped back from the table as Linkola set the toggle switches and pressed a button on a panel at the side of the table.

The body of the man twitched and spasmed, jerking as if he had been woken suddenly. Then he lay still again. A steady rhythmic ticking sound was heard from the monitor displaying each heartbeat as a dot on the screen. After about sixty beats, lines began to connect the dots.

"Let's keep the oxygen on him for a while yet, Korda, but it seems as if we have brought him back!"

Linkola pressed a few buttons on the panel and announced "Ready for total transfer. Siasha, Tawndo's file chip please."

She fitted the data chip into the small indention on the panel. *It will be him... but it won't... Tawndo will be in that body, but he will look different. What if something goes wrong and he doesn't know me?* "Ready for transfer," she whispered.

Linkola pushed another button and lights began to flash; the transfer was in progress. New synapses and pathways were being formed allowing Tawndo to fully assume the identity and control of the body formerly known as Robert Cartwright.

Chapter Nine

WE ARE IN THE ELEVENTH CYCLE

He felt air moving through his lungs and became aware of the beating of his heart. A voice whispered near him; *Tawndo, Tawndo, wake up.*

Slowly he opened his eyes and was pleased to see a beautiful and familiar face watching over him from a chair beside his bed. He smiled. "Siasha," he breathed, reaching for her and feeling the softness of her skin as she took his hand in hers.

"Tawndo," she whispered, resting her forehead against their entwined fingers. "It's good to have you back."

He reached out with his other hand to run his fingers through her long, soft, brown hair and looked deeply into the dark brown eyes.

She kissed his hands; gentle tears ran down her face.

Looking at his surroundings, he recognized the setting. *I'm not in a hospital; I'm in a lab.* He frowned. "What has happened?" he asked.

"What's the last thing you remember?" She asked.

He thought for a moment, and then his eyes grew wide,

and his body tensed. "Nator! Somehow my duality was exposed, and Nator discovered that I am the L'gundo sympathizer the Council of the Selected has been looking for—he stabbed me, tried to kill me!" Tawndo sounded nervous.

"Shhh. It's alright; we're safe here," she said and saw him begin to relax.

"Are you sure we're safe? What happened to Nator? Does anyone else know who I am?"

"Yes, I'm sure you're safe. Nator is dead he won't be able to touch you again—ever."

Tawndo sighed in relief. "What has happened? Tell me."

"Nator found out about you and discovered how to access our secret passageways. He managed to get into one of them and confronted you at the Chasm of Marwolaeth.

"The two of you had a furious battle, and he stabbed you just as you succeeded in pushing him over the edge of the chasm." She looked down sadly. "You both died."

"What? How could that be? I'm alive!" he exclaimed.

"Yes, you are now."

"Ah, they were able to reanimate me?"

"Not exactly." She saw the fear began to grow in his eyes. "You have been given a new body. We were not able to return your body in time for reanimation, but we didn't want to lose your knowledge and expertise, so we managed to transfer your synaptic patterns into storage before they degraded and became unrecoverable."

He raised his hands to look at them and for the first time noticed they looked different, smaller, a darker skin tone. *This is not my body, but it's my mind.* "What happened? He asked.

"As you know, the B'ran scientists started to suspect that

the Council of the Selected had begun using The Healer to further their own objectives as we feared they would. Many of the scientists became L'gundo sympathizers.

"When these scientists refused to make any more of the adjustments to The Healer that the Council requested, the Council coerced some other scientists to make them. The new scientists did not understand the technology, and their tampering had terrible consequences; people began to die by the millions.

"When they tried to shut The Healer down, they discovered that it had become self-aware. It interpreted their shutdown attempt as an attempt to kill it, and The Healer turned on them and killed them. It became a terrible Beast and destroyed everyone who had been implanted with the health monitoring chip."

"But that was most of the population!"

"Yes."

"How is it we are still alive?"

"The reanimated were impervious to the death brought by The Beast and survived.

"Shortly after you were killed, the Council ordered all the reanimated B'ran soldiers to go to the L'gundo facility to attack and capture it. This was done, and according to the last transmission I received, was successful.

"Just as the soldiers succeeded in capturing the L'gundo facility, The Beast unleashed its death. The transport pilots were all killed in mid-flight; all the transports crashed and were destroyed. The soldiers, if there were survivors, couldn't come back, and we haven't heard from them since.

"That was when I was discovered, captured, and held in a cell in the detention area. When The Beast killed everyone, I thought I would die of starvation or thirst, but just as I was about to give up, two scientists from this facility found me. Linkola and Korda are L'gundo sympathizers; the three of us were the only survivors in this facility.

"They gave me food and water, helped me regain my strength, but we became aware of the fact that there was no way to rebuild our society at that time. We knew that there were people who had objected to the health monitor chip and had refused it, so we knew that someday the world would be populated again.

"We decided to enter the deep sleep and wait for someone to discover us. We trusted that it would be a society large enough and intelligent enough that we could merge with.

"A short time ago, men entered this facility which triggered the awakening sequence. They did not find our secret labs. We monitored them to see what kind of people they are and how long we had been asleep."

"And?"

"We are in the Eleventh Cycle."

"Eleventh!" he said looking dumbfounded. "But that would mean we slept for a very long time!"

"Yes, nearly seventy-two-thousand years."

"Do they calculate time the same as us?"

"Yes, there is no difference; the passage of time is based on the Earth's rotation around the sun."

Tawndo was silent as he took in all that Siasha had told him. "Our son?" he asked softly.

"I don't know. He was at the L'gundo installation and hadn't been chipped. Even if he survived the attack, he would be long dead by now -unless he was put in deep sleep and... survived. We don't know... yet."

"How is it that I am alive if I couldn't be reanimated?"

"As I told you, your synaptic patterns were transferred into storage before they degraded. An evil man, John

Brideaux, one of the Eleventh Cyclers, killed one of his own people, Robert Cartwright. Linkola, Korda, and I repaired the damage to his body, reanimated it, and transferred your synaptic patterns into his body."

"You chose me because of my military expertise," he stated without reproach.

"Yes," she said. "And because I love you," she added with a smile.

Chapter Ten

CONTACT

Lights came on automatically as Tawndo stepped through the entrance to the control center.

When Siasha asked him to help restore the facility, so they could discover more about the world they had awoken to, he agreed immediately. He was the only one who had the knowledge and experience to reinstate their communication infrastructure and their only hope to make contact with people from their cycle—if there were any.

Korda, Linkola, and Siasha followed him into the room and stopped just across the threshold—they had never seen such an array of equipment.

"What does all this do?" Korda exclaimed. He began to move around the room looking at the pieces of equipment with intense interest.

Tawndo replied, "If you're really interested, help me to get it up and running, and I'll teach you what I know."

"Yes please!" Korda was excited.

Tawndo smiled.

With Korda as his enthusiastic assistant, Tawndo

restored the control center to full working order in less than a day. Korda was a quick study with natural mechanical and electronic acumen, combined with a healthy dose of curiosity and keen intelligence.

Korda could learn just about anything he wanted to with speed and ease. Tawndo thought as he watched him at work.

Tawndo and Korda spent the next few days getting the communication equipment back into an operational state. As the terminals were brought back to life, Tawndo started tracking down the details of the twelve satellite sites set up across the globe in the days of the 8th Cycle. Each of those sites was equipped and configured as a regional control center, linked to each other and the Central Command and Control Center in the Grand Canyon. He assumed that if there were any people of their kind, they would be in one or more of those regional centers. If they were still in deep-sleep their awakening could be triggered by a command from one of his terminals—if their control center equipment was still functioning.

Siasha arrived at the center, bringing a very welcome meal with her. When they sat down to eat, Siasha remembered how, seventy-two-thousand years ago, Korda had discovered the food storage room within days of The Beast killing everyone.

When they found Siasha in her cell, almost dead from starvation and dehydration, she'd welcomed the tasteless stuff; it renewed her strength. But after suffering through several days of the meals prepared by the men, Siasha was strong enough to be shown where they'd found the food and promptly took over the cooking duties. While it wasn't fresh, their taste buds were much happier after she took over the meal preparations and introduced a bit of creativeness with the various ingredients.

Linkola showed no interest in cooking and was more than happy to leave it to Siasha. Korda, however, was delighted when Siasha agreed to teach him how to cook and was now capable of turning out tasty meals himself. She did have to keep an eye on him, as he sometimes tended to experiment with spices and seasonings that didn't go well together.

Tawndo had activated a search routine to connect with the twelve satellite sites on one of the terminals before he sat down to eat. A few minutes later a sound emanated from the terminal.

"We might have a connection! Tawndo said, setting his plate down.

"What is it?" Siasha asked, moving to his side.

"It looks like there's activity at one of the other sites."

"Can you tell which one?"

"Not yet, just a moment." Tawndo continued to tweak dials and switches then tapped a few keys on a flat, square, silver panel. He took in a sharp breath. "It's the L'gundo site."

"Are you sure? Is it functioning?" She asked.

"Yes, I'm sure, and yes, it's functioning."

Korda and Linkola had joined them, looking over Tawndo's shoulder.

"Wouldn't it be fantastic to make contact with more of our own people," Korda said excitedly.

Tawndo half turned to Korda and Linkola. "Let me first see if I can access their data storage unit and learn what they've been up to. Maybe they survived too and maybe it is possible to establish contact with them and... well, let's first find out if we *want* to make contact with them."

Linkola slowly nodded. "Yes, I agree. Let's not rush into

it. There was a lot of turmoil and some dastardly people in the world towards the end of the 8th Cycle; we shouldn't make any assumptions until we know more."

About mid-day the next day, a deeply perturbed Tawndo made his way down the long, narrow corridor toward the Sanctuary, an enormous cavern where his people had created a beautiful oasis for relaxation. Korda was the one who rediscovered it. Although overgrown in most areas it was still accessible and very enjoyable.

He was troubled by what he'd found in the records from the L'gundo site. Siasha, Korda, and Linkola had invited him to join them at the Sanctuary for a swim some time ago, and he'd agreed to meet them there when he'd completed his work. He hated to bring such ominous news, especially in such serene surroundings, but they had to know sooner rather than later.

Reaching the end of the corridor, he paused for a moment before stepping through the doorway into the haven beyond.

This is truly magnificent he thought looking out over the lush valley created in the cavern. To his left a high waterfall plunged over hundred feet into the crystal-clear cave lake formed by a natural dam across an underground river. Luscious green grass stretched right to the edges of the water while ancient trees with huge trunks grew along the edges of the cavern. Bushes and shrubs intermingled with the forest, ferns, and other shade loving plants filling the areas between the trees.

Artificial illumination that simulated the sun shone high overhead, giving full light to the valley, reflected in blinding flashes off the waves caused by Siasha, Korda, and Linkola swimming in the lake.

"Tawndo!" Korda shouted and waved. "Come join us; the water is tantalizing!"

Reaching the edge, he removed his robe and waded into the water, diving under the surface when the water reached his waist. He rolled onto his back when he returned to the surface and floated peacefully for a few minutes.

"I have always loved this place," he said.

Playfully, he splashed water at Siasha and when he dunked Korda under, a free-for-all frolic erupted. They played until they were tired and returned to the bank to dry off and rest.

"What did you find out about the L'gundo site?" Siasha asked.

Tawndo frowned, he was reluctant to put a damper on the fun, but he thought better of it. "It isn't good," he replied. "We definitely don't want to regroup with them. They have become dangerous—that is my initial assessment of them. I'm afraid we are going to find even more to be concerned about as I continue to dig into their records."

"What did you find," Siasha whispered.

"Based on the research I've done so far; The B'ran were successful in their takeover of the L'gundo site shortly before the Beast destroyed everyone who was chipped. All the transport pilots were killed by the Beast rendering the transports useless, stranding them there with no means of returning to our main site here in the Canyon.

"They obviously had no choice but to make a life for themselves and the captured L'gundo over there.

"They knew, as we did, that reanimated beings are incapable of reproduction. Like us, they also realized that there were, some people who succeeded in hiding from the Council, remained unchipped and survived the Beast's attack. That's when they decided, just like we did, to put themselves into the Deep-Sleep to be awakened sometime in the future when the Earth would hopefully have been repopulated by the offspring of those survivors."

"How long ago were they awakened?" Linkola asked

"In the year 1908 of the current cycle, which would be 115 years ago by my calculations, a shift in the Earth's crust directly beneath the facility triggered the awakening of one of the leaders of the B'ran. He discovered a problem in the volcanic fissures used to power the facility, and although he awoke other B'ran soldiers and the L'gundo scientists, they were unable to stop the build-up of gasses. An explosion occurred that severely damaged the facility.

"After the explosion, it took forty-five years for them to fully repair the damage to the facility and restore it to its former operating capacity. During those years, the B'ran commander, a man by the name of Viktor, forced the L'gundo scientists to create more reanimated beings in an attempt to create a new powerful race called the Re'an."

"How was he able to do that if all of them were already reanimated and couldn't reproduce?" Korda asked.

Siasha and Linkola looked horrified when they understood the implications of what Tawndo was saying.

"Tell me he didn't," Siasha shivered.

Tawndo nodded sadly. "I'm afraid he did."

"Oh no!" Linkola looked as if he was about to be sick.

"What am I missing?" asked Korda.

Tawndo explained. "Viktor ordered the discreet capture of people outside their facility, who were brought back to the facility, killed, and then reanimated as Re'an soldiers."

"How many?" A dismayed Korda asked softly.

"Their numbers had grown to about two-hundred and thirty when the next disaster struck."

"What was that?" Siasha asked.

"About seventy years ago, the military people living on that part of the continent, called Russians, started testing nuclear weapons in the area near the facility. In the year 1954, they exploded a bomb that caused a secondary explosion at the L'gundo site severely damaging it again. It killed many of the Re'an, dropping their numbers back to one hundred twenty."

"And let me guess," Siasha interjected. "they went back to capturing and reanimating people again."

"Well, not immediately. Apparently, that explosion damaged their reanimation technology, and it took them many years to rebuild it. They are still repairing the facility, although my understanding is that it is nearly finished now."

"As horrendous and primitive as nuclear weapons might be—it seems as if that explosion was actually a good thing," Linkola commented with a wry smile.

"That remains to be seen, Linkola. I am still trying to find out how many of them there are now. And what their plans are. I suspect that sooner or later they are going to try and make their way back here."

For a long time, they sat in stunned silence, watching while the simulated sun dipped low over the trees and dusk descended upon them. At last, Linkola stood and announced he was returning inside; Korda followed him leaving Tawndo and Siasha behind.

"I can't believe what has happened at the L'gundo site,

Tawndo. It's terrible." Siasha moved to sit beside him; he put his arm around her in comfort.

"Neither can I," he whispered as he tenderly kissed her forehead.

"Was there anything, any mention of which L'gundo survived?"

"Yes, there was a list of names—your sister and her son are still alive."

Tears streamed down her face. "What about our son? Is he mentioned?"

Slowly, he shook his head. "No mention of him."

Her body was shaking. "Oh, Tawndo—"

He smoothed her hair with his hands, kissed her again, and held her gently while she wept out her grief. The simulated sun had long since set, and they lay back on the grass to watch the lesser light of a simulated moon rise.

At last, Siasha rose and walked into the lake to swim again. Tawndo watched her trim body glide through the water before he got up to join her. She swam to him and, when close, stood and faced him reaching up to kiss him. He returned it eagerly, drawing her in close to his body. After a while, she stepped away, loosened her top, and let it drop into the water.

Tawndo pulled her in and fondled the softness of her skin; she returned his kiss with passion. He picked her up in his arms and carried her to the bank, kneeled on the grass to gently lie her down; then he lay down beside her.

Part II

THE ROWEN

Part II

THE ROVER

Chapter Eleven

THE NOMINATION

Three years later

When former President Nigel Harper finished his speech to John Brideaux and the members of his Supreme Council, the cameras turned to the stunned faces of the council members in the meeting room of The Berlaymont in Brussels—the people who thought they were superior, the untouchables.

In the background, Jack Symonds's voice could be heard instructing his men to handcuff Brideaux and the councilors and take them out to the waiting police vehicles. Jack, a former Delta Force operator, led the mission to Brussels to overthrow Brideaux and his council's world government, arrest them all, and bring them to America.

Jack's team and their prisoners would be escorted by Chief Detective Pierre Bertrand to the Brussels International Airport, about six miles northeast of the city, from there they would fly to Washington, D.C. onboard Air Force One.

JR signaled to a few of the men to follow him to the communications center where the Central Control Unit also known as 'The Beast,' was located. On arrival at the center, JR ordered all the staff out, and he and his team went to work dismantling the Beast. Some of the team took the hard drives out from all the servers and computers in the facility, carefully wrapping and packing them in metal boxes and carried them out to the trucks waiting to transport them to the airport.

At the Rossler Foundation's hidden cave facility in the Gallatin Mountains of Montana, 'the Rabbit Hole', chaotic scenes of triumph erupted in the Robert Cartwright community hall when Jack reported that they were airborne and en route to D.C. Foundation members and their families had fled to the cave in silence, disappearing without a trace, to live and operate hidden from Brideaux and his New World Government. With Jack's success, perhaps their days of hiding would soon be over.

It took almost an hour before the Rosslerites started to calm down and then all of a sudden, almost as quickly as the onset of the jubilations, it went quiet, and everyone was looking at their leader, the founder of the Rossler Foundation, Daniel Rossler and Nigel Harper.

The two of them stopped talking when they became aware of the silence and the people staring at them with a *what-do-we-do-next* look on their faces.

Daniel looked at Nigel and said, "You know Nigel, now I know what it feels like to be the dog that chases a car. We won the war, now we have to win the peace, and I am of the opinion that's going to require political expertise."

Nigel nodded. "Yes, and a lot of it."

"So, as our resident political expert—what's next?" Everyone was listening to them now.

"That was the quickest cop-out I have seen in my life!" Nigel laughed and shook his head, pointing his finger at Daniel. "You are not getting off the hook so easily my friend. You just wait and see."

The group of older men known as the Musketeers were smiling; they knew what those words meant, but they all took an oath to say nothing about it until the time was right.

Nigel continued. "Daniel is correct. We did win the war —no doubt about that. The next challenge is to win the peace, and I'm afraid it's not going to be a road paved with roses. The world is in chaos, and it is going to require wisdom and patience to restore order."

"Do you have any ideas, Nigel?" Daniel's wife and Rossler Foundation co-founder, Sarah asked. "I'm sure a new government will be elected in due time, but in the meantime, the United States is without a government; some sort of interim measures will have to be put in place. Won't they?"

"I don't agree with you that we are without a government at the moment," Nigel replied. "The only issue is that our legitimate government has not been operational for a while. My assessment of the situation is that we had a legitimate government, duly elected, at the time of Brideaux's coup d'état. The elected government has to return to their positions and become operational as quickly as possible."

"Okay Nigel, it sounds easy enough when you explain it like that. The problem is that the elected President has been arrested—by us, I would like to add," Luke, Sarah's uncle and former CIA field agent, said as everyone exploded in laughter. "And the Vice President has been killed—not by us I would like to add," Luke continued. "So, who is now President?"

Nigel replied. "Our constitution is clear about the line

of succession. The President is followed by the Vice President, failing the Vice President, the Speaker of the House of Representatives becomes President, failing which the president pro tempore of the Senate, becomes President. After that, it falls to each of the appointed cabinet members in turn, based on when their respective departments were established. Seeing that the Speaker of the House of Representatives has recently died—of natural causes I would like to add, the next in line is Senator Laurie Campbell, president pro tempore of the Senate."

"Habemus Papam! (We Have a Pope!)," Daniel shouted, quoting the Latin announcement usually given by the senior Cardinal Deacon when a new Roman Catholic pope was elected.

When the laughter subsided Daniel said, "Nigel, I am just wondering if it would be a good idea to give Senator Laurie Campbell a call to offer our assistance in any way we can?"

"Exactly what I had in mind, Daniel. If someone can get me her number, I will call her right away."

It took Sam Lewis, former head of the CIA under President Nigel Harper less than thirty minutes to get hold of Brad Johnston, the former Director of Security in America, under the Supreme Council, and get Senator Campbell's personal number.

Senator Laurie Campbell was awake when her phone rang. She had been following the events as they unfolded from the moment when all TV channels went blank, and Nigel Harper's face appeared as he addressed the Supreme Council. She knew that the Supreme Council was history and quickly came to the same conclusion as Nigel, she was the new President of the United States—whether she liked it or not. And she had no illusions about the mountain of adversities that faced her.

Half of my kingdom to have Nigel Harper by my side at a time like this.

She pushed the green button and answered, "Laurie Campbell."

"Madame President, it's Nigel Harper, allow me to be the first one to congratulate you." Nigel chuckled.

"Nigel! You must have read my mind! First of all, I'm not the President yet; second, if I do become the President, and you ever call me Madam President I will have you arrested. I grew up with you, Nigel; I will never allow you to call me Madame President. Third, where have you been? We need you in D.C. like yesterday."

Nigel laughed. "Wow, slow down Laurie. Let me address your points. First, I'm sure you will be sworn in as President in the next day or two. Two, I won't call you Madame President any longer, you know me, I've never been one to stand on protocol either. Three, I will be in D.C. tomorrow, and I'll tell you everything then."

"Nigel, can I count on you to be my personal advisor. At least during the transition period?"

"Yes, that goes without saying, Laurie. I'll do whatever is required of me. And the other reason for my call is to let you know that you can also count on the support of the Rossler Foundation."

Thank you, Nigel, you will never know how much that means to me right now. Just before your call came through while I was watching you on the TV, and thinking about what's ahead, I said to myself *'half of my kingdom to have Nigel Harper by my side at a time like this'* and then you called."

Nigel laughed. "Laurie, you must remember I'm an old man now; I don't have the strength and energy I had when I was in office—it feels like a lifetime ago. Is there anything at all I can help you with right now? I have to catch a plane to D.C to be there when the Supreme Council and our team members arrive."

"Your team? Are you saying it's your team who did this?"

"No, not my team, Laurie. I am part of the team—the Rossler Foundation team."

"And I guess I'll hear all about it tomorrow?"

"Yes, you will, that's a promise."

"Okay Nigel, before we hang up. What are your initial thoughts? How should I approach this? I have some ideas but would like to hear what you think."

"I suggest you get the Attorney General, Secretary of Defense, Secretary of Homeland Security, Chief of Staff and as many of the other senior appointed and elected officials into a meeting as soon as possible and put them to work. Get your inauguration done right away; the country needs to see their President, immediately. With that out of the way, you will have the power to make decisions and start to rebuild government and the country."

"Thanks, Nigel, that serves to confirm what I have been thinking. One more question. I'll need a Vice President. Any recommendations?"

Nigel had a hard time not to let Laurie sense his big smile. "Yes, in fact, I have, but that can wait until tomorrow. Just one last thought—I don't have to tell you that you have a gargantuan task in front of you. However, I have all the confidence in the world that you will be successful. You are in our prayers, and we will support you all the way."

"Thanks, Nigel. It was really good to hear from you. I'm looking forward to seeing you tomorrow. Have a safe trip."

"Thank you, Laurie. See you at the airport tomorrow."

The Rowen

When the call ended, Laurie Campbell sat back in her chair and sighed. "Oh, Will, how I wish you were still alive to be with me now." She whispered.

She and Will Campbell got married shortly after they both finished University, almost thirty-three years ago. Will was diagnosed with an aggressive type of brain cancer eighteen months ago and died six months later. They had two sons, both of them West Point graduates and officers in the military. Both of them happily married and three lovely grandchildren—Laurie's pride and joy.

Fifteen minutes before the Presidential aircraft commonly known as Air Force One touched down, Nigel was able to meet with Laurie Campbell to give her a quick heads-up of what he was going to say in his speech and get her agreement. Laurie still had a lot to talk about but was happy with Nigel's suggestion and invited him and a few others to continue the discussions as soon as the event was over.

When the Presidential plane arrived, Nigel and Esther Harper were waiting at the bottom of the stairs. Next to him stood Daniel and Sarah, Sam and Susan Lewis, and the rest of the Rosslerites. They had tears of joy in their eyes as they looked up to the five men who'd taken the Supreme Council into custody—the numbers of the Rosslerites were full again.

Their waiting loved ones embraced Jack and his team, and then Nigel Harper walked over to the podium while every news camera in the world followed him.

"My fellow Americans and citizens of the world. A very wise man once wrote the following:

There is a time for everything, and a season for every activity under the heavens:
a time to be born and a time to die,
a time to plant and a time to uproot,
a time to kill and a time to heal,
a time to tear down and a time to build,
a time to weep and a time to laugh,
a time to mourn and a time to dance,
a time to scatter stones and a time to gather them,
a time to embrace and a time to refrain from embracing,
a time to search and a time to give up,
a time to keep and a time to throw away,
a time to tear and a time to mend,
a time to be silent and a time to speak,
a time to love and a time to hate,
a time for war and a time for peace.

Today is the beginning of the time to be born, to plant, to heal, to build, to laugh, to dance, to gather, to embrace, to search, to mend, to speak, to love, and above all, it is time for peace."

The crowd was absolutely quiet until his last words reached their ears and their minds. They began to chant – "Harper for president, Harper for president!"

Nigel held his hand up, and the crowd went quiet again.

"My friends, there is also a time to come and a time to go. I had my time. I am an old man, and the days that God has granted me to remain on this earth are few. It is my time to go. Our country and the world need new leaders to take us into the future. We need people who get courage from their deeply-held beliefs—people who will not waver in the face of adversity."

The crowd exploded in applause while Nigel waited for

them to calm down and for the Musketeers to do as they'd agreed.

Daniel and Sarah didn't know what was happening when the Musketeers and their spouses who formed a half-circle around them moved closer and gently started pushing the two of them towards the podium five yards away. They looked around in bewilderment at the smiling faces. They were holding on to each other as their legs began to feel jittery.

"Sarah, what's going on?"

"I have no idea, Daniel."

When they were close enough, Nigel took their hands and pulled them towards him and the microphones.

"It is today my privilege and honor to introduce to you two of those people. They are half my age, but over the past few months, they taught me two things:

"One. Our present circumstances will not determine where we will go; it merely dictates where we will start.

"Two. Never doubt that a small group of thoughtful, committed people can change the world. Indeed, it is the only thing that ever has.

"I present to you Daniel and Sarah Rossler, the next President and First Lady of the United States of America."

Nigel Harper's last words lingered in the air. The crowd had gone quiet. Cameras started flashing incessantly, and reporters descended on the podium where Nigel stood next to Daniel and Sarah smiling broadly.

Daniel and Sarah's mouths were agape—they looked bamboozled.

"Please, let there be no misunderstanding about what

I've said." Nigel continued. "In terms of our constitution, Laurie Campbell is the new President of the United States of America. I've known her for many years, and I have full confidence in her abilities. I hereby give my full and unwavering support to her as President, and I ask that you follow suit with me, and the Rossler Foundation, and give her and her new administration your unequivocal support as well.

"President Campbell however, has indicated to me that she will complete the remaining term but will not be running for office after that.

"Our next election is in two years, and I firmly believe Daniel and Sarah Rossler will make a fine President and First Lady."

The crowd came to life again, and a person could be heard shouting, "Campbell and Rossler to the White House!" He was soon joined by others, within seconds; the single voice had grown into a thunderous roar of thousands chanting loudly, "Campbell and Rossler, Campbell and Rossler!"

Laurie Campbell appeared on the other side of Daniel and Sarah waving at the crowd.

Daniel and Sarah had turned to stare at Nigel, totally ignoring Laurie. Their beef was with Nigel.

Daniel spoke first, "Nigel Harper what have you done! You have been... what... how... whose idea..."

"Daniel don't even ask," Sarah interjected. "There are the culprits—the conspirators." She pointed to the rest of the Musketeers standing in a semi-circle behind Nigel, all smirking happily: Luke, Sam, Ben, Ryan, John and last but not least Sinclair O'Reilly all with their lovely spouses next to them, wearing equally big grins.

Nigel smiled, ignored Daniel and Sarah, half turned to

Laurie and said, "Ms. President, please allow me to introduce Daniel and Sarah Rossler to you."

"I'm very pleased, and honored, to meet you, Mr. and Mrs. Rossler," Laurie said shaking their hands.

"Likewise, Madame President," Daniel replied. "Please, call us Daniel and Sarah."

Laurie smiled, "Very well, Daniel and Sarah; provided you call me Laurie.

"Why don't we go back to my house to discuss this and get better acquainted? Sam, I'd like you and Susan to come as well."

They all agreed, and as they headed toward their waiting vehicles Laurie whispered to Nigel, "Will you and Esther please ride with me?"

Nigel nodded his agreement, and he and Esther followed Laurie to her car.

General Thomas Hayden, who was the Secretary of Defense when Brideaux ousted the government, growled at the people around him—no one was listening. "A female president in a time like this. Have they lost their minds?"

Thomas Hayden was an angry man as he struggled to get out of the crowd on his way to his car. *"We'll just see about that."*

When the motorcade started moving, Laurie turned to Nigel. "Your support and endorsement mean a lot to me, not to mention your loyalty.

"I like your suggestion, Nigel. Those people of the Rossler Foundation are really something. Anyone that can pull the world out of an all-consuming fire as they did must be part of the leadership and future of our nation. Besides that, their popularity right now is just what we need to get the support of the majority of the American people."

Nigel smiled. "You won't regret it, Laurie—Daniel and Sarah are good people—*the salt of the earth* as the Bible puts it."

Twenty minutes later, Laurie, Nigel and Esther, Daniel and Sarah, and Sam and Susan, were seated in the living room of Laurie's private residence.

If President Campbell had any lingering doubts about Nigel's recommendation for Vice President, they quickly disappeared as Sam and Nigel narrated the events since John Brideaux took over the world and everything that led up to his fall from grace the night before. By the time they'd finished, she could just shake her head in admiration.

"Daniel, Sarah, I don't have words to thank you and the Rossler Foundation team for what you've done. I have to admit, I had some misgivings earlier today when Nigel approached me with his idea, but I have no doubts whatsoever now. Will you please accept the nomination as Vice President? The United States and the world need you and Sarah, and the rest of the Rossler Foundation to get us out of this mess left by Brideaux and his Supreme Council."

Daniel and Sarah were still shell-shocked, but it didn't take much to persuade Daniel to accept the nomination as Vice President. Not because he had any political aspirations —but because he and Sarah knew and understood what role the Rossler Foundation and its people could play in rebuilding the United States, and the world.

With that settled, Laurie and Nigel discussed strategy for the meeting in the Oval Office later in the day. Nigel, Daniel, and Sam Lewis were invited to attend as advisors to the President.

Daniel's nomination would be announced only after Laurie's inauguration as President.

Chapter Twelve

A POWER STRUGGLE

It was shortly after midday when the group of people, invited by Laurie Campbell, walked through the doors of the Oval Office. The Secretary of Defense, retired General Thomas Hayden, immediately went to sit in the chair behind the President's desk. Before anyone could say a word, he looked at the Secretary of Homeland Security and said, "Bob, I need to know the status of our borders, and I need it yesterday.

"Glenn," he said, speaking to the Chief of Staff. "I want a meeting with Secretaries Thompson, Smith, Simmons, and Commandant Allen in one hour—and let Admiral Hensley of the Coast Guard know that they are now under the command of the Navy as I'm declaring a state of war."

He looked over at Nigel, Daniel, and Sam. "What the hell are you three doing here? You two are retired," he said pointing at Nigel and Sam, "and I don't know you from Adam," he said speaking directly to Daniel. "This doesn't concern any of you, so you can clear out."

Nigel stepped forward drawing Daniel with him. "Allow

me to introduce you to the man whose team has just saved all our asses, including yours, Tom. This is Daniel Rossler, CEO of the Rossler Foundation whose tireless and unrelenting efforts brought down John Brideaux, his 'Beast,' and his Supreme Council yesterday.

"The entire world owes the Rossler Foundation, with its handful of brave people, their lives, Tom. That chip in your body and the bodies of billions across the planet was rendered inoperable by the sheer brilliance and dedication of these people. That's why Daniel Rossler is here. He is ready to help and to contribute to the solution of the current issues."

"Oh, well, thank you, Mr. Rossler. Your assistance is highly appreciated. The military will take over now; we're in a war and civilians need to get out of the way. We will arrange a big thank you for you and your foundation at a later date. You are excused."

A sharp silence descended in the room as everyone froze.

Senator Campbell signaled to her aide near the door, and he disappeared into the hallway. She stepped up next to the desk staring silently at Hayden. No one breathed.

"What are you all waiting for? Get moving!" Hayden shouted. "What are you looking at Campbell?" he demanded.

"I believe you are in my chair," she replied with calm authority. "Oh, and just as a matter of interest, who exactly are we at war with? I guess as President I am entitled to that information."

He laughed and looked at those gathered in the room. "Did you hear that?" He snorted. "She thinks she's President—Commander in Chief." He slapped his leg as he laughed. "That's the funniest thing I've heard since this whole cluster-fuck started!"

Laurie bit back her retort and replied, "I'm sorry to inform you, but although I hold no military rank, and neither do you, I am next in line as successor to the Presidency, and I will not step away from that duty."

"Go home and play with your Barbie Dolls, Laurie. This is a military situation and I out-qualify you every day of the week and twice on Sunday."

"What are you two jarheads doing in here? Get back to your guard posts," he shouted at the two Marines who had just stepped into the Oval Office, accompanied by Senator Campbell's aide.

"No one cares if you think you're the most qualified under the circumstances, Tom." The Secretary of Education, Ed Newman, interjected. "The question is, who is the legal successor to the Presidency according to the Constitution—not your opinion."

Hayden was on his feet. "This is a national security situation, and I am the Secretary of Defense. The President automatically assumes the position as Commander in Chief of our military forces, which right now are thin, therefore I am the logical one to step into that role given our current circumstances and my military background."

Ed shook his head and smirked. He'd waited a long time to see this pompous ass put in his place, and he was going to enjoy every second of it. "Even the Secretary of State is ahead of you in the line of succession, Tom. Don't you even know the Constitution you're supposed to defend?"

"We need someone to coordinate our defense efforts, and the best person for that job is me! We don't have time to discuss this or to start taking applications!" Hayden shouted.

"Yes, we do, Tom," Laurie said, still very calm and

collected, with a hint of a smile of amusement, "and as President and Commander in Chief, I'm going to be counting on you to do just that."

Hayden sneered, "I won't serve under a woman."

"Secretary Hayden," Attorney General Scott Jenkins, joined the argument, "I have remained quiet so far, hoping you would see reason. But let me give you the legal position. With all due respect, the Constitution is clear. Ms. Campbell is President pro tempore of the Senate, and as such, since the Speaker of the House of Representatives is dead, she is the next person in the line of succession to the office of the Presidency of the United States."

"Just how do you figure that? The Vice President is the successor, and with him dead, it should go to the next most qualified person, and in a time of war like we're in, that would be the Secretary of Defense—in other words—me!" Spittle flew from his mouth as he spoke.

The Attorney General was incredulous at the audacity and ignorance of this man. His dark eyes blazed in fury—a blush of anger colored his cheeks. "I'm sorry Mr. Secretary, but that is not the case. First of all, no single person, not even the President, can unilaterally declare a state of war—only Congress can do that.

"Second, irrespective of what you think, we are *not at war*.

"Third, the line of succession is very clearly defined in the Constitution—do yourself a favor, sit down, shut up and read it before you make a bigger ass of yourself—the Presidential Succession Act, Title 3 U.S. Code, Section 19."

He tossed a book at Hayden. "The Office transfers to the Vice President first, then the Speaker of the House of Representatives, followed by the President pro tempore of the Senate, then continues through the appointed cabinet members in order of creation of the office they serve. Starting with the Secretary of State, then the Secretary of the Treasury, and only then the Secretary of Defense. In other words, even if she relinquishes the position, it won't go to you. As Attorney General, I fall in line with you, along with the rest of the cabinet members."

"Well, I don't give a rat's ass. A military leader is needed, and I'm that leader—period. So, clear out of here —all of you," he said as he flopped back into the chair.

"Are you saying you are above the laws of this country, General?" Laurie asked with a raised eyebrow.

Hayden looked at the two Marines. "I thought I told you to get back to your posts—get out of here now and take her with you," he shouted pointing at Laurie.

The tall, redheaded, 23-year-old Marine Lieutenant, Rick Jackson, felt his heart drop to his feet. *This is going to ruin my career.* He stiffened to attention, "I'm sorry, Sir, I can't do that."

Hayden was on his feet again. "What!" he screamed. "How dare you! You're finished! Who let you in here anyway?"

Jackson felt an internal flinch but remained steadfast outwardly. "Sir! I was ordered to report to this office by the President of the United States."

"You're crazy. I didn't order you anywhere, except to get back to your post!"

"Sir, I was ordered here by President Campbell. *She* is the President Sir, not you."

"You don't know what you're talking about you little twit."

"Sir, as part of my training to serve as a White House guard I was required to fully understand the order of succession, including the Designated Survivor and obey any order given by the President, aka the Commander in Chief. Due to the deaths of the Vice President and Speaker John Knott, Senator Laurie Campbell became President the instant President Cooper was no longer serving in that capacity."

Thomas Hayden was dumbfounded. He looked around the room but found no support in the eyes of those gathered around him. He harrumphed. "I'll not serve under a woman." His voice had become a mutter.

"What was that?" Laurie asked.

"I said," he stated firmly and loudly, "I'll not serve under a woman!"

"As you wish," Laurie said. "You're relieved of your position—effective immediately."

"You can't do that." Hayden protested.

"I just did." She smiled at Hayden. "You are dismissed." Laurie looked at the two Marines, "Please escort *former* Secretary Hayden out and off the premises."

The two Marines stepped forward and waved to the flabbergasted Hayden to join them.

Retired General Thomas Hayden, now former Secretary of Defense, turned on his heel and walked toward the door, flanked by the two Marines. "You haven't heard the last from me bitch!" he shouted as he was escorted from the room.

President Campbell turned, stepped behind the ornate desk, and settled into the chair. As she sat down, she suppressed a smile when she saw Ed Newman holding the door open.

It won't surprise me if he kicks him in the ass on his way out.

Daniel suppressed a smile, when the thought, *I wonder how JR would have dealt with this situation,* crossed his mind. Patience was not one of JR's strong suits. In a situation like this, with JR having to handle the issue, General Hayden would not have walked out of the Oval Office—he would have been carried out on a stretcher. He was still astounded that JR didn't do John Brideaux any harm in Brussels the night before.

During the course of the argument, Daniel had more than one moment when he seriously questioned the wisdom of Sarah and his acceptance of the nomination. This was a strange world filled with too many narcissistic people, a world in which he had no experience. But he thought about the Rossler Foundation and its people and his late grandfather, Nicholas Rossler. He could almost hear his grandfather's voice; *the Rosslers don't run away from responsibility, and we never give up until we have done our duty.*

"Please everyone, have a seat." The President waved her hand.

"Scott," she said, addressing the Attorney General, "Now that we have that little misunderstanding out of the way I want to thank you for your assistance—and I thank all of you for your support."

"You're welcome, Madame President."

"Scott, to avoid any further legal misconceptions, I want you and the Chief of Staff to issue a press release about my assuming the Presidential duties. Then arrange for my inauguration to take place without delay. And just to be clear about the reason for my haste—the people of America need to see that this country has a leader immediately. Make sure that all of this gets the widest possible publicity.

"Yes, Madame President," Scott replied.

Laurie wrinkled her nose. "Scott and this goes for the rest of you as well, I'm not going to respond to 'Madame President'; my name is Laurie, please address me by my name or as Ms. President. Understood?" she asked looking around.

Scott looked abashed but answered, "yes ma'am" while the others nodded in silent agreement.

Laurie looked at him in wry amusement and just shook her head.

Scott cleared his throat, "yes Ms. President."

"Good! Now that we have that resolved let's move on!" Laurie said with a grin.

We need to look at getting Congress and the Senate up and running as quickly as possible and also to fill the other empty cabinet positions as soon as we can. Secretaries of State, Interior, Defense, Labor, Transportation, and Veterans Affairs all need to be appointed.

She looked at the Chief of Staff, Glenn Baier, "Glenn, I want you to get in touch with those Undersecretaries and tell them I want to see them in four hours so that we can start work on their departments."

Baier nodded. "Yes, Ms. President."

"Ms. President I know it's early days but what are your thoughts on a Vice President?" Scott asked.

"I've already made a decision," she replied without looking in the direction where Nigel, Sam, and Daniel were seated. "But I have to warn everyone, I am going to break with tradition; I'm going to nominate a person who has the skills and the will to do what's necessary—a bipartisan appointment and not to appease party hierarchy.

"I'm not in a popularity contest—I'm here to do a job that I'm expected and privileged to do. And I intend to do it to the best of my abilities, with the assistance of the best and most qualified people available; I don't care about political affiliations, religion, race, color, or creed. The one who is best qualified to do the job gets it—and that goes for all appointments, not just the Vice Presidency.

"As you already know, I don't care about a next term; I'm not running; all I care about is getting our country back on its feet. All that counts are doing the best for this country during the next few years until my term runs out. If my decisions are unpopular with the party hardliners—so be it," She paused for a breath and concluded. "Tough titties for them if they don't like what I'm going to do."

Everyone in the room stood and applauded her. One by one, they got up and pledged their support and loyalty to her and the country.

"Thank you all, it is humbling but also energizing to hear you support me like that."

Chapter Thirteen

YOUR SOLEMN PROMISE

Nigel, Daniel, and Sam remained quiet, and at times very concerned observers throughout the whole saga with General Hayden. When the meeting ended, they readied to leave as well, but Laurie stopped them. "I would like you gentlemen to stay for a while longer; there are a few more things to discuss."

The three of them moved over and took up seats across from her.

Laurie smiled. "Daniel, I was wondering if you had second thoughts after witnessing what I believe would have been your first real political brawl?"

"Madame President..." was as far as he got before she stopped him.

"Daniel, whether you take the job or not, please get used to the idea of calling me by my first name."

"Uh, thank you Ma... ah... Laurie." Daniel stuttered a bit but regained his composure. "Yes, I have to admit there were a few moments when my feet went cold. I got the impression we are in for a rough ride the next few months, if not longer. It made me long for the peace and quiet of the Rabbit Hole."

"You can bet on that rough ride Daniel," Laurie replied as she stared across the room and paused a while before she continued. "You can certainly bet on it."

"Well, Daniel, from your response I gathered you are still on the bucking horse?" Nigel quipped.

Daniel just nodded quietly.

"Good. I'm glad to hear that." The President replied. "Let's talk about the Rossler Foundation."

Daniel's ears pitched immediately, he leaned forward, and was about to say, *the Rossler Foundation will not become government property,* but didn't.

"Daniel, as I have said before, the Foundation's achievements are beyond astounding. There are no words to express the gratitude I have and that everyone on this planet should have."

"Thank you, Laurie. I will pass on your message to the team," Daniel smiled.

"The Foundation seems to be uniquely qualified to be of great assistance, at least during the transition period, and I'm sure in the longer term. I don't know what's ahead, but I'm willing to bet dollars to doughnuts that Thomas Hayden's ego was hurt, much more than he could handle— he is going to make trouble."

"What makes you think that?" Daniel asked.

Laurie leaned back in her chair resting her elbows on the armrests and tapped the tips of her fingers together thoughtfully.

"Thomas Hayden is a proud man and a natural leader; he's career military and comes from a long line of career military people. He's extremely proud of his family's history of service to this country and can trace it back as far as the

Revolutionary War. Men in his family have received honors and decorations during the Civil War, WWI, WWII, Vietnam, Korea, and the Middle East.

"He is a West Point graduate who had an extremely successful military career, working his way up through the officer ranks. He's a highly-decorated Army officer who reached the rank of 4 Star General—there is no higher level except in times of war. His list of medals and citations goes on for pages.

"He exhibited a lot of charisma over the years and became popular among his colleagues. As a popular and successful General, he came to the attention of politicians and previous presidents who drew him into politics in an effort to gain support from the populace. In fact, that is how he became Secretary of Defense.

"My concern is with his popularity, at least amongst the military, and with his charisma, should he decide to cause trouble he could sway many people and possibly obtain a wide following," she concluded.

"What do you have in mind?" Daniel asked cautiously. Daniel and Sarah, right from the beginning, and everyone else who became part of the Rossler Foundation over the years, agreed and stood by their decision that the Foundation would never be ceded to government control. He was worried that Laurie was steering in that direction.

Nigel, who had firsthand experience with the Rosslerites resoluteness about this particular view could see the angst building in Daniel's demeanor and came to the rescue.

"Laurie, I'm part of the Rossler Foundation now. Esther and I are the oldest of the group when it comes to our ages, except for Daniel's grandmother, Bess, but we are the latest of the members. There is one thing that must be made clear right from the beginning, and may I add, is not negotiable

—the Rossler Foundation *must* remain independent. It will not fall under government control, and we want your solemn promise you won't try to bring it under government control."

Laurie held her hand up. "There is no issue with that Nigel. Please don't worry; you have my solemn promise. I can understand what ruckuses it will cause if we brought the Foundation into the fold of government bureaucracy—no, it won't happen, not on my watch.

"I am very aware that it is the independence of the Rossler Foundation which enabled you to turn world events around. That could never have been achieved by any government—not once Brideaux staged his coup in New Delhi."

"Phew." Daniel's sigh was loud and caused everyone to start laughing.

"I am more interested to hear what the three of you think would be the best way the Rossler Foundation can help us," Laurie said. "I am thinking about security and technology."

"Security we can certainly help with, Ms. President," Sam Lewis spoke for the first time.

"Laurie, please Sam. We don't have time for the formalities."

"Mhh, sorry that's going to take some getting used to Ms. President," Sam laughed. "Ah, I mean Laurie."

The President just smiled as she thought, *I still have to get used to being the President.*

Sam continued. "You see, between the technology we have and our relationship with Tectus, we have access to a small but loyal and ready force of ex-military and law enforcement people who would all be willing to do their bit.

"Through Tectus, we have contacts throughout the

country and the world which can keep us up to date while you reestablish Homeland Security, the CIA, NSA, FBI, and other agencies.

"Some of those people might even be ideal to take up interim leadership positions to help reestablish those agencies."

"That's the stuff I like to hear," Laurie said. She looked at Daniel, "Can I leave it with you and Sam to discuss this with the rest of your team and create a plan of action?"

Daniel nodded, "I'll be happy to speak with the team and see in what ways they think they can and are willing to serve. I will try and get a high-level plan to you within the next twenty-four hours."

"Thank you, Daniel; that will be good."

"Anything else on your mind Laurie?" Nigel asked.

"Several things, actually. I'd like to discuss John Brideaux and his Council and what to do with them. I'd also like to review some possible Cabinet replacements with you and get your feel for where we should be heading."

"We have to deal with John Brideaux and his Council, and they are going to be a considerable problem." Nigel started.

A knock sounded on the door, and Laurie invited the person to enter.

A dark-haired girl stepped through the doorway carrying a tray. "I thought you might like some refreshments, Ms. President."

"Thank you, that's very kind and very thoughtful." Laurie smiled.

"Thank you, Elize. How are you and how is your mom?" Nigel said to her as she turned to leave.

"I am good Mr. President; it's great to be back here. Mom is doing fine; she's back here as well. "

"Give her my regards when you see her again."

"I'll do that Mr. President." She said as smiled and left.

"You know her?" Laurie inquired.

"Her mother used to be the head baker here; I watched Elize grow up while I was in office."

"She seems to be a nice girl."

"Indeed, very loyal and conscientious. Now, where were we?

"You were about to tell me what a problem Brideaux is going to be."

"Ah, yes," Nigel said, leaning back on the couch crossing his legs. "Everybody and their brother is going to be out for blood when it comes to Brideaux and his Council members. And I don't think jail sentences are going to suffice where Barbara Cohen and John Brideaux are concerned. The atrocities they committed while experimenting on those people are enough to turn even pacifists and humanitarians into sadistic executioners."

"As much as I don't like it, we can't give in to barbarism. I'm going to have to protect them from that kind of thing until they can be brought to justice in a court of law.

"They'll have to be kept in a secure location under heavy guard, and that in itself will almost certainly give them away."

"You may have to move them and send decoys to several locations so their exact position can be secure," Nigel suggested.

"That's a good idea. I just hope we have enough military and security personnel to pull it off."

"I would use military personnel if at all possible. As Commander in Chief, you will have more control over them should the need arise."

"Good point, Nigel. Okay, I'll get some people working on the logistics and locations for their move and detention."

Laurie got up to get a paper from her desk and handed it to Nigel. "This is a list of people I'm considering for nomination to fill empty Cabinet positions."

Nigel perused the list for a moment. "Hmmm. There are a lot of good people here, Laurie; you'll be able to assemble an excellent team from this list."

"Do you have any recommendations or comments?"

"When I was choosing my Cabinet, the nation was a little more stable than it is right now." He smiled. "I made my choices based on the person's proven track record and qualifications, and whether or not I thought we could work well together.

"In this case," he continued, "you're going to need people you know you can trust without a doubt."

"I thought about that—it would mean replacing a lot of the Cabinet. I'd prefer not to do that right now. I believe some experienced people would be a benefit."

Nigel frowned slightly. "I see your point, but you're a new broom and everyone expects new brooms to sweep clean. I think it's risky to have people with divided loyalties in your midst—like an adder at your bosom."

"Hmmm," she mused, "yes, that's true. I will give it some more consideration before making my final decision."

Chapter Fourteen

ACCOUNTABILITY

After returning to their hotel, Daniel called a meeting of all the Rosslerites who were in Washington, to apprise them of President Campbell's request.

Although they were burning to let everyone know, Sarah, Esther, and Susan, who had returned to the hotel when their spouses accompanied President Campbell to the White House, had kept the secret about Daniel's pending nomination as Vice President.

"President Daniel Rossler—has a nice ring to it," Luke wisecracked, once the group had gathered and before anyone could speak.

Daniel just grinned. "Right now, it's President Laurie Campbell."

"She was a fine Senator, how do you think she'll do as a President, Nigel?" Salome asked.

"She has what it takes Salome—I have no doubts about her. You should have seen her today—it looked as if she'd been doing this for a long time. She handled a difficult situation with grace and competence. She's going to be a great President." Nigel responded.

"She has a world in chaos and a big job ahead of her," Daniel said. "That's why I've called this meeting. She has requested our assistance."

"Oh. What does she have in mind?" JR wanted to know.

"She believes we, the Rossler Foundation, will have a significant role to play in the immediate future."

Luke raised his eyebrows and looked at Salome. "Well, I guess it all depends on what she wants us to do."

"The President is concerned that there will be those nations that will blame the United States for loosing that madman, Brideaux, on the world and will want revenge. Apart from that, there is also law and order to establish and maintain on the home front. She can use our help with both matters.

"She's undoubtedly right and could *need* our help with both matters," Luke agreed.

"President Campbell is about to make appointments to fill the vacant cabinet positions and has called a meeting with everyone later today. I am hoping we can have an answer for her before then. What are your thoughts on the idea?"

"I don't think there will be any objection in principal— we will help where we can— but I don't want this to become the 'Rossler Agency' of the Federal Government. We're not a spy organization or a law enforcement agency. We are custodians of information, and our first priority is to that purpose." Sinclair said.

"I agree with Sinclair," Salome added. "I don't want to see the Rossler Foundation placed under the control of the Government. I don't mind helping to protect our nation and the world using the information from the libraries to benefit all humanity, but to become active members of a government force, I don't agree with. You know our government—give them your pinkie, and they want your hand and the rest of your body too."

"You know some of the Tectus members won't want to have any involvement with the government, so we will need to consider them as well," Raj added.

Daniel allowed everyone to have their say and then told them that they had the President's promise not to try to nationalize the Rossler Foundation and that she understood the importance for the Foundation to remain independent to be efficient. Everyone relaxed.

"So, the question is," he continued, "What is it we can do to help and how can we do it?"

"Well, now that we are assured that they won't try to hijack our operation we can certainly work out a plan," Jack was looking at Sam, Luke, and Salome.

They nodded their agreement.

Sam continued, "Okay let's get all our security and military experts together and start working on a strategy. Madame President," he stopped and grinned, "my apologies, Laurie, wants something definite within twenty-four hours."

"Who agreed to that crazy timeframe?" Luke asked.

"Our new Vice President," Nigel muttered under his breath.

"We have one of those now?" JR asked.

"Well, sort of, maybe, perhaps, almost, more or less, in a manner of speaking." Nigel chuckled.

"Now what the hell is that supposed to mean?" JR asked.

"I think it's best if he tells us himself."

A long perplexing silence spread through the group.

Salome spoke first. "So, when can we meet the Vice President then? Do we know him or her? Does he or she have a name? Come-on, out with it Nigel."

Nigel looked at Daniel. "Your turn Daniel—you heard them. They want to meet you. Introduce yourself. Don't be shy."

Another moment of incredulous silence fell on the group and then, as if on cue, everyone understood what Nigel just said, jumped up and descended on the poor, bewildered Daniel and Sarah.

It took a good half hour to get the group to return to order and discuss the rest of the agenda.

General Hayden's abhorrent behavior in the Oval Office earlier and the potential threat he could pose was first on the agenda. Because the Secret Service, responsible for the security of the President, Vice President and other high ranking government officials, was currently almost nonexistent and hopelessly understaffed, Sam advised including a security strategy in their plan.

Daniel asked his friend and computer expert, Raj, to immediately get in touch with the Tectus hacker team and ask them to put tabs on Hayden and anyone he connected with.

At this stage of the discussions their resident nano-technology expert, Roy James, looked a bit disappointed—it seemed as if there was nothing for him and his team to do.

In a high-pitched voice, sounding a lot like a little boy who has just learned he was not going to get any of the candy being dished out to his friends, he asked, "Is there nothing you want to blow up with my Nano bombs or cut with my laser tools? No use for my spyflies and drones?

Maybe someone you want to put to sleep with my etorphine mosquitoes?"

Everyone started laughing. Salome was just shaking her head as she thought how Roy has changed over the years, *my husband has certainly become an extrovert since he joined the Rossler Foundation. The women-shy, socially inept Roy James is long gone.*

"Don't worry Roy," Daniel laughed. "I was saving the best for last."

Roy beamed—he was going to get some of that candy after all.

"I am of the opinion you need to make sure that all of those gadgets of yours are in a good working condition—ready to deploy at a moment's notice. And, we'll probably need a lot more of them." Daniel said as he looked around to see if everyone agreed. They all nodded.

"What about the Nano-explosives and Nano-nukes?" Roy asked. "Brideaux only destroyed the world's nuclear arsenals; he didn't destroy the capability to build them again."

Nigel and Sam looked at each other and nodded. "Roy's got a good point there Daniel;" Nigel said. "I hate the whole idea of nuclear weapons—it would have been ideal if we have seen the last of them. But that's wishful thinking—in reality, we'll be facing a new nuclear arms race."

"I agree with Nigel," Sam added. "We will soon see nuclear weapons all over the world again. And although I'm not sure that we could make the decision to build nuclear weapons it would be wise for Roy to continue his research on Nano-nukes."

Daniel gave everyone a chance to air their opinion and then concluded the discussion. "I'm seeing Laurie again in two hours and will convey our suggestions."

Later that afternoon Daniel was ushered back into the Oval Office by the same Marine guard who stood up to General Hayden earlier in the day. As the guard turned to leave, the President called him back. "Lieutenant, I'd like a word with you."

"What's your name, Lieutenant?"

"Rick Jackson, Ms. President," he answered, snapping to attention.

Laurie moved from behind her desk, stopping to face him, like a caring mother, she removed a speck of dust from the shoulder of his otherwise perfect dress uniform.

"Disobeying an order of a superior officer is a court martial offense, Lieutenant. You do realize that, don't you?"

Rick swallowed hard. *Court martial! Hayden is retired and wasn't legally Commander in Chief; he had no right to give me an order —besides it was an illegal order.*

He felt dismay wash through him. "Yes, Ms. President, I'm painfully aware of that."

"And yet you disobeyed General Hayden's order to remove me?"

"Yes, ma'am." *I did what was right, but these politicians never see it that way. As a rule, they don't like the military, regardless of the reason. I'll be lucky if I just lose my rank and position—hope this isn't the end of my career.*

"And knowing now that you could face a court martial would you have done it differently?"

"No, Ms. President, I would not."

"That's the right answer, Lieutenant. In my report to your superior officer, I will be requesting you be given special commendation for your service to, and support of, your President."

Rick blinked his eyes. "Ma'am?"

She smiled and reached out to shake his hand, "It's a pleasure to work with someone who knows their job and isn't afraid to stand their ground—not let themselves be bullied. Thank you, Lieutenant."

"Thank you, Ms. President, I'm honored!" he said saluting.

She smiled. The young man reminded her of her sons when they were that age.

Rick, receiving an acknowledgment of his salute, turned on his heel, and exited the office.

"I think you just made that boy's day," Daniel observed with a grin.

"In my book, he deserved it. Refusing that order would have ended his career had things turned out differently with Hayden."

President Campbell motioned toward the matching sofas covered in cream and gold paisley upholstery, before settling onto one in the corner nearest the fireplace.

Daniel took a seat across from her. He noticed that she hadn't wasted any time locating and returning the Oval Office rug with the Presidential seal and the two flags to the room. The American flag and the Presidential flag stood in their rightful places behind the desk. He imagined as the sitting President she would be adding additional personal touches in due time. He noted the walls were bare and that she'd removed all indications of the previous usurpers of the premises.

"So, Daniel, what have the Rosslerites decided?"

"They're in—boots and all. You'll have our high-level plan by this time tomorrow."

"Thanks, I'm looking forward to reading it."

For the next half hour, Daniel gave her a detailed

account of their discussions at the hotel, including the part about Roy's Nano-nukes.

"Daniel, I'm with Nigel on the nuclear weapons issue— I hate them with a passion." She commented. "But it is as your group has so accurately concluded, we can't be sitting around hoping no one else will build nuclear weapons. Of course, I can't and won't give you official sanction to proceed with your plans, but off the record," She leaned forward and whispered, "make sure Roy James and his team give that highest priority. We need those Nano-nukes ASAP."

"Will do," Daniel smiled. "On the record, off the record, official, unofficial, plausible deniability, et cetera— terminology I will have to get used to in this job." He joshed.

Laurie chuckled. "Yes, Daniel, those and many more are part of all politicians' daily vocabulary."

Daniel nodded and returned to the subject. "I believe you may be familiar with our Head of Security, former FBI Profiler Salome James; she has agreed to be your contact with the Rossler Foundation."

"Hmmm. The name rings a bell. Wait a sec; is she not the young girl who took the FBI to task about their monitoring of the stock markets? Or I should say, their flagrant lack of doing so to discover terrorist activities?"

"That's the one," Daniel smiled.

"The Secretary of the Rossler Foundation..." the President mused. "Got a nice ring to it. What do you think?"

"No ma'am, no official office, just a civilian contact. A top secret one, I suggest."

For the next hour, until the President was due to meet with the Cabinet, she and Daniel discussed plans and strategies.

Thus far, Daniel had been highly impressed with Laurie's prowess as a leader, a thinker, and most important of all, a good listener. She instilled a lot of confidence in him and made him feel more at ease with accepting the nomination.

"Daniel, we're about to go into a meeting with the Cabinet, and I appreciate the fact that you are not a politician—yet. But I am sure that's exactly what we need now—a fresh, new, non-political perspective.

"So, allow me to play devil's advocate here for a short while.

"If you were in my shoes right now, having to go into the meeting and nominate new heads of department, what would you do?" Laurie sat back in her chair waiting—and smiling.

"Laurie this sounds a lot like a job interview." Daniel jested.

"There is that," she chuckled, "but what I really want to know is how you think. I'm not going to be a dictator; I want input from the people who work with me."

Daniel nodded, and it didn't escape him that she used the phrase *'work with me'* and not *'work for me.'* "I've given it a lot of thought since this morning. As far as I am concerned, the word is accountability…"

Laurie interjected with a big smile. "Music to my ears. How would you do it?"

"I would get every appointed official in and review their job descriptions with them, including deliverables, time frames, and budget. Then I'd make them commit to that agreement and publish it for the public to see. I'd set up a system whereby they can be held accountable for what they have committed to. That would avoid empty promises and keep everyone on their toes."

"We are going to make a great team Daniel; I can see that."

"One more thing I'd do is to put our jobs, yours and mine, under those same rules. In other words, you and I will agree our deliverables, commit to it in public and allow the public to hold us accountable."

"Nigel knew what he was talking about when he recommended you for Vice President," Laurie smiled.

Daniel blushed. "I would make every appointment subject to a three-month probation period—every three months, performance is reviewed, and underperformers are replaced—that includes you and me."

"Dramatic, even radical, I would say, but I love every bit of it. If we had that in place years ago, we could have avoided the John Brideaux catastrophe.

"The members should be gathered in the Cabinet Room by now," she said as she stood up. "Let's go and break this exciting news to them. For now, you are still part of an *'unofficial'* advisory group attending the meeting on my invitation."

Daniel nodded his understanding and followed her as she exited the Oval Office, strode purposefully down the carpeted hallway to the first door on the right and opened it to enter the Cabinet Room.

Art Deco-style sconces depicting eagles with wings spread decorated the off-white walls of the Cabinet Room, while three modern glass pendant lights hung over the massive elliptical mahogany table surrounded by eighteenth-century design chairs. On the back of each chair was an engraved brass plate that identified a cabinet position.

Heavy gold drapes along the East wall were open allowing sunlight in through the wall of arched lunette windows over the top of French doors. The scent of various aftershaves and perfumes hung in the air.

The floor was covered by a custom-made carpet of golden stars scattered randomly on a field of crimson surrounded by a sapphire line, separating it from the cream-colored border decorated with a pattern of olive leaves. *What a handsome room* Daniel thought as he took it all in.

The room was buzzing with the various conversations going on when they entered.

"Everyone, please take a seat," Laurie said as she entered. Moving toward the Presidential seat at the center of the East side of the table, she indicated to Daniel that he should sit in the chair next to the fireplace. There was one on either side, and Daniel chose the one next to the bust of George Washington. The Chief of Staff took the chair behind and to the left of the President, and a secret service agent sat in the chair on the other side of the fireplace next to the bust of Benjamin Franklin.

A hush descended on the group, followed by the soft scraping of chairs being moved on the carpet and the rustle of papers being arranged and stacked.

"First of all, I'd like to thank you all for responding on such short notice. Our country, not to mention the world, is in a crisis right now. The abrupt removal of that maniac John Brideaux and his Supreme Council, while most welcome, has left every country in the world in leaderless chaos. We have to act quickly to re-establish ourselves as a nation and resume our place in the international community.

"As Brideaux is an American, and our former President was involved in his scheme, I believe there will be a call for retaliation from some countries, if not most of them.

"I fully expect this to turn ugly, ladies and gentlemen, very ugly.

"I'm looking to bring stability at the quickest possible speed, rebuild our defenses, and try to keep us out of a war. We have very little time, and I am counting on each and every one of you to step up and give more than your best and to motivate and lead your staff by example."

She looked around the room for a moment, noting the presence of the six individuals she had asked Glenn Baier, The Chief of Staff, to contact.

"Before I start with the appointments I want to make a few things clear; first, all appointments are subject to confirmation by the Senate.

"Second I am asking you to make the following commitment; all appointments, confirmed or not, are on a three-month trial basis.

"I am aware that's a radical decision, but I suggest we all get used to it. I will publicly and officially put myself on that three-month trial basis at my inauguration. If I don't perform, I will resign. We are in desperate times that call for such measures.

"Everyone, and I reiterate that includes me, will be evaluated every three months. If we perform and deliver as our job descriptions dictate, the appointment is extended for another three months. If anyone fails to perform, they'll be replaced—immediately.

"Any questions?"

The room had gone so silent; one would have been able to hear a pin drop on the carpeted floor.

"I take it the silence means everyone is in agreement then." She didn't wait for responses.

"That's good. Let's get down to business. If you are appointed but don't feel comfortable with the conditions, please feel free to say so and I will make alternative arrangements. But if you accept the appointment you accept the conditions."

She paused, looked around the room, fixing her gaze on each individual in turn until she had a verbal agreement from everyone. Then she continued.

"I'm appointing Bill Simms Secretary of State, Jerry Taylor Secretary of Interior, Cliff Willis Secretary of Defense, Ruth Morgan Secretary of Labor, Tyler Jones Secretary of Transportation, and Shannon Thomas Secretary of Veterans Affairs."

"The rest of you were appointed by former President Cooper. I prefer not to make any further changes to the Cabinet at this time unless it's absolutely necessary. The only condition to your continuation in your current position is that you are now subject to the accountability rules laid out before.

"I hope I can depend on you for your support and loyalty, and that you will do your utmost to work as a team to get our country through this crisis. If any of you feel you cannot discharge the duties of your office under the current administration and circumstances, please let me know now. And remember we are all on three-month probation as of right now."

There was silence for a few moments before she continued. "Alright, it appears as though no one wants to jump ship yet. Thank you all for your willingness to continue to serve.

"With that out of the way, let's start by looking at what we know. Martin, I know you haven't had much time to analyze things, but what can you tell us?"

"Thank you, President Campbell," the Undersecretary of State, Martin Goldsmith, said. "Currently, all other nations are scrambling, as we are, to re—establish their governments. My analysts are suggesting, as you rightly pointed out earlier, that retaliation from several countries, and possibly from independent radical groups in other areas. Nothing has officially come across the wires yet, but the finger pointing among some groups has already begun. I will have a more detailed report for you by this time tomorrow."

"Thank you, Martin.

"Keith, the same goes for you, I know you've had very little time to prepare for this meeting, but what have you got?"

The Undersecretary of Defense, Keith Adams, spoke up boldly. "Ms. President, as we all know, our entire military has been demobilized, and Brideaux intended to destroy all the weapons. The only positive thing about that is the same is true in all other countries as well. He did not succeed in destroying all of our weapons, and I have instructed all remaining personnel to get on the phones and start contacting as many former soldiers as they can, to bring them back to work.

"I'm happy to report that the effort is going well. Word is spreading, and many soldiers are simply 'reporting back for duty' as if they had been on furlough.

"I've got the senior officers verifying that all bases are staffed. The first order of business for those reporting for duty is to secure each base and inventory the weapons and equipment.

"I expect a near full inventory will be available sometime over the next 48 hours."

"Good work Keith." The report was better than she had hoped. Keith's efforts impressed her. "I would like to get an interim report in 12 hours, finished or not. Then I want an update every 12 hours until all our bases are secured and personnel ready for deployment if and when needed.

"Yes, Ma'am."

"Before I give Bob a chance to talk, can you confirm my understanding that the world's nuclear arsenal has been destroyed—there is no nation left with a nuclear weapon?"

"Yes, Ms. President, that is the correct," Keith nodded. "That's unless someone has somehow managed to escape Brideaux's proverbial nuclear Gestapo net."

Laurie shook her head. "This means we are back into the arms race which was supposed to have ended with the fall of the Berlin Wall at the end of the Cold War in 1989."

"I'm afraid you're right about that Ma'am."

"Bob, how are things on the Homeland Security front?"

Bob Thompson cleared his throat. "Brideaux penetrated all our top-secret files. Efforts are underway to re-secure the information as well as developing better security measures for the future."

Oops! Daniel thought, *I forgot to tell Laurie that we have recaptured all that information. In fact, not only the information pertaining to the USA but every nation on earth. I'll let her know as soon as we have a private moment.*

"We are working on re-establishing locations and details about all known terrorists and terrorist groups, and will be working with the Secretaries of State, Defense, and Energy to provide them with the most up to date information possible."

"Not good news, but better than it could have been. I'd like progress reports from you every twelve hours as well."

Yes, Ms. President."

"Since we're on the subject, what is the situation with the Department of Energy?"

"Our power grid is currently stable." Secretary Hank McMillian stated. "Brideaux ordered the shutdown of all nuclear power plants, and we started with those that produced the lowest percentage of their state's overall power. A dozen plants are down, ten of which we can bring back online—the other two were due for decommissioning in the next couple of years, so we'll proceed with an early de-com on them.

"Another fifteen were being prepared for shutdown, but are still functioning at reduced capacity and can be brought back up to full power in a short time."

"George, how's the Treasury Department?"

George Miller shook his head. "Unfortunately, not good Ms. President.

"Brideaux wiped out all debt and then used that damn chip and his 'credits' to replace the currency. With his system down, no one has any way of using the credits they had under his system.

"At the same time, he wiped the electronic records in every financial institution around the world, so the only money that's out there was what was in people's possession at the time of the shutdown. I believe Secretary Richardson of Health and Human Services can give you a better picture of how this is affecting the population."

Laurie nodded for Helen to respond.

"Thank you, Ms. President, George," Helen Richardson, joined the discussion. "Unfortunately, the situation is grim, to say the least.

"In the cities, gangs have taken over control and citizens are forced to deal with them for food and personal needs. Their prices are unsavory to put it politely. Those who trade with them literally trade their body and soul—women, and sometimes their children, are forced into prostitution—men are forced to join the gangs, often losing their lives in the vicious gang wars that are raging.

"Those in rural areas seem to be better off as they have pulled together in groups; working out both a system of defense and a barter system for food and clothing. Those groups are weathering this whole situation much better than the rest of us.

"Urbanites initially went into the cities, but now that they've encountered the gang system, they are moving toward the rural areas, bringing useful tools and equipment, and trading their skills to become part of one of the community groups."

President Laurie Campbell screamed silently, she felt like bursting into tears, grieving for her people. She ground her teeth. "Cliff, I want soldiers in the cities to stop these gangs. When you give the word, I'll declare martial law until we can establish peace and return legitimate commerce to the areas."

As an afterthought, she turned to the Attorney General, "Scott, correct me if I'm wrong, but I do have the authority to declare martial law without having to run it through Congress—don't I?"

"Yes, ma'am, Article II, Section 2, Clause 1, of the Constitution allows you to do that."

She did a double take. "You knew that right down to the clause just off the top of your head?"

Scott smiled grimly. "I thought it might come up so I looked up the reference before this meeting."

"Good. Cliff, as the new Secretary of Defense, do you agree with all this?"

Cliff, whose face had gone pale along with just about everyone else's in the room, nodded.

The President continued. "In that case, I am going to declare Martial Law at my inauguration."

"Richard, what can the Department of Agriculture do to help with the food issue, especially in the cities?"

"Ms. President, we've been sending in trucks of food, but as you've heard; the gangs are commandeering them. We could stop sending in the trucks."

"No. As terrible as it is, the people are able to trade for food," President Campbell responded. "What information do we have on the transportation capabilities of the people in the cities?" she was looking at the Undersecretary of Transportation.

"Ma'am, I'm still gathering reports, but from what I can tell, those that have cars are able to use them where the streets haven't been too badly damaged by the homemade bombs used in the gang wars."

"What about the bus and rail systems? Are they still operational?"

"Most of them are."

"Alright, here's what we're going to do until we have enough military to enforce martial law." The President was up and pacing, her anger evident in her stride. "Richard, in the cities that are under gang control find locations near the outskirts where the food can be safely distributed.

"Ruth, I know you're new to the position of Secretary of Labor, but meet with your people and get as much law enforcement back in place as quickly as you can. They will wait for military reinforcement before moving into the cities to deal with the gangs, but they are to report to the areas where the food is being distributed to provide support and security there.

"Bob, is there anything left of the Federal Emergency Management Agency?"

"Most of the FEMA personnel were moved to the chipping program. What do you have in mind?"

"Carrie," she said addressing the Secretary of Housing and Urban Development, "I'd like to set up and staff emergency shelters at schools, warehouses, and churches – if they're willing to help – near the food distribution points. I think the gangs will try to retaliate against those who seek food from the points we establish and they may need shelter out of reach of the gangs.

"Helen, Carrie, have your departments work with FEMA on getting food and medical attention to those areas as soon as possible."

"Carol, what is our status where commerce is concerned?"

"As you know, Ms. President, without viable currency, domestic commerce is nearly at a standstill. As with what Helen reported, business is pretty much shut down in the cities due to gangs. In the urban and rural areas, there are some functioning organizations, mostly either on good will or a barter system.

"On the foreign front, everything has come to a standstill. We need a meeting as soon as possible with our foreign counterparts to re-establish trade agreements and get things moving again—for their benefit as well as our own. In today's world, trade has become so interwoven that we are all dependent on one another and cannot survive alone."

"Thank you all. One last announcement." She turned and pointed to Daniel. "For those of you who don't already know him, that person there is Daniel Rossler, CEO of the Rossler Foundation. Their organization is the one who liberated the world from John Brideaux and his Council. Ladies and gentlemen, we are here today, free citizens, only because of the brilliance and resourcefulness of this man, Daniel Rossler and his team of patriots.

"As soon as I have taken the oath of office I will be nominating Daniel Rossler for Vice President."

Everyone in the room immediately turned and stared at Daniel. A long silence followed and then, all of a sudden, thunderous applause broke out.

When the room went quiet again, Laurie ended the meeting. "Bill and Scott," she said looking at the Secretary of State and the Attorney General, "I will need to see you after this meeting to talk about Brideaux and his Councilors."

Chapter Fifteen

'NEED-TO-KNOW' AND 'FACE-TO-FACE'

As the room emptied the four of them, which included Daniel, pulled up chairs at one end of the table and sat down.

"I'd like to discuss what we're going to do with the prisoners.

"They created this mess with that technological Beast they constructed and killed millions with. Nearly everyone on the planet had one of those damned biochips implanted, and suffered beyond description because of it. They're going to be after revenge.

"I know what I would personally like to do with Brideaux and his colleagues," Bill Simms, the new Secretary of State, said, "but I'm sure it won't be acceptable."

"It isn't a matter of what we want to do with them, Bill," Scott said. "I think most of us feel like you. Their crimes are against humanity and as such fall under the jurisdiction of the International Criminal Court—the ICC."

"That court is in The Hague in the Netherlands," Laurie said. "It would be difficult for us to try to transport them over there right now. Besides, we don't know what treaties are still in place and what offices are still capable of functioning. Is it legal for us to detain them until things settle down?"

"Under the circumstances, I don't think we have a choice, Ms. President. We brought them back here; we're going to have to protect them until we can hand them over to the ICC—if that's what we decide to do."

"Alright, but I'm of the opinion we only hand over the non-Americans to the ICC. We deal with the American citizens of the Council in our own justice system. That includes Brideaux. Does that sound right, Scott?"

"No, Ma'am; I'm afraid we can't do that. Their crimes were against humanity just like the others and thus fall under the same jurisdiction as the others, the ICC—provided it still exists.

"If we fail to turn them over with the rest of the prisoners, we will be putting the United States above international law. It would set a terrible precedent and encourage other countries to disobey international law—after all, why should they obey it if we don't?"

Bill added, "So if we keep our citizens, the other countries would demand the return of theirs."

"I see," the President said, thoughtfully.

"Currently, they are under heavy guard at Andrews," Bill said, referring to Joint Base Andrews Naval Air Facility. "It seemed the safest place for now since security is already high there as it's the home of the Presidential aircraft, and they flew in there, so they didn't have to be moved elsewhere."

"I didn't know there were detention cells at Andrews," the President said with surprise.

"There aren't, but we have them under heavy guard."

"Not good enough!" the President exploded. "We need those people in proper detention facilities before someone kills them, or they escape."

"I would suggest a military detention center at this point," Bill said, "it would be harder for someone to gain access to them on a military base."

"Agreed. Get Cliff Willis and FBI Director Mike Steele in here; we'll have them work out a plan to move them from Andrews."

Forty-five minutes later both Secretary of Defense, Cliff Willis and FBI Director, Mike Steele were still deep in discussion with the President, Attorney General, and Secretary of State.

"I think it makes the most sense to hold them at the Navy's Joint Regional Correctional Facility in Chesapeake, Virginia," Cliff said.

"We ought to have a couple of decoy locations," Mike said. "I suggest Joint Base Anacostia-Bolling in D.C. and an FBI safe house in Virginia."

"I like the plan. Ms. President?" Cliff asked.

She paused thoughtfully. "Scott, Bill, what are your thoughts?"

"I don't see anything wrong with the plan or in violation of the law," Scott replied.

Bill nodded. "Agreed."

"Okay. Let's make it happen. How long will it take?"

"I'll need several hours to pull together agents for decoys, transport, and staff at the safe house," Mike advised, "say six to eight hours."

"Same here," Cliff stated. "I'll need time to have the troops, transportation, and facilities arranged."

"Good. We'll plan on moving them by noon tomorrow.

You two work together to arrange the timing. Cliff, I have a few more questions for you, the rest of you are excused."

After they had left, Laurie turned to Cliff Willis. "I've been cautioned about trusting the Cabinet members left over from the previous administration."

"Cautioned? By whom?"

"No names, no pack drills" She grinned. Let's just say it was from someone I trust with my life. Scott and Mike are both inherited, not my appointments, and while I want to trust them, I need to be absolutely sure the prisoners are safe."

"Do you want me to set up another decoy?"

"No, we have all the decoys we need. Here's what I want you to do."

As she filled him in, his eyebrows raised in amazement.

"I'll call Admiral Johnson right away."

"No, Cliff. Talk to him in person. Keep this above Top Secret. Communications about this are on a 'need-to-know' and 'face-to-face' basis only. Nothing gets communicated in any way except face-to-face. Understood?"

"Yes ma'am," Cliff said. He got up and left to execute the President's orders. He smiled as he closed the door; *Laurie Campbell is going to be a great President.*

Chapter Sixteen

SHUT UP AND MOVE

John Brideaux paced the room like a caged tiger. He had regained much of his insufferable demeanor and bravado once he realized he was not going to be killed on the spot by JR, in Brussels.

He was back to his old self; incessant blasphemous, foul swearing, and mad rages rolled out of him in waves. It was annoying the two Air Force, Military Police guards to no end, but somehow, they managed to resist any reaction to anything he said and held their guns at the ready.

He had clearly heard the order given by their superior officer: *"If he comes within five feet of you or tries anything, don't hesitate, shoot him in the leg and then call me."*

He assumed the others were being held in a similar manner. It would take time, but he would figure out how to escape, and then the first order of business would be to take care of JR Rossler and all the rest of the 'goody-two-shoes' Rosslerites.

A knock sounded on the door. One of the MP's spoke,

"Turn around and put your hands on the wall above your head."

Brideaux obeyed the command and listened while the other MP unlocked the door. Both men successfully suppressed their surprise when Admiral Ben Johnson walked in.

"Cuff him. We're moving all the prisoners—now."

"Yes, sir."

Brideaux felt the metal of the cuff snap around his left wrist; his arm was pulled down and behind his back. The MP pulled his right wrist down to meet his left and a second snap secured his hands together.

"Let's go," ordered the Admiral.

Brideaux exited the room following one of the MP's. The Admiral and the other MP brought up the rear. In the hallway, he saw the rest of his group lining up single file and walking toward the exit. He fell in line with them.

They were loaded onto a military bus with dark tinted windows. Two MP's rode in the back, two in the front, and two on either side in the middle; one pair watching the prisoners in the back, and the other two watching the front.

The ride was brief, ten to fifteen minutes before they were ushered off the bus and quickly loaded onto a waiting transport plane.

When they deplaned, they weren't in any place Brideaux ever expected to be.

"What the hell is this?" he shouted.

"Move," was the only response he got.

"You..." Brideaux started to object.

"Shut up and move Brideaux!"

Brideaux heard the sound of a rifle being cocked, and he felt the pressure of the muzzle in his back as the MP pushed him forward. He went quietly and started walking.

Chapter Seventeen

A QUIET PRAYER

"How did the Cabinet meeting go yesterday?" Hayden asked his visitor while handing her a martini. The woman, dressed in a short, tight, red skirt that hugged her curves, accepted the drink. Her low-cut, cream-colored blouse trimmed in lace revealed quite a bit of cleavage, and Hayden eyed it appreciatively. She was a remarkably beautiful and sexy woman, and in Hayden's personal experience, she knew how to please a man.

"Have a seat," he invited and sat next to her touching her bare knee for a few moments.

She winked at him and started talking. "Campbell made appointments to fill the vacant Cabinet positions and had a private meeting with Scott and the new Secretary of State, Bill Simms after we adjourned."

"I wonder what that was about?"

"You're in luck," she said with a sly little smile. "The corridor was empty, and I hung around for a while."

"You are one devious woman!" He grinned. "What did you find out?"

"She's going to try to protect the prisoners until she can turn them over to the ICC. Can you believe that? The ICC."

"Only that stupid bitch could come up with something as idiotic as that. Those monsters need to be brought out into the streets and executed in public."

"Well, she's going to move them to a military detention center in Chesapeake, but there will be two decoy transports to make it look like they are going to someplace in Virginia and another base here in D.C."

"When?"

"Noon today."

"Noon today? That doesn't leave much time. I'll get some people in place to take care of them before they're moved," he muttered.

"Why didn't you tell me about this last night," he exclaimed.

"Well, I waited until 2am, but you didn't come over as promised," she pouted. "So, this is the first chance I had to talk to you. You wouldn't have wanted me to risk calling you on your home phone or mobile. I don't have to tell you; phone calls are not secure."

Hayden was not married. As successful as he was in his military career, so unsuccessful was he in keeping a marriage together. He had divorced from his fourth wife four years prior.

"Okay, you're right; sorry about that. I just have a lot on my mind. What else?"

"Well, I have left the best for last. I have also overheard her discussing the arrangements to announce Daniel Rossler as her Vice President."

A long pause ensued. Hayden was speechless. "Daniel Rossler for Vice President! Now I know she is not fit to be the President, forget even mentioning Commander in Chief in the same breath. She is definitely going to lead us back into the dark ages!"

"I agree with you Tom, but what's done is done. Rossler is very popular right now because of his appearance of having stopped John Brideaux and shutting down that Beast."

"I don't care how popular he is—he'll be as bad or worse than Brideaux was if he gets control of everything—and I guarantee you that's what he's up to," Hayden raged. "Call the group members; we've got to put a stop to this."

Within hours Hayden and his protestors descended on the White House carrying signs objecting to Daniel's appointment to the Vice-Presidency, referring to him as the New Beast that would be the downfall of America.

Some claimed he was a dictator who wanted to control the world; others blamed him for giving John Brideaux the technology in the first place. The news media arrived with them and began broadcasting immediately.

Daniel and President Campbell watched from the second floor of the White House as Hayden, wearing his Army dress uniform, complete with its four stars and rack of ribbon bars, climbed the steps to a hastily built platform on the other side of the fence, and began speaking to the crowd on a bullhorn. In no time, he had managed to whip them up into a fit of rage, shouting, and waving their fists in the air.

"Well, it sure didn't take him long, did it?" Daniel said quietly. "And how did he find out about my pending nomination to the Vice-Presidency?"

"We have a traitor in our midst – that's how he found out. Ugly. This is going to turn very ugly," the President stated.

Daniel spoke softly, "Aristotle said, *'At his best, man is the noblest of all animals; separated from law and justice he is the worst.'*"

"He was right about that." Laurie nodded and left for her office.

Daniel watched the demonstration for a few more minutes and then called Luke on the ultra-secure mirror phone developed by Roy and Raj.

"Luke, it's time that everyone returns to the Rabbit Hole. The unrest is building here, and I'm afraid riots are unavoidable."

"Okay, Daniel, we've been anticipating this; we're already packed and will head out right now.

"Peter, Jack, Max, Mark, and Doug have requested to remain behind in case you need help."

Daniel smiled at the names of the five men. Former Marine medic Max Ellis, John 'Doug' MacArthur a former Marine chopper pilot, and Mark Bryant a former Captain in the Marines had all come to the rescue of the Rossler team that was attacked and stranded in the Grand Canyon by John Brideaux. Peter Scott and Jack Symonds were both former CIA operatives who had been indispensable in helping to bring Brideaux and his council down.

"Thanks, Luke. Let the guys know I will be glad to have their help."

Luke added, "Sarah wanted to stay, but I've convinced her it isn't safe."

At that moment, the President returned and motioned for him to follow her. "Luke. Please tell Sarah I'll call her shortly; I have to go now."

"What's up?" Daniel asked as they headed toward the West Wing at a brisk pace.

"We're having an emergency meeting with Bill Simms, Cliff Willis, and FBI Director Mike Steele. It seems our traitor has been busy—someone tipped off the press that the prisoners are being moved.

"Also, that dog and pony show out front is already being broadcast nationwide, and protests are erupting everywhere. They're protesting against moving the prisoners, calling for their public execution. And," she glanced at him, "against your appointment as Vice President."

Daniel stopped and looked at her—stunned.

She tugged on his sleeve to get him moving again. "It seems, Daniel, that Hayden has reinstated himself as 'General' and is raising an opposing army. He's claiming that you were in partnership with Brideaux, gave him the technology and were working with him before you decided you wanted world dominance for yourself and set things up for him to take the fall!

"He's got his followers convinced you'll be as bad or worse than Brideaux and is referring to you as the New Beast—a dictator who wants to control the world. He's even got some of the religious fanatics calling you the Beast from the Book of Revelation."

"You've got to be kidding," Daniel said incredulously as they descended the stairs to the lower level. "We just got rid of one madman; now we have to deal with another."

They arrived in the situation room, and the President asked for an update as she took her seat. "What's happening at Andrew's?"

Cliff said. "The protestors are pouring in, and the streets are blocked for miles.

"I guess the only good thing about what Brideaux did is that with his anti-gun laws, they aren't able to shoot anyone."

"Maybe not, but they are armed with just about everything else they could get their hands on; clubs, bats, pitchforks, knives, swords, and such," Bill added.

"Well, doesn't that put us between a rock and a hard place?" asked the President.

"How so?"

"I don't want our forces firing on unarmed people, but these people aren't exactly unarmed—even though their weapons aren't guns?" she replied.

Cliff and Mike looked at each other uneasily. Was she saying their men couldn't fire on these people to protect themselves?

"With all due respect, Ms. President, these people are carrying weapons that can be just as deadly as guns and more brutal," Cliff objected.

"Relax Cliff; I agree with you. If it becomes necessary, our troops," she looked at Mike, "and agents should defend themselves and government property. I just don't want them to start it.

"Get all military personnel at Andrews to withdraw from the prisoners' detention rooms and take up defensive positions to protect all military installations and their own lives if necessary."

"Yes, ma'am," Cliff replied and left the room to relay the orders.

"Does that mean you're handing the prisoners over to the crowd Ms. President?" Carrie Trent, the Secretary of Housing and Urban Development, asked.

"I'd rather do that than risk the lives of our soldiers to save the lives of those miserable criminals."

Carrie nodded. "I agree with you ma'am; it's a no brainer. My apologies for interrupting. I am actually here to report on the progress of the shelters and food distribution as you have requested. Your orders are being followed, and stations are being set up. The people will have access to food and shelter from now on—not all people immediately, but most within the next day or two."

"Very good, thank you for the update, Carrie."

Carrie left the room.

Cliff returned within thirty minutes. "Ms. President, your orders are being executed as we speak."

"Good, I hope the mob will be happy and disperse after this."

The Chief of Staff entered the situation room at that moment followed by half a dozen other staff members. He grabbed a TV remote control and turned on a second TV monitor. "Ms. President, I think you need to see this—it's a live broadcast from Andrews."

A blurry picture appeared on the TV screen, shouts and screams could be heard in the background as the crowd made a move on the gate and just kept going until they were through and ran towards the rooms where they had been told the prisoners were being held.

Minutes later, the crowd suddenly fell quiet. Someone's voice could be heard over a handheld bullhorn. "They're not here. They've been moved."

The President was beaming broadly. Daniel and Bill wore expressions of stunned disbelief, and Cliff stood quietly, expressionless, next to Laurie.

The rest of the people in the room were flabbergasted. The President stood and explained that the prisoners had been moved the night before—in anticipation of such an uprising.

Before she could finish, General Hayden's face appeared on TV—he looked like a wet chicken. He stuttered and stumbled and sounded incoherent, almost as if he was thing else they could get their hands on; clubs, bats, pitchforks, knives, swords, and such," Bill added.

"Well, doesn't that put us between a rock and a hard place?" asked the President.

"How so?"

"I don't want our forces firing on unarmed people, but these people aren't exactly unarmed—even though their weapons aren't guns?" she replied.

Cliff and Mike looked at each other uneasily. Was she saying their men couldn't fire on these people to protect themselves?

"With all due respect, Ms. President, these people are carrying weapons that can be just as deadly as guns and more brutal," Cliff objected.

"Relax Cliff; I agree with you. If it becomes necessary, our troops," she looked at Mike, "and agents should defend themselves and government property. I just don't want them to start it.

"Get all military personnel at Andrews to withdraw from the prisoners' detention rooms and take up defensive positions to protect all military installations and their own lives if necessary."

"Yes, ma'am," Cliff replied and left the room to relay the orders.

"Does that mean you're handing the prisoners over to the crowd Ms. President?" Carrie Trent, the Secretary of Housing and Urban Development, asked.

"I'd rather do that than risk the lives of our soldiers to save the lives of those miserable criminals."

Carrie nodded. "I agree with you ma'am; it's a no brainer. My apologies for interrupting. I am actually here to report on the progress of the shelters and food distribution as you have requested. Your orders are being followed, and stations are being set up. The people will have access to food and shelter from now on—not all people immediately, but most within the next day or two."

"Very good, thank you for the update, Carrie."

Carrie left the room.

Cliff returned within thirty minutes. "Ms. President, your orders are being executed as we speak,"

"Good, I hope the mob will be happy and disperse after this."

The Chief of Staff entered the situation room at that moment followed by half a dozen other staff members. He grabbed a TV remote control and turned on a second TV monitor. "Ms. President, I think you need to see this—it's a live broadcast from Andrews."

A blurry picture appeared on the TV screen, shouts and screams could be heard in the background as the crowd made a move on the gate and just kept going until they were through and ran towards the rooms where they had been told the prisoners were being held.

Minutes later, the crowd suddenly fell quiet. Someone's voice could be heard over a handheld bullhorn. "They're not here. They've been moved."

The President was beaming broadly. Daniel and Bill wore expressions of stunned disbelief, and Cliff stood quietly, expressionless, next to Laurie.

The rest of the people in the room were flabbergasted. The President stood and explained that the prisoners had been moved the night before—in anticipation of such an uprising.

Before she could finish, General Hayden's face appeared on TV—he looked like a wet chicken. He stuttered and stumbled and sounded incoherent, almost as if he was drunk. But those who knew him well recognized his anger—they had never seen him so enraged.

President Laurie Campbell said an earnest, silent, but very un-Christian-like prayer—*Lord. A stroke or heart attack will solve a lot of problems for us right now. Don't kill him just incapacitate him. That'll be good enough.*

Unfortunately, the President's prayer was not answered.

Half an hour later, General Hayden was shouting to the crowd, "It's time for us to rise up and put a stop to this! The President has betrayed us! She is protecting people who committed crimes against humanity, and she is about to appoint a man as Vice President, who is without a doubt a co-conspirator with these criminals.

"This man is controlling her, and by controlling her, he will soon control this country. He's in possession of the technology the criminals had; in fact, he's the one who gave it to them. His intentions are to control the world.

"He made it look as if the criminals were the villains, and they were, but let me tell you, Daniel Rossler's plan is to make it appear as if he wants to help us. It's all just smoke and mirrors to deceive us. His end game is to gain control of us! If we let him, our lives will be worse off than before.

"They," he pointed to the White House behind him, "are lying to us. They will be our downfall, the end of our nation.

"I am telling you the truth! We have to stop them before it is too late! We want truth and justice!"

The crowd was in a frenzy, shouting and screaming, punching their fists in the air and started chanting; "We want Truth! We want Justice!"

Some in the mob rushed to the security fence surrounding the White House and began to climb it.

Hayden took cover when the White House security force started firing warning shots over the heads of those attempting to breach the fence.

"Call a meeting of our top officers!" Hayden shouted at his aide in panic. "We need a plan of attack to take these bastards out for good. And get some people down to the Joint Regional Correctional Facility in Virginia. We've got to get those criminals out of there and execute them!"

"Daniel! Are you alright?" Sarah questioned breathlessly.

"I'm fine, sweetheart. How's Nicholas?"

"He misses his daddy—just like me."

"I know. Thank you for returning to the Rabbit Hole where it's safe. As much as I miss you, I wouldn't want you to be stuck down here in times like these."

The President, Daniel, some of the Cabinet members, Secret Service men, and others present in the White House Situation Room had quickly moved to the more secure Presidential Emergency Operations Center, six stories below the East Wing, when the first petrol bombs exploded in the streets.

"It's crazy out there Daniel," Sarah exclaimed.

"I know. Hayden has a lot more support than we anticipated and has stirred up a hornet's nest," he said as he watched a silent television screen showing scenes of fighting in the streets, homemade bombs exploding, and buildings burning in the background.

"It's like half the nation's people have lost their minds."

Chapter Eighteen

UNDER NEW MANAGEMENT

There was a sense of urgency amongst the Cabinet members as they realized that General Hayden was stoking a fire that would soon be out of control. The first order of business was to get the President sworn in, and Daniel's appointment as Vice President confirmed by Congress.

Glenn Baier, the Chief of Staff, took it upon himself to make that happen in short order. He gathered the senior White House officials and went to work throughout the night.

By 10:00 am the next day, the President's inauguration was scheduled—it was to take place at noon. With Congress severely reduced by Brideaux's actions there were only sixty of the one hundred Senators, and one hundred ninety members of the House of Representatives, left alive. Nevertheless, the remaining two hundred fifty members of Congress outdid themselves. In an almost unprecedented bipartisan vote, they confirmed Daniel's appointment with an overwhelming majority—only five abstained while another ten voted against.

At noon, the most inconspicuous presidential inauguration ceremony in history took place in the Press Briefing Room of the White House. The room was packed with reporters from every conceivable media outlet who could find a place to stand, leaving almost no space for anyone else to be present. That didn't matter, what was most important was to get the news out across the country and the world, as quickly and efficiently as possible.

America had a new President and Commander in Chief as well as a Vice President in the saddle.

First, Daniel took the oath of office of Vice President, followed by Laurie Campbell taking her oath as President—as was the tradition.

The President made her inaugural speech, keeping it short and to the point as she informed the media of the appointment of officials, and the new accountability strategy that would be put in place for every appointed official, including herself and the Vice President.

She continued, "Due to the civil unrest ravaging our country, I am declaring temporary national martial law until the country stabilizes. This will be implemented in three stages. Stage one, which begins now, is total government control of certain things that I will explain in a minute.

"Stage two will be when the government is able to start releasing the control established in stage one. This will happen gradually as our country stabilizes.

"Stage three will be the complete cessation of all government control established in stage one.

"I've established and communicated the stages to you to reassure you that this is not the establishment of a dictatorship and that it is not permanent. There is a plan in place to remove national martial law as soon as possible.

The duration of martial law will depend entirely on the people of the United States. The quicker we return to order the quicker this will be over.

"As of now, full national martial law is established. Our international borders are closed. No person will be allowed in without proof of American citizenship. Our border patrol officers have been instructed to enforce this order. If you are outside the country and watching this, for your own safety, do not attempt to cross the border at any location other than a legal checkpoint.

"The status of our trade agreements with other nations is unknown at this point. Until this is resolved and trade agreements have been re-established and confirmed, very few goods will be coming into the country.

"All fuel resources are now under government control. We will be producing and refining our own petroleum. Until we are fully operational and capable of supplying our needs, there will be travel restrictions to preserve our existing resources.

"Production, transportation, and distribution of food and medical supplies for public use will have top priority and be unrestricted. Those traveling locally for work have secondary priority.

"Travel for pleasure outside your local area is prohibited. All these travel restrictions apply only to vehicles that use gasoline. You are free to move about by foot, bicycle, paddle, or animal power.

"All farms and farm equipment are now under government control for food production. If you have a farm and or open land, officials will be coming to discuss crops with you. Your land will remain in your possession; we only want crops to feed our people. Your equipment will remain in your possession, and you will only be asked to use it on your land or available land nearby.

"We will be depending on farmers and ranchers who know their areas and which crops will grow best to make recommendations to us for planting and harvesting.

"For those of you who have small properties with room for gardens, we encourage you to plant and farm food for yourselves and to share with neighbors. If you have need of seeds, officials will make sure they are available to you. Personal gardens only large enough to feed your own family will not be touched by the government—we're only interested in mass production to feed our nation.

"Currently we have a serious situation in the cities where gangs have taken control. Military forces are being dispatched to supplement the police force. Those arrested for violence will be imprisoned immediately and their weapons will be confiscated.

"In anticipation of these arrests, those prisoners serving time for non-violent crimes will be released as needed in order of the severity of their crime starting with the least severe first. Those who are released will be sent to work on nearby farms to help with food production. Prisons will be moving to near lock-down status and food will be restricted to the basics. Prisoners will have a bed, blanket, water, and basic food. They will not be treated inhumanely.

"All areas will be subject to a dusk until dawn curfew. I ask all citizens to please cooperate with the military and law enforcement. We need to work together to stabilize our country as quickly as possible so that martial law can be ceased.

"One final note. Radio and TV broadcasts are going to be temporarily restricted to the following conditions: G and

PG rated films may be shown; family shows may be shown; informational and historical shows may be shown.

"Violent movies and shows are temporarily prohibited in an effort to help influence the establishment of peace. The news media is allowed to report facts, and I encourage them to report positive facts and not sensational speculation. Please don't fabricate news.

"There are protests in progress at the moment. Freedom of speech is a right of every citizen, and I don't want to take that away, even temporarily. Therefore, peaceful protests and demonstrations are allowed but limited to groups of fifty in any given area. Groups of more than fifty will be required to split and move to different locations no closer than two-hundred yards. If a protest or demonstration turns violent, military and law enforcement will act accordingly."

A long, shocked, silence descended in the Press Room.

The President used the silence to again plead with the people of America to remain calm and exercise restraint, to help each other and to do their patriotic duty by obeying the laws and cooperating with the law enforcement agencies. She explained the food and shelter provisioning arrangements that were already in progress.

When she stopped, there were a few moments of chaos as every one of the reporters tried to get a question in. The President answered questions for about half an hour, and then she and Daniel left to attend an emergency Cabinet meeting.

The people at the Rabbit Hole watched the proceedings at the White House—as expected thunderous applause went up when Daniel took the oath. Their jubilations subsided when President Campbell moved to the podium and took her oath, then ended completely when she proclaimed Martial Law. Some of them expected the announcement, but for most of them, it came as a big shock.

Martial law was declared only once, nationally, in the history of America and that was at the outset of the Civil War in 1861 by President Abraham Lincoln. Although Congress has never declared martial law, they ratified most of the measures declared by President Lincoln.

When the ceremony and questions ended, the Rossler Foundation leadership group assembled to busy themselves with the tasks at hand.

First order of business was to consider the impact Daniel's new role would have on the functioning of the Rossler Foundation. Sarah and Daniel had already had a long discussion about it in the early hours of the morning and agreed on what they wanted to happen.

Rebecca and JR, Salome and Roy, Raj, Nigel, Ben, Luke, Ryan, Sam, Sinclair and Sarah, were all present in the Robert Cartwright Town Hall.

Sarah informed them about the talk she and Daniel had and opened the topic for discussion.

"I think Sarah did a wonderful job of running this place while Daniel and the rest of us were trying to make our way back from the Grand Canyon site after Brideaux stole the technology and left us for dead," JR said.

"Hear, hear!" Ryan, Sarah's dad, and Ben, her father in law shouted.

"Thank you," Sarah said. "I appreciate the gesture JR, but Nicholas and I will be off to Washington as soon as things have calmed down. So, I am afraid you will have to do without me.

"Daniel and I think it's best to turn the management over to a committee or board of directors."

Ben said. "I still think we'll need one person to be the CEO of the Foundation, or at least the interim head until you and Daniel return. We need someone with a vision for the Foundation who can direct us."

"Well, it could be ten years before the two of them return, Ben." Sinclair laughed.

"What do you mean, ten years?"

"Well, Campbell has two years left in the previous President's term. then Daniel will be President for two terms," Sinclair chortled.

When they stopped laughing they looked at each other, and Sarah said, "You saw the news: gangs running amok in the cities creating terror and race wars. People are killing each other over food, property disputes ending in murder, families and even whole communities starving to death, reports of cannibalism, people dying from lack of medical care, and diseases spreading due to unsanitary living conditions in the most poverty-stricken areas.

"And that doesn't even take into account the political uprising nationally and worldwide! Daniel and I think it is a task beyond a single individual."

Luke agreed. "Do you have something in mind, Sarah?"

"Well, yes, as a matter of fact, I do," she grinned.

They all looked inquisitively at her.

"Sam did an excellent job of leading the Phoenix project, he and Luke have a lot of experience with security and both national and international issues. Nigel is our political expert. My father in law, Ben, and my dad both have been very efficient with setting up and running things locally, Sinclair is the master of the translation project, and

John has really gotten the 'pulse' of the people here since he took over running the school.

"I think they, the Musketeers, would make a great team for running things. Apart from their skills and experience they also have the wisdom of age in their favor. And of course, you all know the old adage, behind every successful man is a woman with a rolling pin." She chuckled.

"Yea, I'll go along with that, just as long as they don't drink themselves into a stupor on the moonshine from that still up in their pub." JR said with a mock serious face.

The seven Musketeers were on their feet. Nigel was the spokesman. He looked at his fellow Musketeers and said, please repeat after me, "We the Musketeers of the Rabbit Hole hereby solemnly swear to uphold the…"

That was as far as he got before another loud roar of laughter interrupted the rest of their oath of office. Sarah finally got them under control, and they all became serious.

Salome said. "I think that's an excellent suggestion." She looked at the rest of the attendees to see if they agreed. They all did.

Rebecca added. "Who better than the Musketeers to lead us!"

"Good! It's settled then," Sarah proclaimed. "Now, who is going to be the leader of your team?"

They all looked at Nigel.

"Oh no," he said, "I'm happy to be on the team to help, but you need someone fully familiar with the Rossler Foundation to be the leader. Besides, Laurie and Daniel are counting on me to advise them. How about Sam? He did a fantastic job with the Phoenix project."

Sarah exhaled, "I already suggested that, and for the same reason."

Sam replied, "No, I agree with Nigel; it should be

someone completely familiar with all the Rossler Foundation information and processes and culture."

After a lengthy discussion, it was decided that Sinclair would be the Team Leader and new CEO as he had been part of the Rossler Foundation from the beginning.

Next, they turned their attention to the uprising fueled by General Hayden and his cronies.

"We'll be lucky if this doesn't turn into an out-right civil war. We have our work cut out for us," Salome opened the discussions.

"Well, the first thing I think we should do is to get everyone back here and tell them what is going on," Sinclair said. "I haven't spoken to many of the people yet, but I can imagine that some of the people here were thinking of returning to their homes and families."

"Good point Sinclair," Sarah commented. "My suggestion is that we ask everyone to remain here in the safety of the Rabbit Hole until things on the outside have settled down."

"Yes, I agree with that Sarah, Sinclair," Nigel joined in. "We'll have to stay here - all of us - and the location must remain a secret."

Everyone agreed, and the rest of the inhabitants were called back to the town hall for a briefing.

Chapter Nineteen

A LOCATION FOR THE EXECUTIONS

General Hayden had gathered his senior officers around him. "We have forces at the correctional facility in Virginia. They are working on plans to break in, get the prisoners, get them into the streets, and have a public execution.

"We've arranged for the media to attend the executions so they can be broadcast live to all parts of the country and the world. We want the world to know that as the new government of the United States, we aren't going to let those lunatics get away with what they did. And we're not going to support their sorry asses in jail while they await trial or serve life sentences—God forbid. They are going to be executed. Dead; just like their victims," he ended with a shout.

"Write that down, Dean," he said to his aide, "that is good speech material."

"Yes, sir!" Dean said and started writing furiously.

"What we need to do now is plan to take over the White House so we have the control and power to bring stability to this country. After all, whoever controls the White House controls the country."

"General, how exactly do you plan to stabilize the country, given the chaos it's in right now?"

"What kind of a moron are you, Alfred?" the General roared. "We're going to use military power to bring peace and stability quickly and efficiently; then we're going to return things to the way they were—with a few adjustments of course. We don't want to repeat the mistakes of the past. Do we?"

"What kind of adjustments?"

"Women are going back in the home where they belong. They should be taking care of their husbands and children, not working. It is this evil thing of working mothers that caught us with our pants around our knees—handing the country, and the world, to a lunatic.

"The freeloaders in society are going to find themselves without welfare checks—they can get out there and earn a living just like everyone else.

"We're going to start shooting illegal aliens instead of capturing them, holding them in detention centers and feeding them with taxpayers' money or sending them back so that they can come back over the border again. That is lunacy. A dead body can be a powerful deterrent.

"We're going to execute criminals too, instead of supporting them in jail for twenty years to life."

"I'm not sure all the states will go along with those idea's, General."

"Of course, they will," the General laughed. "If they don't, they will be branded as criminals, and I just told you what happens to criminals."

"General, I think it's going to be a little harder than that."

Hayden roared. "It won't be harder than that. They'll toe the line, or I'll blast their asses off the planet."

"General?"

"We're going to have the power of the military behind us, Alfred. That means weapons. We'll build nukes again, and I'll drop a nuke on them if I have to. This is going to be a man's country, a military country and we aren't going to have any weaklings, parasites, or dissenters."

Major Alfred Weinberger threw a quick glance around at the other officers. He was the only Major in the midst of Colonels and Generals, yet everyone else seemed enthralled with the General's plans. Weinberger was visibly worried, but he kept his mouth shut.

The General seemed almost murderous at the moment; *perhaps he would be more open to reason later.*

"If there aren't any more ridiculous questions, let's get started with planning the takeover of the White House. Bud, what do you have?"

Colonel Bud Jarmin sat a box on the table. "I brought all the maps and intelligence I could find."

"Excellent! Let's get busy."

Jarmin handed out folders filled with papers. "Here's one on rumored tunnels under the White House that—"

He got no further. "I don't care about rumors," the General snorted. "I know more about the White House than anyone, and I know about the tunnel Ronald Regan had installed and the tunnel to the Treasury Building. There aren't any others, so forget the rumors. Believe me, when it comes to the White House, if it isn't verified, it isn't there."

"But General, shouldn't we at least—"

"No! Forget about rumors and stick to hard facts! Understood?"

"Yes, General."

With architectural drawings of the White House, including the East and West wings, on the table, they began to discuss the most likely places for the President to be. Debating the best paths of attack, assembly, fallback, and regrouping points, prime target areas, et cetera.

Many hours later a Captain entered the room with a report for the General.

"Sir! Our troops in Virginia are set to penetrate the correctional facility, the news media is on standby, and a location for the executions has been prepared."

"Very good! Thank you, Captain. I will let them know when they can move."

"Yes General," the Captain said, with the best attempt at a proper salute he could manage.

General Hayden's troops were mostly angry civilians with no military experience; the rest were mostly low-ranking, impressionable recruits with less than a year of active duty under their belts.

"Alright gentlemen," the General said as he wrapped up the meeting, "We have everything in place. I will let you know when we will execute our plan. In the meantime, make sure you and your men are ready to move into action within thirty minutes from receiving my order."

Chapter Twenty

BUSINESS AS USUAL

The town hall meeting with the entire Rabbit Hole community went better than Sarah had hoped. She expected some dissenters, but there were none. Given the climate in the world outside the Rabbit Hole, everyone agreed that remaining in the cave was the safest and wisest thing to do.

Having concluded the town hall meeting, the Musketeer's turned their focus back to the situation in Washington and Daniel's request for escape routes out of the White House. Sam and Salome headed for Luke's office, locating and taking JR, with them. Luke went to speak with Nigel, who was talking with a small group on the other side of the hall.

"Nigel," Luke said when he joined the group. "Wonder if I could borrow you for a while? We could use your help with some things."

Nodding in agreement, Nigel excused himself from the group and joined Luke on the walk to his office. "What's up, Luke?"

"Sam, Salome, and I thought it prudent to have an escape plan in place should Hayden and his crowd make a move on the White House that can't be repelled. We are going to work on planning escape routes out of the White House and back to the safety of the Rabbit Hole. We'd like your help as you have intimate knowledge of the White House. We've also asked JR to join us for his military expertise – his experience as a Marine should be helpful."

"Sure, I'll be glad to help!" Nigel agreed as they joined the others in the war room.

"Salome, let's bring everyone up to speed with where we are," Luke said taking his seat at the table.

Salome nodded. "Raj and his Tectus friends have successfully deployed their hacking programs against General Hayden and his leadership group, and have set up alarms to notify us if the sniffers they deployed find information of value to the President. We are gathering information from their internet usage, mobile phones, and landlines.

"We've contacted Eric Winchester and Dennis McMahon." Eric was a former Marine Colonel, who is in command of Tectus; his second in command, Dennis McMahon, is a former Navy SEAL.

"They have both activated their members in the D.C. area and infiltrated Hayden's group." She grinned and added, "Two of their members are part of Hayden's leadership group."

Luke grinned as well, "Oh, that's excellent!"

"What we need is several scenarios for escape from different locations in the White House; the most likely being the Oval Office, The Cabinet Room, The Situation Room, and the Presidential Emergency Operations Center," Salome said.

"I think it would be better to plan on directional escape

from general areas rather than specific rooms. That way we have a better chance of success if they are in a room we haven't accounted for, or moving between areas." Sam added.

"You're right, Sam; that would be the better way to plan," Salome agreed

"We can designate which exit they're going to use with a code name so they can tell us which plan they are going to use. North will be Operation Eagle, South will be Operation Hawk, East can be Falcon, and West can be Condor." JR contributed.

"Excellent suggestion, JR!" Salome smiled.

"We're also going to have to consider escape by foot, car, and air," Sam added.

JR crossed his arms over his chest. "I'd hate to have to get them out of there on foot or by car. There is a reason the President's helicopter, is used to move the President from the White House. I think we should try our utmost to make use of it."

"Agreed," Luke said. "But we have to be prepared for any possibility and flexible to change between them as needed. We're also going to need Roy's help once they're in the air. Let's get him in here."

JR was back with Roy in two minutes. "What's up?"

"We need you to hide an airborne 747 for us."

Roy laughed, "oh, is that all? No problem! You just have to know what buttons to push." He was serious.

The others were a little surprised that he thought it would be so easy.

"We can pull the same trick we used for getting Nigel and Ester off their ranch," Roy said.

"But that was a small aircraft," Sam objected. "Here

we're talking about a plane that is over two-hundred feet long with a huge wingspan."

"Two hundred thirty-one feet long, 195-foot wingspan, and 63 feet tall," Nigel supplied.

"It won't be a problem," Roy replied. "My owl drones can be adjusted to account for the size, and the Presidential plane already has electronic countermeasures to jam radar signals.

"We'll bring the drone in, using stealth mode, shut down the plane's identifying transponder, and then engage the electronic countermeasures on the plane at the same time I deactivate the drone's stealth mode."

"Brilliant!" Sam said. "Just don't explain the technical details. It will be a waste of time and breath."

Luke grinned, "Let's take a look at the D.C. information we have and see what we can do to get them safely to the plane." They pulled out maps and photos and got to work.

With Jack Symonds and the rest of his team in D.C. on the mirror phone, Sam and the escape planning team at the Rabbit Hole went over the plans.

"We've decided to go with a basic directional escape plan by area rather than try to plan a scenario for every possible location," Sam said.

"Excellent thinking!" Jack agreed, "That will make things a little easier."

"We've selected four directions and code-named them as follows: Escape to the North will be referred to as Operation Eagle, to the South will be Hawk, East will be Falcon, and West will be Condor.

"Jack, we're going to depend on you to be our onsite team leader. It will be up to you to make the assignments, fine tune plans as needed, and adapt to any changes that arise."

Jack laughed. "No problem Sam, there's only about a million and one things that can change or need to be adapted in a situation as volatile and high profile as this."

"Let's hope it will never come to that. Nevertheless, we have confidence in you Jack; you'll be fine. Let's talk about the details of these plans."

The two groups spent the next several hours reviewing the planning team's recommendations, poring over the maps, planning exact routes and possible deviations, making adjustments and discussing possible scenarios. In the end, they were all in agreement.

"This looks good guys, really good," Jack commented.

"I'm glad to hear you say that, Jack. You guys are the ones who will be dealing with the action if it comes to that. You're the ones who need to feel comfortable with this," Luke said.

"Just get that meeting with Eric Winchester and Dennis McMahon arranged as soon as possible so that we can fill them in and have everything in place quickly. I have this gut wrenching feeling about that Hayden clown."

"We're working on that right now." There was a brief pause, then, "In fact, the meeting is set for 8 pm your time at one of the Safe Houses, I'll have the address for you in a minute. All required members are being notified now and will meet you there for briefing and assignment."

"Great! So, it's back to BAU then." Jack said.

"BAU?" Sam asked.

"Business as usual." Jack laughed.

Sam provided the safe house location address before

they hung up and Jack was surprised to see that it was fairly close to the White House.

Chapter Twenty-One

THE DECOYS

It was 4 pm when Jack's mirror phone rang—it was Sam. "Jack, the holiday is over. I just got off the phone with Eric Winchester, their insider on Hayden's leadership group has important news which he says we must act on immediately. He doesn't have a secure phone, so he needs to meet in person. Eric is going to pick him up now and will meet you at the safe house in an hour."

"Okay let me just get out of the swimming pool, put my clothes on and pull our former Wall-Street-guru-turned-secret-agent, Peter, out of the bar," Jack quipped. "We'll head over there right now."

"Okay Jack, keep us posted," Sam smiled as he disconnected. That's Jack Symonds—when there was a crisis he was as cool as a cucumber, and a humorous side of him emerged that never existed in normal situations.

Jack and Peter were in the rental car on their way to the safe house in less than five minutes.

"I wonder what that crazy general is up to now?" Peter remarked as he put on his seatbelt. Jack was driving.

"We'll find out soon enough."

Eric Winchester, Dennis McMahon, and Major Alfred Weinberger — one of the two Tectus members who had infiltrated Hayden's leadership group — were already at the safe house when Jack and Peter arrived.

Eric, Dennis, Peter, and Jack already knew one another. Alfred was introduced to Jack and Peter, and they all moved to a secured room. The room was scanned for bugs and cameras before Alfred started his report.

Over the course of the next twenty minutes, Alfred gave them a detailed report of Hayden's planning meeting earlier in the day.

"He's got everything in place to launch an offensive against the correctional facility at Chesapeake to get hold of the prisoners and execute them in public. As soon as that's done, he will launch an attack on the White House. He believes that the one who is in control of the White House is in control of the country."

"When's he going to make his move?" Jack asked.

"No specific time has been set. He is keeping that to himself, but all his troops, if you can call them that, are on standby to go into action with 30-minutes notice."

"How many men has he assigned to Chesapeake and the White House operations," Peter asked.

"Difficult to give exact numbers; there is a core group of about two-hundred men at Chesapeake right now, but people are coming in droves out of the neighborhoods, some are spectators, others are joining them. I would say we might be looking at a crowd of between one and two thousand people by the time he launches the attack. I think that is part of his strategy—to get as many sympathizers as possible before he gives the signal."

"And the White House?" Jack asked.

"Same story. A core group of about hundred men who will be first in, but again he's building critical mass amongst the populace, and we might very well be looking at four to five-thousand people by the time he goes into action. It's the White House people we're interested in, I suspect there are going to be thousands of bystanders—many of them might, on the spur of the moment, decide to join in the fun of storming and taking over the place."

Alfred looked at his watch. "Okay, I can stay another twenty minutes then I have to go back. Hayden has an order group at 6:30 pm and I need to be there."

"Alfred, just checking, you are not by chance a member of ISIS, Al Qaeda or some other fanatic group?" Jack asked, pokerfaced.

"Shit no! What the hell…" Alfred protested.

"Okay, no worries Alfred," Jack grinned. "I just wanted to make sure we are not missing an opportunity to send you into that meeting with a suicide vest strapped to your body."

Alfred relaxed and started laughing. "No Jack, I would love to carry a bomb in there but not strapped to my body. I'm afraid we'll have to come up with another plan."

Jack looked at the others. "Any of you guys by chance carrying a few ounces of Semtex or C4?"

They all shook their heads.

"A few sticks of dynamite will also work, even a bit of fertilizer and diesel."

They all smiled and shook their heads again.

"Well, then I guess we have no choice but to do this the old-fashioned way—kick their asses," Jack said.

They all nodded. Peter was used to Jack's shenanigans in a crisis, but Dennis was wondering if Jack was the right man to lead the operation. Eric, assured him later, after they had left the safe house, that Jack's tomfoolery was a sign that he was in operational mode—one hundred percent. He was lethal when he was like that.

"Okay, Alfred," Jack continued. "Step us through Hayden's plan in detail."

Alfred gave them the details and told them about the maps which Colonel Bud Jarmin supplied, the paths of attack, prime target areas, assembly, fallback, and regrouping points.

"And what is his plan if he manages to capture the President and Vice President or any of the other senior officials?" Peter asked.

"He didn't spell that out in any detail, but you can imagine, by that time they will have executed the prisoners in public, the crowds will have an insatiable bloodlust—you can visualize what's going to happen."

Alfred's time was up—he had to leave in the next few minutes.

"Okay, Eric can you give Alfred one of the mirror phones?" Jack asked. "I will get Raj to set it up so that Alfred can reach all of us to keep us up to speed with things."

They showed Alfred how to use the phone while Jack called Raj and asked him to program the phone as required.

By the time Alfred left, his mirror phone was setup. Jack, Peter, Eric, and Dennis started planning a counter for Hayden's plans.

"The problem is we don't have enough police and military forces to fend off an attack on the White House and Chesapeake—not if Hayden is going to do it tonight.

"Yes, the police and military can't even enforce the curfew imposed by martial law, let alone defend the White House and Chesapeake," Dennis added. "I think we'll have to concentrate our efforts on the White House, as you suggested."

It was 6 pm when Jack and Peter got into their car and drove to the White House to meet with the President, Daniel and the head of the Secret Service.

Dennis and Eric were on their way to meet with their leadership group to brief them on the plan.

On their way to the White House, Peter got Daniel on the mirror phone and briefed him on the situation. He requested that Daniel arrange with Nick Clancy, the Special Agent in Charge of the White House Secret Service detail, to allow them access through the Blair House tunnel when they arrive. The tunnel was one of several secret tunnels connecting the White House to nearby buildings including the Eisenhower Executive Office Building, the New Executive Office Building, and the US Treasury building.

When the two of them were escorted into the Presidential Emergency Operations Center by Nick Clancy, shortly before 7 pm, President Campbell, Daniel and Glenn Baier, the Chief of Staff, were waiting for them.

They were all introduced to each other and took their seats as indicated by the President.

"Let's have it," the President said.

Jack gave them the details of the discussion with the Tectus leaders and Alfred Weinberger, then stepped them through the plan and maps which Sam and his team had transferred via the mirror link earlier.

Nick Clancy's face was pallid. He was shaking his head. "I don't have a fraction of the agents I need, the police and the military are hopelessly understrength. Four to five thousand people at the gates... we don't have enough or proper weapons, not to mention ammunition..."

"Tectus will be able to supply about one hundred men," Jack said. "But they don't have much in the form of real firepower either. Pickaxes and shovels are not going to do us any good against a cast of thousands."

"We have two options as I see it," Daniel said. "We move out as quickly as possible—as in right now, or we wait and see if they really attack. But I'm not keen on the idea of abandoning the White House because of a threat."

"Absolutely." President Campbell said. "I'm staying here until it becomes clear that we have no choice but to evacuate. I'm not handing this place to them on a silver platter. Let's send the staff home, and the rest of the people onsite can decide if they want to stay or go. I know it's going to endanger the ones staying behind, but I am not asking anyone to do anything that I am not prepared to do."

She looked around to everyone and got their agreement.

Nick nodded. "No question about it. My people and I stay here, and we defend the President and everyone on site. I agree with Jack and Peter's assessment—the attacks will be tonight. Hayden has the attention of a lot of people now, but their interest will soon dwindle if there is no action—time is not on his side. The longer he waits, the more time we have to bring in reinforcements, and he knows that."

"That's about the size of it," Jack remarked. "I suggest we work out the final details of the escape plan so we all know what to do and expect when the time comes."

"Let's do it," the President said.

Peter got up and spread the maps open on the table. "Here are the possibilities we have."

The first map showed streets and buildings; the second was a satellite image of the same area. Pointing to various colored marks on the maps, he traced the escape routes recommended by Sam's team. As he mentioned each route, he gave her a logistical synopsis of the plan for using it.

The President stood to move about the room. "I know we have at least one Hayden spy in our midst. What do you say we enhance the escape plan with a bit of a twist of our own?"

"What do you have in mind Madame President?" Jack asked.

"Well, I'll have to call an urgent meeting and tell everyone that we expect an attack and provide them with the escape plan, and that could be a good opportunity to feed Hayden's mole some misinformation."

Jack started smiling, *I like this President, she's got a head on her shoulders.* "That could work very well, Ms. President. Do you have an idea who the mole is?"

"Well, I think it is one of the inherited cabinet members, but I am not sure which, and there could be more than one. I just wish we could be certain."

Daniel looked at Jack and Peter. Laurie, there might be a way. Do we have a list of the names of those people with their telephone numbers?"

"Yes, I'll give it to you in two minutes," Glenn said.

"Bingo!" Jack shouted. "Now we're going to nail their asses to the wall. Oh shit... apologies Ms. President." He said as the blush spread over his face.

The President just smiled and waved his apology away. "When you nail their asses to the wall I will be right next to you handing you the hammer and nails Jack."

Daniel just laughed. He was already dialing Raj.

"Raj, Daniel here. Time for you and your Tectus buddies to get some fresh air and do something important for your country."

"Yeah, right Daniel, as if we have never done anything important before." Raj chuckled.

"Okay, Raj, I'm uploading a list of names and telephone numbers as we speak. Please get everyone you can onto this and find out who on that list has been talking to Hayden or any of his officers. You already have tabs on Hayden and his cronies; we are looking for anyone on the list that's been talking to one of them."

"Got it. I'll be back within the hour."

"No Raj, we don't have an hour, I was hoping I could stay online while you get it."

"Daniel, I am good, but not that good." Raj sighed.

"Okay Raj, you've got ten-minutes, tops, please, we need that information. I promise you if you can do it I will put in a good word with President Campbell to allow you access to Area 51."

"I am already onto it. And don't worry if I can't go to Area 51, I will still have it in ten minutes."

Jack walked to the far end of the room and phoned Sam to bring him up to speed with what was happening.

"Daniel, you have some explaining to do," Laurie said in a serious tone.

Daniel raised his eyebrows.

"I get a distinct impression that the Rossler Foundation has been bugging people's phones? Don't you need a court order for that?"

"Martial law ma'am—calls for drastic measures," Daniel grinned.

"I see you're picking up this political game very quickly. And what was that about Area 51?"

"Well, Laurie, that's something I'll have to explain to you when we have more time. But for now, just know that if you ever want to give Raj and his friends a big present, don't give them medals, just allow them to visit Area 51. They firmly believe that the US government has been hosting aliens there."

Laurie looked at Daniel incredulously. "And this Raj guy, he is one of your top technical guys, on the Rossler Foundation board of directors?"

"Yes, and yes, and let me tell you he is the best of the best. You put him and Roy James together, and they'll produce the technology to save the world—as they just did."

Daniel's phone started ringing. He checked his watch it was six minutes. "Tell me you've got it Raj."

"Well, Daniel that offer to see Area 51 did the trick. Your spy is Carrie Trent, the Secretary of Housing and Urban Development. She has made no less than ten calls to Hayden the last two days. One of my hacker group says he recognized her from the TV when he saw her and Hayden together in a wayward restaurant out in Virginia last night."

"I'll be damned. Okay, anyone else on that list had contact with Hayden?"

"No one else. She's the one Daniel."

"Thanks, Raj great job."

Everyone was looking at Daniel. "It's Carrie Trent; not only did she make ten calls to Hayden in the last two days, but they also had dinner at some obscure restaurant in Virginia last night."

Laurie was shaking her head in disgust. "Nigel warned me about the inherited cabinet members. I should have listened to him and fired them all. Anyone else?"

"Nope, she is the only one."

"But how is she getting this information?" Laurie asked. "She hasn't been in every meeting."

"I think she's eavesdropping... hanging around outside meeting rooms, standing close enough to overhear conversations, things like that," Nick said. "I saw her loitering in the hallways quite a bit.

Laurie was beginning to see what a formidable team the Rosslerites were. "Okay, Nick, Jack, Peter, how do you want to handle this?"

Jack said. "My suggestion is we present this to everyone as four general escape options- North, South, East, and West. In other words, we'll tell them 'if you're in the Oval Office; escape to the south; if you're in the Cross Halls go to the North, et cetera—as Sam and his team suggested. What do you say, Nick?"

Nick Clancy nodded. "That sounds good to me. Let's work out the detail."

"How is this going to work with all these options?" Daniel could see a logistical nightmare.

"We'll tell them that you and the President are planning to use the Reagan tunnel to the Oval Office, and then pick up the tunnel going North over to the basement of the Blair house. From there you'll go out the back door, through the West Alley by the Credit Union to be picked up on 17th street and taken to Joint Base Andrews. Later we'll throw in a special piece of information just for Carrie to make her think you'll be going to Anacostia.

"We'll increase Secret Service presence, scattering them in various areas. They'll be instructed that if evacuation becomes necessary, they'll go as a group, making it look like the President, and you, are with them. They'll be decoys. We'll make arrangements to have all escapees picked up at specific locations and transport them to Joint Base Myer, but in the meeting, we're going to tell them they're going to Anacostia.

"You and the President will follow behind the group that takes the escape route out of the East Wing through the tunnel to the US Treasury building. After they are picked up, another car will pick you up and take you to Andrews to board Air Force One.

"You'll be the only ones who know that you'll actually take the tunnels to the Treasury Building.

"That might just work," Daniel said as he looked at Laurie and Nick for their agreement.

When the details were worked out, Peter and Jack left to take up their assigned positions.

The President called an urgent meeting in the Presidential Emergency Operations Center to get an update on the current status from the heads of department and announce the escape plans.

"Thank you all for the updates. Moving on," the President continued. "We have received reliable information that General Hayden is planning to attack and take control of the White House, and thus the country. Needless to say, we must be prepared to move at a moment's notice. An evacuation plan has been made, and I'm handing the meeting over to Nick Clancy to explain how it will work."

Nick stood. "Thank you, Ms. President. Jeff, Martin, Peggy, Sally, Richard, and Ben," he listed the six Secret Service Officers whom he'd informed of the deception earlier, "will accompany the President and Vice President through the Ronald Reagan tunnel and over to the Blair House. From there they will proceed out the back door, through the West Alley by the Credit Union to be picked up on 17th street and taken to Andrews where they will board Air Force One."

There were several looks of surprise and consternation.

Carrie spoke the question that was on everyone's mind, "but doesn't the General have lots of troops at Andrews?"

"He did until the prisoners were moved. We are assuming that most of his troops will have relocated by now. As long as he doesn't know we're heading there, we should have plenty of opportunity for access."

"That's good thinking!" Carrie replied with a smile.

"The rest of you will meet up with the closest Secret Service personnel and escape with them. Those of you in or near the East Wing will go through the tunnel to the Treasury building and out the East side where you'll be picked up and taken to Anacostia where you'll be safe.

"Everyone in or near the West Wing will follow the tunnel to the Eisenhower Building, pass through it to exit on the South side and be picked up for transportation to Anacostia as well.

"These two groups will have designated decoys in them to act as if they are the President and Vice President.

"For those of you going to the North side, there will be a rendezvous point at Franklin Square. To the South, the rendezvous will be at Constitution Gardens."

"Are there any other questions?" he waited a few moments and then continued. "Good, it's all settled then."

The President took over again. "Thank you, Nick. Let's hope and pray it won't become necessary to evacuate, but if we have to, we have a plan. If there are no more questions, the meeting is adjourned."

As the people filed out of the room, the President said: "Daniel and Carrie, I need to see you for a moment please."

As they both approached her, Laurie indicated to Carrie that she should wait just a moment as she took Daniel aside. Carrie looked a bit perplexed but stopped and waited for the President to finish speaking with Daniel.

The President had lowered her voice while she was talking to Daniel, but Carrie could still make out most of what they were saying.

"Daniel, please make sure our aircraft at Anacostia is on standby and ready at all times."

"Don't worry about it. I've taken care of it. Our backgate access is arranged, the plane is fueled and ready to go, and two pilots are on standby at all times. It will be warmed up and ready to fly by the time we arrive."

"Good; Thank you, Daniel,"

The President turned to Carrie and said. "Apologies for making you wait, Carrie."

"No problem at all Ms. President."

"Carrie, I've been thinking about the homeless and have been wondering if we could launch a national campaign to appeal to people with homes to take in some of the homeless? What do you think?"

"That's an excellent idea, Ms. President! Give me a couple of days to work out a strategy and get back to you?"

"That would be good. Thank you, Carrie, you're doing a great job." The President smiled.

As she and Carrie left the conference room, Laurie saw Cliff Willis and excused herself from Carrie's side saying, "I look forward to seeing your strategy, Carrie!"

Laurie made small talk with Cliff until she saw Carrie board the elevator to return to the main floor of the East Wing. When the door opened again and Carrie didn't reappear, she asked Cliff to accompany her back to the conference room.

"Cliff," she said, "Hayden's forces will attack the correctional facility at Chesapeake tonight. Were all the inmates relocated successfully?"

"Yes, ma'am. The regular inmates are being held temporarily at the local jail."

"Good; let's start moving the staff out of there—I don't want anyone to get hurt. Have them put on their civilian clothes as instructed and slip out unnoticed - alone or in small groups. I want the building empty when Hayden's forces get there."

"Yes, Ma'am. I'll start moving them out now."

Chapter Twenty-Two

GIVE THE ORDER

General Hayden was waiting in the hotel room for his mistress. He was excited, Carrie Trent was an energetic woman, but that was not the only reason for his excitement, it was also D-day. He had decided to attack the Chesapeake prison facility at 11:30 pm, get the prisoners out and execute them. While everyone was concentrating on the executions, he was going to launch the attack on the White House.

By one o'clock tomorrow morning, I'll be President Hayden.

When Carrie walked into the room, Hayden put his whiskey down and started to unbutton his shirt. "You might want to hold onto that thought for a moment. Campbell knows you are planning an attack on the White House, Tom."

"What! How did she find out about that; or is she just guessing?"

"I just left a meeting where she told us that they had received information that you are planning an attack. I assume that means someone told her."

"Aw shit! I've got a damn traitor in my group," he said with exasperation. "That's all I need. I'll have to hunt him down and get rid of him."

She moved closer to him, drawing her fingers gently across his chest. "She's made escape plans," Carrie pouted.

He looked at her inquisitorially, "And you know what those plans are?"

"Of course, I do! She and Rossler are going to use decoys! And I know exactly how."

"Oh, you clever and devious woman!" he rejoiced. "You are one sly little fox; you know that, don't you?"

"I'd do anything for you, Tom. You know that."

"If I didn't before, I do now! So, tell me, what is her plan?"

"There are designated escape routes on all sides of the White House. People will be able to escape in one of four directions, and each group will have decoys pretending to be her and Rossler."

"Ha!" Hayden smirked. "Fat chance of that!"

"She, Rossler, and six agents are going to slip through the old Reagan tunnel through to the Oval Office and access the tunnels to the Blair building, exit from the back and be picked up near the alley on 17th street. From there they will go to Andrews and board Air Force One."

"Andrews! With my troops there? Is she crazy?"

"She thinks that you will have removed most of your troops by that time because the prisoners aren't there anymore."

"She's going to be in for a big surprise, isn't she?" he laughed, "And all because of you!" he added, kissing her on the nose.

"But I think she's really going to go to Anacostia, everything she told us at the meeting about her escape was just smoke and mirrors."

"What makes you say that?"

"I overheard her tell Rossler to be sure their plane at Anacostia was ready to go; Rossler confirmed it was and added that the back-gate entrance had been arranged."

Hayden looked at her with admiration. "She thinks she's so smart. We'll just have to see about her little scheme. I'll have that back gate under such heavy guard she'll never get away. She won't be going anywhere near Air Force One or any other plane for that matter!"

"I guess we won't be having any of the usual fun tonight then?" Carrie smiled.

"Unfortunately, not my dear. I'll have to make a few adjustments to my plans. But tomorrow night you can have as much fun as you want with the new President of the United States of America." He grinned with a faraway look in his eyes.

"I'm holding you to that, Tom."

Outside NAVCONBRIG Chesapeake, otherwise known as the Navy's Joint Regional Correctional Facility Mid-Atlantic, a crowd of close to three thousand civilians, Hayden's troops, and news media alike listened eagerly for General Hayden to give the order to retrieve the prisoners. They were going to show the world what true American justice was like.

Hayden looked around him at the mass of people gathered and filled with pride. *True Americans, everyone – they know a leader when they see one! Together we'll set the whole world straight.*

He'd prepared a lengthy speech for this moment but was

anxious to get to the executions. *I think I'll just keep it short and simple.*

"Ladies and gentlemen, I'd like to thank those of you who are here to show your support as well as all the volunteers who have joined my forces! I prepared a speech for tonight, but I'm going to keep it short instead so that we can get on with administering justice.

"And that's exactly what we are going to do! We're going to show the *world* what *true* Americans are like! We are willing and able to do our part and *more* to set the whole world right—starting with the execution of that mass murderer John Brideaux and his despicable Council."

He had to pause several times during his short speech due to all the cheering. At the end, he had to wait nearly two minutes for the shouting and stirring fever that moved through the crowd to subside enough for them to hear his order.

"Move out!"

With screams and shouts, waving their fists and weapons in the air, the crowd rushed the entrance of the facility and paused momentarily while a few of the front runners broke through the doors. Then they poured into the building and spread out to find the prisoners.

Within ten minutes his Captain reported in.

"Sir, they aren't here; there's no one here."

"What do you mean there's no one here. This is a staffed prison facility."

"Yes, sir, but it isn't now."

Hayden shoved the Captain aside and stormed through the doors bellowing like an angry bull. "They're here somewhere! You incompetent idiots just have to find them!"

Thirty minutes later, exhausted from rage, Hayden sat

alone on a couch in the lobby of the facility muttering to himself and looking slightly deranged.

"She did this. She hid them from me—again. Somehow that bitch hid them from me. She won't get away with this. I'll hunt her down; her and the prisoners. I'll hunt them all down and kill them."

By the end of what started as muttering, he was on his feet, pacing the room, screaming. He kicked waste cans, picked up chairs and threw them, overturned a table, scattering magazines across the room, and put his foot through a wall. "I'll kill them all!" he raged.

Storming out of the building into a circle of reporters, he pulled himself up abruptly to give the appearance of authority and control. He stopped and thought for a moment before addressing the crowd.

"Our President has seen fit to deceive the American people! Again!" he shouted. "She lied to us all about the prisoners! She lied to her own people to protect murderers."

The crowd yelled angrily in response, punching their fists in the air and waving their protest signs.

"Our President has chosen to protect men and women who have committed heinous crimes against humanity rather than listen to the voice of the people of America and the world. She has put herself above all of us! By doing so, she has joined the ranks of those who have committed these atrocities."

The yelling of the crowd drowned him out for several minutes. He reveled in the feeling of power he had over the crowd.

"She must be stopped! We must show her how we feel—we will not be led around by the nose! This ends now! Tonight!"

With that Hayden was nearly knocked over and trampled as the crowd swarmed the building, breaking windows, tearing out doors, smashing furniture, uprooting plants, and destroying anything and everything they could get their hands on.

Fights broke out in the streets between the enraged and the curious. News crews were knocked about as they filmed the carnage, broadcasting it around the world.

And the nation responded. Supporters of Hayden took to the streets attacking government buildings and those who supported President Campbell. Self-defense became violent of necessity and streets all across the nation became battlefields in a civil war.

Hayden grinned as he took in the scene around him. "It's time to take the White House," he said to his second in command. "Give the order."

Chapter Twenty-Three

NOW WHAT?

Hayden picked the perfect time to move on the White House. When he and his second in command arrived, protesters were trying to break down or climb the fence, and many were shot. As the bodies began to pile up along the fence, others stepped on the bodies and jumped over the fence, many of them were shot before their feet hit the ground. The bodies of those who made it a little further soon dotted the lawn.

Many inside the White House had gathered in the Situation Room, watching the news on TV in horror as the crowds swept in like a tidal wave. Those in the Presidential Emergency Operations Center watched as well. Cars were overturned, smoke from burning buildings filled the air, brutal fighting was everywhere, and bodies lying dead or injured in the streets and yards.

"They've broken through! They've broken through!" Rick and another Marine guard ran through the White House toward the East Wing shouting the warning to all present.

Household staff scattered and Secret Service agents took up their assigned defensive positions, calling a warning over the radio to those agents assigned to the President.

Daniel felt someone grabbing his left his arm, propelling his body forward even before he could make his feet work properly. He stumbled and found himself held by his arms and moving at a dead run.

"We've got you sir, just keep moving!" the Secret Service Agent said.

Despite the confusion of the flight from the Presidential Emergency Operations Center from six levels below ground, Daniel saw that Laurie was ahead of him amongst a group of Agents accompanied by two Marine guards and an Air Force officer.

As soon as they stepped out onto level five, they encountered gunfire and heard shouting. "Down! Get down! Hit the deck!"

Chips of plaster rained down as bullets struck the walls, the twang and crack of bullets hitting metal and wooden doors rang out, and the air smelled of gunpowder and blood. Several agents lay dead on the floor, and others were firing back at the intruders from their fallback positions.

Hayden must have gathered more troops to have gotten far enough into the White House to push the agents to fallback positions already. Daniel thought.

The group divided. Daniel watched the decoys slip away and open the secret panel that accessed the old Reagan tunnel leading to the Oval Office. Hunkering down even further as a bullet struck the wall inches above his head. He sent up a silent prayer for the brave souls that were putting their lives on the line so he and Laurie could escape. Even as he prayed, he saw one of the agents fall.

He started to move toward the man but felt himself restrained. "We have to help him," he said.

"That's not our job sir. We are to protect you. Others will help him."

Daniel was propelled forward again. "Who?" He shouted looking back toward the fallen man.

"Others sir, keep moving."

A door opened in the wall further down the hall, and the President and her agents disappeared through it. The Air Force officer was close on their heels but suddenly fell to the floor, blood and brain tissue pouring from what was left of his head.

Daniel saw a young girl with a serving tray at her feet cowering in a corner nearby. "Come on!" he yelled.

She rose to join them; her face streaked with tears. Daniel tried to halt to reach out to her, but the agent beside him jerked and fell to the floor as a bullet hit him and he went down. As the remaining agents forced Daniel through the door—he saw one of them grab the girl by the hand and haul her with them.

"Secure the door!" One of the agents yelled. "The rest of you keep moving. Go, go, go!"

They were in the tunnel to the US Treasury building, running as fast as they could, Daniel and Laurie still in the center of their protective circle of agents.

When Jack saw the people breaking the fence and streaming onto the premises, he pulled out his mirror phone and called Sam.

"This is it! The perimeters have been breached; the evacuation is in progress."

"Understood," Sam said. "Get them out and good luck."

"We will Sam," Jack replied.

He and Peter waited in the car on the East side of the US Treasury building. They could see the car sent for the decoys just ahead of them and expected to see them emerge any moment, followed shortly by the President and Daniel.

Instead, the street began to fill with vehicles and people – Hayden's troops – swarming the area carrying baseball bats, pitchforks, chains, swords, whips, ropes, and anything else they could find to use as a weapon.

"Uh oh – this isn't good," Peter said. "They'll never get out that way.

Jack watched in dismay as Hayden's troops swarmed up the stairs to the entrance doors of the five-story building. It was only moments before the four doors gave way and Hayden's troops rushed into the building. "Call them, warn them!"

Peter already had his phone out calling Daniel.

Jack was on his phone to Sam.

"I can't reach Daniel! He's not answering!" Peter shouted.

Hayden and his troops were waiting in the Oval Office when the decoys emerged from the tunnel. His men shot and killed the first two agents that came through the door and captured the rest. They were unable to turn back as Hayden's troops had followed them into the Reagan passageway.

Looking at the decoys for Laurie and Daniel, Hayden

exploded "She tricked me! She tricked me again! The lying bitch! I'll kill her!"

"Where are they General?" One of the men asked.

"Where do you think they are, moron! They lied to us! They've taken another way out of the White House. Some of you follow me to the East Wing; we'll check the tunnel leading to the Treasury building. The rest of you spread out and check the other exits. Find them!"

The decoys were completely forgotten as the General and his troops ran out of the Oval Office and down the hall toward the East Wing.

Several members of the staff had been herded into the room adjoining the Oval Office when the alarm was given. They and the two agents who were guiding them were headed for the parking lot of the West Wing when they had to hide quickly because they heard Hayden's men approaching.

Fortunately, the door between the room and the Oval Office was closed, or they would have been discovered if Hayden's men had taken the time to check the area. Instead, they overheard the scene in the Oval Office.

As soon as they heard Hayden and his men leave, one of the staff members said, "Let's get the hell out of here!"

"Come on!" one of the agents said and he left the Oval Office running toward the West Wing exit.

"Is it safe outside?" someone questioned as they ran.

"We won't know until we try," someone else answered.

When they reached the exit to the parking lot, they stopped short. It was full of Hayden's troops. Their flashlights and burning torches gave off an eerie light in the darkness that sent chills along several spins as the group looked out on the site in dismay.

"Now what?" someone asked.

"This way," one of the Secret Service agents spoke up. "Follow me; hurry!" And he headed back the way they came.

Chapter Twenty-Four

THEY'RE GOING TO NEED SOME HELP

"I'm telling you, right now *no one* knows where they are, Luke; it's like they just disappeared into thin air!"

"They have to be somewhere, Jack, find them!" Luke was trying hard not to lose his temper, but things were finally starting to get to him, the disappearance of both the President and the Vice President had put him over the top.

Sam stepped over and put his hand on Luke's shoulder to calm him. "Let me talk to him for a moment, Luke."

Jack was on speaker phone—the polite gesture helped to distract and ease Luke slightly.

"Sorry Sam," he said stepping away, "go ahead."

"Jack, give me a run-down of the situation."

"Peter and I were on site as planned, but I guess the ruse with the decoys didn't work—Hayden's people arrived shortly after I talked to you and broke through the doors of the Treasury.

"We stayed on site just in case they were able to find a way out, but no one came out. We've been trying to reach

Daniel, but he isn't answering his phone. The Tectus members on the other side ..."

But that was as far as he got before Sam interrupted.

"Wait, wait a minute, Jack. What do you mean no one came out? The decoy team should have come out at least."

"I'm telling you, Sam; something went wrong. Absolutely no one came out of that building, not even Hayden's people."

"What?"

"The Tectus surveillance team is telling me that no one has exited the White House—or any other building in the area, Hayden is barging around like an enraged bull—it seems *he* can't find them either, and he's mad as hell."

"So, the decoy team that was supposed to exit at the Blair house didn't show either?"

"Nope. No one showed up at any of the designated or backup sites."

'*The best-laid schemes of mice and men go oft awry,*' Sam remembered the line from a Robert Burns poem.

"Alright, we have a missing President, Vice President, and their staff. We have not one, but two missing decoy teams, and as yet are unable to account for the welfare of the White House staff and anyone else who may have been inside.

Jack replied. "Yep, that's an accurate summary. However, I must point out; Hayden obviously hasn't found the President and Vice President either. So let's not get desperate.

"Is it possible that the President found a hiding place inside and is evading Hayden that way?" Sam asked.

"At this point, I'd say just about anything is possible, Sam."

"Alright. Tell everyone to hold their positions and let's

see if anything shakes loose. Jack, get Tectus to send a few team members into Hayden's camp to see if they can learn anything. The rest of us here will put our heads together and start work on alternatives."

When Jack hung up, he looked at Peter. "Well, what do you think?"

Peter sat silently for a few moments deep in thought. "I think we need information; I'm going to take a look inside."

"I'll go with you," Jack said.

"Let's do it!" Peter grinned.

They made their way boldly across the street in plain sight of anyone who might be watching, stopping to pick up weapons on the way. Peter chose a baseball bat that was covered in blood and Jack an axe with skin and cloth still hanging from it.

Just as they reached the entrance to the building, a man with a pitchfork came around the corner. "Hey! You there! Stop!"

"Hi! How'd your area check out?" Peter asked as the man approached.

"I haven't seen a sign of them. You?" the man replied.

"Nothing yet, still looking. The General asked me to check the Treasury building."

"Again?" the man asked incredulously. "We've checked it twice!"

"Well, I guess it's my turn—want to come?"

"Hell no! There're too many dead bodies in there—gives me the creeps. 'Course it isn't much better out here," he said surveying the remnants of the most recent civil war skirmish. "I think I'm going to go get a drink somewhere."

"That sounds like a grand idea!"

"Wanna come?"

"Nah, I'm gonna make a quick check of this place,"

Peter inclined his head toward the building, "and then head home to my girl," Peter winked.

The man grinned back at him, "In that case, I wouldn't waste my time with the building, but have it your way!"

Jack looked at Peter. "I can see I don't have to worry about you. They trained you CIA spooks to think and lie on your feet. Well done!"

"The best defense is a good offense! Fit in first, fight second; listen and learn; they gave us all kinds of training," Peter grinned. "So many people think spy work is about sneaking around with a gun and breaking into places for information. It's really about how well you can fit into a situation and function as one of the group—being a chameleon."

"Let's go... ya big lizard!" Jack laughed.

"Careful, friend," Peter cautioned with a smile, "the Komodo dragon is also a lizard - and a big one!"

Peter knew that twinkle in Jack's eyes meant he would probably never live this down.

Stepping inside the Treasury Building, they quickly but carefully made their way through the darkened hallways toward the tunnel entrance. The tile floors gleamed softly in the dim lighting of the building. They passed by beautifully designed spiral staircases and many columns reminiscent of the Greek Revival style architecture of the building. Had the building been fully illuminated, they would have been able to see the baroque designs on the ceilings.

When they reached the tunnel, they paused to listen and then, hearing only silence, cautiously stepped inside and began to make their way toward the East Wing.

With room for three to walk abreast, the tunnel, with its low ceiling, concrete block structure, and concrete floor was in stark contrast to the wide, high-ceilinged, richly decorated hallways they had just passed through. They moved stealthily through the tunnel, pausing to listen every few steps, and stepping over bodies, watching for anyone they knew.

They'd identified two dead Secret Service agents, picked up their guns and magazines, checked the guns and moved on into the East Wing. There was no sign of Daniel's party or the decoys—nor had they seen a living person. The East Wing seemed to be just as deserted—only dead bodies in the hallways.

It was evident that quite a battle had taken place near the tunnel entrance. Aside from the bodies, the walls were riddled with bullet holes, pictures hung askew on the walls or lay on the floor beneath their mounts, and a serving tray, its contents scattered nearby, lay abandon in a nearby corner.

"Wherever they went, it looks like they got there by the skin of their teeth," Jack whispered.

They listened for a moment and decided it was safe to proceed into the hallway.

"I think, on the off chance that they had somehow managed to shelter in the Presidential Emergency Operations Center, I'm going to check there first," Peter told Jack, "and then I'll check the Reagan tunnel and over to the Blair House."

"I'm going to check the lower floor and sub-basement, then return to the car," Jack advised.

"Okay," Peter agreed. "Pick me up on 17th Street when you're done."

Jack nodded, and they went their separate ways.

Taking the stairs to the first floor, Jack passed through the Lobby and Garden Room, made his way along the East Colonnade through the Visitor's Foyer and into the Center

Hall of the White House ground floor. He took the stairway immediately to his right and entered the sub-basement.

He'd barely taken two steps toward the hallway when he heard a voice behind him, "Don't move, hands up."

Jack froze as a Secret Service agent stepped in front of him, gun drawn and leveled, ready to fire.

"I'm not one of Hayden's people; my name is Jack Symonds; I'm with the Rossler Foundation."

The agent before him sized him up for a moment. "If that's true, name the rendezvous point."

"Which one?"

"You pick."

"Southern exits were to meet at Constitution Gardens."

The agent still didn't lower his weapon.

"That's a logical guess. What else?"

"If the President were going to exit from the West Wing, Vice President Rossler would have called her plan to the Foundation referring to it as Operation Condor."

The agent lowered his weapon. "You took one hell of a risk coming down here. Why?"

"We're looking for the President and Vice President. They called in that they were leaving through the East Wing, but never appeared. I decided to check down here."

"The last I heard over the radio they did leave through the East Wing as planned. We came down here and have been leaving, alone or in groups of twos and threes through the courtyard above as if we are part of Hayden's troops. We mingle with the troops, then the crowd, and work our way to the North rendezvous point. There's only a few of us left down here."

"Do you know anything about the other groups?"

"No, shortly after I heard the report of the invasion,

Hayden's men took over the radio system and we have been maintaining radio silence."

"Okay, go ahead and get the rest of your group out, and go with them. I'm going to check a few more places and then leave myself."

The two men shook hands. "Good luck," they said almost in unison.

Jack did a quick check of the storage rooms, the air conditioning center, and the dish wash area, counting five people in addition to the two agents. Then he took the stairs on the west end of the hallway to the basement under the North Portico.

He checked the carpenter shop, storage areas, Nixon's bowling alley, and the flower shop but saw no signs of anyone. Just as he started up the stairs to return to the ground level, he saw two of the people from the sub-basement emerge from the stairwell and slip out the door into the west courtyard.

At least I'll have some good news when I get back—some of them have gotten out.

Peter got to the Presidential Emergency Operations Center; it was the one area free of damage and bodies.

They had obviously been here but got away.

Don't want Hayden digging himself in here.

He checked the door mechanism and found that it was still operational. The door had been blocked open by someone's shoe. He removed the shoe and secured the door.

Only an authorized fingerprint can open this door now.

From there he worked his way back up to the fourth level and moved toward the access door to the Reagan tunnel, following it to the Oval Office. Being inside the White House, this narrow corridor was equipped with lights, and he was relieved when he didn't come across any more bodies.

If they came this way, at least they were safe—this far at least.

Before Peter reached the door to the Oval Office, he heard Hayden's shouting.

"What do you mean you lost them? How can you lose a room full of people?" Hayden shouted. He had completely forgotten that he too had just managed to lose the equivalent of a room full of people.

"They were all right here in this office when we left with you for the East Wing to capture the others. When we returned, they were gone."

"You didn't think to leave someone here to guard them?"

"No sir, you said they were decoys, and we were after the President and Vice President, so we didn't think you wanted those people held."

"Idiots! I'm surrounded by complete idiots!" he shouted shoving the unfortunate soldier away from him. "Do I have to think of everything? Do I?"

The General's eyes were bulging, and saliva was beginning to dribble from the corners of his mouth. Those around him looked at one another in alarm and tried to, unobtrusively, step away from him. They all knew the General was a tightly wound man, and right now he was becoming slightly undone. No one was sure what he was going to do next.

The room became silent as the General paced, pulling himself back together.

"Alright. Forget about the decoys. I want this place and

the tunnels searched—every closet, cupboard, alcove, bedroom—everywhere!"

"But sir, we've already searched the House, the Wings, the tunnels through to the Treasury and Blair house, and they just aren't here."

"Ask the staff—beat the information out of them if you have to."

"The staff have vanished as well, sir."

"What! They didn't just disappear. They're here somewhere—all of them. Find them! Find them now!

"And send reinforcements to both Andrews and Anacostia. If they did get out, they aren't going to get to either one of those planes."

Oh oh. Peter thought. *That's going to cause problems if they're still trying to make it to Air Force One. But what was that about another plane?*

He heard people leaving the office and decided it was time to move on and meet Jack. He carefully stepped through the door arriving near the President's private bathroom outside the Oval Office and fell in with the group as they filed out to search the premises again.

Starting off toward the stairs that led down to the tunnel to the Blair House, he stopped and checked each room as if he were one of Hayden's troops.

He was alone when he reached the entrance to the tunnel. He double-checked that it was clear and stepped inside. He switched on the flashlight app on his smartphone. This tunnel was older and narrower than the one to the Treasury Building.

Again, he was relieved to find the tunnel free of the dead or injured. He reached the basement of the Blair House without finding any evidence that anyone had come this way.

He left through the back door, made his way quietly across the courtyard and down the alleyway, appearing on 17th street just as Jack was starting to worry.

"You're not going to *believe* this buddy," Peter said as he got into the car with Jack. "We need to get HQ on the line."

Jack dialed, and as soon as Sam answered, he put the phone on speaker.

"Sam, everyone," Peter said, "the White House is empty except for dead bodies and Hayden's people."

"You mean Daniel and the President, and everyone is dead?" Sam asked horror-stricken.

"No! Sorry, that's not what I meant!" Peter corrected. "I mean that Daniel, the President, the decoys, the staff, everyone is gone."

"How did you find this out?"

Peter related his excursion through the White House and what he heard in the Oval Office.

At the conclusion of Peter's report, Jack added, "I checked out the sub-basement and found two remaining Secret Service Agents and a few staff members. From their report, they are escaping alone or in small groups through the courtyard by blending in with Hayden's troops and then making their way to the North rendezvous point."

"That's good news!" Sam said.

"Peter, Nigel here. How many Secret Service Agents were down?"

Peter thought for a moment counting silently. "No more than half a dozen."

Nigel frowned. "I may have an idea where they went, and if I'm right, given what you've just told us about reinforcements at the two bases, Peter, they're going to need some help."

Chapter Twenty-Five

A BACK-UP PLAN

After coming to a dead end at the West Wing parking lot, the agent led the decoys and staff members deserted by Hayden on through the lobby, across the hallway, and into an opening that accessed a stairwell to the lower floor.

From there he checked to be sure the way was clear of Hayden's people and led them across another hallway and into an infrequently used office.

The office was unadorned having only a desk, two oak-finished filing cabinets, oak paneling on the right-hand wall, and a full-wall oak bookcase on the opposite side. Stepping to the left corner of the bookcase, he pulled the spine of one of the books open and pressed a button. To the astonishment of the people with him, the center section of the bookcase swung open revealing a dark stairwell.

He pushed another button, and a dim light appeared at the foot of the staircase. He motioned for everyone to proceed quietly and follow the tunnel below. After the last person had started down the stairs, he carefully closed the wall, took the stairs two at a time, and sprinted to catch up with the leader of the group.

"Where does this go?" Someone asked.

"To the Blair House."

"But the General's troops are all over the place; we won't be able to get out of there either."

The agent grinned. "Oh yes we will!"

When they emerged into the empty brick basement of the Blair House, several people started for the stairs. The agent stopped them. "No, not that way. Come this way!" And he opened a door marked 'mechanical room' and stepped inside.

The room contained what looked like a boiler, water heater, water filtration system, and a few other things that were not identifiable. A panel marked 'Master Control Unit' was installed on the right-hand wall. He approached the panel, pushed a couple of buttons and part of the wall slid aside revealing a concrete platform and several maroon underground monorail cars gleaming in the overhead lights. Tracks disappeared into the tunnel in both directions. "Hurry, get in!" the agent encouraged.

With stunned expressions, everyone quickly made their way onto the platform and boarded one of the cars. By this time, one of the other agents had taken a seat in the front compartment of the monorail and as the last agent stepped aboard it began to move.

"Where are we going now?" someone asked sounding half amazed half scared.

"To Camp David!" The agent said with a big grin as the cars smoothly picked up speed.

They had just entered the Treasury building when Daniel heard a gunshot and saw the leading agent fall. "We're trapped!" yelled a second agent, "Fall back!"

"Can we get to the basement of the Treasury building?" Laurie asked one of the agents.

"No, ma'am. With Hayden's troops covering this tunnel entrance, there is no way to exit and reach the basement stairwell safely."

Several agents ran forward to lay down fire, "Get them to safety," one of them yelled referring to Laurie and Daniel. The remaining agents turned, and Daniel found himself being propelled back the way they'd come.

He managed two steps before he felt a tremendous blow from behind and was knocked to the floor. He heard someone shout "Veep down" just as his brain registered searing pain tearing through his left shoulder.

He was lifted bodily and flung over the shoulders of someone who began to run again.

"We're going to run into Hayden's forces this direction too!" Rick shouted.

"No!" the girl said. "I know a way out! Quickly, come this way!"

The agents looked at one another for a moment. "She grew up in the White House," one of them shrugged, "what do we have to lose?"

They followed her another 30 yards where she stopped and disappeared into an alcove.

"There's nothing there! It's just an old storage closet without a door," one of the agents said.

She stuck her head back around the corner of the alcove. "Hurry!"

They could hear Hayden's men approaching from both directions.

"Follow her," the President ordered.

"Put me down," Daniel told the agent. "It's a shoulder wound; I can walk."

Daniel found himself set on his feet inside the alcove illuminated only by the light from the tunnel. He was astonished to see that the left side of the concrete block alcove was actually fairly deep, but there was no one in it. He turned and stepped quickly toward the end, but when he arrived, he found a narrow passageway to the right and stepped through.

The only light was given off by someone's smartphone screen, but Daniel could see they had entered a small cave that appeared to be man-made.

"Shhh," The girl whispered. "We have to be very quiet; they might still be able to hear us."

Daniel saw the others standing around in the small area, all trying to catch their breath. When the last agent stepped through the narrow passageway, the girl quietly pushed what looked like a narrow wall of concrete blocks into the opening.

"They're fake," she whispered.

Turning back to them, she stood stock still and put a finger to her lips in a gesture for silence.

They heard running footsteps in the hallway. Everyone froze when they heard General Hayden bellow, "Where the hell are they?"

"They came this way General; we chased them from the Treasury building. You should have seen them."

"Would I be standing here asking you where they were if I'd seen them, you oaf?"

"I'm sorry, sir," the soldier stammered.

"Don't be sorry, find them, dammit! Search the tunnel, check every nook and cranny!" the General ordered. "What's in here?"

In their hideout, they all stopped breathing as they realized the General had stepped into the alcove to inspect it. They heard him step to the end where the narrow passageway was; there was a pause, and then he returned to the entrance. Then they heard a loud thud near the bottom of the wall followed by a curse "Ow! Son-of-a-bitch!"

The all had to suppress their laughter at the General's frustration.

"That's a solid wall, start checking the rest of the tunnel. They have to be in here somewhere!"

They started breathing again when they heard the soldiers start to move away.

The girl motioned for them to remain still and quiet. After a minute or so she put a finger to her mouth again, signaling them to remain quiet, but motioned them to follow her and she started off following a dark tunnel in a southerly direction.

Several had taken out their smartphones and activated a flashlight application.

In the dim lighting, Danial saw that the passageway was literally a tunnel, not a hallway. It had been dug out of the earth—the walls, ceiling, and floor were dirt and rock, and it was just large enough for them to walk through upright in single file.

After they'd walked about five minutes, the girl stopped and turned to them. "It's ok to talk now but keep it soft. Are you alright Mr. Vice President?" she asked.

"I believe so. It's a bit sore, but it's just a shoulder wound, I'll be fine," he responded with a smile.

The agent next to him inspected his shoulder and whispered quietly, "Liar."

Daniel grinned and shrugged, instantly regretting the move.

Laurie stepped forward. "You're Elize, aren't you? President Nigel Harper introduced you to me when you brought us tea a few days ago, in the Oval Office."

"Yes, Madame President."

"How did you know about this tunnel? Do you know where it leads?"

Elize blushed. "Well, growing up in the White House with all its secret rooms, trap doors, and hidden hallways leads kids to explore and find things. My best friend and I found this tunnel about ten years ago, and we used it many times.

"It's one of the old tunnels that Harrison Gray Dyar, Jr. dug while he was working at the Smithsonian."

"Who?" Rick asked

"Harrison Dyar, Jr. He was an entomologist that worked for the Smithsonian, at the National Museum of Natural History. His expertise was in mosquitos, but his hobby was building tunnels – he said he did it for exercise. He lived near here and dug quite a few tunnels. This one leads to the Museum where he worked."

"Well done, Elize. We owe you our lives," the President praised.

Elize smiled brightly.

"If we could get from there to the Air and Space Museum we could ..." one of the agents started to say but was stopped when the President raised her hand.

"All the Smithsonian museums are connected by tunnels," Elize volunteered. "We can easily get to the Air and Space Museum."

"What's over there?" The agent asked.

"Let's get there first, shall we?" the President responded.

"I think we need to check Vice President Rossler's shoulder and try to stop the bleeding," one of the agents said, stepping over to help steady Daniel, who was showing signs of lightheadedness.

"I'm fine," Daniel insisted.

"Really?" the agent asked holding up a blood-covered hand. "I think you'd better sit down sir, and let us take a look at that before you lose any more blood."

After being persuaded to sit down, Daniel allowed them to inspect his shoulder.

Someone held a phone flashlight on the wound while one of the agents took off his own shirt and, tearing it into squares and strips, made a bandage to cover the wound.

"The bullet's still in there—no exit wound," he said as he applied the bandage causing Daniel to wince in pain.

"Try not to move your arm if you can, sir." He pulled Daniel's bloodied shirt back on and buttoned it for him with his left arm against his skin. "It will help you to keep from moving it if it's tucked inside your shirt," he explained.

"Sit here and rest for a bit, I think I have another patient to attend to," he said looking at Rick.

"You're hit, son."

Rick looked at him, "Not bad sir; it's just a graze."

"Let's take a look at it."

Rick lifted his shirt, and the agent examined the wound, dabbing at it gently with a leftover piece of cloth from the bandages he'd made for Daniel.

"You're right; it's a flesh wound. It will need treatment so it doesn't get infected, but it's already stopped bleeding. You'll be alright."

"Thank you, sir."

While the agent inspected Rick's wound, Laurie had taken a seat next to Daniel. A word with you?" she asked.

"Sure, what's up?"

"With all that's been happening, you haven't had a chance to receive any training from the Secret Service."

"I need training?" Daniel asked in surprise.

Laurie smiled, "Yes, you do. I know you were trying to help back there in the hallway, but your actions could have gotten an agent wounded or killed.

"These agents put their lives on the line to protect us, Daniel; we have to trust their judgment and follow their lead without question.

They've been highly trained for their positions, but their training is only as good as we allow it to be. If they don't know what we're planning to do, they can't protect us. They can't read our minds. Just follow their orders."

Daniel thought for a moment and then nodded his understanding.

"Good!" she smiled, "are you able to travel?"

"Yes. I'm good to go."

"Let's get moving then; we still have quite a bit of territory to cover;" the lead agent said.

He helped Daniel to his feet, and it was then that Daniel realized he hadn't checked his phone. He pulled it out to have a look. "Hey, I got a message from Peter telling me to abort Operation Falcon!"

The agents looked at each other and started laughing.

"No shit Rambo," said the lead agent quietly.

Only the President heard him, and she smiled.

"Let's hold off on returning that call for the moment, Mr. Vice President," the lead agent said. "I'd like to have a little better idea of our situation before we let our whereabouts be known. We could easily be trapped in here if the wrong people get wind of where we are."

"Okay, Nigel, let's hear it," Luke said.

Nigel looked at Salome, Luke, and JR. "Aw hell, I don't need to tell you guys about top secret and need-to-know.

"There is a secret underground monorail system between the White House and several destinations around the general Washington, D.C. area. Only Presidents, Vice Presidents, and a few specially cleared Secret Service Agents know about them and how to access them. I think they may have accessed it."

The three of them just stared at Nigel in shock for a moment. Then they started to smile.

"How can we be sure that's what they did?" Salome asked.

"Until we have contact with them, we don't," Nigel replied, "but it's the only thing that makes sense, based on what Peter told us."

"Where does this monorail go?" Luke asked.

"Let's have a look at it on the map," Sam suggested, placing a map of the city on the table.

Nigel looked it over, then took a highlighter and circled the Pentagon, CIA Headquarters, Camp David, and the Capitol building.

"For the group that was in the Oval Office and West Wing area, I'm guessing the agent had them escape using the tunnel to the Blair house."

"But Hayden's men searched that tunnel and the house and didn't find any trace of them."

"Unless they were expert trackers or someone left a deliberate trail, they wouldn't. The monorail access platform is through a hidden wall in a room in the basement.

Once on the rail, depending on which route they took, they would have direct access to any one of those four locations.

"If it were me," said JR, "I would try to get them out of the area. I'd take them to Camp David."

"That is my thinking too, JR," Nigel said.

Sam and Luke looked over the map and agreed. "Camp David seems the most logical destination."

"What about Daniel's group?" JR asked, worried about his brother.

"If they made it to the basement of the Treasury, they would have direct access to those locations except for Camp David. In addition, they could directly access the NSA, FBI, Anacostia, Myers, and Andrews."

"The question is," Salome said, "did they make it to the basement? From what Peter overheard, it doesn't sound like they made it into the Treasury building."

"Where else could they have gone?" Sam asked.

"As far as I know," Nigel replied, "the only ways out of the White House from their last known location, are the ones we planned for or the basement of the Treasury."

"So, where the hell are they?" Luke said exasperated, flicking his pencil onto the table in frustration.

"I think we have to anticipate where they are most likely to go and try to set things up to help them," Sam said.

"I agree," Salome nodded. "Since the primary objective in these circumstances was to get them out of Washington and to the Rabbit Hole. I'm guessing they are still going to try and make it to Andrews and onto Air Force One. But it sounds like they may have a backup plan in place for Anacostia.

"I think we should proceed as if they are sticking to the original plan at Andrews and shift some Tectus people to Anacostia to be ready for support if they show up there."

Chapter Twenty-Six

SEE YOU AT THE RENDEZVOUS

They reached the National Museum of Natural History without further incident. The tunnel had been tight, and more than one of them started to feel slightly claustrophobic by the time they reached the end. They all felt a sense of relief after stepping out into the large, well-lit open space of the storage room in the museum.

"Elize, do you know your way from here to the Air and Space Museum through the tunnels?" The lead agent asked.

"Yes, sir, this way," she said and led them out of the storage room, down a short hallway, and through double doors that opened into a large main hallway that had the feel of a shopping mall. She turned to the left and headed off. "The hallways to the other museums are all clearly marked; it will be up this way on our right."

They continued along the main hall for about ten minutes passing more double-doors marked 'Smithsonian Castle/Freer Sackler Gallery,' 'Museum of African Art,' and 'Hirshhorn Museum' before coming to the doors marked 'Air and Space Museum'.

Elize turned right, leading them through the double doors, along another corridor and into a large basement area stacked with hundreds of boxes and crates. Space suits with helmets and gloves, rocks—presumably from the moon, pieces and models of aircraft, pictures, books, and much more filled the area.

Neatly organized chaos, Daniel mused. He was starting to feel dizzy again from shock and blood loss, but he managed to stay on his feet and keep up with the group.

The President turned to the agents, "Do any of you know where it is?" She asked.

Three of the agents looked bewildered; the other two looked at each other and nodded.

"I do, Madame President," one of them said.

"Please, lead the way."

He led them further into the basement of the museum and then into a small conference room. Pictures from the surface of the moon hung on one wall, and those of astronauts were displayed on a paneled wall across from them. A large TV sat on a low shelf at the far end of the room, a conference phone was centered on the rectangular table, and a small electronic control panel was inlaid at the closest end of the table. The agent entered a code on the control panel, and part of the paneled wall opened revealing an acid-finished platform and Hunter Green monorail cars.

The group looked at one another in astonishment.

"Let's go, people," the agent said, "we don't have all day!"

As they loaded into the monorail cars, Laurie turned to Daniel, "It's time we contact the Rossler Foundation."

Daniel, feeling extremely grateful to finally be able to sit down again, pulled out his mirror phone and called the Rabbit Hole.

"Daniel! Thank God! Are you ok? Is the President with you and is she ok? Where are you—where have you been?"

Daniel laughed, "Easy Luke, one thing at a time. Yes, I'm ok and so is the President. She's with me, along with five Secret Service agents, as well as Cliff Willis, Bill Simms, one of the Marine guards, and Elize, a beautiful young lady who saved our skins."

Elize blushed and managed to look both shy and proud at the same time.

"The President wants to talk to Nigel; is he handy?"

"I'm right here Daniel—it sure is a big relief to hear from you guys, we've been worried."

"Nigel," Laurie broke in, "I'm sorry, I don't mean to be rude, but we still have quite a way to go before we're out of this, and we need to get moving again."

"I understand," Nigel replied.

"Ms. President, ah Laurie," Sam broke in. If you don't mind waiting just a moment, I'd like to get Jack conferenced into this call—he will be able to provide you with the support you're going to need."

"Make it quick, Sam, I have a feeling we're running out of time."

There was a brief pause, then "Jack here; what's happening Sam?"

"The President is about to bring us up to speed on the situation."

"The President; great—I'm all ears!"

Laurie understood their relief, but she was worried

about what they still faced, yet she tried not to show her impatience at these small delays.

"Nigel, about security issues ..."

"Don't worry; I've already briefed them on what they *need* to know."

He emphasized the word 'need,' so he's told them about the monorail system but left the classified information out. "Very well. We just boarded at the Air and Space Museum and are heading for Andrews as originally planned."

"Good, we thought you might be doing just that, and the team is already assembled as planned."

She sighed with relief. *Finally; something is going right!* "Do you have any word on the others?"

"Some of them have escaped through the courtyard, but that's all we know at this time."

"Everyone disappeared, just like you did." Nigel said and relayed Peter's report from having eavesdropped on Hayden in the Oval Office. He also included Jack's description of the escapees he'd found.

"We're pretty sure the ones that were captured in the Oval Office went to Camp David, but won't be able to confirm that until we hear from them. A couple of Tectus members are on their way. They both have medical training in case anyone is injured."

Laurie grimaced at the thought of injuries, "Thank God. I'm glad to know they made it out of there."

"We'll be arriving at the base by monorail obviously, which changes our access to the plane. Have you made adjustments for that?"

Sam replied, "Yes, we have. Jack is already on board Air Force One and is in charge of the operation; he can provide a better brief. Jack?"

Jack cleared his throat, "President Campbell, I will pick

you all up in a covered utility cart at the station access point and ferry you to the plane.

"We can't have you trying to board by the stairs, so we lowered the cargo ramp at the back. We'll board that way.

"Hayden's troops are scattered all over the area and have been watching closely, but they are starting to get bored and have become less attentive. Military and Secret Service guards are in place as usual. The pilots boarded as mechanics. Additional Secret Service agents and military guards are buzzing around the plane as mechanics, and other agents have boarded as housekeepers assigned to clean the plane and prepare it for the next use.

"We've already tested the engines once and advised Hayden's troops that we will be testing them again. As soon as I'm off the phone with you, we'll begin another test, so the plane will be ready to fly as soon as you board."

"You make it sound easy Jack."

"No, it isn't going to be easy." *So far nothing about this operation has been easy.* But he kept his thoughts to himself. "There're still about half-a-million things that could go wrong."

Laurie looked directly at Daniel. "Very well, Jack. We are in your hands and will follow your lead."

Daniel nodded, understanding her message: *Remember what I told you in the tunnel.*

Jack swallowed hard as the responsibility for the lives of America's top two leaders settled firmly on his shoulders.

"We'll see you at the rendezvous then," Laurie confirmed.

"See you there Ms. President," Jack responded, "God speed."

Chapter Twenty-Seven

COME RIGHT THIS WAY

Jack looked over at Peter, who sat as if shell-shocked. "This isn't going to be a walk in the park, Jack," he said slowly. "This could turn into a bloody massacre."

"We'll have to see that it doesn't. Let's go. Get the pilots to warm up the engines again."

They left the conference room on board Air Force One still dressed as mechanics, carefully concealing their guns. Peter headed toward the cockpit, gathering the agents he came across as he went. Once he had them all around him, he briefed them on the plan and sent them to their positions.

Jack was already approaching the rendezvous with President Campbell's group when Peter took his place in the cargo hold along with a few agents prepared to lay down protective fire for those who would be boarding.

He heard the engines start up and saw a few people near the cargo-hold approach the military guards. He couldn't hear what was said, but it looked like they were demanding to know what was going on.

Time to play my part again.

Descending the cargo ramp while appearing to wipe his hands on a 'grease rag,' he approached the guard most in danger of being overrun by those surrounding him. "What's the problem?" he shouted over the noise of the engines.

"We want to know what's going on!" the man said pointing at the guard, "he says this is routine maintenance, but I don't believe him."

Peter looked over the motley crew. Since taking over the base, they had all found real weapons to replace their bats and pitchforks... guns—military issue guns.

"Well, he's telling you the truth!"

"I don't think I believe you either!" the man retorted, poking Peter in the chest with his index finger for emphasis.

Peter restrained himself from breaking the man's arm. "Why not?" Peter questioned acting genuinely surprised.

"I've never seen any airplane get so much attention from so many people."

Peter could see this man was going to be trouble. "Sir," Peter said firmly, "this plane carries the most powerful person in the world, the President of the United States. Nothing is ever overlooked when servicing the President's plane—everything has to be in perfect working order. That's our job.

"Can you imagine what would happen if we let our President die because his airplane wasn't serviced and checked properly?"

The man thought for a moment. "Well, why do they keep testing the engines? Isn't once enough?"

"They test them after every adjustment to make sure that the work they performed didn't have a negative effect on any other system. Aren't you one of General Hayden's troops—President Hayden I should say?"

The man stiffened proudly, "Yes, I am."

"General Hayden just became the President." Do you want to explain to him why Air Force One isn't prepared for use when he needs it? Or do you want to be the one who gives him a firsthand report that the service has been completed, and Air Force One is at his disposal?"

"What do you mean?" he asked suspiciously.

"Since you're so concerned about the President's plane, how about I take you aboard and assign one of the mechanics to give you a thorough tour and explanation of everything that's been done to ready the plane. Then you can give a full and complete report as to flight readiness to President Hayden when you next see him."

Looking around at his colleagues for agreement, which he received, the man grinned. "I'll take you up on that offer!" he said enthusiastically.

Peter led him up the ramp into the plane—just in the nick of time too—he could see Jack approaching with the service cart.

They stepped around a pallet of boxes to reach the front of the bay. Peter called one of the 'mechanics' over, "Smith," he yelled, not knowing the agent's name, "I'm turning this fine gentleman, a representative of President Hayden's over to your capable hands. Give him a complete tour of Air Force One—he needs to give President Hayden a flight readiness report ASAP.

The agent smiled in understanding. "Of, course Jonesy! Come right this way sir," he said to the man.

"That's right kind of you fellows; I guess there really is nothing going on here after all. Hey!" he screamed as he found himself face down on the floor and felt the cold metal of handcuffs snap around his wrists. "What's the meaning of this? Help! It's a trap!" But the sound of his voice was already muffled by the rag shoved into his mouth.

He was out of sight of his colleagues, and no one could hear his calls for help over the roar of the engines.

"Leave him be; they're here," Peter said turning back to the cargo ramp just as all hell broke loose.

Chapter Twenty-Eight

HAND ME THE SCALPEL

Jack parked the service cart and its attached boxes as close to the ramp as he could. The Secret Service agents got out first, then Rick, followed by the President, Daniel, the two Secretaries and the last two agents.

Although they were all dressed as mechanics, their feet had barely touched the ramp before one of Hayden's troops recognized them and opened fire. Two of the leading agents were hit in the first barrage of fire.

Suddenly, the President bent over sharply and fell forward. Rick threw himself on her shielding her with his body.

Jack half turned and started firing at the attackers with one hand while pushing the Secretaries forward shouting "Go, go, go!"

Out of the corner of his eye, he noticed two of the agents had already surrounded Daniel and were dragging him up the ramp.

"Take off!" Jack screamed into his mic. Within seconds, the huge aircraft began to move.

Secret Service agents lined the top of the ramp, firing at the men running towards the plane, dropping several which slowed those behind them. Two agents ran down the ramp to the President's side, one of them fell as a bullet hit him in the chest. The other reached the President, lifted her in his arms, and ran up the ramp as it began to close.

Jack, still firing, jumped onto the ramp and pulled a blood-covered Rick away from the edge.

"Leave me, sir, take care of the President," Rick said.

"We don't leave anyone behind, Rick, you know that," Jack yelled as he flung the boy's body over his shoulders and started up the ramp. He felt a bullet graze his left leg and stumbled for a moment but quickly regained his balance and kept running.

Hayden's troops reached the plane, and about a dozen of them jumped onto the edge of the ramp. But just as the ramp leveled out, Air Force One accelerated for take-off, and everyone at the end of the ramp was thrown off onto the ground.

Having made it further up the ramp, Jack was thrown onto his back, landing on Rick, who screamed in agony and then mercifully lost consciousness. Grabbing a tie-down ring with one hand and wrapping his legs around Rick's torso, Jack kept them from rolling out the back of the plane as its angle increased with take-off.

He saw three of Hayden's men slide to the end of the ramp where two were thrown out onto the tarmac. The third clung to the side of the rising door, half in, half out of the plane. Before the plane leveled out for cruising, the man's agony was over, as his body was crushed by the powerful hydraulics that operated the ramp.

Just as Jack felt the pressure ease from his body when the plane leveled out, gunfire erupted over his head. He rolled behind some cargo containers, dragging Rick with him and saw some of Hayden's troops, who were inside, had regained their feet as had the agents and were exchanging fire.

Bullets were striking randomly throughout the hold.

I hope they don't hit anything vital! Jack thought as a piece of the wooden pallet splintered next to him.

He reeled back, pulled Rick deeper behind the pallet and peeked around the other side. As near as he could tell, five of Hayden's men had made it onto the plane. Based on the rate of fire being returned, he guessed that they were severely out-gunned, so it was only a matter of time before the fight was over.

From his position, he saw several agents making their way around behind Hayden's men. Jack fired three quick rounds, blowing off half the head of one of the unwelcome passengers and hitting another in the shoulder. His fire kept their attention away from the approaching agents.

One of the men made a run for a better position and was picked off by an agent; another fell to the marksmanship of one of the military guards. *One left.*

Jack noticed that it was becoming a little harder to breathe and realized that the plane must have passed twelve-thousand feet. *Something's wrong; the compartment hasn't pressurized! We have to get out of here before we die of hypoxia!*

Just then he heard a minor explosion and the plane tilted to the left.

Sounds as if we've lost an engine! Some of the shots from Hayden's men on the ground could have damaged it.

When the plane tilted, it threw some of them off balance, and they fell to the floor. The remaining man of Hayden's outfit slid from behind his cover toward him.

Jack had held on to the cargo straps and pulled himself to his feet in time to kick the gun out of the man's hand.

The man grabbed Jack's ankle to stop his slide and pulled him down. They wrestled across the floor—the man got on top of Jack.

He grabbed Jack's head and tried to slam it into the floor, but Jack struck him with the palm of his right hand in the throat, breaking his larynx and cutting off his air supply. The man grabbed at his throat, making gurgling sounds as he fell to the floor. He would be dead within minutes.

The plane had leveled out and was stable.

Jack got up and made a quick assessment—two of the agents were down—wounded. The remaining three were in good shape. Hayden's men were all dead.

"The altitude and pressure—we have to get out of here!" He shouted.

The three able agents helped the two wounded while Jack went to help Rick. They needed to get out of the cargo area, but, due to the dropping pressure, they didn't make it to the cabin—all of them collapsed short of the door.

Max and the doctor worked feverishly over the President trying to stabilize her.

"One bullet went through her right lung and exited through the right shoulder," the doctor reported.

"Another is lodged somewhere in her abdomen; she's bleeding severely. Have you ever assisted in surgery, Max?"

"Simple surgeries, yes; but nothing like this. But, I'm probably the best qualified you've got at the moment."

"So be it. Can you administer anesthetic."

"Yes, sir but minor surgery only—you'll have to guide me."

"Good. Get it going; I'll prep her for surgery."

Max placed a mask over Laurie's face, and the doctor quickly inserted an IV, injecting several medications and then wiped the blood from her abdomen as best he could.

The doctor called to an agent, "Can you please come and apply firm pressure to her shoulder wound—try to slow or stop the bleeding. Max, hand me the scalpel."

Chapter Twenty-Nine

A LION EXAMINING ITS PREY

Hayden stood frozen at the demolished gate of Joint Base Andrews, the engine of his car still running. His aides stood behind him, watching Air Force One's nose wheels lifting off the ground as the wings caught air and pushed the plane aloft.

His driver quietly eased himself back into the driver's seat while the General's aides swallowed hard and stepped back. Who knew how he would react to this? For fear of his wrath, everyone was silent.

Hayden stood watching until Air Force One was out of sight then turned around, his face was nearly purple with rage; he was shaking. His aides took a few steps back.

"Get me back to the White House—now!" he hissed through clenched teeth.

When he was settled in the seat of the limousine, he called his top commander at Andrews. "Who was on that plane?"

The aides held their breath while the General listened to the report.

"Are you positive it was them and not decoys?" He listened for another minute and then hung up the phone without another word.

He sat quietly for a few minutes, but his stiff posture and constantly working jaw muscles told his aids it was all a façade—the calm before the storm.

"Brandon," he said quietly to one aide, "call the senior staff. There will be a meeting in one hour in the situation room."

"Yes, sir," he responded and started making calls.

Hayden was silent for the rest of the trip. While the General's rage was frightening, this calm silence was terrifying.

When he reached the White House, he entered the Oval Office, ordered his aides to 'keep everyone out' and shut the doors.

He descended the stairs into the Reagan tunnel and walked its length, coming out where the fiercest of the fighting took place—where the President had gotten away from him. He paced between the bodies. "Shit," was all he said and then returned to the tunnel and the Oval Office.

Brandon was waiting for him when he returned. "I thought I told you to keep everyone out!"

"Yes sir, you did, but we became concerned when you didn't answer, and I came in to check on you. The others have gathered in the Situation Room as you ordered."

"Let's go then," he led the way out of the office, down the staircase to the Situation Room.

The room grew deadly silent when he walked in; no one knew what to expect next. The General appeared calm and totally in control— to them, a truly petrifying occurrence.

"Air Force One, carrying Laurie Campbell, Daniel Rossler, and God knows who else, lifted off from Andrews less than two hours ago, I don't know how they got out of the White House or how they gained access to that plane. It doesn't matter—what's done is done.

What matters now is what we do next." He paced slowly around the table—a lion examining its prey.

Just as the doctor began tying off bleeders in the President's abdomen, an agent carrying Rick, rushed in. "Bullet wound to the chest." Several others followed carrying more agents.

"Shit!" responded the doctor as blood sprayed out of the President's gut splattering on the wall. "She's sprung another leak!"

Max quickly stopped the flow of blood from the ruptured artery and the doctor repaired it posthaste.

"Max, she's under, I'll take it from here, see what you can do for the boy. Agent!" he was speaking to the man who carried Rick in, "Get over here!"

The agent paled but stepped up to the table that held the body of the President. "Is she alive?" he whispered, taking the suction tube from Max and watching as blood flowed through it from the abdominal cavity.

"Barely. Hand me instruments as I tell you what I need, and do exactly what I tell you when I tell you. Understood?"

"Yes, sir."

"Max! How's the boy?"

"Multiple gunshot wounds, the worst is to the chest. Preparing to tie off bleeders."

"Who else in here is wounded?" the doctor demanded as he finished with the last bleeder and moved to inspect Laurie's spleen.

"I have a wound from earlier but the bleeding has

stopped," Daniel said, "and I have basic first aid skills; I'll check the others for you."

Another agent stepped into the room, just in time to hear Daniel's offer. "Stay where you are sir, I'm Stan. I'm trained as a First Responder. I'll check everyone."

"What about the agents that were just brought in? Are they injured?" the doctor asked.

"Most of them have minor injuries. Jack Symonds took a bullet through the left calf; I will bring him in shortly. The cargo hold is riddled with bullet holes and couldn't be pressurized. They couldn't make it out before the plane gained too much altitude—they're unconscious but still breathing. We brought them into the cabin."

"They'll be alright before too long - although they may wake up with one hell of a headache." He told the agent which instrument he needed next and began removing the spleen.

"Alright, if you're not injured and not here to help, clear-out and give us some room to work," the doctor ordered.

While the doctor fought to save Laurie's life and Max worked to stabilize Rick, Daniel watched as Stan treated several agents with bullet wounds in arms and legs. Most of them were grazes with only one that tore through an agent's wrist shattering the bone.

Stan had tried to check Daniel first, but Daniel would have none of it. He insisted that the recently injured took precedence over him. Their discussion started to become heated until one of the wounded agents stepped in.

"Excuse me, sirs. My wound is only a scrape on my side. Let me check Vice President Rossler's shoulder while you start on the others. I have some first-aid training and can let you know if it needs immediate attention."

The young agent helped Daniel to take off his shirt.

"Tell me what you see, Ken," Stan ordered.

"Yes sir, give me a moment to get to the wound."

Daniel winced when the blood-soaked bandages were removed.

Just then the doctor uttered a string of swear words that would make a sailor blush. "There is only so much damage a human body can withstand and only so much I can heal! What the hell am I supposed to do with this …" and he seemed to run out of steam. "I'm sorry; I'm so sorry Madame President," he whispered. "There is only so much I can do."

"Doc?" Stan shouted. "Can I help?"

"No. Only God alone can help now."

"What is it?"

"Her liver — her right kidney — her heart … where do you want me to start?"

Stepping beside the agent helping the doc Stan said, "the others are stable and can be treated with first aid. I'll help."

The agent stepped away looking relieved when the doctor nodded.

"We need to address the bullet lodged above her heart … it's injured the right pulmonary artery and it could fail at any moment," the doc said even as he began the process.

"Looks like half her liver is gone," Stan commented appalled.

"More than half — must have been hit by a hollow-point. We'll be lucky if there's enough left to keep her alive."

"Can she live without a liver?" Daniel asked.

"Without one? No. But if we can save at least twenty-five percent she can ... it is one of the few organs in the body that can regenerate over time."

"Excuse me gentlemen," Ken said and started his report on Daniel's shoulder for Stan. "The blood has started to dry, and some of the bandages are sticking to the wound; I'm going to soak them off with some saline solution." It took him a few minutes and then he continued.

"Hmmm. There's no exit wound, so the bullet is still in there. The wound is red and angry but isn't actively bleeding. I'll clean it up a bit and re-bandage it until the doc can take a look at it."

"Thank you, Ken," Daniel smiled.

Chapter Thirty

I CAN, BUT YOU WON'T LIKE IT

Half an hour later, Daniel left the press-section-turned-medical-bay area of the plane with Jack, who was limping from the bullet wound in his lower leg, sporting a shiner on his right eye, and had one hell of a headache. The doctor, Stan, and Max were still busy with the President, and the two men went in search of Peter for a status update.

Moving forward along the left side of the plane, they spotted him coming out of the Main Galley with a cup of coffee.

He saw them as they approached and grinned. "You two are a site for sore eyes!" Then he grew somber, "How's the President?"

"Not good," Daniel answered. "The doctor and Max are doing everything they can. What's happening here?"

Peter frowned, "Come on, let's go talk to the pilot—he can answer that better than I can."

They followed him up the stairs to the upper deck and took a seat in the Communication Center. "Daniel, why don't you call Sam and the guys while I fetch the pilot," Peter suggested.

"Good idea" Daniel replied pulling out his mirror phone to get the Rabbit Hole on the line.

A few minutes later the pilot joined them, introducing himself as 'Chuck,' shaking hands with Daniel and Jack as he sat down.

"Well gentlemen, that was certainly the most exciting take-off Air Force One has ever had, but we're not out of the woods yet."

"It felt like we lost an engine just after take-off," Jack said.

"Yes, we lost the number one engine just after we got airborne—damage from bullets is my guess. The problem is that the number two engine was also damaged and is showing signs of impending failure as well."

Daniel paled. "Can a plane this big stay in the air with only two engines?"

"Yes, Mr. Vice President; this plane can fly with one engine," Chuck replied, "but I won't have much fun—especially when it comes time to land."

"Mhh, well, if you say so but…"

Chuck smiled. "Mr. Vice President, this plane has armored windows, a shell that can withstand the Electromagnetic Pulse from a nuclear blast, countermeasures to hide it from radar, and flares to confuse heat-seeking missiles. She's a tough bird, and she even has a glide ratio of fifteen to one—at this altitude, we could glide for over one hundred miles if necessary.

Daniel looked impressed, "What's the plan then?"

"I had them set course for Dallas as planned and the decoys are supposed to arrive soon, then we'll be able to change our heading to Denver—Owen is there waiting for us," Peter said referring to their writer friend and pilot who owned the ranch, known as Mount Ararat, which they used as a base to the nearby Rabbit Hole.

"We're going to need another plane, to transport everyone from there," Daniel said.

"Okay, we'll see what we can do—maybe we can commandeer a jet," Sam replied. "

"The problem is, Owen and I aren't trained to fly jets," Peter said.

"I can fly pretty much anything that has manmade wings," Chuck grinned. "I'll get you where you're going."

"Alright, we'll see what we can have ready for you when you land," Sam replied.

Just then the noise of the engines grew slightly quieter, and the plane dipped softly forward and to the left, correcting almost immediately.

"Excuse me, gentlemen, I believe that was engine number two," Chuck stood and headed quickly for the cockpit.

Sam and the others were on speaker from the Rabbit Hole, listening to the discussions.

"So, let me see if I understand your situation correctly." Sam started. "The President is shot up pretty bad, along with a young Marine; Daniel took a bullet to the shoulder; you copped a bullet through the left calf muscle, and there are quite a few others with less severe injuries and wounds.

"In addition, gunfire damaged two engines which have now failed, plus the cargo bay is full of holes, so you had to seal the lower decks completely in order to pressurize the rest of the plane.

"In other words—things aren't going very smoothly—

but at least you have a spare engine because the plane can still fly with one engine."

"Sam, you'll definitely have to see a professional person about that sudden life-threatening streak of optimism that overtook you," Jack replied.

Daniel and Peter started laughing, but Daniel's laughing was short-lived as a blinding pain shot through his shoulder.

In the background, the laughter coming from the Rabbit Hole could be heard.

"So, I take it that's the size of it, Jack?" Sam asked.

"Yep, you've got it," Jack replied.

"As I understand it, Sam, we're about two-and-a-half hours out of Denver. We're going to try to stabilize everyone so they are ready to be moved when we arrive," Daniel said.

"Okay, sounds good. Roy says his decoys are in position now Peter; you can let the pilots know."

"On my way," Peter replied as he disappeared toward the cockpit. He still marveled at the 'toys' Roy created. In this case, a drone designed to look like an owl would fly up close to Air Force One, create an electromagnetic field that would make it look like a 747 to radar, and then fly off in a different direction. It would look like Air Force One was headed to South America, but four hours into the flight the drone would self-destruct in an explosion that would leave no trace—vaporized.

Within minutes of the phone call from Daniel, Rebecca was hurriedly gathering the instruments and supplies she thought she would likely need, packing them into a bag in a semi-orderly fashion. Not really knowing what to expect, she planned for the worst.

Her sister, Cyndi, helped her pack medical supplies. Cyndi was a Nurse Practitioner, and Rebecca welcomed her assistance in treating whatever was coming their way.

"I can't stuff anymore supplies into these bags," Cyndi said. "But I can't think of anything else we should take with us anyway."

Rebecca surveyed the room. "I can't either, and even if we did, how in the world would we get it there? I can already hear Aaron and the others complaining about us using them as pack animals."

Aaron poked his head into the medical center and whistled at the sight of the supply bags. "We need to talk about getting some pack animals," he said.

Rebecca gave Cyndi an 'I-told-you-so' look—Cyndi just smiled.

"So, are you two just about ready to leave?"

"Yes, we've got everything we can think of."

"And then some, it seems. All right; I'll get the guys, and we'll be on our way."

Nigel, JR, Aaron, and the brothers Jack and Shane Walker, had volunteered to accompany Rebecca and Cyndi on the hike to the farm.

Sarah was going to stay behind at the command center to wait for updates. "Luke and I will leave for Mt. Ararat as soon as they're off the ground in Denver."

"We'll see you there—hang in there Sarah, he's going to be just fine," Rebecca encouraged.

Sarah's eyes brimmed with tears, she swallowed hard and said tightly, "Thank you Rebecca; I hope and pray you're right."

"That's all we can do for now, Max. She's stable, but..." The doctor swallowed the rest of his words.

Daniel and Jack had returned a few minutes before and heard the glum report.

"How bad is she?" Daniel asked.

Shaking his head the doctor answered sadly. "As you know, I removed her spleen. I was able to repair the damaged pulmonary artery and stop all the internal bleeding, but she lost most of her liver, her right kidney and left lung. She also lost a lot of blood and barely has the minimum volume left to stay alive. We used the supply of O-negative blood aboard just to get her through the surgery."

"But there's other blood in storage."

"Yes, but it isn't O-negative, which is the only type compatible with all other types. Without knowing her blood-type, I can't risk using the other."

"Will she recover?"

The doctor bit his lower lip momentarily. "Barring a miracle ... no."

Daniel stood silently, swallowing several times with his jaw muscles clenched. "How's the boy?" Daniel asked looking over at Rick's unconscious form.

"He'll pull through."

"He'd better," Jack said tightly. "That's one of the bravest Marines I've ever seen. He shielded the President with his own body—twice—taking bullets both times. Every bullet in him was one less in the President."

Another quiet moment passed before the doctor spoke again. "I hear we're about an hour out of Denver. How about I take that bullet out of you Daniel?"

"Can you do it with me conscious?"

"I can, but you won't like it," the doctor warned.

"Then that's how it will be. With the President unconscious, I need to stay alert."

"Have it your way—take a seat. I'll use some local to help dull the pain."

Chapter Thirty-One

GET THIS BIRD READY TO LAND

Just as Daniel sat down on the chair so the doctor could look at his shoulder, a flash of lightening brightened the inside of the cabin and shortly after the pilot's voice came over the intercom.

"Everyone take a seat and strap yourselves in; we've got some nasty weather ahead."

"Must be pretty bad if he's making that call," the doctor commented. "Help me get these two secured," he said, pointing to the President and Rick.

Peter, arriving from the flight deck, helped them strap Rick and Laurie to the seats that had been adjusted as improvised beds. "The captain says we just passed over the Oklahoma City area, and there are fierce storms all across the state—high winds, tornados, flooding and such. He says it's worse on the ground, but it will be a rough ride up here too since we're flying at a lower altitude than normal."

"Can't he move us to a higher altitude?"

"Not with only two engines and being less than an hour from landing," Peter replied

"Isn't it dangerous to be flying in a thunderstorm?"

"Thunderstorms are the most hazardous weather there is when flying. With the high winds, turbulence, lightning, heavy rain, and wind shear, it's not just dangerous; it's more like suicidal. Sometimes, like now, it can't be avoided and you either get through it, or it kills you."

Daniel looked at him in stunned disbelief. The plane hit a wind shear and dropped dramatically. Instinctively Daniel grabbed the armrest of his seat, followed by a grunt of pain escaping his mouth. "Swell," he said through clenched teeth.

For the next fifteen minutes, the plane bumped, rattled, dropped and rose as it rode the air turbulence like a rollercoaster. People's bodies grew tenser with every passing minute. There was a flash of lightening; the plane lurched terribly, the lights dimmed and then went out completely.

The captain's voice came over the intercom almost immediately. "Peter, I could use your help up front."

Peter pulled out his smartphone, switched on the flashlight app and made his way over items scattered around the walkway.

When he reached the flight deck, Peter saw that Chuck had his hand's full. His white shirt was splattered with blood that dripped from the side of his head, and he had both hands firmly on the controls, his jaw clenched in concentration.

One of the communication officers was checking the co-pilot who was unconscious in his seat. "What happened?"

"He was getting up to secure some of the stuff in the back when we hit that air pocket, and he hit his head on the instrument panel above him."

Peter helped the officer disconnect the co-pilot's harness

and ease him to the floor then used the intercom to call the doctor to the flight deck.

"You'll have to take the co-pilot position, Peter," Chuck ordered.

"What!" Peter exclaimed. "I've never flown anything bigger than a twin-engine prop, let alone a 747."

"Don't worry about that now," Chuck said, "It's exactly the same, only different."

Peter did a double-take, "huh?"

"The principles of flight remain the same. Right now, I need a second set of hands on the controls. I'll tell you what I need you to do."

"Okay," Peter said. As he settled into the co-pilot seat, he couldn't help but grin.

"How is he doc?" Chuck asked shortly after the doctor arrived and checked to co-pilot

"Concussion, I think he'll be alright."

"See if you can secure him in a seat. We're just about out of the weather, but we still have to land and it ain't gonna be smooth." Chuck said.

The communication officer came forward again to assist the doctor.

"Nick," Chuck called to the officer. "Go with the doc, have everyone move back to the Guest Section. I want everyone behind the wings.

"Will do," Nick responded as he and the doctor descended the stairs.

As they left the top deck, they heard Peter ask, "What's the situation, Chuck?"

"We're down to one engine; number four was struck by that last lightning flash you saw."

Peter paled. Almost breathlessly he asked, "I know you

can fly with one engine but can you land this thing on one engine?"

"Sure!" Chuck replied.

Peter was surprised by Chuck's and calm demeanor.

"Wow! How many times have you done it?"

Chuck looked at him with a grin, "Four or five times—in a simulator."

Peter's pleased amazement changed to a worried frown. "A simulator? You mean you've never actually done it for real?"

"Think about it, how else can you learn to do it? You have to learn it in the simulator before you can do it. It's the same with landing on water—you can't go dumping planes into the water to get practical experience—can you?

"Look at it this way. If I don't try it we'll all be dead, so what do we have to lose?"

Peter dead-panned him. "I hate your logic."

Chuck laughed. "Help me get this bird ready to land; we're all gonna be just fine."

Chapter Thirty-Two

INTO THE EARLY MORNING SKY

Emergency lighting came on while the doctor was gone and Daniel looked around. Everyone seemed to be secure in their seats or improvised beds.

"What's going on up there?" Daniel asked as the doctor returned and took his place.

"It sounds like we lost another engine from a lightning strike."

"What?" Daniel released his seatbelt and headed for the flight deck.

"They're kinda busy right now," the doctor said to Daniel's retreating back.

Stumbling in the dim light, Daniel made his way forward and up the stairs, gritting his teeth in pain. As soon as he reached the communications center, he pulled out his mirror phone and called Sam.

"Hi, Daniel! What's happening?"

"I'm about to find out. Sam, I'm putting you on speaker now. I've just joined Chuck and Peter in the cockpit.

"Sam, we've had some trouble up here. Chuck, what's our status?"

"As you know, we lost two engines due to bullets. We also hit a severe thunderstorm over Oklahoma and our number four engine was shut down by a lightning strike."

"Dear God!" Sam exclaimed. "Can that thing be landed with only one engine?"

Chuck and Peter looked at each other. Chuck shrugged, and Peter said, "It sure can—Chuck here is an expert at it. Done it four or five times before."

Daniel saw Chuck break into a grin and wondered what was up but decided not to ask.

"Wow," Sam said, "I had no idea!"

Sarah's voice came over the phone. "Peter, are you sure?"

"Don't worry Sarah, Chuck has done it quite a few times." He just hoped no one would realize he was lying—sort of. Even if they did, there was nothing they could do—other than worry and panic. "We just started dumping fuel to get rid of unnecessary weight, and we'll slow our air speed before touching down, so it won't be a problem."

"Oh, ok. I didn't realize it would be so easy," Sarah responded with relief.

Peter froze momentarily and glanced at Chuck from the corner of his eye and mouthed, "*easy?*"

Chuck grinned again, shrugged slightly, and busied himself with the controls.

The silent communication between the two did not escape Daniel, but before he could say anything, Sarah spoke again.

"How's the President and the young Marine?" she asked.

"They're holding their own for the moment, but we need Rebecca to meet us."

"She's already on her way," Sarah replied.

"Alright, Daniel," Chuck said, "we're on final approach, time to get yourself strapped in."

"Everything is ready for you in Denver," Sam said. "We'll see you soon."

"See you soon," Daniel replied. *I hope.*

"What are you guys not telling us?" Daniel asked.

"Later," Peter said. "Strap yourself in a seat."

Chuck was a bit surprised to hear how Peter was talking to the Vice President and frowned at him.

"Don't worry we're old friends—he's not a stuck-up type of guy," Peter said softly.

Daniel didn't hear that as he was already on his way back to the crew lounge. He buckled himself in a seat near the flight deck door and felt an uncomfortable pinch in his stomach—it wasn't from hunger. It grew into a cramp as he listened to the two talk on the flight deck.

"Er, Chuck? When should I stop dumping fuel?"

Chuck checked the fuel levels. "Not yet."

"Um, ok," Peter said looking at him nervously. "Uh, how much more do you think we need to dump?"

"Oh, we're on final approach and only have about fifty miles to go, don't worry about it."

Peter was silent for a minute and then whispered, "shit, I just realized you're emptying the tanks."

Chuck looked at him and nodded slowly. He pushed a couple of buttons to lower the landing gear.

"But, why? You'll kill us all! You're one of Hayden's men, aren't you?"

Chuck blinked at the absurdity of Peter's comment. "Of course, I'm not!"

"Then why?"

"Because the nose gear is damaged and can't be lowered for landing," he said pointing to a flashing indicator on the instrument panel. "This lady is going to belly flop, and I don't want to risk an explosion with all the fuel onboard.

"But we'll fall out of the sky like a rock!" Peter objected.

Chuck snorted a laugh. "Weren't you listening earlier? Contrary to popular airline disaster movies, this plane can glide for nearly one hundred miles under the right circumstances, and we're only going to need about thirty."

At that moment, the last engine failed—it was out of fuel.

Chuck checked the instruments. "Good, we got further than I thought; we're only twenty miles out."

"Why hasn't the control tower contacted us?"

"I turned the radio off; don't want them to know who we are until the last minute, which I guess is about now."

Chuck flipped a switch and adjusted the radio to Denver's frequency. He started clicking the transmit button on the mic in slow irregular intervals and spoke in a slightly excited voice, "Mayday! Mayday! Denver tower this is SAM28000; do you read?"

"Unidentified aircraft this is Denver tower; repeat your last transmission."

"Mayday! Mayday! Denver tower this is SAM28000; do you read?" Chuck repeated as though he hadn't heard.

"Unidentified aircraft this is Denver tower; your transmission is breaking up repeat. Are you declaring an emergency?"

"Denver tower, SAM28000, emergency, emergency. We've lost all engines."

Owen and the local Tectus members who were assisting him watched as Air Force One approached the runway, descending closer and closer to the ground. It was obvious the plane was having difficulties; it was too low and moving too slow.

What the hell else has gone wrong up there?
Engines.
No engines!
Shit!
A coffin with wings.

They watched in horror as the plane touched down fifty feet shy of the runway. The weight of the plane drove the wheels into the soft earth, and the landing gear snapped off like matchsticks.

The mid-section of the plane's belly touched the ground at the beginning of the runway and began skidding along the tarmac. The flash of sparks illuminated the darkness of the early morning. The nose of the plane slammed down—that's when Owen realized the nose gear hadn't been extended.

Everyone held their breath, waiting for an explosion—but it never came. Sparks continued to light up the night as the plane skidded down the runway, some of the metal was glowing red by the time it came to a stop—intact.

Owen, and everyone with him, was slack-jawed. Slowly the cargo door at the back began to lower.

"Let's get going!" Owen shouted, and they moved toward the plane.

Because it was resting on its somewhat crushed belly, the cargo door couldn't be deployed entirely, but it was enough to get everyone off.

They hurriedly sorted and loaded everyone according to their destination.

The President, Daniel, and Rick, accompanied by the doctor, Max, and four Secret Service Agents, along with Cliff Willis, Bill Sims, Jack, Peter, and Chuck were all taken to a waiting bus which transported them to a private airstrip not far away. There, a nineteen passenger, twin-turboprop Fairchild Swearingen Metroliner airliner, which Sam and Luke had managed to find, was waiting for them.

Everyone else was taken to waiting cars and then on to local Tectus safe houses before Hayden had time to figure out what happened and send in his troops.

Beds had been improvised along each side of the Metroliner for the President and Rick. Everyone else took their seats as Chuck and Owen taxied to another runway for take-off.

Owen called Roy. "We're going to take off in a few minutes; are your decoys ready?"

"Ready and waiting, I'll get them airborne right now."

Chuck and Owen ran through the pre-flight checklist quickly, double checked their instruments and revved the engines for take-off.

When Chuck released the brakes, the plane began to roll, and Owen reported to the Rabbit Hole, "we're on our way; see you soon!"

The sleek Metroliner roared down the runway, caught air, and lifted into the early morning sky, the faint light of sunrise off the starboard wing.

Chapter Thirty-Three

THAT'S MY WIFE YOU'RE HOLDING MISTER

General Hayden and his senior officers were startled when a young clerk barged into the room shouting, "they've crashed, they've crashed!"

Hayden grabbed him by the arm, angry at being interrupted, but too exhausted to spare the energy of rage. "What's the meaning of this? How dare you…"

"Air Force One, sir," the clerk said excitedly, "she's crashed! Look!" he said as he turned on the TV in the room.

"… that's right Sally," the newsman said to a woman sitting next to him. "And now we go live to Mike, who is on site at Denver International Airport. Mike?"

"Good morning Dave—what a way to start the day. Airport authorities say that an unidentified plane called in a Mayday and requested an emergency landing, reporting that they were coming in 'dead-stick' which means they were without power.

"Control tower staff were stunned to see the low-flying

plane was none other than the Presidential plane, Air Force One, and even more shocked when it came in short of the runway, crashed, and skidded nearly half the length of the field.

"We are told that rescue personnel were on site and unloaded the passengers, but took them to an unknown location. It is not known if the President was indeed on board or what her condition is after the crash.

"Airport security has secured the plane and is awaiting the arrival of the FBI."

"That is an incredible story, Mike! Did anyone see somebody getting off the plane alive?"

"Dave, several airport employees did indeed say they saw people climbing from the cargo ramp and walking across to board a service vehicle. They also said they saw at least two people being carried out on gurneys."

"That's not much to go on."

"No, Dave, it isn't, but keep in mind the plane came in almost unannounced, and that it was just before dawn and the only lights were those on the runway itself, there wasn't much time to prepare and visibility…"

"Got you, bitch!" shouted Hayden over the voice of the reporter on the TV. "We found them!

"Contact our troops in Denver; get them out to the airport and have them start looking for those guys—they have to be there somewhere. Tell them to check the hospitals and clinics—someone's going to need medical attention after a crash like that!"

The Metroliner smoothly leveled off and settled into a north-westerly heading. Everyone on board was pleased to hear the muffled roar of healthy engines that carried them toward safety at close to three-hundred miles per hour.

Chuck called back over the intercom in his best happy voice.

"Good morning ladies and gentlemen, I'd like to welcome you aboard Air Force One. All systems are functioning normal and flight time to our next destination is about two hours. Please sit back, relax, and enjoy the flight."

"Air Force One?" Owen asked.

"Yes, any plane that is carrying the President gets the 'Air Force One' call sign."

"Mhh, never too old to learn new things," Owen mumbled.

The group of exhausted, disheveled travelers sporting black eyes, cuts, bruises, broken bones, and gunshot wounds looked at each other and then burst out laughing. It was the laughter of relief, knowing they had escaped from the jaws of hell.

Owen looked at Chuck and grinned. "You're quite a guy to get them laughing after what they've been through—they look like they were in hand-to-hand combat with a speeding train."

Chuck smiled, "Thanks, Owen, all in a day's work—oh, and by the way, congratulations on your promotion."

"What are you talking about?"

"Becoming an Air Force One pilot."

Owen grinned, "you're the pilot, I'm along for the ride."

"You're rated on twin-engine aircraft, aren't you? That's what Peter told me."

"Well, yes, but nothing as big as this…"

"Aw, the principle is the same. Time for a bit of on-the-job training. I'm going to take a nap, so you're the pilot now."

"But ..."

"Wake me up if you need me. Enjoy!" and with that Chuck donned a baseball cap and pulled the bill down over his eyes.

Owen stared at him for a moment, before looking out the window at the rapidly brightening sky, glanced at the instrument panel without seeing it, and then turned back to Chuck and settled a bit further into his seat.

"Well, I'll be a son-of-a-bitch... I'm flying Air Force One!" Owen mumbled.

Chuck smiled, but Owen was already looking over the instrument panel again, seeing it this time.

As tired as the passengers were, most of them remained awake.

Daniel's shoulder was throbbing, but he tried his best not to show his discomfort.

Max and the doctor stayed close to their charges, Rick and the President, checking their vital signs and trying to keep them as comfortable as possible. The doctor frequently shook his head, obviously worried, but said nothing.

To everyone's relief the flight went without incident, and Chuck awoke when Owen tapped him on the shoulder.

"Wake up old timer," he teased. "I've got her lined up for you, and we're on final approach."

"What did you wake me up for then? You're doing fine!"

"I've never landed a plane this big, and while the principle may be the same, with all the injured we've got on board, I'd prefer that someone who knows what they're doing land the plane."

"Well, if you insist—I guess I can't let some young upstart out-fly me now can I?"

"After that landing at Denver, I don't think anyone can out-fly you!"

Chuck checked the instruments and looked out the window. "You've lined us up dead on. Good job! I couldn't have done it better myself!"

Within minutes the plane touched down gently, rolled out, and taxied toward the gathered welcoming committee.

Chuck was the last to leave the plane, and Sarah walked over to him, put her hands on her hips and glared at him, fuming.

"So, you're the one who has *lots* of experience landing a 747 on one engine— *simulator* experience? Huh?

"And you dumped the entire fuel supply? Right?"

He stood looking at her, bracing himself—he had no illusion that he was facing a mother grizzly ready to tear him apart. He took a step back, "I ah ... I ... I ..."

"I ought to tear you apart for lying to us," she started to cry and threw herself at him wrapping her arms around him, "but I'm just so grateful to you for bringing them all here safely—thank you!"

Chuck was astounded and uncomfortable; surely this beautiful woman was someone's wife; he patted her haltingly on the back, saying "that's my job ma'am."

Just then someone tapped him on the shoulder—the Vice President.

"Yes, sir?"

"That's my wife you're holding mister."

"Oh, geez, sorry sir," Chuck said looking abashed and trying to step further aside.

Daniel smiled and offered his hand. "Thank you for bringing me home to her. If it's ever up to me, I want you as my pilot from now on when I fly anywhere. You have a permanent place in the Rossler family."

Chapter Thirty-Four

YOU BETTER RUN AND HIDE

Kelly, Peter's wife and former TV celebrity, and Alison, Owen's wife, were a little overwhelmed by the influx of people suddenly needing food and places to sleep at Mount Ararat. However, they were able to accommodate everyone.

They already had a buffet style breakfast of coffee, eggs, bacon, potatoes, toast, and fruit ready. People gratefully served themselves and found places to sit wherever they could. When they finished eating, they were distributed between the two houses to clean up and get some sleep.

One of the rooms at Kelly's house had been arranged as a two-patient improvised hospital room for Rick and Laurie with Max and the doctor taking it in turns to check on them.

Rebecca and Cyndi treated other injuries throughout the morning. Mostly it consisted of cleaning up minor cuts, suturing a few more serious wounds, providing analgesics, wrapping sprained appendages, and setting and securing a broken bone or two.

The doctor left Max in charge of the two hospital

patients while he tended to Daniel's shoulder—Sarah present, like a broody hen, during the procedure.

It was a relief to Daniel when the local anesthetic eased the pain radiating from the wound.

"You're lucky it stopped where it did. Otherwise, it would have shattered your Scapula—the shoulder blade."

Daniel grunted as the doctor applied a clean dressing over the sutures. "Thanks, Doc."

"You're welcome. Here, let's get this sling on you to give that shoulder some rest, and then *you* need to get some rest."

Smiling slightly Daniel replied, "Oh that I could, but I think that is going to be awhile in coming yet," he nodded toward the approaching Max.

"Daniel, the President is awake and wants to talk to you and Nigel immediately; Nigel is on his way," Max reported.

"I'll be the judge of *that*," the doctor said hurrying away toward the President's room.

"Come on, Max," Daniel said, "This ought to be interesting."

"What?"

"The doc trying to make the President behave."

When they arrived, they heard the doctors voice… "Absolutely *not*. You are in no condition to receive visitors!"

"Then I will get up out of this bed and go meet them somewhere else."

"But you can't, you're in no state to go anywhere!"

"Doctor now is not the time for this. We are in the middle of a crisis, and I don't have the strength to argue with you. Either get Daniel and Nigel in here, or I will go to them."

A brief silence followed and then the rustle of covers being thrown aside was heard.

"All right, I'll get them, just please stay in bed, and *please* keep it short."

"Thank you, doctor," she said weakly.

Daniel stepped into the room, "I'm here Laurie, relax."

"Daniel," Laurie gasped, "we have to let the people know what has happened... I mean what is happening..." she looked around puzzled, taking in her surroundings for the first time. "Where are we anyway?"

"We're in one of the Rossler Foundation safe houses, don't worry, you're going to be fine," Daniel tried to sound upbeat, but the tightness in his throat made it impossible.

"No Daniel, I am not going to be fine," she said softly. "I need to get on television and radio and let the people know what Hayden has done and is planning to do."

"Okay, it will take a little time to set things up—I'll get it done right away."

She shook her head in frustration. "I don't have time, Daniel." Her eyes were closed, and her voice was dropping off. "I need to do it now! Use a smartphone to make a recording if you have to."

Nigel had just arrived and pulled out his phone. "One moment, Laurie."

She tried to adjust herself to a more comfortable position but grimaced from pain.

"Okay, ready. Go ahead, Laurie."

She looked directly at Nigel's phone. It was clear, she was in pain and was mustering all her strength to speak, "My fellow Americans. Our nation is at a crossroads, and we must act wisely. The criminal John Brideaux and his Council have left this nation and the world a legacy of death and destruction. We must act to change that. We must join together to rebuild this nation, and the world, for the good of all people." She gasped for air momentarily and then continued.

"Retired General Tom Hayden has attempted to overthrow this government and brought about civil war. His attack on the White House last night cost many lives, and I have been mortally wounded.

"We have intelligence reports that he is planning on setting up a military government to help him attain and keep his control. This is a nation of democracy and General Hayden's plans are those of a dictatorship."

The President coughed, and a trickle of blood began to run from her nose and the corner of her mouth. "I beg of you to stop fighting, join together to support your next President, Daniel ... Rossler, ... and restore ... this once ... proud ... na ... ation ... to ..." she got no further; she slipped into unconsciousness.

"Shut that damn thing off!" the doctor said, rushing to her side. He checked her pulse as she began to stir slightly.

Daniel could see her slipping away with every passing moment and tears began to fill his eyes.

She spoke to him, "I won't last much longer, Daniel. You are going to have to make the decisions." She paused, her breathing labored. "Lean on Nigel, trust my appointees, they're loyal—you can do it, Daniel. I've seen you at work—I know you're the right man for this." Her voice was barely audible."

"Don't worry; I'll 'hold the fort until you're better, Laurie."

Her face had grown pale; she tried to smile, "Daniel, the prisoners ..." she faded out.

"Yes?" he said bending down to get his ear close enough to hear. "What about the prisoners. Laurie?"

"They're ... they're ... Cl ... liff..." and she exhaled her final breath.

Daniel hung his head, allowing the tears to flow freely. The doctor shoved him out of the way, yelling for Max's help.

Max began mouth to mouth resuscitation while the doctor prepared the defibrillator.

After several minutes of trying unsuccessfully to restart her heart, the doctor reached out to brush her eyes closed and pulled the sheet up over her face.

Nigel stood quietly with his hand on Daniel's right shoulder, struggling to regain his composure.

It was several moments before anyone stirred. Finally, Nigel spoke softly, "Daniel, this has to get out to the people."

"I know," he whispered, "go ahead."

"No, Daniel. You are now President. The people need you."

Daniel was white in the face, he clenched his fists and hissed through his gritted teeth. "You better run and hide, Tom Hayden. Today, you've made an enemy out of the Rosslerites."

Nigel felt goosebumps over his body when he heard Daniel's words. He knew what it meant, and he almost felt sorry for Hayden.

Chapter Thirty-Five

YOU WILL BE HIS SLAVES

Fifteen minutes after Laurie Campbell let out her last breath, a meeting of the Rossler Foundation leadership was called in the hanger at Mount Ararat. Daniel, Sarah, Nigel, JR, Rebecca, and Luke were present in the hanger. Sam, Salome, and the other leadership dialed in on Daniel's mirror phone from the Rabbit Hole and were on speaker.

"President Campbell is dead," Daniel said bluntly and paused to get his quivering voice under control. He waited through the exclamations of distress coming over the phone.

"She died about a quarter of an hour ago, while recording a speech for the nation." Daniel's voice broke, and he paused to clear his throat.

"This message needs to get out to the media and the nation as soon as possible. Can a link be set up here, or would it be better if I come back to the Rabbit Hole?"

"Stand by, Daniel," Sam responded in a solemn tone. The line went silent as it was muted.

Daniel looked at Luke and Nigel. "What's that about?"

Nigel shook his head, and Luke just raised an eyebrow and shrugged his shoulders.

Sam's voice came over the phone again. "Daniel, I assume then that you are now President and will be addressing the nation as such; is that correct?"

Daniel nodded glumly, and then realized that Sam couldn't see him, "Yes, that's correct."

"We could set you up there, but we all think it would be better, and just as fast, for you to come here—for a number of reasons. That's if you are in good enough physical state to make the trip here."

"Very well, you can explain your reasons to me later," Daniel said, "Just make sure everything is set up and ready to go when I arrive."

"We'll be ready. Oh, and please send us that recording over right away so we can work on it to remove any background noise and disturbances."

"Will do," Daniel replied and ended the connection.

"Let's get Daniel on his way. JR and some of the others can stay and take care of things here," Nigel suggested. "Sarah, Luke, Rebecca, and I should accompany Daniel."

Everyone agreed.

"Come on, let's go see Peter," Luke said. "He and Kelly have a few horses—that will get us to the Rabbit Hole much quicker."

They departed the hanger and made their way across the yard to the house.

"Peter!" Luke called as he entered the house.

"Over here!" Peter replied from the kitchen.

Luke pulled him to the side, out of earshot of the other people in the house and said. "Daniel, Sarah, Nigel, Rebecca and I need to get to the Rabbit Hole immediately —I was hoping we could use your horses?"

"Help me get them saddled," Peter replied without hesitation.

Twenty minutes later the five horsemen rode across the meadow and disappeared into the tree line. Rebecca had tried to persuade Daniel not to make the trip but in the end had to give up after a heated argument. She gave him a painkiller injection and strapped his wounded arm tight to his body to prevent it from too much movement.

The afternoon air was warm, and the coolness between the trees felt good. The peacefulness of nature stood in sharp contrast to the turmoil in their minds, the misery and suffering brought upon the people of America again, by another madman.

Despite the morphine shot Rebecca gave him, within five minutes Daniel was clenching his teeth in pain. Sarah was leading Daniel's horse, Nigel and Luke kept their horses on either side of his, close enough to support him if the need arose. As Daniel tried to divert his mind from the pain in his shoulder, he managed to look around him and breath.

If it weren't for Laurie's death, the pain in my shoulder and the national crisis, I could have enjoyed this.

They arrived at the Rabbit Hole in less than two hours. Daniel was in agony from the jarring his shoulder took with the motion of the horse.

Rebecca and the rest just shook their heads in disbelief that Daniel was able to make it to the Rabbit Hole without passing out. A shoulder wound was one of the most excruciatingly painful wounds one could sustain. It is nothing like in the movies where the hero gets shot in the shoulder and is still able to knock the villain out with a world-class uppercut or hook.

The Rowen

A warm but worried welcome awaited them in the Robert Cartwright Town Hall, and despite the urgency of the message he carried, Daniel, as pale as bleached white linen, took a bit of time to greet his family and the rest of the Rosslerites.

Finally, he motioned to Sam that it was time to get down to business and Sam led him away from the crowd, to a room that had been set up to resemble a formal office—no sign that they were in a cave. A dark blue fabric hung behind a desk framed by two American Flags on stands. He had no idea where all the decorations came from and how they were able to set it up so professionally in such a short time. Then again, those were the Rosslerites for you—give them a challenge and they will meet and exceed any expectations.

"You can sit at the desk, Daniel. We'll play the recording from President Campbell and then switch over to you for your address to the nation."

"Thanks," Daniel said. Despite the fact that Nigel had coached him and helped him prepare what he had to say he was still nervous.

Nigel, who had just joined them, stopped himself from slapping Daniel on the shoulder and simply said, "You'll do fine, Daniel. Just do it—you've got it."

Daniel was dressed in a dark suit, white shirt, and red tie; his arm was in a clearly visible sling. As previously agreed Nigel was also suited up and took a seat next to Daniel.

Raj and Roy pulled off the same stunt they did a few days ago with John Brideaux when they took over all broadcasting stations and communications satellites across the globe.

Daniel waited while they played President Campbell's

recorded message to the American people, fighting to subdue the turmoil of emotions when he listened to Laurie's voice again.

When Sam pointed to him, he began to speak.

"My fellow Americans, it is with deep regret and profound sadness," his voice cracked a little, "that I have to inform you that President Laurie Campbell passed away a few hours ago. She died of a gunshot wound inflicted when General Thomas Hayden and his men launched a domestic terrorist attack on the White House last night..." He paused.

Hayden was agape when the TV screen all of a sudden went blank. He stared as Daniel and Nigel appeared and gave a startled jump as Daniel began to speak. "Stop it!" He yelled. "You idiots. Get them off the air!"

The aide jumped to get hold of the remote, frantically pushing buttons to no avail. Every channel had been compromised. Daniel's and Nigel's faces were everywhere.

"Nothing we can do sir." The jumpy aide said. "It looks like he has somehow hijacked all TV and radio stations. You want me to turn the power off?"

"No, you moron! Get hold of the TV stations and order them to get this retard off the air. Tell them if they don't I will personally see to it that they're shut down. Incompetent bunch of apes." He was shaking with rage and frustration.

Then all of sudden it dawned on him, a wild almost elated expression settled on his face, and he started shouting, "I got her! I got her! The bitch is dead! And I am President!"

His few moments of delusional glory were interrupted as he again became aware of Daniel's voice and turned to the screen.

"General Hayden's dastardly actions have caused more than fifty deaths, hundreds are wounded, and chaos and disruption have erupted in our towns and cities," Daniel said while Nigel nodded.

"He still refuses to abide by the presidential succession rules of the Constitution of this country. Instead, he has chosen to ignore it and overthrow our democracy, killing and hurting innocent people just to declare himself President.

"General Hayden has created a regime and intends to rule the United States with force after this illegal coup. What he has done and is busy doing is unconstitutional. It's undemocratic. It goes against everything America stands for.

"General Hayden, I have a message from the American people for you today; we cannot and *will* not accept it. We have just rid ourselves from the chains of an insane dictator —we *will* not accept that of another—never.

"We, the American people, will bring you to justice for your reprehensible actions."

Hayden exploded again. "You, you... snotnose! Who are you to threaten me, the President of the United States! I *will* get hold of you! And I *will* make you regret every word you have uttered." The spit was flying from his mouth. "What the hell is going on with those TV stations! When are they going to shut this damn circus down?"

He didn't realize that he was the only person in the room. Everyone had scampered out of his way when he started raving.

"Hayden is not a peaceful man. He is not upholding the ideals and principles of the Constitution of the United States of America, which he swore to defend when he entered the Army. General Hayden has reneged on his oath; he has betrayed his country, he has betrayed the American people.

"You have heard, President Laurie Campbell's last words ..." Daniel slowly and measuredly repeated her exact words, "*I beg of you to stop fighting, join together, and restore this once proud nation.*'

"She spoke from wisdom. We don't need a dictator, we don't need a military regime, we need to come together and work together to raise this nation from the chaos created, first by John Brideaux and his Council, and now by General Hayden.

"We have a constitution which has guided this great nation for centuries—let's respect it and follow it. Let's defend it and uphold it—against all enemies, foreign and domestic. The time has come for us to rise up and defend our Constitution.

"Hayden is a vulture. He's exploiting a vulnerable situation; instead of working together to bring restoration, stability, and peace, he has chosen himself and his own selfish goals which brought nothing but death, destruction, division, and civil war.

"He is responsible for the death of President Laurie Campbell—he is a murderer. I was there; I saw what he and his men did.

"In terms of our Constitution, which still exists, whether General Hayden likes it or not, the Vice President becomes President when the sitting President dies while in office. There is a very specific order of succession—it is not something that's decided on the whim of a delusional power-hungry man.

"Unfortunately, General Hayden has decided that he is greater and more important than our Constitution, and is somehow beyond the laws of our country.

"As the constitutionally appointed successor of the late President Laurie Campbell, I give you my solemn promise that I intend to bring a swift and just end to this death and division. I will work with duly, democratically elected, and appointed members of our government to restore law and order, to return democracy to our nation.

"The unspeakable atrocities committed by John Brideaux and his Council will not go unpunished, neither will those of General Thomas Hayden.

"My fellow Americans I call on you, one and all, to abandon Thomas Hayden, defend our Constitution, turn your back on lawlessness and chaos. Join us to restore our democracy. With Thomas Hayden there is no future, you will be his slaves, and you will lose your freedom in the same manner that you lost it when John Brideaux and his council ruled.

"May God bless you and may God bless America."

Across the entire country, TV screens and radio stations went blank and remained off the air for twenty-four hours. This brought absolute frustration and annoyance to General Hayden who had no way to get any messages out to the public.

At the end of the speech, Daniel was totally exhausted. He slumped forward onto the desk. He was barely aware of the waves of deep grief and nausea that rolled through him. Some part of him wanted to scream, to punch something, to kill Hayden, but he had no energy left.

Rebecca, Sarah, and Nigel helped him to his feet and lowered him onto the gurney which Cyndi had rolled in.

Daniel opened his eyes, looked up and saw Raj standing close to him, pale in the face and very worried. "Raj can you please get Peter, Jack, JR, and the others on the video link," he said softly, "I want a meeting with them and the rest of our team in the planning room as quickly as possible."

Then he turned his head and looked at Sam and Nigel. "Sam I'd appreciate it if you could help to get the rest of the leadership team together."

Rebecca pushed Daniel out of the room in silence, directly to the clinic to attend to his wound. She tried, unsuccessfully, to persuade him to rest. No amount of arguing could change his mind, not Sarah, not Nigel, not his parents, in the end, they gave up and let him be. He refused another pain-killing injection.

Chapter Thirty-Six

A LITTLE CARRIED AWAY

When the TV screens went blank again, Thomas Hayden bounced out of his seat and executed a silly dance while chanting; "I got her! I got her! That bitch won't cause me any more trouble now!"

He punched a button on his phone to reach his secretary. "Sheryl, I want a meeting in the cabinet room in three hours. Make sure Generals Nguyen, Potter, Frayser, and Neeley, and Colonels Baum and Stillwater are there. Get Hold of General Lucas Nguyen first and tell him I want to see him immediately." He didn't even wait for her to reply before he hit the disconnect button.

He continued his ludicrous dance around the office singing "Yee-haw, I got her, I got her, yippee-ki-yi-yay, I got her. I'm President now. Yee-haw."

Carrie Trent had a somber demeanor as she entered the office and saw Hayden's elation.

He grinned at her. "You heard the news? The bitch is dead. Now we're going to get somewhere!"

Carrie frowned. "I heard Tom." She said softly and

managed to suppress the, *'I don't think it's a reason to be dancing around in the Oval Office'* comment.

"What's your problem? Aren't you happy that she's out of the way?"

Carrie was crying now. "I thought you'd make her see reason ... how much the country needed you ... I certainly didn't think you'd kill her."

"Well, now you know different." Hayden snapped bombastically. "Let this be a lesson to everyone—don't mess with Thomas Hayden."

"Tom, you're scaring me."

"There's nothing to be scared of darlin'. I've called a meeting and we're going to start running this country right now—we'll turn it back into the best country in the world in no time. I'm going to get rid of the freeloaders, put women back in the home where they belong, and make men work whether they want to or not. I won't have any mamby-pamby lazy-ass men who won't take care of their families. They can man-up or get out of the country."

"That sounds great, Tom," she whispered, too afraid to get into an argument with him. In the last minute or two, she had discovered Thomas Hayden's true nature. A tsunami of guilt threatened to drown her as the biblical account of Judas's betrayal of Jesus rose in her mind.

"I'm the President now and the people *will* follow my orders or suffer the consequences. Come on; we've got about 20 minutes before the meeting, let's go upstairs and 'celebrate' while we wait." Hayden, totally oblivious of her emotional state winked and smiled.

Carrie was repulsed but managed to hide it when she said, "Please Tom, not now. This is not a good time..."

Hayden grabbed her arm and started to drag her from

the room. "I said we're going to go upstairs and celebrate and that's exactly what we're going to do."

She pulled back. "You'd force me?"

He turned to face her. "I'm the man here and women are supposed to obey men, so you'll do as I say."

"I'm not going to *obey* you or be submissive to any man," she shouted. People passing in the hallway heard her.

Hayden slapped her with such force it knocked her off her feet. She landed on the couch, he jumped on top of her, pinning her down with one hand covering her mouth. "If you cry out, I'll kill you too."

He started ripping her clothes off as she continued to struggle and when she scratched his face, he hit her in the face with a clenched fist. Mercifully, she lost consciousness.

A few minutes later he became aware of people who had entered the office and jumped up from Carrie's body. He fell to the floor with his legs tangled up in his pants which had fallen to his knees.

"What the hell ..." he exclaimed. "How dare you! This was a private moment between us. Get out!"

"Begging your pardon, General, but it didn't look or sound like the lady was participating of her own free will."

"Of course, she willingly participated! What are you insinuating? She likes to play rough... it turns her on. What kind of a man do you think I am?"

"She's unconscious, sir."

"Yes of course she is, pea-brain, she faints when she climaxes."

"Sir..."

"Now get out and keep this to yourself... we wouldn't want to embarrass the lady."

"But, sir..."

"Don't you but sir me! Get out of here. NOW! And keep this quiet! That's an order!"

"Yes, sir."

The three men exited the room looking nervously at each other. When the door closed behind them one of them started, "Do you…"

His comrade grabbed his arm and hissed, "Shut up!" then beckoned with his head for the other two to follow him and headed down the hall away from the Cabinet Room.

When they reached the parking lot, he spoke quietly, "Keep your voices down."

"That wasn't willing participation … He knocked her out and raped her!"

"Yes. Our leader has been a source of concern for me. And what we just witnessed is totally unacceptable, it takes my 'concern' to a whole new level."

"I agree. I'm beginning to worry about his mental stability. We all know he has a temper, but this is barbarism if you ask me."

"What should we do?"

"For now, let's attend the meeting, and we'll meet at the club afterward. In the meantime, I'll send Sheryl in to check on Carrie."

General Thomas Hayden straightened his uniform jacket and looked in the bathroom mirror to assure himself his image was picture perfect. He brushed imaginary dust from his trousers and turned to re-enter the Oval Office.

His secretary, Sheryl, bent over Carrie still lying on the sofa. She was just regaining consciousness. He walked over to her and brushed a strand of hair from her forehead. He had a mock embarrassed smile when he said to Sheryl, "I guess we got a little carried away."

Sheryl stared impassively at him and drew a deep breath. "Of course, sir."

"She'll be alright in no time. Why don't you fetch her a glass of water?"

"Yes, sir. I'll be right back." She rushed out of the room, in a hurry to get out of Hayden's presence.

As she disappeared into the bathroom, Hayden leaned over Carrie, seeing the fear developing in her eyes, grabbed her by the throat, "If you say anything, even one word, I'll kill you. Do you understand?"

Carrie's eyes grew with terror, then brimmed with tears that overflowed and rolled down her face. She nodded silently and glanced toward the door through which Sheryl had exited the room.

Hayden's eyes followed hers. "I'll kill anyone you tell, too… don't think for a minute I won't do it. And don't think you will be able to get away from me."

Carrie started to cry in earnest just as Sheryl returned.

"You were wonderful, honey," Hayden said smoothly and kissed Carrie on the top of the head. "You just lay here and rest. I'll see you later."

As Hayden left the room, from the corner of his eye, he saw Sheryl hand Carrie the glass of water and heard the women whispering…

"Carrie! Did he just rape you?"

"No! No, I … I … just got a … a … little carried a … away."

Hayden smiled. *Clever girl.*

"General, you called for me?" Lucas Nguyen said as he was led into the Oval Office by Sheryl about fifteen minutes later.

"Yes, thanks for coming so quickly, Lucas. I've got a small but critical matter I want you to take care of before the Cabinet meeting." Hayden grinned.

"Just say the word, sir."

Hayden first explained what Nguyen's role was going to be in the new administration.

Nguyen was beaming when he heard what his old friend had in mind for him. But his elation was short-lived when he realized that the adage 'there's no such thing as a free lunch' was very true when Hayden told him about the 'small but critical matter' that he had to take care of before he could take up his new position.

Chapter Thirty-Seven

YOU'RE ALL DISMISSED!

Striding purposefully into the Cabinet room, Hayden took his seat at the head of the table and looked at those seated around its perimeter, noting the absence of several Cabinet members, and then at the six military officers standing along the far wall. The others were taking notice of them as well but had no idea what the purpose of their presence was.

"Thank you all for coming. While we are under martial law and rebuilding our government and country, I'm going to make a few changes to the traditional Cabinet Offices to help streamline things until we are back on our feet," he laughed. "I don't want to have too many chiefs and not enough Indians!

"So, the cabinet offices will be the following: Attorney General, Secretary of Defense, Secretary of Interior and Agriculture, Secretary of Health and Education, Secretary of Housing and Labor, Secretary of Treasury and Commerce. That's it. That's all we need and all we can afford."

Everyone looked around the table in surprise. Finally, someone spoke up. "You're reducing the Cabinet from fifteen members to six?"

"Good!" Hayden brimmed with sarcasm, "give that man a gold star; he can do math!

"Yes. While we are rebuilding this country, we need to be well-organized, and in my experience, too many cooks spoil the broth."

The Cabinet members stared around the room in dismay, wondering who would be given the boot.

"Having explained that...," Hayden paused and grinned, "you are all dismissed."

A stunned silence filled the room followed by several voices, "what? You can't..."

"Yes, I can, and I just did." He smirked. "You heard me; you're all dismissed! Thank you for your services. While we're operating under martial law, only military officers will take up seats in my Cabinet until such a time as this new Cabinet deems it prudent to hand responsibility of leadership back to civilians."

Slowly the room emptied as the stunned, redundant, ex-cabinet members left.

The six officers in formal military dress, medals and all, remained. Hayden invited them to take seats at the table with him.

Lieutenant General Kurt Frayser took his seat first. Hayden had known him for years and, as an Army JAG officer, he had saved Hayden from disciplinary actions several times in his early career. He would make a fine Attorney General and, having studied international law, would handle the Secretary of State position with equal skill as well.

The Rowen

Hayden had earmarked General Lucas Nguyen for Secretary of Defense. They had graduated high school together and both been accepted into West Point. They remained the best of friends even after graduation when their career paths took them in separate directions. Nguyen had entered Military Intelligence and would be in control of the Transportation and Energy departments as well as direct the FBI, CIA, and the NSA, all under the umbrella of Homeland Security. Lucas took a seat directly across from the General.

Colonel Howard Baum and Colonel Cameron Stillwater took seats on either side of Nguyen. They had come to the attention of Hayden during the war in Afghanistan when they were serving under his command. Both had keen minds, and during their time together Hayden had found they shared his ideals of how things should be in the United States. He had chosen Baum to take over the Secretary of Interior and Secretary of Agriculture positions and Stillwater to cover as Secretary of Housing and Secretary of Labor.

General Joe Potter was another West Point graduate. Although two years behind Hayden, their attendance at this prestigious institution had overlapped and they had been teammates in several competitive sports. Potter had pursued medicine and become a highly-regarded Army Surgeon. Hayden was placing him in charge of Health, Education, and Veterans Affairs. He sat next to Hayden.

Brigadier General Stephen Neeley was the last to sit down. Hayden had become friends with Neely in their early military careers during the action in Vietnam. At that time, Neely ran a black-market operation that provided many things to the soldiers. Back then Frayser had helped shield Neeley from disciplinary measures as well. Hayden could think of no one better to assume the duties of Secretary of Treasury and Commerce.

"All right, gentlemen. Let's get this country back on its feet!"

The men grinned in unison. "What do you have in mind General? Rossler has a pretty substantial following, and the country is divided in their loyalty between the two of you. And from what I have established so far, unfortunately only about forty percent of the populace has a favorable view of you."

"General Frayser has a point, General. How are you going to win over those who currently support Rossler and the previous administration, short-lived though it was?"

"Polls! Don't tell me you guys are paying attention to polls." Hayden responded. "Don't you get it? This is not a democracy, its martial law, military rule, my way or the highway. We're in this shit-heap because of idiotic political leaders who got mesmerized by public opinion and listened to the polls.

"Those polls are always fiddled with; none of them are ever the truth. Lies, lies, all of them. Politicians did everything just to please the public and get re-elected. And the pollsters, all of them liberal bigots, controlled the polls.

"The people out there have no idea what's good for them—they can't see the big picture; they don't have the information we have to make sound decisions. That's what we're here to do. Decide what's best for the American people and give it to them."

He paused for effect and to breathe. "Please promise me that the day I start caring about opinion polls is the day you —this cabinet—will form a firing squad and execute me on the spot."

The cabinet members exploded in laughter. General

Hayden had a way of making things very clear— sometimes.

"We're going to give the people what they really need, not what they think they need, or what the liberal media and polls tell them they need!"

Six pairs of eyes stared at him, waiting for him to continue. None had the backbone to challenge him.

"The Campbell bitch and her puppy dog, Rossler, did us a big favor by declaring martial law. We will use it. We're going to give the people good news and things they've needed for years!" Hayden said with glee.

"We're going to give them a smaller government, reduce spending, and we'll give them jobs— jobs for every single man. There'll be immigration control, and we'll turn this country back into a God-fearing nation again!"

Each and every one of the cabinet knew him long enough, personally and by reputation, to know that this was not a good time to question this fearsome man. But the unspoken question on everyone's mind was; '*How the hell are you going to do all that with the present state the country is in?*'

"First we're going to hold a press conference and announce exactly what I just said.

"We're also going to make sure to tell them that there was discord between Campbell and Rossler, which was the reason why my men and I were summoned to the White House. Campbell called on me and my men to come and help her to get rid of Rossler. But unfortunately, we were too late.

"Rossler used the confusion at the White House to abduct her. We have eye witnesses who will go on TV and tell the American people how they saw it happen."

He paused and looked at Nguyen. "You already have some of those witnesses lined up. Right, Lucas?"

Lucas Nguyen nodded slowly and managed to hide his surprise.

The general was on a roll now, making things up as he went. *Lies and deceit come naturally to this man.*

"We'll let it be known that we are searching for Rossler to answer for the abduction and murder of President Campbell.

"With Secretary of State Bill Simms missing, either incapacitated, dead, or too lily-livered to shoulder his responsibilities, as Secretary of Defense I am next in line to assume the Presidency. Since Campbell's appointed Secretary of Defense is also missing, I have stepped forward to lead our nation in this very trying time in our history."

"What about George Miller, Secretary of Treasury? Isn't he in the line of succession before you? Lieutenant General Kurt Frayser had decided it was better to put that in the form of a question rather than a statement. He knew he was correct but was not prepared to take the risk of telling Hayden what the actual legal position was. It was obvious Hayden was not interested in the facts.

"Yes, you're right, he was. But... I've just received the dreadful news that Secretary George Miller was killed by an unruly mob who stormed his house. This country is in shambles; we have to stop this lawlessness immediately.

Fraser slowly nodded as the realization of what Hayden was saying sunk in.

Nguyen didn't blink an eye. He just stared at the table in front of him. *He has earned his Cabinet position.*

Hayden continued, "Lucas, as my Secretary of Defense and Homeland Security, I want you to take charge of the FBI, CIA, and NSA. Appoint whoever you need to get the departments up and running. I take it you already know what your first task is?" At Nguyen's slight inclination of his head, he continued.

"Thank you, Lucas, I knew I could count on you. Your second job will be to get the alphabet soup agencies searching the Eastern seaboard for the missing prisoners… they have to be here somewhere. Tear it apart if you have to. Leave nothing to chance."

"Yes, sir."

"Third, I want you to send some agents looking for Rossler. But don't put too much effort into it, he isn't a politician and has already run with his tail tucked between his legs, I doubt we'll hear much more from him."

Lucas frowned slightly but confirmed his orders with a 'yes, sir.' He wasn't about to do a slack job of trying to locate Daniel Rossler. The man had brought down Brideaux and his council, and no one he knew had the slightest inkling how that feat was pulled off… Rossler was definitely not to be underestimated.

"Last, but not least, I want you to start rounding up some illegal aliens and have them ready to deport. We are going to make a big spiel about that in the media. That sight will be good publicity for the second press conference."

Lucas smiled, "good thinking, Mr. President!"

"Howard," Hayden continued, "I'm appointing you as Secretary of Interior and Agriculture. I want you to get the people in those departments moving. Find every scrap of food and food resource available, note where it is and how much of it there is … in case it is needed for reserves."

"Understood Mr. President."

"Cameron, you're my new Secretary of Housing and Labor. Use the resources in those departments to find out the size, condition, and location of every home in this country. Also, find out how many jobs are held by women, how many people are unemployed, and how many jobs are available."

"You got it, Mr. President!"

"I also want to know about every prison ... how many cells each one has and how many prisoners are housed at each one."

"Yes, sir!"

"Potter?"

"Yes, sir?"

"I want you, as my Secretary of Health, Education, and Veterans Affairs. You will look into the health system and come up with a way for medical, dental, and vision care to be available for everyone at little to no cost ... and for God's sake, DON'T name any programs after me!"

Everyone chuckled.

"I also want you to let it be known that the Pledge of Allegiance and prayer are to be returned to the classrooms at all schools—without any delay or debates about it. It's a Presidential decree, and it *will* happen. This is our country, and we'll pledge and pray whenever and wherever the hell we want to!"

"Yes, sir!"

"And get a status on our veteran's programs. We *will* take care of our veterans!"

"Right away, sir."

"Stephen, you are now Secretary of Treasury and Commerce. Get hold of all the fiscal information and come back with a plan to put the financial puzzle of this country back together so it can function properly again."

"I'll get right on it, Sir."

"Last but not least, for Secretary of State and Attorney General I will be depending on you, Kurt."

"Ready to serve, Sir."

"I want to know what's happening outside our borders. What kind of trouble is brewing, who is likely to attack us, who is likely to be willing to form alliances, etcetera."

"Dean," he said speaking to his aid, "set up a press conference as soon as possible. I need to address that incendiary broadcast Rossler made."

"Yes sir, General, ah… sorry, Mr. President. Right away."

Chapter Thirty-Eight

SEE TO IT THAT THEY DON'T

Hayden stood waiting to enter the room and appear before the cameras as President of the United States for the first time. He brushed at imaginary dust on the sleeve of his uniform jacket and checked the medals and bars on his left breast to be sure they were perfectly aligned. He was dressed to impress.

Taking a deep breath, he slowly released it and walked out on the stage to stand at the podium. With the flag of the United States and the Presidential flag behind him, in his dress uniform, he knew he presented an imposing picture.

"Ladies and gentlemen, it is with deepest regret that I confirm the death of President Laurie Campbell." He started with a faux-somber voice. "We are still investigating the causes and circumstances of her death, but early indications are that there was discord between President Campbell and Vice-President Rossler. It appears that he attempted a takeover of the White House. During the upheaval, he took President Campbell hostage, tortured her to create the video you saw depicting *me* as the aggressor," he pointed to himself, "and then killed her."

Sounds of dismay, disbelief, and confusion ran through the crowd, and Hayden signaled for quiet.

"Be assured, law enforcement officials are currently searching for Daniel Rossler and his associates. They *will* answer for the wrongful death of our beloved President Campbell. During Rossler's attempted takeover of the White House, Secretary of State Bill Simms also disappeared, and the Secretary of Treasury, George Miller, was killed.

"During this attempted coup, Rossler and his cronies have removed the prisoners, John Brideaux and his Council members, and took them to a secret location. We believe Rossler and his bandits are in cahoots with those evil doers.

"As Secretary of Defense, I am next in line to assume the duties of the Presidency. I willingly and humbly accept this responsibility and will do my best to get this nation back on its feet as quickly as possible and see to it that John Brideaux and his Council members as well as Rossler and his band of outlaws are tracked down and brought to justice.

"To that end, I have all federal law enforcement agencies searching for Rossler and his followers, as well as John Brideaux and his Council members. My office will keep you apprised of any developments.

"In re-establishing this country, it will be necessary to temporarily maintain martial law. There is nothing to fear; we will work fast and efficiently to restore our country and hand the reins back to democratically elected officials. I believe in our democracy, and believe me, there is no one more eager than me to return to it. However, for a short while, we'll have to live with martial law. That's what's required now.

"My staff is currently undertaking an exhaustive survey of food resources, housing, and job opportunities. My goal is to see every *man* employed and able to provide adequate food and shelter for his family."

Only a few of those present took note of Hayden's emphasis on the word 'man.'

"We are going to stop wasteful government spending and use the savings to provide free medical and dental care to everyone."

Cheering and applause interrupted him at this point, and it took several minutes to re-establish order.

"I have business and financial experts assigned to comb through all available financial institution records to see what can be done to restore our monetary system.

"Last, but by no means least, we are Americans, and this is our country. Immigrants will come to this country legally or not at all. We are going to go back to our roots; we're going to take pride in our country as Americans again. From this moment on, prayer is reinstated in our schools and public gatherings. We will pledge allegiance to our flag when and where we want to!"

The response to this last statement nearly brought the house down, and it became obvious he would get no more said for the moment. Stepping back from the podium, he waved to the crowd, raised his hands in a 'two-thumbs up' salute, and left the stage.

Across the nation, shouts of jubilant and joyous celebration flowed from Hayden's followers while doubt and anger spread among those who supported Laurie Campbell and Daniel.

At the Rabbit Hole suspicion reigned. *"What's he doing?*

What has he got planned?" Daniel wondered as he watched Hayden's harangue. Back at the White House, in the Oval Office, Hayden's cronies were congratulating him.

"That was great, Mr. President!" Howard praised, "the people love you ... you had them eating out of your hand!"

"Of course, I did," Hayden responded, "tell people what they want to hear and they'll believe you and follow you.

"People these days can't think for themselves, they only *feel* and *need*. Meet their needs and make them feel good ... they don't care about anything else. No wonder true democracy doesn't exist anymore.

"The people have allowed greedy politicians, with selfish aims, to gain control of government. They became the puppets of those who were supposed to work for them and the good of the nation. They have lost their ability to think and act for themselves—politicians did everything except breath, for them. Now they need a strong and capable government to take care of them, and that's what we're going to do."

Frayser was frowning, and Hayden noticed. "Something troubling you Kurt? Do you disagree?"

"Nooo, not exactly." Frayser responded cautiously, "I'm just thinking that there are still people left who do think for themselves and question things ... true, they are most likely the minority, but they are there, and they could be troublesome."

"When they see how much better things are under my command, they'll come around."

"Hmmm. Perhaps, but we should be careful not to underestimate them."

"I suppose you have a point, but I'm sure Lucas will be

ready and able to deal with any ... issues that might develop. Right, Lucas?"

"Yes, sir!" Lucas replied, without hesitation.

"Speaking of issues, Lucas... have you anything to report on the whereabouts of the prisoners or Rossler and his gang?"

"I've chosen three of my top intelligence officers to head the FBI, CIA, and NSA. They are putting together teams and organizing a thorough and meticulous search of the Eastern States."

"Excellent! Keep me posted. Gentleman, it's late. I suggest we retire for the evening and meet again early tomorrow. There is a lot of work to do."

The small group of men nodded and got up to leave.

"Lucas, a moment please?" Hayden called as the others left.

"Yes, Mr. President?"

"Hank McMillian, Richard Westfield, and Bob Thompson I think are three people that might ... cause problems." He didn't tell Nguyen that they were the three men who saw what happened between him and Carrie Trent earlier. "They are the type that 'think for themselves' as Frayser put it, and could make things difficult if they discuss their opinions with others. See to it that they don't."

Silence three former Cabinet members? That's going to take some care not to create suspicion. "Yes, sir."

"Oh, and before I forget, add Carrie Trent to that list."

Four former Cabinet members. "Yes, sir."

"Thanks, Lucas. I knew I could count on you."

The next morning the nation was rocked by the news that former Secretary of Homeland Security Robert 'Bob' Thompson was caught in the act of leaking top-secret information to the Russians. He resisted arrest, a gunfight ensued, and he was fatally wounded.

Two days later, former Secretaries of Agriculture and Energy, Richard Westfield and Hank McMillian, were in the same vehicle with their wives, on their way to a social dinner, when a semi-truck blew a front tire causing the driver to lose control of the giant vehicle. It collided head-on with the car the four were traveling in; the car exploded on impact. Tragically all involved were killed.

The body of a woman was found in the woods on the outskirts of D.C. a week later ... it had been mutilated and burned beyond recognition, but DNA testing revealed it was the missing Carrie Trent.

Friends and family rallied around Carrie's husband, in shock.

President Hayden issued a press statement lamenting her death and reaffirmed his promise of stepping up law enforcement measures to bring an end to senseless killings like this. He included his personal promise to order the FBI to find the killers, no matter what it took.

He also sent a beautiful bouquet of flowers and offered his personal condolences to her grief-stricken husband at the funeral.

Chapter Thirty-Nine

'STUBBORN' IS THEIR MIDDLE NAME

The leadership team was ready when Sarah and Rebecca assisted Daniel into the Rabbit Hole's war room where they held so many important meetings in the past. Daniel looked like death, but some inexplicable force kept him on his feet and kept him going. The people in the room and on the video feed were all alarmed when they saw him, the murderous look in his eyes and the anger radiated by his body language.

A soft groan escaped Daniel's lips as he sat down. He looked around the room and at the video screen and started in a low, raspy voice, almost mumbling. "I don't care how we do it; I want Thomas Hayden taken out." By the time, he said the last word he was shaking with rage and fever. The dark circles under his eyes were accentuated by the bloodshot sclera from lack of sleep. The pain and the effect of the morphine gave him a slightly deranged look.

Everyone looked at him with disquiet—no one, including Sarah, had ever seen Daniel in such a poor shape.

Rebecca, who had been watching him like a falcon, hoping the rest of the people in the room would support her, said, "Daniel, you are exhausted and overwhelmed. Please, you have to get some rest, just a few hours. We know what you want, we can deal with it. You MUST get some rest now, please."

"Absolutely not!" Daniel shouted, shocking everyone with the sudden outburst and intensity in his voice. "I want Hayden out! You hear me. Out!" He struggled to get to his feet; his eyes were wild.

"Daniel, Rebecca has a good suggestion," Sam said softly. "Why don't you get a couple of hours of rest while the team puts together a plan? We'll have it ready by the time you wake up."

"No, Sam. I want a plan ready to go within the hour. Within the hour, we move. I want that bastard gone! Gone!" his voice had dropped to a whisper. "Gone!" He muttered as he slumped back into the chair.

"Daniel, be reasonab...." Sam tried again.

"I said NO!" Daniel yelled. "I'm part of this team, and I will be here when we plan this." His speech has become slurred.

Sam shrugged and nodded to Cyndi who was standing in the doorway. Daniel, staring at the table, didn't see his sister-in-law entering the room. She quietly slipped in behind Daniel's chair and quickly pushed the needle into his right shoulder and depressed the plunger.

Daniel whirled around angrily, grunting in pain from the sudden move. "What the hell did you do?" He started swaying slightly, Nigel and Luke were up and caught him as his body relaxed and started slipping off the chair.

Sam turned to Rebecca. "Good call Rebecca, and

Cyndi. You two nailed that one. Thanks for arranging the nap for him."

"No problem," Rebecca and her sister replied in chorus. "We're married to the rest of the Rossler brothers," Cyndi giggled as she pointed to Rebecca and herself, "'Stubborn' is their middle name."

This little interlude broke the staid atmosphere, and everyone started laughing. Nigel and Luke placed Daniel on the gurney and rolled him out of the room.

"Rebecca, is it okay if we take him to our quarters?" Sarah asked over her shoulder.

Rebecca nodded. "Yes, I'll come and check on him there. He'll rest better in his own bed."

A few minutes later, Daniel was in his own bed with his mother sitting next to him, keeping an eye on him.

"Alright everyone…" Sam said.

"Sam," Jack interrupted from Mount Ararat, "before you get started; Secretary of Defense Cliff Willis just told me that it is imperative that he speaks with Daniel. Apparently, he has pressing information which he can only give to Daniel and no one else. I also have four very worried Secret Service Agents on my hands, pestering me about Daniel's whereabouts."

"Do you know Willis? Is it safe to bring him here?" Sam questioned Nigel.

"Laurie trusted him, and I've known him for many years. Yes, we can bring him here. If he says it's urgent, you can believe him." Nigel smiled, "as for the agents, Jack will probably have no peace unless you get them to Daniel. Those guys were trained to protect the President of the United States—they will not be pacified until you bring them to his side. I know Ken and Matt personally; you can bring the two of them in with Willis."

"Okay Jack, there's your answer, get someone to bring the three of them out here ASAP."

"Will do," Jack replied and smiled. "Seeing that you have helped us onto our feet by taking all the horses earlier, you can expect us about three to four hours after the end of this planning session."

Chapter Forty

THE FIRST PLANNING SESSION

With Daniel, out of the way and the Secretary of Defense Cliff Willis on his way with his urgent matter, Sam was ready to continue the meeting.

"Let's start planning how we are going to get rid of our fake President.

"Rebecca promised to keep our real President sedated for at least six hours. I suggest we have enough of a plan ready by the time Daniel wakes up that he doesn't throw all of us in the slammer for conning him into that nap.

"However, before we get into any specifics allow me to sketch the current political climate for you.

"In the days leading up to Hayden's coup d'état, Nigel, Luke, Salome and I formed an Intelligence Committee and coopted a few of the other inhabitants of the Rabbit Hole to help us monitor and analyze domestic and international news. We believe it is important to keep up with what is going on across the USA and the globe.

"Since Hayden's unilateral declaration of his presidency and after his first public press conference today, it became clear that he had succeeded in grabbing the attention of the populace. Opinion polls taken a few hours after his speech show that there was a drastic and instant swing away from Daniel Rossler's presidency to that of Thomas Hayden. He now has close to a seventy-five percent approval rating, that's if the early polls are to be believed.

"So, here's the thing; shocking as it may be; if Hayden is so popular, it means the people don't care about how he got to power, as long as he would improve their lot. There will be very few voices questioning the way in which Hayden ascended the throne. That means our plans to overthrow him would be met with very strong resistance and would probably fail."

The feeling of despondency that flooded them was articulated by Sinclair, "We have just rid the world of the worst tyranny imaginable, and this is the thank you we get for it?"

Nigel shook his head. "No, don't get disheartened. I am of the opinion this love affair is going to end fairly soon. Every president gets a so called 'honeymoon' period after the inauguration. It's a time where everyone lays off and gives the new president a chance, a period during which the new president rides on the crest of the wave of popularity. The media goes soft, and critics temporarily remain quiet.

"And in Hayden's case," he explained, "he has the benefit of the reigning chaos, threatening famine, and hardship caused by Brideaux's new world order. People are hungry and desperate, and they will follow anyone who promises them food and shelter. It's like the proverbial dangling carrot in front of the mule…"

"And forget that it was Daniel Rossler and his people who actually liberated them from that monster by deactivating their microchips," Sinclair remarked bitterly.

"That's true," Nigel replied. "But survival is at the top of the human pyramid of basic needs, and gratitude is right at the bottom - if it even features. You can't blame them; gratefulness is not going to provide them with food and shelter. And on top of that Daniel, and the rest of us, have just been made out to be the worst criminals alive."

Some of them nodded, others were shaking their heads.

"So, I am saying it is not our time to make a move yet." Nigel continued. "But that doesn't mean we shouldn't start planning and preparing. The little bit I know and have seen of the man scares me. He is a self-serving man, not a trait you want in a President of the United States. That trait is the embryo of failure—especially if you have to lead this country. His popularity won't last long. I predict within a few weeks from now the people will be demanding his head."

Everyone nodded. They respected Nigel, he was a thoughtful man, and he brought with him the wisdom of two terms as President of the United States. He was one of *the* most popular Presidents in the history of the country.

After a few moments of quiet as everyone digested what Nigel said, Sam continued. "Alright, let's get busy. Daniel obviously wants to kick Hayden's ass and so do I. Is there anyone here who feels differently?"

To everyone's bewilderment, Roy stood up and with a serious expression declared, "I don't think we should kick his ass."

They were all exchanging looks of surprise, and Salome was about to get up and feel Roy's temperature when Roy leaned forward and put his hands firmly on the table. "Kicking his ass *will* not cut it for me. He killed our President, wounded my best friend and Vice President, still my best friend but now President, and you *only* want to kick his ass? No, let me tell you; here's what we should do, we go and nuke him and his ass to the hottest spot in hell!" Roy was trembling with anger. "To that end, I already have a few Nanonukes ready… let's use them."

Sam had a mock serious look when he turned to Rebecca and said, "Looks like we might have another candidate for your sleep treatment. Is Cyndi still around?"

Relieved laughter flowed through the room.

"Okay Roy, that's one plan of action—and I'm not opposing it, yet," laughed Sam. "Let's hear what the others have to say."

Roy smiled as he took his seat.

"How about we make use of the medical data and Nanobots we have?" Raj asked.

"What's your idea?"

"We have all the personal and medical data of nearly everyone on the planet thanks to the information stored on the servers we captured along with The Beast.

"Roy could design Nanobots based on the DNA of Hayden and his leaders that would incapacitate them—inflict some serious pain or death if you want to," he said with an evil grin. "We could use Roy's drones to drop the bots."

"Mhh, good ideas, keep them coming," Sam encouraged them.

"What if we turned the tables on them?" asked Peter.

"Yeah! Give them a taste of their own medicine," Jack added. It was obvious the two ex-CIA agents had already been conspiring before the meeting.

"Tell us about it," Sam said.

"Why don't we terrorize *them* for a change? We should spy on them, gather information, and then start making Hayden's top men disappear. You know, like the Gurkhas from India. We sneak into their camp, so to speak, and cut off every second or third man's head. Demoralize and scare the living shit out of them!" Peter was getting enthusiastic.

Sam smiled as he remembered the words of Sam Manekshaw, a former Indian Army Chief of Staff Field Marshal, *'If a man says he is not afraid of dying, he is either lying or is a Gurkha.'*

"You want to kill Hayden's men?" A worried Nigel asked.

"No, not kill them... kidnap them... just make them..." Jack grinned evilly, "disappear."

"Okay, that's another good idea," Sam responded.

"We'll have to keep in mind that there might be crowds to contain once we take over," Sarah said.

Roy got excited, "well if you don't want to shove Nanonukes up their asses, I have microwave beams that we could use to disperse the crowds. It won't kill them, but it would certainly give them a very painful suntan—it'll heat up their skins to the point where they'll be discouraged from hanging around and causing trouble."

"All good ideas," Sam grinned, "keep them coming. I would suggest we keep Roy's Nanonukes as a last resort... We also have to think what to do with Brideaux and the other prisoners. That's if and when we find them and can get to them."

"We also need to think what we can do to bring to safety those officials and cabinet members who are loyal to Laurie and Daniel," Nigel said. We have to try and establish contact with them as quickly as possible—I believe their lives could be in danger."

"That's a good point, Nigel; we need to get that communication set up right away. Let's look at that and the safety of the cabinet members first.

"Jack, can you and Peter work with Nigel and take care of that? Ask Tectus to help, if necessary."

Jack and Peter nodded.

Sarah said. "Sam, I believe the Secretary of State, Bill Simms, is at Mount Ararat and received only minor injuries. He or Secretary Willis would be good representatives to send back to Washington to work as liaisons with the Cabinet Members."

"I'm not sure I agree with that Sarah," Salome interrupted. "Hayden may know they were on the plane with the President and if he gets hold of them, he might use them to try to locate Daniel."

"Good point," Sam responded.

Sarah conceded.

"I think we can call on Tectus to have them get word to their members to meet at a safe house where we can use our secure phones for a conference," Jack said.

"Great idea! That will kill two birds with one stone, at least in the short term." Sam said.

"What we're missing folks," Salome said, "is the fact that we now have a power struggle between Daniel and Hayden, and we don't know where everyone's loyalties are right now. Loyalties might change soon; in fact, we've just seen how quickly they can change. And politicians are known for setting their sails to the wind."

Nigel nodded his assent. "Very true Salome. Let's be careful in our dealings with them. I'm not saying we shouldn't protect them, but we must make sure we don't put them in a position where they can sell us out."

"Which brings us right back to where we started; dealing with Hayden," Sam noted.

"I suggest we get Tectus to start deploying some of

Roy's spyflies in the White House to help us to start collecting firsthand information," Jack suggested.

"I'm afraid we would need a lot of them to cover the entire White House," Nigel said, "and there are security measures in place to detect bugs…

"Roy, you don't perhaps have some trick that you could build into the spyflies to evade detection?"

"First, we may not need as many as you think," Roy grinned.

"How's that?"

"With the biochip DNA information, I can set the flies to follow certain individuals and use them in combination with the general surveillance ones. That way we don't have to cover so many areas, we just follow the key people around."

"Brilliant! What about detection?"

"That's my second thought," Roy said slowly. "Nothing is impossible; some things might just be a bit more difficult than others. Give me a bit to work on that one." He didn't tell them about another gadget he had quietly been mulling over on for a while now. Roy never talked much about his ideas until he had it figured out in his head.

Sam and Nigel shared a quick glance and a grin. This was the Rosslerites in action, and those words 'nothing is impossible' should be the motto printed on their t-shirts.

"Alright, Roy, get your spyflies ready, and we'll have Jack arrange for their delivery and deployment. I'd like to deploy some for general surveillance first so that we can find out what Hayden's routine is and who his cronies are before we get the DNA specific flies on site."

The planning session continued for another two hours before everyone understood what was required and went to work.

Before they stood to leave, Nigel stopped them. "There's one last thing. Laurie Campbell. We have to get her body back to her family…"

"And we should have a memorial service for her here at the Rabbit Hole," Sarah added before Nigel could continue.

"Yes," everyone said in chorus.

"Agreed," Sam said. Jack, Peter, will you two make arrangements with Tectus to help track her sons down and to get her body to her family?"

"Yes, of course," Jack replied.

"That's the least we can do," Peter added.

"Nigel, can we leave it with you and Sarah to make the necessary arrangements for the memorial service?"

"Consider it done," Nigel replied as Sarah wiped a tear away and nodded.

Chapter Forty-One

THEY HAD TO MAKE CONTACT

"They've killed their own President," Korda whispered to himself in disbelief. "They've killed her... These people are savages; we can never assimilate with them."

After Tawndo's reanimation, he had helped Korda to adjust their systems to allow them to tap into the television and radio broadcasts in the United States and other countries across the globe. For Korda, it was a bizarre experience to learn about the enigmatic history and culture of the people of the Eleventh Cycle. The worldwide political turmoil of the last few years was a cause of concern for him and the rest of the Eighth Cycle team at the canyon.

During their joint meals, Korda would usually share his latest learnings with the rest of their team, often finding them gaping at him in disbelief.

Korda ran to get Linkola and take him to the control center where Tawndo and Siasha were working.

When they were all together, Korda immediately spilled the news, "They've killed President Campbell; they killed her!"

The others were speechless and Tawndo sat down heavily on the nearest chair. "Something tells me this is bad news."

"Very bad news indeed," Linkola agreed.

Tawndo had been focusing his energies on the activities of the B'ran, at the Tunguska site and what he had learned about them the past few days worried him.

"I'm afraid I have more bad news," Tawndo added when Linkola stopped talking.

They all looked at him inquisitively.

"As you know, I've been able to access the information center at the Tunguska site without the B'ran knowing about my explorations into their data centers. Late yesterday afternoon I managed to get access to a new area in their information store and what I learned is troubling.

"They have spent the last seven decades building an army for world conquest, despite the setback of that second explosion in 1954."

"How many of them are there?" Siasha asked with a deep frown on her forehead.

"I'm still gathering information and records, but so far I've been able to confirm one thousand seven hundred."

Siasha was dumbfounded. "One thousand seven hundred; how is that possible?"

"After the explosion in 1954, their leader, Viktor, sent some of his best soldiers out to join the Russian military. Over the years, unknown to the Russian leadership, several of them managed to infiltrate the ranks of senior officers and formed a top secret covert group.

"They have about one thousand five hundred B'ran or as they now call themselves, Re'an, spread throughout the various divisions of the Russian military complex. Another one hundred fifty of them are highly skilled Special Forces operators. The B'ran scientists have killed, re-animated, and enhanced, these people before inserting them into the military.

"In short, all the B'ran soldiers are highly trained. If their enhancements and the Eighth Cycle's technologically superior weapons are taken into account, each of these Re'an soldiers becomes a one-man fighting force that can easily take on and overcome odds of a few hundred to one in any battle." "Wait," Siasha interrupted, "what do you mean 'enhanced'?"

"Apparently, Viktor had the scientists experimenting, and succeeding, with augmenting specific areas of the human anatomy and senses… intelligence, strength, endurance, vision, hearing, and much more.

"From what I can tell, it seems that the chip that is implanted in the brain can be adjusted in the lab without removing it.

"Since these re-animated soldiers don't age, they leave the military service after about ten years, unless they are one of the elite officers, and relocate to the Tunguska site where they help to rebuild the site and become part of one of the teams there. That's where they receive further training and enhancements which shape them into the force Viktor plans to use to conquer the world."

"How do they provide for that many people?" Korda wanted to know.

"They have developed highly efficient systems for underground food production, storage, and preparation. They also expanded the facility as they rebuilt it, and they have an extensive research division dedicated to the development of new types of weapons, transport, and communications.

"And… although I am still trying to confirm it, it looks

as if they have also placed some people in deep sleep. In other words, stockpiling them…"

Still somewhat shocked by the death of the President and the news he just heard, Korda spoke as one dazed, "Do you know what his short and medium term plans are?"

Tawndo shook his head. "I've only scratched the surface since the discovery yesterday. Nevertheless, it is abundantly clear to me that they are preparing themselves for war."

"Why do you say that?" Siasha asked. "Surely, a few thousand soldiers, irrespective of their skills and training, are not enough to take on the world?"

"Yes, you are right about that, but you are forgetting about the weapons they have. Let me give you a few examples, and keep in mind these are only the weapons I know of at this stage."

Korda, Linkola, and Siasha were visibly troubled as they stared at Tawndo, waiting for him to continue.

"They have particle-beam weapons that utilize high-energy beams of subatomic particles to damage or destroy targets by disrupting their atomic and molecular structure. Depending on the power of the weapon it will vaporize targets in the blink of any eye. Their soldiers are all equipped with short-range particle beam weapons which would be effective up to a mile or more. They also have long range versions of these weapons that could take out targets in the air and on land—some of them can destroy targets up to a thousand miles away."

Linkola spoke softly, almost whispered. "No one on earth, including us, will be able to stop them."

Tawndo slowly nodded. "And that's only one of the many deadly weapons I have learned about so far.

"Part of their soldiers' equipment is lightweight liquid body armor that doesn't restrict movement at all but protects them against projectiles fired by any handgun or rifle in use today."

A long silence followed as everyone processed the gravity of what they have heard.

Korda broke the silence. "You know; I've been studying the people of the Eleventh Cycle for some time now and after seeing their barbaric ways, especially the past few days, I've reached the conclusion that many of them are savages who have not yet reached the level of development where we could assimilate with them.

"However, that's not the case for all of them. They're not as advanced as us in many ways, but many of them have good intentions and are good people. "They have no idea what is in store for them if the Re'an attack them. I'm beginning to wonder if we should warn them. But I'm not sure they would be able to stop it."

They all went quiet; they knew there was no choice; they had to make contact, not only to save the Eleventh Cyclers but also to save themselves.

An evil grin appeared on Viktor's face as he leaned back in his chair. "So, they have killed their President; their Vice President has gone into hiding like a coward allowing this General Hayden to take over the nation with his ridiculous antics."

He rose from his chair and began to pace. "John Brideaux left the entire world in a dysfunctional mess. It's going to take a lot of time for all the nations to stabilize and begin restoration. Now is the ideal time to act for world domination. We can go in, restore order swiftly and establish our control.

Soltan nodded in agreement.

"We have spent many years building our forces, and our weapons systems, now we can reap the benefits," Soltan said.

"We need a planning session. Contact our senior officers and arrange a meeting with all of them for tomorrow afternoon."

Chapter Forty-Two

SPYFLIES AND SPYDERS

Daniel was still sedated; Rebecca and Cyndi had checked in on him a few times, taking his blood pressure, heart rate, replaced his dressings, the IV drip, and administered more sedatives, anti-inflammatories, and antibiotics. They were satisfied that he was over the critical stage and would recuperate quickly.

Peter, JR, and Jack had arrived back at the Rabbit Hole, accompanied by Secretary of Defense, Cliff Willis and Special Agents, Ken and Matt. The three newcomers received the same hearty welcome which every visitor always received at the Rabbit Hole.

Of course, Ken and Matt insisted on seeing Daniel the moment they walked in. They were taken to his bedside where they assured themselves that he was alive and in good hands. It took Nigel to persuade them that they could leave Daniel's quarters; that their new President would be safe even if they were not right next to him.

Once Cliff, Ken and Matt were happy about Daniel's safety and care, they were fed and given the royal tour of the facilities, and like everyone before them, their mouths were hanging wide open as they tried to process everything they saw.

Roy, Raj, Jack, and Peter gathered in Roy's lab. In the hours since the meeting in the war room, while JR, Peter, and Jack returned from Mt. Ararat, Raj had accessed the recovered servers, located Hayden's personal information and dug through it.

Roy had been busy experimenting with his special toys.

"Guys! I've solved the spyflies' detection problem," Roy announced in a monotone as if he was reading from a book when the three men walked in.

"Excellent!" JR shouted. "How did you... ah don't bother I'm technically challenged, won't understand even if you explain it. But are you sure it's working?

Roy smiled, "yeah hundred percent. You want me to give you a demo?"

Jack looked at Raj and said, "Raj just tell us you have tested it and agreed with Roy and that'll be good enough for us."

Raj nodded. "Yep, been there done that, it works as intended."

Roy explained excitedly. "I've made a few adjustments to the flies so that they can detect surveillance sweeps and shut themselves down!"

"How does that help?"

"Bugs are only detectable when they are operational—switched on. By detecting the sweep when it initiates and shutting down immediately, they can avoid detection."

"It's as easy as that?" Jack asked.

Roy nodded, "Yep, more or less, without going into technical details."

Jack motioned to the others, "that's good enough for me. What do you guys say?"

"Even I understood that," JR laughed.

Jack said. "Okay, that takes care of our surveillance issues then. We just need to deploy them now."

Roy held his hand up. "Before you saddle your horses and charge the White House, Raj and I have another gadget that might come in handy. We call it a 'spyder,' we have a prototype which we can show you now, it's not working hundred percent yet, but you will get the general idea when we show you."

"Spiders? As in those hairy eight-legged creepy-crawlies?" JR shivered.

Peter exploded in laughter. "The big JR Rossler has arachnophobia!"

"I hate the damn things," JR mumbled, a bit embarrassed to admit it.

"Well, JR," Roy chuckled, "if it makes you feel any better we spell it with a 'Y' instead of an 'I,' you know, 's-p-y-d-e-r-s.'"

"Okay, I get it. Can't say it does anything for my fear of them, though. What's new with them?"

"They have the same anti-detection abilities as the flies, but they can also disappear into their surroundings, like a chameleon..."

"Wait; hang on there for a second Doctor James," Jack stopped him. "You saying this spyder thingamabob of yours can become invisible?"

"Like Harry Potter's invisibility cloak type thing?" Peter asked incredulously.

Roy and Raj were laughing and nodding.

"You're not shitting us, you guys are serious... keep on talking," Jack said.

Roy continued. "Apart from the disappearing trick, they have tiny but powerful speakers that can project a voice anywhere in a room."

"An invisible, talking spyder you say..." Jack murmured and then his face broke into a broad smile. "Bring it on Roy; bring it on, lots of them. We're going to have Hayden and his leaders shitting in their boots before this show is over."

"We could use them to make Hayden think the White House is haunted, like the rumors of the Lincoln Bedroom.

"When looking through Hayden's personal records, I discovered that his boyhood hero was Abraham Lincoln! We could make it seem like Lincoln was talking to him! Or anyone else for that matter;" Raj informed them with a grin.

"But that's not all," Roy continued, "these spyders are also very powerful in relation to their size and can move objects, such as pencils, pens, and other small things, around if required."

JR laughed. "We're going to drive that son-of-bitch insane. I like it!"

The three of them didn't see Roy and Raj winking at each other.

As Roy spoke, Raj's coffee cup began to move smoothly across the table.

"What the hell!" JR shouted and jumped off his chair. "You have one of those hairy damned things in here? Now?"

"I think we've just seen a demonstration of a spyder!" Peter laughed.

Daniel's voice came from the other side of the room, "you certainly have!"

They all spun around to look, but there was no Daniel.

"Bloody hell," JR said. "This is absolutely brilliant guys." Peter chuckled.

"That was a recorded voice from the spyder!" Raj laughed.

Looking back at the table, JR asked, "where the hell is the damned thing?"

Roy stared at the table for a moment and then pointed to an area just slightly off the center. "There."

Everyone looked but couldn't see anything. Finally, JR spoke up "I don't see a thing. How can you tell?"

Roy grinned "Isn't that the point? To not be seen?"

"But *you* can see it! Or do you have some super vision?"

"No, but I know what to look for. See the faint line near the center of the table?"

"The thing that looks like a thin strand of hair or a flaw in the table?" JR asked.

"Yes, that's it. That is the shadow outline of the spyder on the side away from the light. As you can see, it is very small and faint, so unless you are actually looking for it, you wouldn't be likely to see it."

"Wow! They must be hard to find if you drop them in your office."

"Nope." They all watched in amazement as a small black spider materialized on the table.

JR cautiously took a step away.

"They're easily found when out of camo mode!" The spyder crawled quickly to Roy, then onto his red shirt, stopped, and disappeared. "It's back in camo mode now."

"Thank you, Roy and Raj!" said Daniel's voice from next to Jack.

Jack jumped and turned expecting to see Daniel, but stared only at empty space.

"You were right about these little gadgets," Jack said

when he got his breath back. "They will *indeed* come in very handy. How long will it take you to make ten of them?"

"Raj and I should be able to have five or so ready within the next twenty-four hours, I reckon. But there is one more feature we want to add to it first."

"What's it?" JR asked.

Roy and Raj shook their heads in unison. "You know us. We don't tell until we can show."

"Okay, go for it. I can just see how we are going to use these little buggers." Jack grinned.

"Agreed," Peter said. "Let's keep all of this secret for now. I would like Roy and Raj to give the leadership team a demonstration when we meet again."

JR, Jack, and Peter gave Roy and Raj a high-five before they walked out.

Chapter Forty-Three

THIS IS INHUMANE

John Brideaux paced in his makeshift cell, two steps, turn, two steps, and turn. "This is inhumane. I'm going to figure out how to get out of here, take control, and kill every single one of these bastards!" he muttered, then started yelling at the guard posted on the other side of the door, "you hear that? I'm going to kill every one of you bastards!"

Captain Locklin had made arrangements to keep Brideaux separated from the rest of the prisoners... he didn't even get to eat with them. He was totally isolated, and the only time he left his cell was to go to the bathroom. *How the hell can I plan an escape from this hell-hole when I don't have access to anyone or any information? I'll kill Laurie Campbell for this when I get out!*

He banged his fist on the door, "Bathroom!"

"Stand back," the guard snapped.

When the door opened, Brideaux was surprised to see the Captain standing alongside the guard.

"Well, well, well. Captain Locklin, come to check on

John Brideaux. I'm honored!" Brideaux said with a mocking grin.

"I didn't come to check on you, Brideaux. I had a message that you wanted to see me. What do you want?"

"That was days ago!" he replied incredulously.

"I'm a busy man. What do you want? Spit it out now or forget it."

"I want time with my friends... a meal, a game of checkers. Keeping me isolated is inhumane and criminal! I have rights!"

"As far as I'm concerned, you gave up your rights as an American citizen and as a member of the human race the instant you turned that Beast on. If it were up to me, you'd already be dead. I'm under orders to transport you, but that doesn't mean I have to give you any luxury or special consideration. Be thankful I gave you bathroom privileges instead of a bucket to use in your cell."

"You're a true humanitarian, Captain."

Captain Locklin turned and strode away down the narrow corridor.

"You need to take a leak or not?" the guard asked.

"Yeah."

"Let's go then."

Brideaux walked ahead of the guard with his head held high. A plan was taking shape in his sick mind.

Chapter Forty-Four

TO THE TREPANG

Daniel stirred beneath the covers and opened his eyes. His first sight was of Sarah sitting across the room from him, reading, Nicholas asleep next to her.

"Sarah?"

"You're awake!" she said softly so as not to wake Nicholas. Gently she put the book down and moved to sit next to Daniel on their bed.

He ran his fingers appreciatively through her hair and then stifled a sharp groan as he tried to sit up to kiss her.

"What happened?" he asked sinking back on to the bed in pain.

"You were shot."

"Shot?"

"Yes, during your escape from the White House."

It all came flooding back to him then; fleeing through the tunnels, escaping on Air Force One, the crash in Denver and the flight to Mt Ararat. "Laurie's dead," he said quietly, grief washing over him again. "Hayden's men killed her."

"Yes," Sarah nodded, brushing his hair gently from his

forehead and caressing his cheek. "The doctor did everything he could; the bullets just did too much internal damage."

Daniel squeezed his eyes together and several tears rolled down the side of his face. "She was a wonderful person, Sarah. I wish you'd had the chance to get to know her."

"Me too," she said softly. "Now it's all on you."

"What funeral arrangements have been made for Laurie?"

Sarah told him what was decided earlier.

Daniel nodded, "That's good. Thank you."

They remained silent for several minutes before Daniel spoke, "I'd like to get up; let's see if I can try it again without causing myself so much pain."

Sarah moved to give him more room, and he rolled onto his good side, eased his legs over the side of the bed, and sat up with a hiss.

"Well, it wasn't quite as painful that way. I sure hope this heals fast. There is so much to do. I can't spend my days in bed while everyone else is working hard."

Sarah just smiled and helped him get cleaned and dressed. As she was adjusting the sling that held his arm, he caught her in his other arm and kissed her. "I love you, Sarah! Thank you for taking such good care of me."

"I love you too! But you will have to thank your sisters-in-law for getting you through this, they really took good care of you—I just watched.

"Now let's have breakfast and then I believe the leadership is expecting you to join their meeting."

Daniel flushed and looked embarrassed. "I believe I made a bit of an ass of myself in the leadership meeting..."

"Well, it's over and done now. You're rested *and* forgiven."

"Just whose idea was it to have me drugged anyway?"

"Sorry can't tell you; I've been sworn to secrecy."

"Hmm. Never mind. If it wasn't you, it had to my sister-in-law… or both of them, come to think of it. I vaguely remember seeing Cyndi's face last… she and Rebecca would about be the only ones who would dare …"

"Come eat your breakfast," Sarah giggled.

They ate breakfast and made their way to the planning room where they found the others gathered, deep in discussion, cups of coffee in hand, and an enormous, sinfully delicious looking coffee cake in the middle of the table.

The room fell silent when Daniel walked in. He looked around at everyone and then smiled. "It's ok, I'm back, and except for my shoulder, I feel just fine. I'm not mad at anyone—well I may be a little bent out of shape at one person here and possibly another not currently present. Just follow my eyes and you will know," he said as he fixed his eyes on Rebecca.

Rebecca grinned at him. "I love you too, Daniel; get over it!"

Everyone laughed. The tension in the room eased and the talk began again as everyone found a place to sit so the meeting could start.

Daniel, back in command, addressed the group. "All right people. I have a feeling you've all been hard at work while I've been sleeping; but as you know that sleep was not out of my own volition."

"Yeah right," Sinclair said. "We all know how capable you were to participate in the planning when you were in here last time."

Daniel just grinned sheepishly and continued. "Why

don't we start by you bringing me up to speed? Give me an overview and then we'll come back to the details later."

Everyone looked to Sinclair. He held both his hands up in surrender. "Oh no, I don't do presidential briefings. I'm in charge of the Rossler Foundation only." He looked to Sam, "the floor is all yours."

Sam nodded. "Okay then. But before I give you a synopsis you will have to talk to Secretary of Defense, Cliff Willis. He apparently has some critical information for your ears only. We brought him over from Mount Ararat while you were sleeping.

"Shall I go and get him? We'll clear out this room so you have privacy."

"Thanks for that Sam." Daniel replied, nodding.

A few minutes later Nigel led Cliff Willis into the meeting room.

Daniel noticed the perplexed look on the man's face. "Something wrong?"

"Not at all Mr. President; in fact, I am amazed at what your people have done here. It is absolutely remarkable."

Daniel both smiled and grimaced inwardly at being addressed as 'Mr. President', it was going to take some getting used to. He would prefer to be addressed by his name but thought that for the moment a sense of hierarchy and discipline should be maintained. And as far as he was concerned it was the respect for the office of President and not the person.

"Thank you, Mr. Willis. What can I do for you? You indicated this meeting was urgent."

"This information is beyond Top-Secret and on a

'need-to-know' and 'face-to-face' basis only." He glanced around the room. "Is this room totally secured?"

"You may speak freely here, Mr. Willis," Daniel said, a little irritated.

Willis glanced around again, leaned toward Daniel, and said in a low voice, "It's about the prisoners."

"You know where they are?"

Willis only nodded.

"Alright Mr. Willis, I am an inexperienced President, and I depend on former President Nigel Harper for guidance. I want to ask that you disclose your information to both of us."

Willis thought for a moment and then nodded his agreement and Daniel buzzed Nigel to join them.

Nigel and Cliff Willis knew each other. They exchanged a few pleasantries and then took their seats.

"Sirs, the late President Campbell said that she had been cautioned about trusting the Cabinet members that were left over from the previous administration.

"Therefore, after all the arrangements had been made to house the prisoners at the facility in Virginia and the decoy plans were in place, she gave new orders that were strictly need-to-know and face-to-face, as I have noted before.

"She had me contact Admiral Johnson, and several hours before the planned transfer to Virginia, under her orders the prisoners were flown to a nearby submarine base and transferred to the USS Trepang under the command of Captain Reese Locklin.

"Captain Locklin's orders were to proceed to Bangor Naval Base in Washington State via the polar route. Upon arrival, the prisoners were to be secretly transferred to the

Northwest Joint Regional Correctional Facility near Fort Lewis.

"Unfortunately, President Campbell was killed before the final arrangements at the Fort Lewis facility could be made. The Trepang is currently cruising slowly under the polar ice cap—an additional security measure."

Nigel and Daniel both leaned back in their chairs, stunned. Then Nigel grinned "Brilliant!"

"Yes sir," Cliff agreed.

Nigel slapped Cliff on the shoulder. "This is the best news I've had in a while."

"How do you communicate with the sub without jeopardizing it?" Daniel asked.

"Before she put to sea, Admiral Johnson, myself, and Captain Locklin met aboard the Trepang and devised a schedule of pings at irregular intervals that allow us to track the Trepang's general location and to serve as an 'all is well'.

"Should she miss one of the pings we are to assume something has gone wrong. For that scenario, we have a list of rotating frequencies we use, again at specific but irregular intervals, to establish contact. We also established a specific course and depth for the sub to follow. Any ping that deviates from that course or depth by more than ten degrees is also to be considered as a sign that something has gone wrong. Only the three of us at that meeting have the pre-arranged schedules and frequencies."

"Excellent!" Daniel responded.

"I don't recall us having a sub designated USS Trepang during my time," Nigel said.

"No sir, officially, we don't. We, Admiral Johnson and I, took the name from a World War Two Balao Class submarine commissioned in 1942. After the decommission and sinking of the original Trepang, a Sturgeon Class sub launched in 1969 that also carried the name Trepang. She was decommissioned and sunk in 2000.

"We took the name as an additional security measure in an effort to protect the current sub carrying the prisoners. It is one of our Virginia class subs."

"Okay," Daniel said. "From now on, the three of us will use the words 'Snow Cone' if we need to meet to discuss the prisoner situation and the sub. If the matter is urgent, use the word twice. This will continue to be on a 'need-to-know' and 'face-to-face' only basis."

"If anyone asks, this meeting was about National Security and the information is classified."

"Agreed," Cliff and Nigel said.

"To the Trepang," Nigel saluted.

"To the Trepang," Daniel and Cliff echoed as they raised their coffee mugs.

Chapter Forty-Five

RAVEN ROCK

When Willis left the room, Sam quickly assembled the leadership team and gave Daniel an overview of their plan. He also gave Daniel and update of the political climate in the country and told him that it was the Intelligence Committee's considered opinion that they should plan and prepare, but not launch any offensive until such time as the tide has turned against Hayden.

Daniel listened carefully and nodded. "I agree with the Intelligence Committee's views, frustrating as it might be, it is wise council.

"I also agree with Nigel's view; this euphoria is not going to last long. I saw the man in action a few days ago, and I'm sure he is delusional. He is a windbag and is not going to achieve anything. He reminds me of some dictators in history, they build a following with promises and lies, get to a position of power, lead people by the nose and then one day the people wake up and realize they have been taken for a ride."

"You've hit the nail on the head, Daniel," Nigel

responded. "That's more or less how I see things playing out as well. And in Hayden's case, given the people's desperation levels, it's going to happen very soon."

"That's all the more reason for us to get our preparations in place ASAP," Sam said. "If everyone is okay with that I would like to move on?"

Everyone nodded, and he continued.

"Roy has formed a team devoted to building new spy gadgets and upgrading our existing arsenal to enable us to spy on and terrorize Hayden. Salome will assemble a small team to design a psychological warfare program." Sam asked Jack to give Daniel the details.

"I've been in touch with Eric Winchester and Dennis McMahon to mobilize Tectus, and as always they are ready to help us with everything they have."

"That outfit has been a real knight in shining armor whenever we needed them," Daniel remarked in appreciation. "It's good to know they're still on our side."

"Salome and I have also been looking for a safe place to hide those Cabinet members and other officials loyal to you," Jack finished.

Salome provided more details of their progress. "We had been reviewing the safe houses available when Nigel came up with a very good idea—Raven Rock."

"I thought that place was sealed up years ago," Daniel said.

"It was," Nigel agreed, "which makes it a perfect hiding place."

"What is Raven Rock?" several voices asked at once.

Nigel settled back in his chair as if getting ready to tell a campfire story.

"Its full name is Raven Rock Mountain Complex or RRMC. It was once an underground military installation designed during the Cold War to function as something like the Pentagon and an emergency operations center for the military during a nuclear strike. It was built as a secret project authorized by President Truman in the early 1950's.

"A huge hole was blasted out inside a granite mountain, and five three-story structures were built inside... office-building type structures.

"In its heyday, it was a small city that had nearly everything people in hiding could need: living quarters, a fitness and medical facility, dining hall, chapel, store, its own underground water reservoirs, a waste water treatment plant, hell, it even had its own barber shop. It had two power plants and could sustain a population of 3,000 for 30 days in a complete lockdown situation."

JR whistled. "So where is this place and can we still get to it?"

"It's near Blue Ridge Summit in Pennsylvania," Luke said. "Its last use was during the 9-11 crisis of 2001.

"After that, due to the expense required to upgrade the facility, it was decommissioned, and the four access portals were sealed up from the cave side by filling them with nearly a mile of concrete and then collapsing them the rest of the way to the entrance. There's no way anyone is going to get in there now."

"Too bad," JR sighed. "It sounded so perfect. As you all know, we love living and working in caves; it's our specialty."

"Actually," Nigel interrupted, "Luke is not entirely correct. See the thing is, although the site was officially decommissioned years ago, as Luke said. Much more than what was 'officially' said was left intact should it ever be needed again. It remains accessible from the underground rail system Laurie and Daniel used to reach Andrews. Also, the tunnels were only filled with concrete for the first 300 feet from the roadside, and the tunnels were not collapsed."

Luke's chin dropped. "I didn't know that!"

"You're kidding!" JR exclaimed. "You mean we're going to set up shop in another cave again?"

Various other expressions of surprise erupted around the table, and everyone began talking at once.

"I know you're all excited to move into another cave but let's hear the rest of it before we start packing." Daniel said loudly and turned to Nigel asking, "How sure are you?"

Nigel grinned, "One hundred percent sure. I've seen it myself!"

"You and who else?"

Nigel's grinned widened. "Esther. Do you know how hard it is to be truly alone when you're President of the United States? I found out about it and Esther and I went there occasionally—to be alone."

"Sounds like we should change the name to the Presidential Love Nest." Sinclair chuckled to the amusement of everyone.

"Does it have anything like cells or secured rooms?" Jack asked.

"Not that I saw, but I didn't explore the whole facility."

"We need to get a look inside that mountain, Daniel," Jack commented.

"I agree, Jack. You, Peter, and Nigel put your heads together and figure out a way to get there and get in.

"JR? I want you and Raj's team to start looking through all the classified documents we recovered from Brideaux's servers. Find every scrap of information on what was in that site and estimate what might still be usable and useful to us.

"If we're lucky, we may have just found a secure place for the prisoners and a safe refuge for our people in D.C."

"Nigel, what do you think about the idea of getting hold of Elize and asking her to help us? She saved our lives with her knowledge about that hidden tunnel to the museum. She grew up in the White House and may know more about it than anyone. She might know of some more tunnels and passageways that no one else has discovered. Should we ask her if she's willing to help us and if she is, should we bring her on board?"

"Well, she has more than proven her value during your escape I would say. If everyone agrees I'll get in touch with her right away."

Everyone agreed and began speaking excitedly again.

Daniel raised his voice, "Let's meet back here in six hours and see what we have to work with."

"Yes, Mr. President!" came a chorus of replies as if they have been practicing it.

Daniel just smiled at the lively antics of the group; *we could get our country back on its feet with a group like this* he thought.

Sarah and Rebecca assisted him back to his bed for more rest and medication.

Chapter Forty-Six

MY LIPS ARE SEALED

On board the Trepang, inside his makeshift cell, John Brideaux lay on his bunk considering his circumstances and despising those responsible for putting him in this tin can. He needed a way to gain control of the contraption and get off it. He needed allies; he needed an 'inside man,' he needed out of this prison... *prison! That's it!*

Folding his hands behind his head, he closed his eyes with a smile and began plotting his escape. By the time his guard knocked on the door announcing it was time for dinner he was ready.

"On your feet Brideaux; chow time."

Brideaux growled obscenities under his breath but put a smile on his face and announced, "Ready."

The door opened with the usual caution, one man pushing it open, a second pointing a gun in his direction, ready to fire.

He held his hands in the air, "Thank you, boys! I really appreciate you letting me out."

"Come on Brideaux, shut up and get moving."

"No, really," he said as he stepped across the threshold. "You two are my favorite guards. You're much more efficient than the others. They aren't consistent like you two. You know, they sometimes let things slide a little, yes, they do. But not the two of you; nope, I always know what to expect with you. Spit and polish, no-nonsense; you do your jobs well. Why, if I were your commanding officer, I'd see you got a promotion!"

When his guards didn't respond, he knew he had them. *These ducks are going down easier than I expected, and they'll take the rest of their crew with them!* He thought with glee.

Upon reaching the mess, the younger of the two guards took a seat across the table from him while the other moved to the door, both of them keeping a weapon trained on Brideaux.

"You know; it is a little disconcerting to eat while you're staring down the barrel of a gun; gives me severe heartburn."

"Shut up and eat, Brideaux," the guard at the table said, but Brideaux noticed he allowed the tip of his gun to drop and move to the side slightly.

When they stopped at the bathroom on the way back to his bunk, saying he felt grungy, he persuaded them to give him an extra minute for personal grooming.

The next day when their shift came again, and he was seated in the mess hall with the young man, he continued his ruse. "So, Lieutenant, what is your job on this fine ship, aside from guarding me."

The boy's face reddened. "It's Ensign; I'm not a lieutenant... and this is a boat, not a ship."

"Ensign, Ensign. Sorry, my boy, I didn't mean to

promote you too fast, although I'm sure you deserve it! Look at what a fine job you're doing of guarding me. Do you know I heard one of the other guards saying what a fine job you're doing and that he tried to emulate your example?"

The boy reddened further, "just eat your food and shut up."

Later that evening, though he was loath to do it, Brideaux begged the boy to give him an extra bathroom break saying he wasn't feeling well and really didn't think he could hold it.

For the next few evenings, Brideaux tried to engage the boy in conversation and although it was mostly one sided, he did glean some information. He knew he was on a Virginia class nuclear-powered submarine that had been awaiting dry-dock time for conversion to conventional engines at the time when the Beast was destroyed.

He also learned that its 16 Tomahawk nuclear-tipped missiles had not been converted to conventional warheads yet either as that was also scheduled to be done during the engine conversion. *The imbeciles couldn't even work fast enough to have at least had THAT done,* he thought with disgust.

A few nights later, when the boy was pulling the door closed after returning from dinner, John commented. "You know, I sure wish I had something to read in here, something to help me pass the time. Do you think I could have a book to read?"

"We're not supposed to give you anything, Brideaux."

"Oh, I know, I know. I'm sure you're not supposed to give me anything that's *dangerous*, but do you really think that applies to a book?

What harm could come from a book?

Couldn't you just slip one in to me, something to help

me pass the hours? No one else would have to know; it'd just be our little secret, I promise!"

"I suppose a book wouldn't hurt. Alright, I'll see what I can find, but you can't tell anyone."

"My lips are sealed," Brideaux said with a wink.

Chapter Forty-Seven

IN TWO DAYS' TIME

With another 12-hours of rest and medical care from 'the Confederate of the Evil Sisterhood,' as Daniel now called his sisters-in-law, he felt like a new man. His shoulder still reminded him to take it slow every time he made a sudden move, but his mind was clear, the fever was gone, and the infection stopped in its tracks.

Aaron was instructed by the 'evil sisters' to build a wheelchair for his President-brother and, being married to one of them, he complied without arguing.

Although he was fully capable of walking on his own two legs the 'evil sisters,' supported by Sarah, would have none of it. He was unceremoniously told that he had a choice, he could stay in bed or get pushed in the wheelchair; and they left him no doubt as to what would happen if he didn't comply, when Cyndi produced a syringe, still in its wrapping, and placed it on the bedside table.

Daniel wanted to visit Roy's and Raj's technical division before the next leadership meeting. Sarah had sent word about Daniel's impending visit, so the two teams were all assembled in Roy's lab when Daniel was rolled in on the homemade wheelchair. The chair sported, on both sides, a Ferrari emblem complete with a black prancing horse on a yellow background and the letters RHSF for Rabbit Hole Scuderia Ferrari below it.

"Good morning Mr. President," they all echoed like a class of first graders greeting their teacher first thing in the morning.

"Now listen, you bunch of propeller-heads. I have been Daniel to you since the day I met every one of you, and that's how it's going to stay. Are we clear?"

"Yes, Mr. President!" Came their practiced chorus again. They all started laughing hysterically when they saw the look of disgust on his face.

Daniel, first looked at Sarah, she shrugged her shoulders in a *'don't look at me; I didn't put them up to this.'* Then he caught the grinning exchange between JR and Jack who were also present.

"I'll deal with the two of you in due course." He said in a feigned serious tone before turning his attention to Roy and Raj.

"Now please show me what you have been working on, spyflies and everything else. I heard a rumor; it could also have been a dream, about something called a spyder."

Daniel's wheelchair was pushed closer to the table and a mug of coffee placed in front of him. Roy started by giving Daniel a run-down on the new features added to the flies, the development of the spyders, and their plans to 'haunt' the Whitehouse.

"Look at your coffee cup." Roy said when he finished his explanation.

"I don't see anything," Daniel said.

Just then his coffee mug started to move slowly across

the table away from him. Daniel pulled his hand away in alarm. "What the hell? How did that happen?"

"Okay, look carefully now, keep your eyes on the bottom of the mug, Daniel."

There was a bit of movement, and a small black spyder materialized out of thin air. Then another one appeared and crawled around the side of the mug and joined its compatriot on the edge of the mug.

Sarah and Daniel gasped in surprise. "That's impressive Roy!" Daniel exclaimed.

Raj had a big grin when he held his hand up to get attention. "You ain't seen nothin' yet." He nodded at one of the technicians.

Across the table from Daniel, in one of the lab chairs, Nigel appeared—smiling. Daniel and the others blinked their eyes, then looked around as if to say, *where did he come from?* There was only one entrance to the lab; they were sure Nigel didn't hide under the table until now. How did he get in there? None of them said anything, assuming they must have somehow missed his presence when they came in. What other explanation could there be?

"Ah, mhh, Nigel, sorry I didn't see you earlier. How are you?"

"I'm good Daniel. I trust you had a good rest and are feeling better?"

"Yeah, thanks to the unscrupulous attention of the evil sisterhood, I am on the mend." He chuckled.

The next moment Nigel's seat was empty. Daniel and the others blinked, their eyes gawked at the chair and then darted around the room. JR bent down to look under the table—nothing there. He and Jack had previously seen the disappearing act and heard the voice projection of the spyders. They instinctively knew that this had something to do with the other feature Roy and Raj had been talking about, but how did it work?

"What is going on here Roy, Raj?" Daniel demanded.

Before Roy could start, Nigel walked through the door, laughing. "Amazing, isn't it? I have no idea how these geniuses did it…"

"Teleporting, like in Star Trek," Jack babbled before anyone could answer "you know like, beam me over Scottie?"

"Huh, what?" Daniel emitted.

"Wait, wait, I know." JR started. "Holograms! Is it not?"

Roy and Raj were beaming. "You've got it, JR." Raj replied. "We are using holographic telepresence technology we are…"

"Bloody hell! Jack interjected as he could immediately see the possibilities of this powerful tool. "You're telling me you can make anyone appear and disappear like that anywhere you want? And make them talk with their real voices?"

Roy laughed, "more or less, yes, as long as we have a spyder or two deployed in the same place."

Roy continued and explained that holographic video conferencing was still very much an evolving technology in the rest of the world, but they borrowed some ideas from the Tenth Cycle Library to construct these phantom spyders and incorporated the holographic capability.

Jack and JR looked like their smiles were tied behind their ears as their minds were racing with possibilities of what they could do with these new gadgets.

"You guys are really scary sometimes," Daniel said with proudness in his voice. "I'm glad you're on our side! Well done team! This is excellent work."

A round of loud applause followed.

A few hours later the leadership reassembled in the war room. The meeting was kicked off with a bamboozling demo of the new generation spyflies and the spyders. Those who hadn't seen the new technology in action reacted with initial fright and bewilderment, and finally, rapturous excitement when they realized what powerful means they had been handed by the technology division.

Roy continued. "These can be dispersed throughout the White House by Tectus while our team prepares Raven Rock for the arrival of prisoners and others. We'll be able to see and hear what is happening in the White House both here at the Rabbit Hole and at Raven Rock. We'll also be able to control the spyders and spyflies from either location."

Roy and Raj told them that they already had twelve the spyflies ready to go and would have another twelve ready in a couple of days. The spyders were a bit more complex, but they would probably have six of them ready to go in that time.

Sam was shaking his head in amazement when he voiced the thoughts of the ex-spies in their midst, "These are the type of spy gadgets we couldn't even dream of back in my days."

Luke laughed. "And to think all those years Sam and every other spy boss in charge of me sent me on those dangerous missions while they could have sent one of these spyders instead."

"Yeah, Hayden's going to have his ass handed to him," Peter commented. The room erupted into excited chatter for the next several minutes.

Salome and her psychological warfare team consisting

of Sam, Luke, Rebecca, and herself were brimming with excitement. Rebecca started chanting;

Ghosts will haunt you
Invisible spyders will taunt you
Undetectable flies will thwart you
Oh my, oh my...

Daniel let the good-natured talk flow unheeded for a few minutes and then brought the meeting back to order, "Okay people, let's get back to the task at hand. What have we found out about Raven Rock?"

JR responded, "From what we can tell, in its glory days, it was indeed a veritable city unto itself. Completely self-sustaining… they even had hydroponic gardens although not many people knew about that.

"We're still going through the records. But we already know that leaving it intact for possible future use suggests that the site was carefully shut down and preserved rather than being destroyed and haphazardly abandoned. The site was sealed up about twenty-five years ago, so as far as the power systems and technology go, they will be out of date, but they could still be functional.

"Food and water could be a concern, but if the power systems are still working, then fresh water shouldn't be a problem."

"Excellent! Do you think the existing technology will be sufficient for our needs, and if not, can it be upgraded?" Daniel asked.

"Since we're just talking about housing people in a safe and hidden environment, the site itself should meet our needs well—we think.

"As for the technology, if you're planning to fight a war I'd say you'll probably get your ass kicked. If you just need clandestine housing, communication, and observation, it will serve the purpose."

"That's a good start. Thank you, JR."

JR nodded.

"Jack? What has your team come up with?"

"We believe that we should send in a small team to make a firsthand assessment and report back. The team that goes in should have diverse enough skills to be able to do the work needed to bring the complex back to life and install secure cells for the prisoners."

"I've shown them a recommended access route," Nigel added. "It's a hotel near the White House that has access to the underground rail system from where they should be able to get to the site unnoticed."

"The team will consist of four members," Jack continued, "Doug, Max, Aaron, and I."

"That is an interesting combination." Daniel said. "Care to explain?"

"I'll lead the team. Max is the medic and computer specialist, Aaron the construction specialist, armed with Roy's laser cutting tools, and Doug is the pilot in case we need to fly somewhere.

"Max will setup our communications equipment and we'll be able to give you regular updates."

"And I'll stand guard and shoot anyone that interferes with my team," Jack said in a serious tone which sent everyone into laughter.

Daniel drummed his thumb on the edge of the table for a moment, deep in thought. "I'm happy with that, except you're missing one member though."

"Who?" Jack asked a little surprised.

"Moi, yours truly." Daniel pointed to himself.

"You?" Jack blinked.

"Yes. I'll be going with you. I need to be in Washington with my Cabinet members."

Silence reigned for a few moments while they all considered ways to dissuade Daniel from going. Sam and Nigel gave Rebecca a quick glance as if to ask, *you ready for another round of sleep treatment?*

"Daniel…"

"Don't, Jack. Don't even try. I'm going. And as for you sis," he looked at Rebecca, "I'll have you and Cyndi locked up until I'm out of here."

"An executive order, I guess." Jack grinned.

A few eyebrows raised, but no one said anything. What Daniel said did make sense, although they were all worried about his condition and his safety.

Rebecca just grinned. She'd give Max instructions and enough sedatives and show him how to use it if the need arises.

Before anyone could start, Daniel said. "I want to be ready to leave, including Roy's flies and spyders, in two days' time. Has anyone figured out how we're going to get there?"

"Yes," Peter replied. "We'll use the Metroliner… it's being repainted and reconfigured to carry cargo and a limited number of passengers as we speak. The team will be traveling along as 'medical and equipment technicians.'"

"How do we get a shipment for her?"

"She's already scheduled to pick up a shipment of medical supplies bound for L.A. from Baltimore at the Washington National Airport in three days," Peter replied. "We'll use the help of some of the Tectus members to move our team and equipment from the airport to the hotel."

"Alright!" Daniel smiled. "Sounds like we have a plan! Let's get moving and make the final preparations."

Chapter Forty-Eight

WE SHALL CONTINUE

The next morning when he returned from his scheduled bathroom trip, Brideaux felt a hard lump under the pillow on his bed. Reaching under it, he pulled out a book titled 'Kiowa Trail' by Louis L 'Amour. "Wouldn't you know, the kid is a fan of westerns," he muttered.

By now Brideaux had the young guard thoroughly under his control. When he took Brideaux for dinner that night, Brideaux filled his plate as normal, but feigned tripping and dumped it on the floor. While the guard jumped aside to avoid being splattered with food, Brideaux slipped a knife up his sleeve.

"Oh dear, look at the mess I made!" he exclaimed.

"Brideaux!" the other guard shouted, "What the hell are you doing?"

"I'm so sorry," he faked his contrition. "I tripped and lost my balance. Clumsy me; I'm really sorry; here let me clean it up."

"Sit down and shut up, Brideaux" the guard commanded. "Littleton, get a mop and clean up the mess," he ordered the younger guard. "Mickelson, bring the prisoner another plate."

"Oh, you don't have to wait on me; I can get it," he said as he started to get up.

"Just stay put. We'll bring it to you. One disaster tonight is more than enough."

Brideaux shrugged helplessly and sat back down, suppressing a grin as he felt the knife against his skin inside the sleeve.

He ate his dinner calmly and went back to his room without protest. Once inside he pulled the knife out and began to work it against the metal of the bunk, sharpening the piece of simple flatware into a sharp and lethal weapon. As he worked, he reviewed the information he'd been able to wrangle out of the kid over the past few days.

The Captain had moved eighteen of his crew to the torpedo room two decks down where additional bunks were set up. This enabled the Captain to keep him and his comrades in the three compartments vacated by the men; six each in two compartments and him in solitary confinement in the third.

They were only allowed access to the galley once per day and were served cold cereal for breakfast and sandwiches for lunch in confinement. Dinner was the only hot meal they were allowed, but he was not allowed in the mess hall at the same time as his fellow prisoners.

The next day after lunch, he spent the time in his quarters quietly performing the most taxing exercises he could think of that wouldn't alert his guards to what he was doing. By the time he knew his fellow prisoners were sitting down to the dinner meal in the mess hall, he was dripping with sweat. He lay down on the bunk tucking the sharpened knife ready to hand but out of site, curled into a ball on his side and pounded weakly on the wall of his quarters. "Help! Help me!" he cried, "I'm ill!"

"Stand back," the guard commanded.

"Help me!"

As the door opened, he feigned semi-consciousness and delirium. The guard took one look at him and called for help. "Look at him! I think he's really sick," he said.

Too bad it's the kid ... I actually kinda liked him.

Brideaux curled tighter and groaned, "Please, help me." The young guard moved closer and leaned over him.

Quick as a snake, Brideaux flung the unsuspecting Ensign over his body, slamming him into the wall with stunning force. At nearly the same instant he grabbed the knife, slashing it across the softness of the other guard's belly, instantly disemboweling him. Mercifully his next thrust went through the man's heart putting him out of his misery.

Brideaux grabbed both of the guns the guards had dropped and pulled the Ensign to his feet planting the muzzle of the gun on the young man's temple. "Make one wrong move, and your brain will be dripping down the bulkhead. Understand?"

Afraid to move, the Ensign blinked and swallowed hard. "Tell me how to get to the bridge."

"Bridge, sir?" the Ensign asked confused, wondering why he would want to go up in the sail.

Brideaux shook him roughly, "the bridge, the control center of the ship you idiot!"

"Uh ... the ... the bridge is ... is in the s .... sail of the boat, b ... bu ... but the c ... control center is in ... in the control room one ... one deck down, un... under the sail."

"Where are the Captain and officers now?"

"In ... in ... in the ... in the wardroom."

"And, where is it?"

"B ... be ... below us."

"Alright, let's move."

Keeping the Ensign in front of him for protection, they moved out of his compartment and down the steep stairs to the next deck and the entrance to the mess hall.

Another guard stood just inside the door of the mess hall. He didn't see Brideaux and his prisoner before it was too late. Brideaux put the gun to the back of the guard's head and ordered him to step back quietly. The guard did so, and before he could do anything else, Brideaux had cold-cocked him and grabbed his gun.

Stepping into the mess hall, Brideaux shot the guard across the room in the right eye, and before the second guard could move for his holstered gun, his chest exploded with another shot from Brideaux's gun.

By now Brideaux's fellow prisoners had all dropped to the floor out of the line of fire. Shoving the Ensign ahead of him, he made his way through the mess hall, shouting at his comrades to get the guns of the dead guards. As he passed two of his most trusted founders, he gave them each one of the guns he'd recovered and ordered them to follow him.

Keeping his hold on the Ensign, Brideaux made his way to the wardroom, shot the man coming through the door, and pushed the Ensign through ahead of him. The Executive Officer started to get up, and Brideaux shot him in the shoulder then swung the gun on the Captain.

"Don't, even think of it," was all he said. He stepped out of the doorway so that there was a wall behind him and instructed the man that followed him to guard the door.

"Hands flat on the table where I can see them, all of you," Brideaux ordered.

At that moment, an alarm sounded and a voice came over the speaker in the Wardroom.

"Gunfire aboard, secure all compartments."

"Your crew reacts quickly, Captain." Brideaux snarled with an evil grin.

Captain Locklin remained silent, glaring at Brideaux in contempt.

"You will contact whoever is in the control room and tell them to stand down."

"Never."

Brideaux pulled the trigger shooting the executive officer in the other shoulder. The man screamed in shock and pain.

"Brideaux kept his gun pointed at the executive officer and snarled. "Your call Captain Locklin ..."

Locklin moved slowly to the wall for the communication mic, flipped it on, and shouted "Brideaux is loose…"

Brideaux fired another shot through the Exec's head and watched him slide down the wall.

The rest of the warning died on Locklin's tongue as he watched the gun level at another officer's head.

"Captain!" A voice came over the speaker.

"Your call again, Captain," Brideaux hissed, holding the gun to the Ensign's head.

"Stand down! Stand down!" Locklin yelled into the mic.

"Captain?"

Brideaux grabbed the mic from the Captain's hand, "Your Captain told you to stand down idiot. I suggest you listen to him before I put a bullet through his head," he shouted.

Silence followed.

Brideaux lowered his gun a little and stepped back. "You see Captain you just have to know how to command people. I'm surprised they gave you command of this tin can considering your lack of skill. Now, where are we?"

No one stirred.

Brideaux nodded, chewing on his lower lip. "I see… that's how you want to play it." His knife flashed, and an ear landed on the white table cloth, droplets of blood trailing from the side of the head of the former owner followed by a groan of pain.

"Where are we?"

"Under the polar ice cap."

Brideaux sighed heavily, "and where are we headed?"

"The Northwest Joint Regional Correctional Facility at Fort Lewis, Washington."

"Thank you, Captain." Brideaux bowed mockingly at Locklin. "You see, that wasn't so hard."

The men remained frozen at the table, glaring at Brideaux. He just smiled at all of them. "I know what you're thinking, all of you. You'd like to kill me. I suggest that you don't try. I'm more than a match for anyone of you. But of course, you're welcome to test my claim if you want to. I just thought you might want to heed good advice."

Turning back to Captain Locklin he said, "You're going to change course to …"

"Not a chance, Brideaux," Locklin cut it. "This boat stays on course."

Brideaux leaned toward the Captain slightly; "Really?" he drew the word out.

Brideaux grinned as he looked over the men at the table, picked the one next to Locklin, and pointed his gun at his head. "You will change course or …"

"You can threaten all you want, and kill us one by one," Captain Locklin said, staring directly into Brideaux's eyes, "but I will sooner scuttle this boat than let you have control of it."

"Hmmm. We'll see about that." Brideaux moved toward the door, dragging the Ensign with him.

"Get a couple of our people in here now, he ordered the man who had followed him."

In less than a minute, two of his Council members stood outside the door.

"Take all these officers, except the Captain and this Ensign, and lock them in cold storage. Have the doctor brought up here... one of the officers needs medical attention," he said pointing to the man holding the side of his head where his ear used to be, blood dripping between his fingers. "Make sure you secure the storage area so they can't get out. Shoot anyone that resists or tries anything."

By the time the officers had been put in cold storage, the Corpsman had arrived.

"Move them both to the cold storage area," he said indicating the man with the missing ear and the medic, "he can treat him in there."

"You can't keep us in cold storage, we'll die!" The medic protested.

"You would prefer that I just kill you all outright? What kind of a man are you? What kind of a man do you think I am? I don't kill people for no reason!" Brideaux shouted, his eyes wild.

The Corpsman looked at him, astonished. "Excuse me?"

"I said I don't kill people for no reason," he rose to his feet, "however, if I have a reason, I'm quite effective at it. Now get on with it!" he shouted, "Before I have a reason to kill you!"

Brideaux turned away as the men were lead from the room and leveled his gun on the Captain. Taking the mic from its cradle, he keyed it and said, "This is John Brideaux.

You will turn this ship around now, or I will shoot the officer before me."

"No way, Brideaux; give it up, you have nowhere to run," came the reply.

Brideaux adjusted his aim, keyed the mic, and pulled the trigger. The Captain fell to the floor screaming.

"That was the sound of a bullet removing your Captain's right knee cap. I'll give you thirty seconds to think about that, and then I'll remove the other kneecap."

"Are you ready to give me control of this ship yet Captain?"

"Go to hell, Brideaux," he said through clenched teeth.

"Wrong answer." Brideaux left the room, and they heard him rummaging around in the galley.

When he returned, two of his colleagues grabbed the Ensign, sat him in a chair, and pulled the shoe and sock from one foot. "You are responsible for the lives of those under your command, are you not, Captain?"

Locklin just stared at him with hate filled eyes.

"This is your responsibility Captain. Key the mic," he ordered. Then he pinned the boy's leg tightly and began removing the toenail from the big toe with his knife.

Ensign Littleton screamed at a blood-curdling pitch. By the time Brideaux had the nail off, everyone was covered in sweat.

Brideaux held the mic in his bloody hands. "Turn the ship around."

"No way, Brideaux," the voice replied over the speaker.

"Captain?" he inquired.

Breathing heavily with pain Captain Locklin shook his head, "No."

"Key the mic," Brideaux ordered as he turned back toward the Ensign.

"No!" he yelled. "Oh God! Someone stop him! Please!" His pleading became screams as Brideaux amputated his big toe.

Again, he returned to the mic and keyed it with his bloody hand. "Turn the ship around."

"No."

"Captain?"

"No."

"Very well, we shall continue."

Chapter Forty-Nine

MERGE US

"We are going to need help," Siasha said in a soft but very concerned voice as she looked at Tawndo, Korda and Linkola in turn.

"Yes," Tawndo nodded. "The question is how are we going to get it? None of our other satellite sites have responded, and it would be difficult to bring any of them here anyway without alarming the Eleventh Cycle population. We can't just walk out of here and announce to the people out there we are from the Eighth Cycle; we're about sixty-two-thousand-years old and need your help. Can we?"

"What about Robert?" Korda asked.

Tawndo looked at Korda. "Who?"

"Robert. As you are aware, it is his body you inhabit. He was a member of the Rossler Foundation, the people who brought Brideaux down recently. I've studied every bit of the history of the group."

"Yes, I know this body was Robert Cartwright's before, but you never told me about my history. Actually, I never asked—it never bothered me; I never had a desire to know. But now it seems to be important that I know."

Korda nodded. "The man that is now President, Daniel Rossler, and his team gained access to the history and technology of the Tenth Cycle people and have been protecting the knowledge ever since. They've only shared the parts of it that could be used to make life better for the people of this cycle.

"They also found a Ninth Cycle site at the South Pole of the planet—they call it Antarctica. Unfortunately, that discovery released a dreadful disease on the population of the world. Fortunately, they also found a cure for the disease otherwise it would have been the end of their cycle.

"Because the disease attacked only people of a certain genetic makeup, the Rossler Foundation was blamed, and enemies arose which drove them to the brink of an all-out nuclear war. A fanatical group who called themselves The Sword of Cyrus infiltrated the Rossler Foundation and almost succeeded in gaining control of the world, but the Rossler group found out about them just in time and was able to defeat them.

"Not long after averting that disaster, the Rossler Foundation discovered our site here at the canyon. This man, John Brideaux, took the Beast from them and in the process, killed Robert Cartwright," Korda pointed at Tawndo, "and got control of the world, just like the Council of the Selected of our cycle did.

"We reanimated you within hours after Brideaux killed Robert Cartwright, using his body to host you. From that point onward, you know what happened.

Tawndo interjected. "So, what's all of that got to do with me?"

"You were part of the Rossler Foundation before you

were killed by John Brideaux. They will be able to recognize you. You are the only one of us who can get in touch with the people of the Rossler Foundation to tell them about the danger they are in and perhaps get them to help us."

Tawndo nodded slowly. "That's if I can somehow bring them to believe I am who I say I am. In their world, there is no such thing as coming back from the dead."

Korda was looking down and away from Tawndo when he spoke. "As far as I can see we don't have much of a choice Tawndo. I ... I think we should use Robert ... bring him back ... and ... and use him to contact the leaders of the Rossler Foundation, for help,"

Tawndo quietly stared at the floor for a long while before he spoke. "That means I have to die and then be brought back as Robert?"

Korda slowly nodded.

Siasha shook her head. "No, we also need Tawndo's knowledge of this facility and our technology."

"Yes, we need them both," Linkola said softly, "but we can only *have* one."

They all sat silently, each of them deep in thought for several moments.

Korda broke the silence clearing his throat and said with determination, "I volunteer to become Tawndo so he can become Robert."

"Korda!" Linkola roared.

"No!" Siasha added, "You can't. We need you as you are now."

An argument broke out between the three; Korda had many logical arguments for why it was necessary, the other two had equally logical arguments why they had to keep him as Korda. The discussion had become quite heated, and Linkola was on his feet when Tawndo's voice stopped them.

"Merge us."

"What?" Linkola asked with astonishment. "What did you say?"

"I said merge us ... Robert and me ... merge us, make us one."

"That's what I thought you said, but you don't know what you are saying!"

"It makes the most sense."

"No," Linkola responded, "it doesn't make any sense. It's never been done. It's a crazy idea. It would most certainly kill both of you."

"Has it ever been tried... or even theorized?" Tawndo asked.

Linkola clenched his jaws and stared defiantly at Tawndo, refusing to answer. It was obvious that this idea had caused him a tremendous amount of distress. But no one knew why.

"Has it?"

"It's a crazy idea." He mumbled, "It can't be done."

Tawndo rose to face Linkola, brow furrowed, eyes slightly narrowed and his jaw tight.

"Answer me, Linkola. Has it ever been tried?"

Linkola turned away in fury. "Once," he hissed. "It killed the man, we lost two identities, and it was horrendous. The poor man quite literally tore himself apart."

Tawndo paled, "what went wrong?"

"We don't know. It was shortly before the Healer became the Beast and we never had time to look into it."

"I suggest you look into it now then and do it quickly," Tawndo said in a commanding tone, a determined look on his face.

"I will not, *ever*, try that again. You have no idea what you are talking about or what that man went through. It happened so fast we weren't able to stop him. The answer is NO; I won't do it."

"Siasha, find the records and review the process," Tawndo ordered.

"Tawndo, I can't. Please don't ask me to do this," she cried.

He took her by the arms, looking deep into her eyes, "you must. Siasha, this world is unaware of the danger of the Re'an. We are the only ones who can help them understand the danger they are in and our only hope of survival. We can't do it on our own."

She buried her head in his chest. "I know," she sobbed, "I just don't want to lose you—again, this time probably forever."

He encircled her in his arms, kissed the top of her head, and smoothed her soft hair, running it gently through his fingers. "You won't. I know you and Linkola can do this if you work together." He swayed gently with her until her sobbing subsided.

"Okay, I will look at the experiment information." She said softly, "but I won't try it without Linkola, and neither of us will try it if we can't find what went wrong."

"Fair enough," Tawndo said. "Will you agree to help, Linkola?"

He sighed heavily and swallowed hard. "Under the circumstances, and with that understanding, I will look at the data," Linkola agreed. Then he said angrily, "but if we find it can't be done, I will destroy it so no further attempts or research can be done."

"Agreed," Tawndo said, turned and walked away.

Chapter Fifty

GRITTING HIS TEETH

Jack was going through the last preparations before the advance team departed for Raven Rock. "The team going to work at Raven has grown a bit due to the added security detail needed for the President," Jack grinned at Daniel.

"Two Secret Service men will accompany us as well as Cliff Willis. Chuck, the pilot who successfully got us to Mt Ararat, will pilot the aircraft to Washington with Owen as co-pilot.

"Peter will remain at the ranch to take over while Owen is gone.

"I'd prefer not to leave the plane until we're ready to transfer to Raven Rock, especially the President, but it's too hot to sit inside the plane on the tarmac this time of year. So, once we're in Washington, Tectus members will pick up and transport our team, at staggered intervals to safe houses.

"Max, Aaron, and I will go first and check in to the hotel. Once we're checked in, Aaron and I will proceed to the site and verify it is still accessible and secure.

"After dark, Daniel and the Secret Service Agents will be transported but they will go directly to Raven Rock rather than checking into the hotel.

"Doug and Cliff will be transported last. Doug will come directly to Raven Rock while Cliff will check in to the hotel.

"Max will be our contact point with Tectus, and Cliff will work with us on the outside to coordinate and bring in the Cabinet members when we are ready for them.

"Over to you Aaron."

Aaron cleared his throat. "We will use Roy's laser cutters to remove enough of the concrete in one of the tunnels to allow a vehicle the size of a semi-trailer through.

"Two semi-trucks will bring in needed supplies and remain hidden inside. They will be driven by Doug and Max or if needed, Tectus members.

"Roy is building additional spyders to create a holographic covering of the tunnel opening." He nodded at Jack to continue.

"A second team consisting of JR, Raj, Roy, and Secretary of State Bill Sims, will join us on the Metroliner's next transport run. We've also asked Rebecca to join us to serve as the medical provider for the facility should the need arise.

"Tectus members will deploy the new flies and spyders in the White House, and once we see what is happening inside, we will be able to form a plan to proceed with operations there."

Sam and the rest nodded approval of the plans so far. Jack nodded for Nigel to provide his input.

"As soon as Daniel arrives he will start working with his Cabinet members to come up with plans for the stabilization of the country and foreign affairs.

"Once Aaron has the holding cells built for Hayden's

top advisors, we will begin removing them one by one to their new... ah... quarters." Nigel smiled.

"What about Camp David?" Luke asked. The tunnel to RRMC passes through there. Does access still exist, and if so, what do we need to do to secure it?"

"Good point Luke," Nigel said. That access point still exists and will have to be secured. My understanding is we have two Secret Service agents still recovering at the Ranch. Their wounds were minor. I suggest you take them with you; they might prove to be very useful."

"Good idea," Jack responded. "I think it would be good to take Elize if she's willing to come with us. Her knowledge of the White House could be invaluable."

Nigel hesitated, "She is young, and I don't want her exposed to unnecessary danger."

"We'll bring her to Raven Rock with the second group. She'll be safe there."

"If you could locate her mother and smuggle her in as well, you'd have meals fit for a king," Nigel smiled.

The others laughed.

"Okay," Daniel said. "I am impressed with the arrangements you and the team have made Jack. Thank you. Do we have consensus on these plans so far?" He looked at everyone in turn and got the nod.

"JR, you and anyone else you can find to help you, please keep looking through the documents we have and let us know of any additional information you find on Hayden and the RRMC site... or anything else you think could be helpful in any way. Every bit of information could be useful."

"Sure, no problem," JR agreed.

He concluded the meeting with, "Those of us departing

tomorrow, let's get our things together and be ready to go at first light." Daniel was gritting his teeth at the thought of another trip on horseback to Mt Ararat, but it was still better than walking.

Chapter Fifty-One

ONLY A MATTER OF TIME

Captain Locklin lay on the deck; blood splattered around and over him. The still-breathing body of the Ensign Littleton lay next to him, one foot was toeless, and his back, belly, and legs had large raw patches where the skin had been removed. He had finally given in to Brideaux when he started to literally skin the boy alive.

The corpsman was shocked by the scene greeting him upon entering the Wardroom, but quickly recovered and treated the Captain's knee as ordered, giving him morphine to ease the pain.

"Get him on his feet," Brideaux snarled.

"You're a barbarian, Brideaux!" The corpsman yelled.

"Take him to cold storage and take the boy with him," Brideaux ordered.

"Alright Captain. Tell your men in the control center we are coming in. They are to surrender and report to the mess hall."

Locklin nodded.

Brideaux keyed the mic, "this is Brideaux; your Captain wishes to speak to you."

"Stand down. Surrender and report to the mess hall immediately." The Captain said with a voice laced with pain.

"Captain?"

"You heard me. Brideaux and I are coming to the control room. You are to surrender."

"Aye, Sir."

"Well done, Captain!" Brideaux exclaimed triumphantly. He signaled one of his men to assist the Captain, and they left the Wardroom moving forward to the control room.

When they stepped into the nerve center of the boat, Brideaux whistled as he stared at the monitors and state of the art electronics. At least a half dozen double-stacked monitors lined each side of the room with more across the front. Two stations in the middle of the room held monitors as well, one of them in a horizontal position - a mapping station.

"Stop. Tell me what all this is."

Starting at the left Captain Locklin indicated each station in a soft and labored voice, "photonics and navigation are closest to us, then sonar, up front is ship control, combat control is on the right, and over there is the radio room. The console at center front is the Officer of the Deck station, and the flat top is the mapping station."

"How do you drive this thing?"

"You don't. The pilot and co-pilot work together along with the maneuvering room to control the depth, speed, and course of the boat."

Brideaux approached the control stations, looking carefully at the displays. "There's no picture of what's out there! How do you know where you're going?"

"It's too complicated to explain in a few minutes. I will order my men to follow the course you want. You need all of them to successfully maneuver this boat."

"No tricks, Captain, or I promise you; you have only seen the beginning of the fate of your crew."

"No, Brideaux, no tricks." Captain Locklin replied in a tired voice.

The lone pilot nervously watched the display panels as the submarine continued its silent course through the dark and icy waters under the polar ice cap.

Locklin had succeeded in convincing Brideaux that they were closer to exiting from under the ice if they proceeded than if they turned back. Unfortunately, Brideaux continued to think of the sub as an underwater airplane, believing that a single person could maneuver it through the watery depths. It was only a matter of time before he found out differently.

He had allowed two men to remain in the maneuvering room with two guards and secured the rest, including those that had been held in cold storage, in their quarters with a guard at each end of the corridor.

The corpsman made regular visits to the control room to attend to Locklin since Brideaux would not allow him to leave.

"How is the crew, Doc," Locklin had asked on the doc's last visit.

Looking around to be sure Brideaux's attention was elsewhere he whispered, "two are unaccounted for, Littleton is stable, but in critical condition, the rest of us are ok."

"Don't give me as much morphine as you did last time, I need my head to be clear," Locklin hissed. "It's only a matter of time before this boat hits something."

The Doc nodded, completed his ministrations and was ordered from the control room.

Chapter Fifty-Two

WELCOME TO THE TEAM

It was two hours before dawn when the seven team members started off to Mt Ararat. Jack rode at the head of the group with Peter, discussing all the ways they were going to torment Hayden with the spyflies and spyders. Daniel and Cliff Willis rode side by side talking in low voices; no one could hear what they were discussing. Agent Ken Mason was about twenty or so yards ahead of them and agent Matt Smith about the same distance behind, while Doug brought up the rear.

Max and Aaron waited for them at the ranch. Having been apprised of the plan the previous day, they were ready to go. Chuck and Owen had finished the paint job on the Metroliner while the others had worked late into the night to complete the conversion to a cargo plane.

They'd pulled out nine seats, replacing them with tie-down areas that would allow half the plane to be filled with cargo.

Kelly and Alison, having already prepared and loaded

sack lunches into the plane for everyone, had breakfast waiting for them when they arrived.

They ate quickly, appreciating the hot breakfast, and boarded the plane.

Chuck and Owen ran through the pre-flight checklist in the cockpit, and when they were satisfied the plane was ready, Chuck turned to Owen, "are you ready to fly this thing?"

"Me? I thought I was the co-pilot!"

"You are, but every Air Force One pilot and co-pilot is fully capable of handling the aircraft they fly. You handled the plane just fine in flight; now you get to learn to put her in the air."

"Do you think I'm ready?" Owen asked.

"Whether you're ready or not, you have to be able to do it, so let's get started."

"Okay," Owen agreed, took a deep breath and made a quick cross over his chest, although he was not Catholic it felt like the right thing to do.

"Don't worry," Chuck assured him, "it's exactly like any other plane... only different."

"Exactly the same, only different," Owen moaned, "you're real funny, Chuck."

"Thanks. I always thought I would make a good standup comedian if this pilot job didn't work out." He smirked and began coaching Owen on the take-off for the Metroliner.

As Owen listened to Chuck's instructions he realized that take-off in the Metroliner was nearly the same as the plane he was used to—but a little bit different.

At the conclusion of Chuck's instructions, Owen taxied the plane to the end of the runway, revved the engines, released the breaks, and let the plane roll down the runway gathering speed.

When the plane reached lift-off velocity, Owen pulled back on the stick, and the sleek plane rose smoothly into the air, climbing quickly towards the rising sun on the horizon.

Upon reaching cruising altitude, Owen leveled the plane off and grinned at Chuck. "That wasn't so bad!"

"Piece of cake. I told you so!" Kicking back in his seat he added: "she's all yours; wake me if you need me!"

"Wake you? Don't you ever do anything besides sleep?" Owen frowned.

"Sure, I do," Chuck said with a wink, "why do you think I need sleep?"

Owen stared at him for a moment and then laughed.

"Alright, fine. I won't ask. But I can only guess you're practicing standup comedy in your off time."

Chuck opened one eye to look at Owen, "wise man," he said and closed his eye. "Besides, I always did sleep best on a plane."

Owen just shook his head and returned to the business of guiding the plane through the air.

The flight to D.C. was uneventful, and as they started the descent, Chuck began coaching Owen on landing the plane. This led to further conversation about avionics in general, and Chuck realized he'd found a kindred spirit in his love of flying.

When Owen set the plane down in Washington, the landing wasn't quite as smooth as he would have liked, nevertheless Chuck congratulated him. "That was a very good first time landing for a plane this size," He chortled.

"Oh, my God!" Owen suddenly exclaimed, "I just practiced landing an unfamiliar plane with the President of the United States on board!"

"And you did very well," Chuck said. "Don't worry; I wouldn't have let you try if I didn't think you could do it."

Tectus members were waiting with several cars and immediately took everyone to safe houses. Max and two Tectus operatives, Kimberley and Stan, went to a nearby safe house where they were given a change of clothes and disguises.

Kimberley and Stan, now dressed casually, were dropped off a few blocks from the hotel and strolled to a coffee shop across the street from it. They went inside, ordered their coffees and took seats at a table by the window.

A few minutes later they watched as a limousine pulled up in front of the hotel, and a handsome business man wearing a very expensive looking suit got out and went inside. They giggled as they watched Max pull at his collar. "He sure isn't used to wearing suits, is he?" Stan commented.

"Nope, and I get the feeling from the expression on his face he isn't happy about it either!" Kimberley giggled.

Max entered the hotel feeling all tied up in the fancy suit. *I could have gone all year without having to put on one of these things.*

"I have reservations."

"Yes, sir. Your name sir?"

"Vincent Meyers the Third."

"Yes, sir, I have your reservation right here. It says it's pre-paid by MacArthur Labs and Engineering."

"Correct."

"Sign here please, sir," the desk clerk indicated a line at the bottom of the paper.

Max signed and impatiently waited for the key to his room. *Hurry up kid; I can't wait to get out of this monkey suit!*

"Thank you, sir." Handing Max the key, he pointed to the elevators across the lobby, "You're in room 336. Take the elevator to the third floor and go to the left when you step off. It will be about halfway down on the right. My apologies for not providing a porter, but with all the unrest going on in the city lately, very few people have turned up for work.

"Thanks. Don't worry I can carry my own bags," Max said and headed for the elevators.

He had his tie undone and his suit jacket laying on the foot of the bed almost before he sat his luggage down. Pulling the mirror phone out of his pocket he called Jack, "Team one in position," he reported, knowing Kimberley and Stan were waiting at the coffee shop.

"Great. Team two departing now."

While the three members of team one were getting situated, the Tectus members had taken Jack and Aaron to a safe house where a heating and air-conditioning service vehicle awaited. The two men were supplied with, and had already changed into, the uniforms of maintenance staff and put their duffels into tool boxes.

As soon as the call from Max ended, they were in the service van and on their way.

They pulled up behind the hotel and went in through the service door in the back.

The housekeeping crews that had finished their room blocks were lining up and restocking their carts for the next day.

"Hi!" Jack said. "We're here to check your HVAC units. How do we get to the basement?"

A woman pointed to a door on the other side of the room and mumbled, "over there."

"Thanks!" Jack replied.

He and Aaron quickly disappeared through the door and down the stairs.

"There should be an exterior door over there," Jack told Aaron, pointing to the left. "Check it out and get those agents in here while I locate the entrance to the tunnel."

Aaron hurried off in the direction Jack indicated, located the door and opened it. Taking out his mirror phone he called Kimberley, "We're in, come on over."

Kimberley and Stan gathered their things with natural ease and set off toward the hotel hand in hand, acting like lovers. They headed down the side of the building as if to use one of the exterior access doors, but quickly stepped aside and descended the stairs into what appeared to be a pit. At the bottom, under the overhang of a walkway, Aaron waited with the door ajar.

They stepped through and watched as Aaron put duct tape over the latch-bolt and attached a small box to the inside of the door and another one directly across from it on the door frame.

"What are you doing?" Kimberley whispered.

"Making a way for Daniel and the others to get in. The tape will keep the latch from working, leaving the door open, but the handle will be locked. This is a type of magnetic lock. It's battery operated and will only last for about six to eight hours, but will secure this door until our other two teams are in. Each team has a key that will demagnetize the locking mechanism long enough to allow them through. Doug will remove it when he comes through. Let's go," Aaron whispered as he finished.

Aaron had found and opened the section of wall they spotted on the old maps and was waiting for the others when they arrived. They stepped through the wall with him onto the platform, and he pushed a small gray button in the platform-side wall causing the imitated the concrete block door to slide back into place, hiding the entrance.

The trip from the hotel to Camp David took about 45 minutes. On arrival, Jack and Kimberley got off to check the area. Passing through an opening in the wall, they started across the basement toward the stairs to the main level.

"Stop! Put your hands in the air," a stern voice said from the shadows of the dimly lit room.

They froze.

"Who are you?" Jack asked.

"Agent Harrison. Who are you and what are you doing here?"

"Gary?" Kimberley asked. "Gary Harrison?"

"How do you know me?"

"It's me! Kimberley Andrews."

"Kimberley? How did you get here?"

"It's a long story, how about you? The last I knew you were in the White House when Hayden attacked."

"I was. We escaped and came here."

"Um, excuse me," Jack broke in, "can we hold the romantic talk for later and put our hands down?"

"Depends," Harrison said. "Who are you working for?"

"The President," Kimberley replied.

"Which President?"

"There's only one President, political whiz kid, Daniel Rossler," Jack snapped.

"In that case, yes, you can put your hands down, but don't make any sudden moves. Turn around and go back the way you came. I'll follow you."

Once they were back out on the landing, Harrison told them to turn around. He recognized Kimberley immediately, but not the man with her. Inside the monorail car he also saw two more men he didn't recognize.

"What's going on here? How did you know about this tunnel?"

"President Nigel Harper told us about it," Jack said. "How did you know about it?"

"Several of the senior Secret Service Agents are told of the tunnels and how to access them should there be a need to evacuate the President. We are sworn to secrecy. Why would President Harper tell you about them?"

"It's a long story, and as I've said before, we don't have time for all this talk," Jack replied. "The late President Campbell and Vice-President Rossler used them to escape from Hayden and the White House. Kimberley and Stan were part of the team that got them out and to safety. Now let's cut out this idle chatter and move our asses."

"You guys are going after Hayden?" Harrison asked. "Please count me in and tell me how I can help."

Jack weighed his options quickly—*any reliable help that knows how to shoot straight will be welcome.* "Who else is here with you?"

"There are two staff members and one other agent. The other five staff members we managed to get back to their homes."

"What are your plans for the other two staff members?"

"Agent Williams is taking them home tonight after dark."

"Do you know where his loyalties lie?"

Harrison stiffened, he looked offended, "with all due respect, *Mister*," he spoke tightly, "I don't know who you are and what you know about Secret Service Agents but we have sworn to give our lives to protect the President of the United States. Hayden is *not* the President and we will *not*, I repeat *not*, support him."

"Sorry Harrison," Jack replied. "We need someone to secure this entrance to the tunnel. If you two could work with Kimberley to do that, it would be a huge help."

Harrison holstered his gun and offered his hand to Jack, "you got it Mr.… ah…"

"Jack Symonds," he replied as they shook hands. "Welcome to the team!"

Jack stepped aboard the monorail as Aaron closed the wall behind them.

"Let's go," he urged.

Chapter Fifty-Three

THEIR FIRST MISSION

Travel time from Camp David to the platform at Raven Rock was about ten minutes, but to Jack it seemed to take forever. The fact that others at the White House knew of the tunnel system made him nervous and he was no longer sure the facility would still be abandoned. By the time they arrived, he had made his decision.

He called Daniel and had him get the team at the Rabbit Hole to join the call.

"Aaron, Stan, and I have arrived at RRMC. We found two Secret Service Agents at Camp David who used the tunnel system to help seven members of the White House staff escape when Hayden took over. Kimberley is with them. I have serious concerns about the security of the facility, not sure that it's still deserted. I want to confirm that it's secure before proceeding."

"Who were the agents at Camp David?" Nigel asked.

"Harrison and Williams."

"Gary Harrison?"

"Yes, he is the one I spoke with."

"I'll vouch for his loyalty, and that of Williams if it is the same 'Williams' that is usually partnered with Gary—tall, lean guy with blond hair," Nigel said. "If it's them they will support you."

"That's good to know; thank you, Nigel," Jack responded. "I want to postpone Daniel's arrival here until tomorrow night. Send in Doug and Cliff; Max, you come too. I want to search this place from top to bottom before we proceed and I can't do it without losing precious time if it's just the three of us. If all checks out, we'll have Daniel brought out tomorrow night."

"Very well, Jack. You're on site and calling the shots. Feel free to bring in more Tectus members if you feel you need them," Daniel said.

Jack paused briefly. "Hmm. Good idea, Daniel. Give me a sec." Jack addressed Max. "Okay. Max, get in touch with Eric Winchester and Dennis McMahon. Ask them if they're willing to join us."

"I'm on it, Jack," Max replied. "Doug, Cliff, let's meet in the basement in an hour—I'll have Eric and Dennis with me if I can." And with that, Max left the call.

"Sorry for the delay, Daniel," Jack apologized.

"No need to apologize, Jack. You're doing a fine job. I'm anxious to get there, but I trust your judgment."

"Thanks, Daniel. I'll be in touch again soon," Jack ended the call.

Kerinski set the last of the spyflies in the Oval Office. Like the five spyders before them, they quickly disappeared when they were activated.

Raj and Roy, operating the spyflies remotely, dispersed

them throughout the office. A few were settled in to be eyes and ears for those at the Rabbit Hole; the majority were waiting to escape when the door opened. They would be moved to other areas of the White House to gather information.

"Okay, Kerinski, that's the last one," Roy confirmed. "We're done, thanks for the help. Mouse should be there any minute."

"Roger that, we'll be on our way out in a few," she whispered

Kerinski and Mouse had joined Tectus at about the same time and had formed a bond of friendship that was closer than brother and sister. Kerinski's husband of six months and Mouse's younger brother had both been lost on a military mission gone terribly wrong.

Kerinski sought a way to fulfill her husband's ideals - to protect the country against enemies foreign and domestic. As far as she was concerned, the government had become a domestic enemy, and with the onset of Brideaux's insanity, she, like many of her husband's friends and their families, had joined Tectus to do what she could to make a difference.

One night, while serving on shift together, Kerinski and Mouse had discovered their connection in the loss of their loved ones. They talked long into the night, sharing their grief, frustration, anger, and struggle to cope. The sharing brought a small measure of comfort and healing to each of them, and since then their bond of loyalty and friendship had grown and solidified.

They worked well together, and Tectus acknowledged them as a top-notch team of operators. Thus, they had been chosen by the leaders to be one of the teams to work closely with the Rosslers to penetrate the White House, plant the spy hardware, and kidnap Hayden's top men.

Their first mission in this operation was to deploy the spyders and spyflies in the East and West Wings. Kerinski was assigned to the West Wing, and Mouse to the East Wing.

They had completed their mission, met at the predesignated location and were returning to safe house where President Daniel Rossler and his agents awaited the 'all clear' from the team leader. They would accompany the Presidential party to RRMC.

She closed the connection with Roy, and started back down the stairs, stepping into the circle of light created by Mouse's flashlight at the bottom. They high-fived - no easy task as Kerinski was barely five feet in height and Mouse towered over her at six feet three - and headed out through the tunnel to the Blair House.

Kerinski marveled as she followed the dim outline of Mouse's shadow through the tunnel. The man was huge! Tall, heavily muscled, and yet he could move with the grace of a dancer and stealth of a hunting tiger. The man was amazing! His given name was Leonardo, Leo for short, but his agility, speed, and stealth had earned him the nickname 'Mouse' – a pun on his height – given to him by his special forces buddies. His body carried the scars of the many deployments he'd seen; he was a highly decorated and honored officer when he left the Recon Marines.

Chapter Fifty-Four

A BRIEF MESSAGE

Rafael Martinez stared at his coffee, anger and grief washing through him like the tides of the ocean that enveloped the submarine carrying them through its murky depths. *I will kill John Brideaux if it's the last thing I do.* He swore to himself for the hundredth time. *I will kill him or die trying.*

Martinez was not one of the men Brideaux had entrusted with a gun; perhaps he remembered the threat Martinez had made to kill him in the council chambers when he shot and killed Martinez's friend Ruben Weinstein.

Nevertheless, the opportunity would come, and he would be ready for it he promised himself.

He considered the present circumstances. There were thirteen of them and at least one hundred crew members as best he could estimate. *It's only a matter of time before we get too tired to watch them or they figure out a way to overpower us.*

He considered the possibility that some of the crew might have weapons in their quarters. He also considered that neither he nor any of the other council members were a match for trained military personnel. There would be more deaths, and God knew the world had seen enough death since Brideaux had set that Beast loose on everyone.

Maybe if the crew was armed, his fellow council members wouldn't fight back, and there would be no more deaths - *except for John Brideaux*, he promised himself again.

A plan began to form in his mind as he headed for the control room and John Brideaux. "John," he said, stepping into the control room. He came to a sudden stop as he marveled at the technology in the room.

"What do you want Martinez," Brideaux growled.

"We can't all stay awake indefinitely. We will need sleep to guard the crew effectively. There are only twelve of us and over one hundred of them."

Brideaux frowned slightly, "yes I suppose you are right. Very well. Allow six to sleep while the other six perform guard duty - twelve hours shifts. Two in the maneuvering room, two at either end of the corridor guarding the crew, one guarding the officer's quarters, and one up here with me."

"There are no more quarters for our people to sleep, I assume you will be in agreement with them sleeping in the torpedo room?"

"I don't care," Brideaux said irritably, "just make it happen, Martinez."

"Right away, John," he said in a subservient tone as he left the room.

Stopping at the Captain's cabin, he looked around and then stepped inside, quietly closing the door behind him. He found a writing pad and quickly wrote a brief message on it, tore the paper in half and repeated the message and placed both pieces of paper in his pocket before he left the room.

He was passing the galley when he noticed that several trays of sandwiches were waiting to be taken up to the crew for their noon meal. He offered to help and then took a plate of sandwiches back to the crewmen and guards in the maneuvering room.

Chapter Fifty-Five

WE MUST RISK IT

Linkola and Siasha had been hard at work, pouring over the information to find a way of merging two identities and reviewing the results of the failed attempt. They were exhausted and had reached an impasse.

"I'm telling you, Siasha, that couldn't have been the cause."

"It's the only thing that makes sense, Linkola; there is nothing else!" she exclaimed, slapping her hand on the table.

"It can't be that simple!" he shouted.

"Look at the data, Linkola; it speaks for itself!"

At this moment Korda arrived. He stopped mid-stride and stared at them. "Shouting and screaming won't get you anywhere. I suggest you both take a break."

Siasha and Linkola glanced at each other in embarrassment.

"Korda is right," Linkola said. "Let's take a break."

The three of them got up and went for a swim and returned refreshed after an hour.

"Alright, Siasha, where were we?" Linkola said when they were back in the lab.

"I was telling you that the reason for the failure of the previous experiment was that you tried to merge two B'ran - two individuals from the same race. Both had strong, warlike personalities and training; they both tried to dominate the other and ended up destroying the host body and thus themselves."

"It was such a horrible and violent death, Siasha. I can't watch something like that happen again. It's still haunting me."

"Then you will leave the room," a voice said from behind them. It was Tawndo.

"Tawndo," Linkola begged, "think carefully about this. "If we start this procedure, there is no going back. Once started, it cannot be aborted. If it doesn't work, it will kill you, Robert, and the host body—forever. There will be no reanimation possible."

"I know that, but if what Siasha is telling you is true, then there is a good chance this will work. I am a soldier and a dominant personality. This, Robert, was not a soldier; he was a peaceful man. Yes?"

"Yes, but he is a descendant of the X'ran, the most ferocious, war-loving people ever known and you are of the B'ran. There's no telling how the merging of an X'ran and B'ran would be tolerated in a single body. And even if it can be done, no one knows if the human body is capable of handling the personalities of two people. The one time it was tried it ended in disaster."

"We must risk it," Tawndo said.

"No!"

"Linkola," Siasha interrupted, "I don't like this idea any more than you do, but I think Tawndo might be correct. He is a dominate personality, a soldier, and from a warring race. However, he is a peaceful man and fully supports the L'gundo beliefs and culture.

"He is highly intelligent and will fully understand what is happening. Because of this, he will likely be able to maintain dominance and control over Robert until we can explain what has happened and he has a chance to adjust."

"And if he can't adjust?" Linkola shot back.

Siasha paused, then said quietly, "I suggest we destroy and remove his chip."

"You can't… possibly… be serious!" he said aghast.

"Quite serious. I believe Tawndo's intelligence would allow him to survive the separation, and that the possible damage to the brain could be repaired."

"You are *both* completely insane!" Linkola stated in undisguised terror. "And I will *not* be a party to any of it." He stormed out of the lab.

Siasha sat down at the table. "Well, that actually went better than I expected."

"Glad to hear it," Tawndo said with an uncertain look toward the door through which Linkola had exited.

"You do realize, don't you, that he is not exaggerating what happened in the experiment. This could kill you."

"Yes, I realize that, but there is no other way."

"Just how do you plan to contact the Rosslerites if we do successfully merge you with Robert?"

"I have been working on that with Korda. We will have Robert tell us who he thinks would be most likely of the Rosslers to respond to him and then we can project a holographic image of me to that person first and take it from there."

"It sure seems like there is an awful lot that can go wrong with this whole idea."

"There is, but we must risk it. If you have a better idea, then let me have it."

"Very well. I will speak to Linkola again after he calms down. In the meantime, how about a swim?" she asked slyly.

Tawndo read the message in her eyes, "I'd love it; lead the way!"

They left the lab together, hand in hand.

Siasha, seriously worried about how much longer she would have her beloved Tawndo with her.

Chapter Fifty-Six

SO MANY BIG BATTERIES

When Max arrived, almost two hours later, with Doug, Cliff and the two Tectus members in tow, Jack had already explored the tunnel leading to portals C and D. It was clear and usable, and both portal entrances were filled with concrete just as Nigel said.

While he explored the access tunnel, Stan and Aaron walked the entire circular tunnel that was the roadway for the site. One lane went in each direction with no cross tunnels. They guessed this was done to help maintain the structural integrity of the mountain rather than risk opening up the entire cavity.

Light and the sound of a light rail car moving along the tracks alerted them to the arrival of another of the monorail cars. The three stepped into the shadows and waited to see who had arrived.

Max stepped off the car first, and they all breathed a sigh of relief. Doug and Cliff followed, and then two unfamiliar men joined them on the platform.

Jack stepped forward greeting the men. "Welcome to Raven Rock guys."

Dennis whistled, "I've heard rumors about this place, but never thought I'd ever see it."

"As you know, Daniel intends to use this as a headquarters from where we will launch our operation to overthrow Hayden. We are here to secure it and get it operational before he arrives.

"That means checking every corner of this place, verifying the water is potable and that all support systems are functioning as they were designed to do.

"We need to split into four teams of two each and work as fast as we can while still being thorough.

"Max, you and Aaron start with the power plant on the far side. See if you can get it up and running, and then find the water reservoir. Test the water and make sure it's safe to drink and that the water treatment plant is functional. Then check the ventilation control system."

"Right," Max replied.

"Dennis, you and Cliff start by checking portals A and B, then move on to the power plant on this side. Make sure it's secure and check for any signs of damage that could indicate it might be non-functional. Then move on to buildings D and E. Search and secure them, every floor, every room, every closet. Got it?"

"Yes, sir!" Dennis said with a salute.

"Doug, Eric; you two take the strip mall. Again, search and secure every room inside.

"You got it, Jack," Doug acknowledged.

"Yes, sir!" Eric echoed with a smile.

"Stan and I will take buildings A and B. We'll meet you at building C, and the four of us will search it together. Any questions?"

When there were no questions, Jack dismissed them. "All right, let's get to it. We'll all meet at the entrance to building C when we're done."

Max and Aaron made their way quickly down the roadway to the left of the platform and turned to the right at their first opportunity. The map of the area provided by Daniel indicated that there was a freshwater reservoir ahead and to the left, and the West side power plant was straight ahead.

Aaron had expected to find a huge cavern with a small city inside. So far all he had seen were tunnels. "I'm beginning to feel like we should see Fred Flintstone and Barney Rubble any minute."

Max laughed. "This is a bit surreal, isn't it?"

"It's weird alright. It feels like a cave, but it doesn't smell quite like a cave exactly. It has a mechanical smell to it or something."

"Yeah, that's the paved roads and concrete along with the car and diesel exhaust that got trapped in here over the years. Their ventilation system worked good enough to keep them from being poisoned but didn't eliminate all the odor.

"They probably focused on the living area and didn't worry too much about the tunnels since they didn't expect foot traffic in them."

They came to a turn to the left but didn't see a power plant.

"Now what?" Aaron asked. "Where's the power plant?"

Max examined the wall for a few moments, then shown his light down the left tunnel followed by the right tunnel. He thought he saw an odd shadow in the tunnel to the right. "Let's go this way."

Aaron followed him, and in a few dozen steps they found a large rolling door on the left side of the tunnel. To their surprise, it opened easily, and they stepped inside. It was the control room to the power plant.

Aaron studied the control panels and workstations. "It's solar!" he exclaimed. "They must have one hell of a battery farm! Let's see!" He stepped through a door at the back of the control room and entered what resembled a long warehouse filled from floor to ceiling with rack after rack of huge batteries running the length of it.

Max stepped inside with him. "Wow. I've never seen anything like this!"

"It's amazing!" Aaron replied with excitement.

"Can you get it powered up?"

"From what I could see, the batteries are fully charged; let's give it a try."

Stepping back into the control room he flipped a switch that brought the instrument panel and computer to life. Once the computer booted up, it waited for a password.

Max took a small device out of his backpack, inserted it into the computer's 3.5-inch floppy drive and waited while it searched for the password.

"Wow! I can't remember the last time I saw a computer with a floppy drive!" Aaron said.

"Yeah, these computers are seriously out of date, nearly antique. It's a good thing Raj has a hobby of messing with old technology and thought of this scenario." The computer beeped and the screen changed, giving Aaron access to all the systems.

"First thing I'm going to do is change the password!" he grinned, doing just that.

It didn't take them long to figure out the system and get it up and running.

"We better check the generators and the diesel fuel levels just in case."

At the far end of the battery room was another door which opened to reveal eight large generators sitting side by side, four on each side of the room. At the back hung a regular looking fuel hose and nozzle, except the hose was long enough to reach all the generators.

"There must be a tank below the floor or in the ground behind it. But the gauge on the wall here says the tank is nearly full."

"That's good. We've done what we came here to do, let's move on."

They left the power plant and stepped out into a dimly lit tunnel.

"Well, the power is on. I guess they had the vehicles depend on their headlights."

"Probably. Come on," Max started off back the way they had come.

Like the power station, the entrances to the Water Treatment Plant and the Waste Water Treatment plant were simple roll up garage doors opening into equipment filled caverns in the rock.

Both facilities had been left in stand-by mode, and as soon as power was restored to them, they went back into operation.

Aaron checked the equipment in both locations, and announced they were operational. "We really need someone who knows about water treatment to verify both of these. I can vouch for the physical operation of the machinery, but I don't know anything about chemical levels and such that are actually used in the treatment process."

"Alright," Max said, "we'll make sure that is included as a request in our report. Let's test the water in the lake."

They continued to follow the tunnel which came to a sudden end on a wooden dock. There were lights around the dock, and a spotlight light shining out over the water, but visibility was limited. The cavern ceiling was less than fifteen feet high where they were standing and tapered off toward the waterline in the distance.

A small boat was laying upside down on the dock. Aaron flipped it over into the lake and got in. "I'm supposed to take the reading away from shore."

"Okay, be careful."

Aaron rowed to what he hoped was about the middle of the lake, retrieved the small test kit from his backpack and proceeded to perform the tests as he'd been instructed to. He carefully recorded the results in the log book he'd brought with him from the Water Treatment plant.

When he had finished, he noted that the boat had drifted more than he expected. "Hey! I think there's an underground river feeding this lake; there seems to be a current here."

"There'd just about have to be; either that or a spring, otherwise this water would be no good."

"I wonder how deep it is; it sure is cold," he said shaking his wet hand after rinsing the test container, "my hand is nearly numb!"

"Let's not find out right now, come on back."

"On my way," he said as he began rowing back to the dock. *Between the ultra-quiet, the dim light, the musty cave odor, and the echo, this place is eerie.*

They stored the little boat back on the dock and headed back into the tunnel.

Moving on to the ventilation control room, they found it already in operation. It too had powered up and started running as soon as the power was restored.

Aaron performed a quick check but didn't see anything suspicious or damaged and pronounced it functional.

"Okay, well done Aaron!" Max praised. "Let's see if we can find the others and lend a hand."

"Right behind you!" Aaron answered with a grin.

Walking back down the tunnel past the power station, they found another tunnel leading off to the left and followed it. When they stepped from it into the habitation area, Aaron stopped abruptly and stared. *This is more like what I had been expecting.*

A large parking lot lay before them in a massive cavern that had been opened in the granite. It was at least fifty feet high at the center and had five-foot-square columns of granite, floor to ceiling, at evenly spaced intervals to provide stability to the cavern ceiling.

Commercial street lights provided illumination for the parking lot and exteriors of the buildings—a city of perpetual night.

As they headed across the parking lot toward building C, Doug and Eric emerged from the west end of the mall.

"Did you find anything?" Max asked

"Empty buildings," Doug replied. "Thanks for getting the lights on, that helped a lot!"

"Anything for my buddies!" Aaron laughed.

Dennis and Cliff were waiting outside building C when they arrived.

"Find anything?" Max asked them.

"Nope; the blast doors were sealed, but the power station seems intact. I've never seen so many big batteries all in one place. Must be solar powered," Dennis replied.

"Yeah, it is!" Aaron replied excitedly. "Have you ever seen anything so amazing?"

Chapter Fifty-Seven

QUIETLY DOWN THE TUNNEL

Jack moved quietly down the tunnel, Stan a few steps behind them. Max and Aaron had moved away from the platform first and were already quite a way ahead of them.

When Max and Aaron disappeared into what they assumed was the power plant, Jack and Stan continued, turning left into another adjoining tunnel. Several yards into the new tunnel it turned sharply to the right, and within a few steps, they found they were no longer in the tunnel but in an area of blackness so vast their flashlight beams could not penetrate to the end.

"Stop," Jack commanded. "We can't go wandering off into that. According to Nigel's information, the buildings are to our left. We'll stay next to the wall and walk in that direction."

They'd gone no more than a few dozen steps when the glow of light appeared above them, and they were able to identify a parking lot to their right and several buildings ahead.

"Well, that will make things easier," Stan said.

"If it doesn't get us killed," Jack commented under his breath. Realizing how exposed they were if there were people in the cavern, he hustled Stan ahead of him toward the buildings at a fast pace.

Stan, suddenly realizing what Jack's concern was, broke into a run and arrived at the shadowy edge of the building alongside Jack.

"Building A," Jack said pointing at the square sign affixed to the side of the building above their heads. Looking around he said, "Let's go," and moved cautiously down the side of the building.

At the center, they found a covered entry way. Stan laughed quietly and shook his head. "Some things never change. Do you think they were expecting rain in here?"

Jack laughed with him. "Have to keep up appearances, my friend!"

They proceeded to enter the building and explore the first floor. Jack went down the first hallway to the right and Stan to the left. Thanks to JR's research, and Roy's and Raj's talents, they each had 'master key' of sorts that allowed them to enter each room.

After searching all the rooms in the first hallway, they moved to the next hallway and then up to the second floor where they found exactly the same layout. Each door opened to a modestly furnished studio apartment with a neutral color scheme and decorations. Some of the apartments had adjoining doors.

When they reached the third floor, they found one bedroom apartments with neutral color schemes just like the studios.

Satisfied that building A was empty, they moved on to building B where they expected to find a similar layout.

Instead, the ground floor of building B had a common

area with comfortable looking couches and chairs at one end, along with a couple of game tables. The middle, held tables and chairs set up like a large dining room, and at the far end, a large kitchen and buffet style cafeteria.

The kitchen had been cleaned and shut down in an orderly fashion, but everything was still in place: stoves, griddles, ovens, pots, pans, skillets, mixers, and toasters, etcetera, were all awaiting use.

Jack wiped his fingers along the counter top, noting the thick layer of dust. "The maid has apparently been on leave," he joked.

The second and third floors were identical to those in building A; studio and one bedroom apartments

Building C was again housing; studio and one bedroom apartments, on the first and second floors. In this building, the third floor contained two bedroom apartments.

"Guess they didn't have many families staying here ... must have been mostly singles."

"That and it is reminiscent of military barracks. Studios for the recruits, one bedrooms for the junior officers, and two bedrooms for the senior officers.

"Knowing the secrecy surrounding this place, I doubt anyone would be allowed to bring children in."

"Yeah, you're probably right."

"Well, let's go see what the others found."

Doug, Eric, Dennis, and Cliff all set off together, following the tunnel to the right of the platform. Shortly after it made a sharp bend to the left, they came to an intersection.'

"Nigel's drawings say portals A and B are this way," Eric

said pointing to the right. "I guess this is where Doug and I leave you."

"Watch for bears," Dennis teased, knowing of his friend's love and respect for the magnificent creatures.

"Don't worry, if there's one in here I'll have him so tame he can be my bunk-mate!" Eric responded with a grin.

Dennis laughed, "I'm sure you will!"

"See you guys at building C!" Eric said as he and Doug turned down the access tunnel to the portals.

They found the blast doors closed and were unable to open them. "Jack said the other blast doors were open and he was able to access the portal tunnels. I wonder why these are closed." Doug murmured.

Eric considered the question for a moment and found an answer. "They probably used one of the other portals as the final exit, so no one remained to shut it and then shut the power down."

"Why wouldn't they shut it, shut the power down, and then leave by the monorail system?"

"Either the monorail system didn't exist or come this far then, or only a few people knew about it, and they didn't want to let anyone know there was another, secret, access point to the facility."

"That makes sense," Doug nodded. "Well, let's see if we can find the power plant."

They turned back and followed the same tunnel Cliff and Dennis had taken but didn't see any sign of them.

Shortly after, they found a large rolling garage door on the right side of the tunnel. Although they didn't know it, it was identical to the one that Aaron and Max found.

When they compared notes with Aaron later, they would find that the two structures were identical.

Moving on through the tunnel, they came to another

tunnel off to the right just as dim light appeared overhead. "Hey! He got the power up!" Doug exclaimed.

"He sure did, and just in time too. This should be the tunnel to the housing area," Eric said.

They followed it a short way, made a sharp left and found themselves on the edge of a huge parking lot. "Wow!" Doug said astounded, "would you look at the size of this place!" as he ducked back into the shadowy cover of the tunnel.

They both knew the light made them moving targets if there were any hostiles in the cavern, so they proceeded with caution.

Eric sized up the situation and made his decision, "Okay, here's what we're going to do. You're going to cover me while I run to the first granite column, and then to the second. When I'm stopped at the second, I'll cover you while you move to the first column. Then I'll move again, leapfrogging until we reach building E."

"Got it," Doug said lifting his gun to the cover position. "Go!"

They reached Building E without incident. *Maybe there isn't anyone here.* Eric thought. *Better safe than sorry though.*

The entrance to building E was on the side facing building D. They made their way quickly to the entrance and, using the special key Roy had made, slipped inside.

The lobby area where they entered divided the ground floor evenly in two. One side they quickly discovered held site security and communications offices, a small efficiency kitchen, and a few general offices. The other side was a large conference hall and restrooms.

Examining the walls of the conference hall, Eric stated, "these walls are concrete block, probably reinforced with rebar and filled with more concrete. This area could easily be modified to house prisoners."

"That's good news!" Doug said

After discussing the possibilities for a few minutes, they agreed that constructing three cells along both the longsides of the hall so there was a central hallway made the most logical use of the space. Satisfied with the decision, they moved on to the second floor. In its prime, the area had been a top of the line command center with computer stations, large screens, telephones, and all sorts of electronic gadgetry.

"Wow, this would make a great museum display for a Cold War museum," Doug said.

Eric whistled softly, "Unbelievable."

The third floor appeared to be the communications hub for the command center. It was also filled with antiquated electronic equipment that had been state-of-the-art in its day.

"Man, the Smithsonian would have a field day if they knew all this existed!" Doug exclaimed.

Both men were still marveling at their discovery when they entered building D. They found the ground floor consisted of several meeting and conferences rooms, but they were quite elegant looking compared to those of building E, and great care had been taken in furnishing and decorating them.

Continued exploration of the rooms finally revealed a room that was unmistakably a Presidential situation room similar to what might have been found in the White House during the Cold War.

"I think we found the Presidential building," Doug said.

They completed their check of the ground floor and proceeded to the second floor where they found rooms for the housekeeping and kitchen staff, a good-sized kitchen, and a large dining room and living room with fine furniture, rich wood, paintings, thick carpeting and draperies hung as if to cover non-existent windows.

"Definitely Presidential," Doug said.

On the third floor, they found the Presidential suite. It was luxurious. The bedroom was huge; the bathroom had a large Jacuzzi in addition to a garden tub and a separate shower. The living room was comfortable and again, richly furnished; there was a large study, a small private gym, a movie theater room, and a room that must have been used as a salon and spa - it contained a barber's chair, a sauna, and a massage table.

"Rank sure doth have its privileges," Doug whispered.

"And the taxpayers pay for it, my boy," Eric said slapping him on the shoulder.

"Don't make me sick."

"It's true."

"I know. I just don't want to think about it. Do you know how many homeless people... Aw, don't get me started," Doug said. "C'mon. Let's go meet up with the others before I get really depressed."

Chapter Fifty-Eight

SECURE THE BOAT

Seaman Michael Sumner and Chief Petty Officer Perry Guinn hunkered down in the maintenance area at the bottom of the sub, under the maneuvering room three decks above them.

As soon as the 'secure the boat' order had been given they'd closed and locked the hatch that allowed access to the engine room.

When the order was given to surrender, they knew that the Council members would be searching the boat, rounding up the crew. They'd opened the engine room deck plate and crawled into maintenance area, securing the deck plate behind them and hoping that the Council member who searched the area wouldn't recognize it as a movable deck plate. As further insurance against detection, they'd opened and crawled through the water-tight hatch into the maintenance area they now occupied and waited.

"I haven't heard anything for hours," Sumner said. "I wonder what's happening."

"I think it's time we found out. Let's do some reconnoitering," Guinn suggested. "You go back through the engine room and see if you can get to the maneuvering room. They have to have someone working in there."

"I'm going to go through the battery room as well as the torpedo maintenance area and see if I can get near the control room, find out what's going on up there. Let's meet back here when we're done."

The two shook hands and went their separate ways.

Sumner gently raised the engine room deck plate, watching for nearby feet and listening for unusual sounds that would indicate the presence of someone in the room. After a time, feeling it was safe to emerge, he left his hiding place carefully and quietly replacing the deck plate.

He checked the room below the maneuvering room and found it empty of personnel. The air conditioning equipment hummed quietly without anyone watching over it. Knowing that if there were guards in the maneuvering room, they would most likely be faced forward because of the positioning of the equipment, he returned to the engine room and climbed the port side ladder to the platform that allowed access to the overhead lockout hatch for the mini subs they occasionally used.

Pressing himself tightly against the wall, he slid quietly next to the hatch to the room and listened.

He heard the familiar voices of two of his crewmates using standard communication for controlling the throttle to the turbines and the nuclear reactor. *There should be another crewman in there; where is he?*

"Did Brideaux say when he planned to have us relieved?" asked an unfamiliar voice.

"I didn't hear anything. I can cover these two for a few minutes; why don't you find someone to take your place?"

"Good idea. I'll send someone back shortly."

Sumner had heard enough for the moment and returned to the ladder, slid down it, landing as quietly as a cat. Moving stealthily back through the air conditioning room, he listened at the door to the reactor room. Hearing no voices, he peaked through the hatch; all appeared to be clear. He was down the stairs and across the floor of the reactor room in seconds.

Listening for a moment, he got control of his breathing then quietly ascended the ladder that accessed the auxiliary hatch to the upper deck and peered into the corridor that ran between the crew bunks to the lockout trunk. He jerked his head back. There were guards at both ends of the corridor. *They must have everyone confined to quarters.*

Deciding he'd discovered all he could, he retraced his path back to the engine room and was just securing the deck plate in place over the maintenance access when he heard someone crawling through the access hatch to the next compartment. He froze. *That better be Guinn!*

"Sumner? That you?" a voice whispered.

"Guinn?"

"Yeah, it's me."

"What did you find?"

"The Captain is in the control room with Brideaux and another guard. It sounded like the Captain may have been wounded and Brideaux is letting the doc up to check on him every so often. I think Sanders is the only pilot right now."

"That idiot is going to get us killed running into something!" Sumner exclaimed.

"I know. What did you find?"

"The crew is confined to quarters and under guard. The AC compartment and reactor room are clear; there are two crew members in the maneuvering room along with two guards.

"Okay. There are thirteen of them including Brideaux; two of them are in the maneuvering room, Brideaux and one other in the control room. That's four."

"I saw at least two guarding the crew on the upper deck, and there are probably some guarding the officers... maybe two there too. That's eight."

"What do you think the other five are doing?"

"I'm guessing they are probably in the mess and galley. Someone has to be making food, and they can't all stay awake all the time; sooner or later they're going to have to start trading off to get some sleep.

"Let's see if we can contain the two in the maneuvering room."

"With four of us and two of them we should be able to," Guinn said.

They climbed quietly back into the engine room and ascended the ladder to the access platform. Guinn stole a look into the room then whispered to Sumner where the two guards were.

They each identified which guard they were going to take and then on a quiet count of three they rushed into the room, tackled the guards and had them restrained almost before their comrades knew what was happening.

Reacting quickly, the two crew members swept up the guns and leveled them at the Council members who had guarded them.

Guinn and Sumner tied them up and were just dragging them toward the stairs to the engine room when Martinez walked through the doorway carrying a plate of sandwiches and pointing a gun at them. The four of them froze in their tracks.

Martinez grinned at the sight. "Are you boys hungry? I've brought some sandwiches. Looks like it's a good thing I picked up some extras!"

He kept the gun steady, stepped to the console, sat the plate down, and backed toward the door. Looking directly at Sumner and Guinn he said, "Make sure you have them tied well."

Their facial expressions changed to stupefaction. Martinez looked at the crewmen again, "And be ready; your crewmates are about to escape."

With that, he pocketed his gun, turned, and left the room.

Six men lay on their bunks in the small room they shared. The bunks were narrow with a shallow storage compartment beneath and stacked three high. Only three men could stand in the room at one time and then they could barely move. They were marveling at the strange turn of events that had come with lunch.

A knock had sounded on the door, and a voice had called out, "lunch!"

Seaman Yoder had climbed off his bunk and accepted the plate of sandwiches for all of them. He had been surprised when the man handed him a short stack of napkins that was stiffer than it should have been. He'd looked inquiringly at the man who had just winked and backed out of the room.

After handing the plate to his hungry roommates and examining the stack of napkins, he'd found a hastily scribbled note. "Guys! Look at this!" he'd whispered excitedly.

"That man just left us a note telling us how the guards are stationed, and that he's willing to help us!"

'Brideaux + 1 bridge, 2 maneuver, 2 crew, 1 officer, 6 sleep torpedo, I secure 6, be ready.'

"Why would he do that?"

"Maybe he has turned against Brideaux and wants him stopped as much as we do."

"Yeah, right," someone said sarcastically.

"No, it's possible," another voice spoke, "one of the prisoners has been very quiet and withdrawn the whole time he's been with us... the olive-skinned one with black hair and mustache."

"That's the one that brought us the sandwiches with this note!"

"So, we might have some inside help. Now, how are we going to use it?"

"If one of the guards is helping us and secures the six in the torpedo room, that leaves seven for us to subdue. We capture the two on this deck and leave them with our helper. Two of us take the one guarding the officers, one of us guards the control room in case Brideaux comes out, and three of us take the two in maneuvering. Once they're secured in the torpedo room with the others, we can take care of Brideaux."

"We need to let the others know what we know."

"How are we going to do that?"

"Easy. They don't pay any attention which rooms we go to. Next time we go for dinner, when we come back a couple of us can switch with guys from other rooms and then spread the word."

"That's only good for the three other rooms they allow us to eat with."

"Well, twenty-four of us knowing is better than just six of us; don't you think?"

"Sure, it is!" said someone else enthusiastically.

Chapter Fifty-Nine

GET DANIEL OUT HERE

Jack and Stan exited building C just in time to hear Aaron providing a brief lecture on the use and benefits of solar power.

"Buildings A, B, and C are empty. What did you find?"

Eric and Doug took turns reporting their discovery of the secured blast doors, the identical power center and the antiquated electronics in the command center.

"Building E also has a large conference hall on the ground floor. I think the walls are reinforced, so with a blow torch and some metal pipe, it would be fairly easy to build some holding cells for the prisoners," Eric reported.

"That's excellent!" Jack replied. "Once we get a report from Cliff and Dennis, you, Aaron, and I will take a look at the area and see what we can do."

Just as he finished speaking, Cliff and Dennis joined them.

"Did you two have any problems?"

"Nope," Dennis replied. "This place is amazing, though. It has just about everything anyone could need."

"What's over there?" Aaron asked excitedly.

"Well, there's a small six-lane bowling alley, a movie theater, and a barber shop," Dennis said.

"And a commissary that still has quite a bit of merchandise in it, plus a coffee shop complete with bakery and deli. It looks like they might have made hamburgers and things too," added Cliff.

Dennis continued, "there's also a fitness center with a swimming pool and tennis courts."

"And a small medical office," finished Cliff.

"No signs of anyone?" Jack inquired.

"No, I'd say this place hasn't seen a soul since it was abandoned," Dennis replied.

Jack decided to keep Nigel and Ester Harper's visits to himself.

"Okay," Jack said. "Let's get in touch with the team, give them a report, and make plans to get Daniel out here."

Max had the communication equipment set up and the conference call with the team at the Rabbit Hole, Daniel, and the Tectus team was underway.

"As we expected, the power plant is tied into the local power company; it has both solar and diesel generator backup. I was able to get it operating on solar power to avoid detection by the power company."

"Good job, Aaron!" Sam praised. "How long can we keep it running on solar?"

"I can't say, but it's only logical that the more power we draw, the faster the batteries drain, and it takes time to recharge them.

"I recommend we shut down all the power except in

buildings B, D and E. Building B has the cafeteria, common room and housing for our people. D is the Presidential building for Daniel, and building E has the command and communication center, as well as being the chosen location for holding the prisoners."

"Very well. Any objections to Aaron's recommendation?" When no one objected, Sam continued, "okay, Aaron. Shut down whatever you think isn't needed."

"One more thing Sam."

"What's that?"

"When you send the trucks in, put a good supply of LED rope lights and LED replacement bulbs for regular lights in one of them. LED lights will be much less of a power drain, and the rope lights we can use to light the path between buildings... as you might imagine, without any lights it's beyond dark in here."

"We can do that. How is the water situation?"

"I believe the water is safe to drink, but I'd feel better if we can run a proper test on it as soon as possible. We don't want to find ourselves incapacitated with dysentery.

"The reservoir is fairly large. The water is taken into the water treatment plant at the end closest to the buildings, treated and sent to the buildings for use. The gray water is sent through the waste water treatment plant at the far end before it is returned to the lake."

"Yuck!" Several voices shouted in chorus.

"It's not like that guys. It's actually cleaner water than any waste water treatment plant can ever produce." Aaron explained.

"The process of recycling of wastewater and sewage to turn it into potable, drinkable, water is older than most of us. In Windhoek, the capital of Namibia in Africa, the process has been in operation since 1968; it's also been in use in some places here in the USA since the seventies and in many other countries."

"And just to help you get over it, the water we have here is only used as sink and shower water. The toilets are incinerator toilets, so all that stuff is dealt with differently. It's burned to a sterile ash and then removed about every six months.

Sam swallowed hard and changed the subject. "What about getting the supply trucks in?"

Jack took over. "Since the blast door for the D and C portals is already open, I suggest we cut an opening through D portal and bring them in. There is plenty of room in the parking lot for them until they are needed again.

"I don't want to leave the portal open, though; we'll work on a way to close it up again."

Daniel spoke up, "I suggest a false brick wall. There was one blocking the entry to the escape tunnel we used to get out of the White House. It was the face of concrete blocks that matched the wall, mounted on plywood."

"We'd want it to match the look of the other portal," Aaron said. "It's a solid concrete wall, so a thin layer of concrete on plywood ought to do it."

"We could use holographic imaging to hide it as well," Roy added. "It wouldn't be hard to tap the solar power supply to power a couple of stationary imagers to make it look like a solid wall of concrete."

"Great idea, Roy!" Jack said. "Can you have them ready to send out with the second team?"

"Unless they're leaving today, I don't see why not."

"The plane is due back tomorrow and has another pickup in Washington three days later, so you should have plenty of time," Sam reassured him. "We'll send the second team of medical, technical, and support personnel out in two days."

"When can we expect the trucks?" Daniel asked.

"My team in Washington is handling that," Eric spoke up. "Two trucks of food and medical supplies, plus your other requests, will arrive in four days."

"We're not taking supplies destined for starving people, are we?" Daniel asked, concerned.

"No, Daniel, Tectus members had a stockpile in their homes and warehouses throughout the city before things went south. We are drawing from those supplies.

"And before you ask, Tectus all over the country have these stockpiles and are using them as needed to help those in their community."

Daniel smiled. He really liked these Tectus teams. "That is great to hear Eric, thank you! And please, thank your teams for their efforts!"

"You got it Daniel, err, Mr. President," Eric responded, and the others started laughing.

"You had it right the first time Eric. It's Daniel to you," Daniel smiled.

Sam grinned, "Alright everyone, is there anything else?" No one spoke up, so he continued after a brief pause, "ok then, in two days, JR, Raj, Roy, Rebecca, Secretary of State Bill Sims, and Elize will join you at RRMC."

Chapter Sixty

GET US TO THE SURFACE!

Brideaux paced the deck of the control room becoming more and more agitated by the minute. Muttering to himself he looked at the monitors although they were meaningless to him; he stared over the helmsman's shoulder at the controls and monitors - also meaningless.

"I've had enough of this," he exploded turning to Captain Locklin. "Get us to the surface!"

"Not possible; there's too much ice over us."

"Don't lie to me. I've seen pictures of subs stuck up through the ice."

"Yes, I'm sure you have, probably in movies and definitely not in this part of the ice canopy. The ice is too thick here to surface through it."

"You're lying. Surface this ship. Now."

"It won't work, Brideaux. We could surface through ice as thick as six feet, but it's more than twenty feet here."

"I don't believe you, and I don't care. Get this ship to the surface. *Now!*" Brideaux shouted.

"Please wait until we're closer to the edge of the ice canopy or you'll kill us all!"

Brideaux grabbed the helmsman, violently twisting his arm causing it to snap. The helmsman cried out in pain and swung at Brideaux who reacted by knocking the man to the floor, unconscious. He pulled his gun to shoot the man.

"Brideaux!" Locklin yelled.

Brideaux spun in surprise, bullets flying from the gun in his hand, and pieces of glass and plastic rained down on Locklin who dove to the deck.

Leveling the gun at Locklin's head Brideaux spoke through clenched teeth, "never yell at me, Captain; next time it will cost you your life."

"You have to quit killing and injuring people, otherwise you won't have anyone left that knows how to run this boat."

"Then get someone up here who can surface this boat or I swear I will kill every man on board and you will be begging for death long before we die together," Brideaux was shaking with rage.

"Have Lieutenant Copeland sent up," Locklin ordered.

Kicking his guard who had also taken refuge on the deck, Brideaux ordered "take that lump," he pointed to the helmsman, "out of here and bring back Copeland… on the double!"

When the guard returned with Lieutenant Copeland, and Locklin told him they were going to surface on Brideaux's orders, Copeland looked at Brideaux, "Are you out of your mind? The ice is too think here; we'll never get through."

"How the hell do you manage to function with a crew that questions your every order?" Brideaux snarled at Locklin.

Locklin chose not to answer. "Get ready to blow the tanks Copeland, and hold on to your ass."

"Aye, sir. Holding onto my ass," Copeland said dismally.

"Before you blow the tanks, sound the collision alarm and make sure you have something to grab hold of."

"Aye."

Locklin sat down at the helm and prepared to brace himself. "Alright, blow the tanks!"

Copeland pressed the button to sound the alarm and pulled the levers that would rapidly blow air into the ballast tanks.

The sub surged forward and up, rapidly gaining speed as it ascended.

Chapter Sixty-One

NO, ABSOLUTELY NOT

Before leaving the Rabbit Hole, Daniel asked Nigel's advice about the people to appoint to the Cabinet. He knew he wanted to keep the members Laurie had appointed or trusted to keep, add Salome as head of Homeland Security if she would agree, and fill the rest of the positions with experienced, trustworthy people.

Nigel had made suggestions of three people for each open position and helped Daniel pull résumés on all of them.

Daniel made his decisions and was ready to send teams out to collect the currently serving members and the newly chosen ones and bring them to RRMC for protection until they could oust Hayden.

Upon arrival at Raven Rock, Daniel was taken to the Presidential Suite. He found the accommodations luxurious, too luxurious—he wanted to be with his team who were being housed in building C. He had always been part of the team, and it was not going to be different now.

"No, absolutely not. I won't be staying here." He said when the agents wanted to unpack his bags in the suite.

The two agents stared at Daniel, not quite sure what to make of the situation. "Please, Mr. President; these are the Presidential quarters. They are designed and set up with your privacy and protection in mind."

"I said no," Daniel replied tightly, in a low voice. "I will not stay in such extravagance and be separated from the rest of the team!"

"But, sir, your safety…"

"Is not in question here," Daniel interrupted. "These are my friends and teammates. I will stay in regular housing with them and eat my meals with them. Is that clear?"

The agents looked at one another in consternation. "Yes, sir," they replied together in submission but clearly not happy about it.

"Look, I'm not trying to make your job harder," Daniel spoke in a friendlier tone. "If we were outside this facility it would be different, but there isn't anyone on this team that I wouldn't trust with my life, and that includes the two of you. I will be fine with them."

"As you wish sir." With reluctance, the agents accepted his choice of a one-bedroom apartment on the third floor and appreciated that he at least let them have rooms on either side of him with the teams sharing the apartments directly across from him.

Anyone else coming in would be housed on the second floor, so they were satisfied that they had a measure of security around him.

Aaron felt sorry for the lambasted agents, but he knew his brother. He meant no disrespect to them; Daniel was just not the type of leader who led from the rear. He wanted to be in the thick of things.

As soon as this was settled and Daniel's bags were unpacked in the apartment, he accompanied Eric, Aaron, and Jack to view the holding cells for the prisoners which had been hastily constructed from materials found at the site.

At the back of several of the buildings, shrouded in darkness, Aaron had found stacks of metal and PVC pipe, lumber, concrete blocks, bricks, wiring, and other building materials. He'd seen a machine and maintenance closet in the West power building and raided it, producing torch welders, masonry drills, bolts, hammers, and nails.

With the help of Jack and a few others, Aaron had constructed six 8x10 holding cells, each complete with a table, chair, and bed confiscated from apartments in building C.

Chapter Sixty-Two

FINDING THE TREPANG

At dinner, the second night after Daniel arrived at Raven Rock, Cliff looked across the table at Daniel as dessert was placed before them. "You know what I wish I had? A Snow Cone. I really miss Snow Cones. I haven't had one in ages."

Nodding at Cliff, he said, "I know what you mean."

Daniel calmly finished his cake then got up to leave the table, "please excuse me, and continue to enjoy your meal."

Cliff followed Daniel with his eyes for a moment and then got up himself and made his way through the room, stopping briefly to speak with one person and another. After casually circling the room once, he wandered through the exit into the hall in time to see Daniel enter an office a few doors down.

Casting his eyes along the hallway in both directions, making certain he was alone, he followed Daniel, paused at the door to check the empty hallway again, and then entered the room where Daniel was waiting.

"What's happened?" Daniel asked without preamble.

"Mr. President, the Trepang missed her last two scheduled contacts. We have to assume something has gone wrong," Cliff reported.

"There could be any number of reasons for that. Is that not true?" Daniel responded.

Cliff nodded. "But the fact that we haven't had a signal from them in the last twelve hours is disquieting, sir. If they had technical problems, I would like to believe that they would have been able to resolve it within that time."

"Okay. I hear what you're saying, but there's not much we can do at the moment. Is there? It's not as if we are able to send another sub, or any vessel for that matter, to go and look for them?"

"Yes, sir. Unfortunately, thanks to General Hayden, that's the painful position we are in right now."

"It's agonizing and infuriating," Daniel said. "Do you think we might be able to get someone in the Navy, in control of one of the submarines to go rogue and go looking for the Trepang?"

"That's one option, sir…"

"We know the coordinates from where they were the last time they made contact don't we?"

"Yes, sir; that's correct."

"What about sending in a team of Navy SEALs on a commercial vessel?"

"That's a possibility sir, but the Trepang is traveling around on a preset course under the polar icecap, specifically to avoid detection. It's not going to be possible to get close to them with anything but another sub. Even if we could airdrop a team of SEALS, they will somehow have to get through the ice."

Daniel shook his head. "I'm not ready to give up on them Mr. Secretary. There has to be a way, or we will *make* a way. I don't care a hoot about Brideaux and his fellow prisoners, except maybe for Rafael Martinez, but as for the rest of them... well, let me rather not go there.

"My only concern is for Captain Reese Locklin and his crew. We *must* do everything humanly possible to rescue them, that's if they need rescuing."

"My sentiments exactly Mr. President."

Daniel paced thoughtfully for a moment, "Why don't you contact Admiral Johnson and see if he has any ideas on what we can do to find and help them?

Willis smiled. "Actually, sir, I anticipated your request and have already been in touch with him by brief code. This situation is need-to-know and face-to-face only as you know.

"And?"

"His response was very brief; 'confirmed, David.'"

Daniel raised his eyebrows and spoke incredulously, "what the hell is *that* supposed to mean?"

"To anyone else who might hear it, absolutely nothing. To me, it means that he is aware of the matter and wants me to meet him at Camp David.

"At least it's close; how soon?"

"As soon as we can both get there. I'll leave immediately and wait for him. With the dusk to dawn curfew in place, he may not be there until early tomorrow morning."

"Alright. Please let him know that we have former military people who would be willing to provide assistance and safe houses available for meetings if needed."

"I will."

"Very good; I'll be waiting. And Cliff, before you go, stop and see Raj or Roy. Tell them you need to keep a meeting top secret and have them give you one of our special pens and show you how to use it. Better safe than sorry, even if it is at Camp David."

"Will do," Cliff said and quietly left the room.

Cliff stepped into the living room of the Camp David house and was surprised to see Admiral Johnson sitting on the couch studying a map laying on the coffee table before him.

"Good evening Admiral," he greeted as he sat down.

"Good to see you Mr. Secretary," Johnson responded.

"How did you get here so fast?"

"I left as soon as I sent the message and managed to get out of town before dusk. I brought along some night vision goggles so I could drive with the headlights off for the last bit."

"Smart. So, what's the situation?"

"Here, have a look," Admiral Johnson invited, gesturing to the map before him.

Willis sat down looking at a map like he'd never seen before. It was mostly blue with white and tan areas. He looked at Johnson, "what's this? It isn't like any topographic map I've ever seen."

"It's a bathymetric map of the ocean floor in the Arctic. Similar to a topo but this one shows the ocean floor relief with the depth notation instead of elevation above sea level.

"The last ping originated from here," Johnson said indicating an area near the middle of the map, "just after they crossed over the Spitsbergen Fracture Zone and were about to enter the Barents Plain at the South-East end of the Nansen Basin." Johnson indicated the location of each of the places as he named them.

"Their next ping location was supposed to be here, as they crossed over the Nansen Ridge and were entering the Fram Basin."

"Has there been any intelligence at all as to their whereabouts?"

"No, nothing. As far as anyone knows that sub is in drydock as scheduled."

"Any ideas on how we find her?"

"That's the big problem. With Hayden in control of the military, I can't use our detection system or satellites to try to locate her.

Thinking of what he has learned about the incredible abilities of the Rossler technical team, Willis was inclined to believe *they* could probably locate the missing sub themselves.

"Admiral, with your permission, I would like to bring a few of President Rossler's top team members in on this. They may be able to locate her for us without anyone else knowing, and they are one hundred percent trustworthy. President Rossler is very concerned about the disappearance of the sub and anxious to find her."

The Admiral raised his eyebrows, "Do they have that kind of equipment?"

"I don't know *what* kind of equipment they have, but they were able to bring Brideaux down *and* shut down all his operations, worldwide, within a few hours. I desperately want to believe they are capable of locating a submarine ... especially when we have a general idea of where to start looking."

"Good point," Johnson agreed. "Alright Mr. Secretary, we don't have much of a choice. Let's bring in the Rossler people, but keep it limited to as few as possible and let's continue with the need-to-know and face-to-face communication. When they find her, I want to meet with you and the team to discuss interception, rescue, and recovery scenarios. We won't know exactly what is needed until we find her."

Johnson folded the map and handed it to Willis. "You know the route they were taking. I suggest they start looking for the sub in the Fram Basin and then the Makarov Basin. If they don't find it there, have them look back at the Norwegian Sea and the area along the East Coast of Greenland and Iceland. If Brideaux or his Council members somehow got loose, Captain Locklin may have been forced to turn the sub back."

"That's not a pleasant thought, Admiral."

"A nightmare is what I'd call it."

"Alright, I'll take this information to the President, and we'll get the team working on it."

"Mr. Secretary?"

"Yes?"

Pausing briefly in consideration, Johnson finally said, "Let them know that I am ... overseeing a project ... that has produced something that may be able to get us to the sub without Hayden knowing about it ... but they have to find it first."

"I'll do that."

Looking at his watch, Johnson said, "I'm heading back to town, it will be dawn by the time I reach the outskirts."

The two men shook hands, and Johnson stepped through the door into the cool, early morning air.

"I hope to hear from you very soon Mr. Secretary."

"You will, Admiral."

Cliff caught Daniel's eye across the room and nodded. Daniel nodded covertly in return and excused himself from the breakfast table.

Daniel stopped to refill his coffee cup and filled a second

one to take with him. When he entered the room where Cliff was waiting, he handed him the coffee.

"You look like you could use a cuppa joe."

Cliff grinned. "Thank you, sir! I certainly can!"

"Good! I've done my good deed for the day! Now, how did your meeting with Admiral Johnson go?"

Cliff spread the map on the table and explained to Daniel what Johnson had told him about the last known contact with the sub.

"The Admiral can't use his normal resources to look for the sub because of Hayden, so I recommended that we bring your team on board to help us find it."

"Good thinking! What did he say?"

"He agreed, but he's very cautious. He wants as few people as possible involved and insists that this remain on a need-to-know and face-to-face communication basis."

Daniel nodded. "That shouldn't be too much of a problem."

"He also suggested that if your team can find the sub, he may have a way of getting a team out to her without Hayden's knowledge."

"How?" Daniel asked, surprised.

"He didn't elaborate, just mentioned it might be possible."

Daniel drew a deep breath and let it out. "Ok, let's get going on this. Let's start by bringing in Raj and Roy, between the two of them they can do just about anything with technology.

"Find them and discreetly let them know I have a special project for them that they are to keep to themselves. We'll meet in Roy's office in thirty minutes; you will brief them and then we'll see what they think can be done."

"I think we could probably be there in ten minutes."

"I'm sure you could, but I want you to take a bit of time to get some breakfast ... I'm betting you've been up all night and haven't had anything to eat."

"You're right," Cliff said sheepishly. "Breakfast sounds good. We'll meet there in thirty minutes!"

Raj and Roy listened carefully as Cliff outlined the situation.

"So, you want us to try and locate her," Roy said, nodding his understanding.

"That's the idea, yes," Cliff responded. "Can you do it?"

Raj piped up, "I can hack into the military's satellites and ..."

Cliff cut him off, "No. Because of the risk of Hayden finding out, we have to do this outside of the usual resources."

"That's a different story," Raj replied frowning. "Roy?"

Roy's eyes were unfocused, his expression flat, and he didn't respond.

"Roy?" Raj snapped his fingers, "you ok?"

Roy jumped, "What? Oh, yeah. If she's deep, satellites won't find her anyway. I don't know the full capability of the Skywalker satellites. I was wondering if they might be able to search for her?"

"Skywalker satellites?" Cliff asked.

"Long story for another time," Daniel answered. "Can the two of you, using our technology and resources, start searching for the sub?"

"Sure!" Roy said.

Cliff grinned. "Good!" He opened the map Johnson

had given him and showed the two men the subs last known position and provided Johnson's recommendations on where to start looking.

"We'll get right on it!"

"Okay, guys put your people to work on this and then please join us in the situation room so we can get busy with getting rid of Hayden," Daniel ended the meeting.

Chapter Sixty-Three

TUCK AND ROLL

With the spy gadgets successfully deployed throughout the White House, the information started flowing in quickly. It was their first meeting in the RRMC situation room, Daniel chaired. There was a general feeling of excitement in the air as they gathered. Joining them via the mirror satellite video link were the rest of the leadership team at the Rabbit Hole, as well as Eric and Dennis from the Tectus headquarters.

As soon as everyone was seated, Roy, who was controlling the spy gadgets from his laptop, started. "Let's begin by introducing you to all of Hayden's top players. They all happen to be in a meeting as we speak and our spy gear has provided us with front row seats."

With that, the large monitors in the room came to life revealing a picture of the White House cabinet room occupied by Hayden and seven men.

Roy made an adjustment to one of the controls on the panel before him and focused on a short, bald man wearing wire-rimmed glasses whose rounded cheeks suggested a portly body. He nodded at Salome.

"This is Hayden's Attorney General and Secretary of State, Lieutenant General Kurt Frayser," Salome started. "He was an Army JAG officer and studied International Law. He and Hayden go way back. Evidence suggests he is probably responsible for keeping Hayden out of trouble and in the Army as he protected Hayden from being disciplined several times in his early career."

The focus shifted to another face. "This is Hayden's most trusted confidant and friend, General Lucas Nguyen. The two were boyhood friends, graduated high school together, attended West Point together, and although their military careers took different paths, they have remained trusted friends.

"Nguyen is highly regarded in the military intelligence field, and Sam suggested he should be our first target for abduction when the time comes."

"What office did Hayden assign him to?" Daniel asked.

"Secretary of Defense as well as Transportation, Energy, and Homeland Security… which now heads the FBI, CIA, and NSA."

Daniel whistled softly, "top dog indeed."

"Yes," Sam confirmed, "and most likely to be a thorn in our side, which is why I suggest we take him out first."

"Good thinking," Daniel nodded.

Returning to the screen, Roy focused on a tall man, with thick blond hair and blue eyes. He appeared somewhat younger than the previous two men.

Salome continued. "This is Colonel Howard Baum, Hayden's Secretary of Interior and Agriculture. He served under Hayden in Afghanistan and earned Hayden's trust and respect. As did," the screen shifted again to a man of average height, wavy red hair and blue eyes, "Colonel

Cameron Stillwater, Hayden's new Secretary of Housing and Labor.

"Hayden rolled the Secretary of Health, Education, and Veterans Affairs into one office and appointed this man, General Joe Potter, to the position." The picture shifted to show a gangly looking man with dark hair whose appearance belied his talent as a surgeon. "Potter is also a West Point graduate, and although two years behind Hayden, the two formed a friendship based on common interests and ideals.

"Last, but not least, Brigadier General Stephen Neeley has been appointed Secretary of Treasury and Commerce. Neeley was a black-market operator in Vietnam and friends with Hayden since those days. Frayser also aided in shielding him from disciplinary measures from time to time."

"And Hayden appointed him Secretary of Commerce and Treasury? That's like sending the fox to guard the henhouse!" Luke objected.

"Pretty much," Sam agreed.

"Roy, can you and Raj give us a quick live demo of what those spyders can do? But only if you are sure it won't compromise our spy gadgets," Sam asked.

Roy and Raj beamed like children opening their Christmas presents and went to work.

Everyone watched as Hayden sat his pen down. It rolled to the edge of the table and fell on the floor. Hayden frowned as he picked it up and sat it back on the table at a different angle.

Once again, the pen rolled to the edge and fell. Picking it up again, he sat it further away from the edge and watched it for a bit while listening to the reports being given. The pen remained still. When Hayden looked away, it began to roll toward the center of the table. Hayden grabbed it and stuck it in his pocket.

Everyone in the situation room at Raven Rock and the Rabbit Hole chuckled at the look of consternation on Hayden's face. A few moments later, Hayden noticed his tablet had moved; he looked worried when he rose hastily and called an abrupt end to the meeting.

Nigel shook his head in amazement. "Hayden, that fall off your high horse is going to be a bitch... I suggest you tuck and roll."

Chapter Sixty-Four

TURN YOUR MEN LOOSE

Lieutenant Larson stared at the piece of paper which had been stuffed in the napkin that came with the plate of sandwiches. "Would you take a look at this?" he said to the other two officers in the room. Like the crew's quarters, their bunks were stacked three high, but there were only three of them instead of six, so they had a little more room.

"What's that you've got?"

Larson read the same information that Seaman Yoder read to his bunk-mates just minutes earlier.

"Well, what do you know about that!"

"Do you really think we can trust him?"

"I don't see why not. I also don't see that we have other options."

"Let's plan this and do it right."

At that moment came a bone breaking lurch and the sound of screeching metal.

Picking himself up, Larson tried to run out the door to the control room but was stopped by a Council member with a gun.

"I need to get to my station."

"You will remain in your quarters."

"You don't understand. We've hit something and may be in trouble. I'm needed in the control room."

"You will remain in your quarters or I will shoot you."

Larson fumed but stepped back inside and shut the door. A few minutes later, the Council member outside announced that his cabin-mate was to report to the Captain.

Shortly after his departure, Larson heard a quiet thud outside the door, then it opened again, and one of the Council members stood before him offering him a gun, butt first. He pointed to the ladder to the upper deck, and with a finger to his lips he said, "there is only one left; go, quickly."

Larson didn't hesitate, although he wanted to, he stepped over the body outside the door and looked at the council member who gave him the gun.

"He will recover," the man said. "Turn your men loose; they're in their quarters."

Larson stepped to the ladder and quietly began climbing. Reaching the top, he stepped into an empty alcove and peered down the corridor. A guard leaned lazily against the wall about twenty feet from him, looking the other way. Moving like lightning, Larson threw the man on the ground and pinned him down.

Hearing the commotion in the corridor, several crew members peeked out their door and then came to his aid.

Chapter Sixty-Five

TO FIND A POSITIVE SOLUTION

When Siasha returned to the lab, she found Linkola standing before the Itran unit, pointing a small hand-held laser weapon at it.

"Linkola! What are you doing?"

He spun around, pointing the weapon at her. "Don't try to stop me Siasha."

"You can't do this, Linkola!"

"I can, and I will."

"But why? Nothing has been decided yet!"

"As long as the possibility remains, the argument will continue. I will not be a part of another test to merge individuals."

"Linkola, you're a scientist; you live to learn and discover. You're a logical man. Don't let emotion control you."

"I once was a scientist, but no longer," he said sadly. "I've become a murderer."

"What are you talking about?"

"I killed them, the two men in the test."

"What?"

"*I* killed them. *I* should have destroyed the equipment, and I didn't, and so the two men died... needlessly and horribly—because of me."

"Linkola, I'm not following you. Please," Siasha begged, "can we just sit down and talk about this?"

"No, I am going to destroy the equipment, but I'll tell you why first. Perhaps it will help to ease my guilt-ridden conscience and bring me some peace if I tell someone the truth."

Siasha decided that arguing with him would get her nowhere. "Okay, Linkola," she said as she slowly backed away and sat down, "I will listen." She was relieved to see his shoulders and face muscles relax a bit.

"What isn't in that report," he began, "is that there was a previous test that ended much the same way. After reviewing the data, I wrote the report and told the team the merger process wouldn't work, but they wouldn't listen."

"But the research says..."

"I know what the research says!" he yelled. "I wrote it! But you are looking at a report written under coercion. This," he held up a data chip, "this is the real report, the true report.

"They wanted to continue the experiments, try again, so they suppressed my report and forced me to write the one you read, suggesting that the merge is possible."

"Are you saying the report I read was false? Why would you write a false report?"

Linkola was visibly shaking now. At first, I refused. But they killed my wife," he cried. "When I continued to refuse, they brought in my brother and his little girl. They started to torture his little girl right in front of us," Linkola began to sob. "What they were doing was terrible. I couldn't let it continue - the screams - the begging of that innocent little girl," he sank to the floor.

"They were using my research. I killed them!" he said as the tears continued flowing down his cheeks, wracked with guilt. "I killed them."

Siasha went to his side. "I'm so sorry, Linkola. That is a terrible burden you've been carrying," she soothed as she pocketed the weapon that had fallen from his hand.

Linkola gradually quieted, and Siasha helped him to stand and move to a chair.

"I can't go through that again, Siasha," he whispered, "I won't allow it to happen again."

"I understand," she said. "I promise you; I don't want to see anything like what you described. And yes, it may have been your research, but it is they who chose to use it so despicably. You were not to blame."

"I should have destroyed the equipment."

"Maybe, but they might have just killed you and re-built the equipment. We will never know. Playing with the 'should haves' and 'what ifs' will only continue your pain, Linkola. You must try to let them go."

"I don't know that the memory of that day will ever stop haunting me."

"It may not, but we need to find a way to bring you peace. Did they conduct a third experiment?"

"Not that I know of."

"Okay. I'll tell you what. This has troubled you for some time, and you are full of guilt and grief over it. How about you and I sit down together, study your original findings and then look for some other solution?"

"There is no other solution," he said angrily. "Weren't you listening? The merge of two identities isn't possible and never will be!"

"Yes, Linkola, I heard what you said, and I'm not talking about finding a way to merge Tawndo and Robert. I'm talking about perhaps finding a way to access Robert's memories to know who to contact at the Rossler Foundation, or perhaps finding a totally different way of dealing with the Re'an issue."

"Sorry. I didn't mean to snap at you," Linkola said.

"It's okay. You are a good scientist, and I know you don't want to see anyone suffer or die. We will work together to find a positive solution. Okay?"

Linkola nodded, "okay."

Chapter Sixty-Six

ARE WE CLEAR?

Salome and her Intelligence Committee kept Daniel and the team at Raven Rock well-informed of the political sentiment in the country during their daily intelligence briefings. Part of the briefing covered the information gathered from the White House through the spy gear deployed there.

The information gathered by the spy gear immediately highlighted several major problems Hayden had.

First of all, his staff feared him; it was abundantly clear that the man had a serious lack of people skills. He terrorized his staff and even his cabinet with his brusqueness, disrespect, and frequent temper tantrums. The spyflies and spyders picked up a number of privately whispered conversations about Hayden's insufferable mannerisms. It was just a matter of time before people would turn against him and start leaving him.

Second, was the lack of security. He had less than a third of the number of Secret Service Agents who protected any of his predecessors. Hayden had tried his level best to track down all of the Secret Service Agents who served before and lure them back to the service. He had very little success. Many former agents knew him from the time when he served as the Secretary of Defense and therefore refused to work for him. Many of them who were desperate enough to take any job that would put food on the table for their families turned his offer down once they spoke to the agents already in his service.

Compliments of Roy's and Raj's spy gear it became abundantly clear that there was growing disgruntlement in the ranks of the Secret Service agents. Hayden and his cabinet treated them like children, and quite a few of them had voiced their intentions to resign as soon as they could find other employment.

Hayden had no choice but to resort to the military for his protection. The problem was those recruits had no training and only caused more of a burden for the already overloaded Secret Service agents who now had to look out for the recruits as well.

The third issue was Hayden's biggest headache—his rapidly declining approval rating. He and his military cabinet, or 'junta' as the media started calling them, were not able to deliver on his promises. Some of the media outlets started running a 'Dissatisfaction Barometer" and updated it daily. It was heading in one direction only — up.

His seventy-five percent approval ratings had already plummeted to below fifty.

His cabinet tried to persuade him to walk back some of his promises, to start managing expectations but Hayden would not heed their advice.

For the populace, the situation became more and more desperate by the day. The promised food trucks never arrived, millions of families were without food, water, electricity, and other basic needs. More promises were made, but the crowds quickly realized that's all it was—promises.

And they had no choice but to return to the way they survived during John Brideaux's reign—stealing, looting, and killing if necessary - whatever it took to survive.

In one of the cabinet meetings, Hayden exploded in a rage when one of the members brought the matter of the growing dissatisfaction and civil unrest up again.

"That's the problem, you idiot! Can't you see it? That's what's wrong with this country, people have no discipline, no respect for authority. What they need is a heavy hand… order. What we are going to do now is deploy the National Guard and the military in support of the police, and we are going to restore law and order.

"You all remember Napoleon Bonaparte, don't you? He brought an end to the chaos caused by the hysterical masses during the French Revolution when he issued his troops live ammunition and ordered them to clear the streets of Paris.

"That gentlemen are exactly what we're going to do. For God's sake, we have martial law, let's use the powers we have. Forget about rubber bullets, water cannons, and tear gas."

"Lucas, you're the Secretary of Defense, Transportation, Energy, and Homeland Security. You have the FBI, CIA, and NSA at your disposal. Why haven't you taken care of this problem?"

On the display screens at Raven Rock and the Rabbit Hole, the spectators watched as the color drained from Nguyen's face. "I… I… didn't want to interfere with police matters, sir. But if it is your wish…"

"Well, now you know what my wish is. No wait, let me be more succinct, I'm ordering you to restore order, and I am ordering you to use live ammunition."

"Mr. President," General Joe Potter, Secretary of Health, Education, and Veterans Affairs started, "I'm afraid those kinds of measures are going to alienate the people even more. I..."

"Joe, listen carefully." Hayden interrupted him. "This is not a democracy; this is martial law. The reason why we have Martial Law is that we have a crisis. In a time of crisis, it is sometimes necessary to take drastic steps. That is exactly what we are going to do right now.

"Oh, and by the way, I am not asking for anyone's opinion about this—I'm issuing an order, and I expect it to be followed; to the T. Are we clear?

The cabinet members nodded. They were all clear about that, but very few of them agreed. However, they were soldiers, and soldiers followed orders, they did not question them.

"This meeting is over."

Chapter Sixty-Seven

YOU'RE GOING TO REGRET IT

Listening to Hayden's exchange with his cabinet filled the audiences at Raven Rock and the Rabbit Hole with revulsion.

"We have to stop that lunatic before he fills the streets of this country with the blood of innocent people," Daniel whispered.

"No 'ifs, and's, or buts' about that Daniel." Sam concurred while the others nodded in agreement. "Let's make an assessment of our readiness right away."

Daniel nodded for Sam to continue.

"Salome's psychological warfare team is satisfied that they have enough surveillance in place to kick-off the first phase of psychological warfare.

"Jack's team is ready to start 'disappearing' Hayden's cabinet members."

Speaking via the secured phone to Kerinski and the man called 'Mouse' in the tunnels below the White House, Sam asked, "Is everything in place to start removing Hayden's men?"

"Yes, sir!" Mouse replied eagerly. "We know Nguyen's routine. He always leaves through the West Wing. We'll be waiting for him and transport him by wheelchair to the monorail and on to RRMC."

"Good. Make it happen at the first opportune moment. As soon as he is taken care of, we'll let you know who's next." Jack ordered and ended the call before turning to Roy for his report.

Roy grinned evilly as he activated the big screen so everyone could see. "Watch this!"

On one screen was the view from the spy fly riding on Hayden's shoulder while he was moving alone toward the Oval Office, while another screen showed the closed door from inside the Oval Office.

When he opened the door, Hayden saw a very relaxed Laurie Campbell sitting calmly behind his desk. He froze. His faced paled, and he breathed "what the hell?" Speaking louder he said "What... no... you're... you're dead. You're... you can't be... Get away from me!"

Laurie looked up at him and smiled, *"you shouldn't have killed me, Tom."* She said.

The sweat on Hayden's face was clearly visible as Laurie slowly rose and added, *"you're going to regret it, Tom. You're going to regret it."*

Hayden screamed in terror as Laurie turned and walked through the wall, disappearing from view. The Oval Office spy-camera showed his large form retreating more hastily than was decent from the office door, wiping his brow with the sleeve of his shirt as he went.

The situation room erupted into applause, hoots, whistles, and laughter. Roy and Raj found themselves being pounded on the back in congratulations.

"Oh well done, guys! Well done! You scared him witless!" Nigel chuckled.

Daniel leaned back in his chair, shaking his head with a big grin on his face. *I couldn't have imagined it better myself!*

Chapter Sixty-Eight

DWINDLING ENTHUSIASM

Hayden strode purposefully up to the podium to address the media representatives in the room. He was a worried man. He always maintained a macho image in front of his subordinates, including his cabinet, waving off opinion polls and media reports as fluff, lies, party-political con-jobs, and grandstanding. But he knew better than that—there was enough truth in those poll results to spur him to action and try to do some damage control.

"Good evening ladies and gentlemen! I want to thank all of you who are working diligently to cooperate with local agencies to enforce and abide by the restrictions of martial law. Your help and cooperation are much appreciated! You are true patriots.

"I want to take a few minutes to provide you with the updates I promised.

"The good news is that we have turned the corner, the worst is over, and things are going to start looking up in a matter of days now! I want to give you the reassurance that my cabinet and I are working around the clock for you, the

American people and you will soon see and feel it. Soon the basic needs of everyone will be taken care of. There will be food, shelter and medical care for all. With some of our plans in the making, the job market is about to explode; soon there will be jobs for every man, there will be more jobs than people. You will be able to feed your families and provide shelter for them."

There were a few halfhearted attempts at applause, but it died down quickly. They'd heard this before.

Hayden was unnerved. He fancied himself a great orator who could motivate people with his words—tonight it was not working. At least not yet.

"I'm going to give you a brief overview of some of the most important initiatives my cabinet and I are working on in addition to addressing the food and housing shortages, which has been and still is our paramount priority.

"We *are* going to decrease government spending. There will be cutbacks in some programs, and complete elimination of others. Let me give you some examples.

"Keeping inmates in prison is costing the United States taxpayers nearly one-hundred billion dollars a year. We are going to cut funds to the prisons by fifty percent immediately. No, this doesn't mean a reduction in guards, nor does it mean we are setting inmates free. It means a reduction in the luxuries the inmates have been enjoying. Incarceration is intended to be punishment, not a summer camp experience. Prisoners are going to find prison life much less comfortable than they are used to. They will each have a bed, a blanket, and a dry place to sleep. They will be provided with three meals per day that consist of basic and healthy nutrition. Those who maintain good behavior will have the privilege of being outside in the prison yard for one hour a day for fresh air and exercise.

"All other activities they have been enjoying are over. No gyms, no television, no libraries, nothing of that kind. They will spend most of their time in their cells. That measure alone is going to reduce the cost of keeping prisoners by one-third."

This time the applause running through the room was much more enthusiastic. Hayden smiled, *I almost thought I'd lost my touch.* When the noise abated, he continued.

"We're going to quit funding ridiculous research projects that have no direct correlation to specific human illnesses or technological advances," he paused for a moment. Let me give you a few examples of what previous governments have been spending your hard-earned money on. More than a quarter million dollars were spent on a bird-watching project, three-quarters of a million dollars to investigate the methane gas emissions from the belches of dairy cows, close to fifty thousand to write an article about Russian smokers…"

Some people started laughing, and some were shaking their heads.

Hayden snatched the opportunity, "Yes, ladies and gentlemen if it didn't take the food off your tables, I would have joined those of you who are laughing at the absurdness. "One-hundred-fifty thousand dollars to study why politics stress us out! Sixty-five thousand to figure out what bugs do near a lightbulb. It's criminal! I say the gravy train has stopped; We will have no more of this wasteful spending. It's gone. You've seen the last of it."

This time the applause was even better. Hayden was energized by it.

"And on that same topic of wasteful spending; the entire space program is out the door. We've been to the moon, we've sent probes to Mars, Venus, and other planets and nothing has come of it. We've been looking for ET for decades; he has not arrived or contacted us—ET either does not exist or doesn't want contact with us. Whatever the case may be, it's time to stop wasting exorbitant amounts of money on these ridiculous pursuits and start putting that money to work for our citizens!"

This time wild applause, whistles, and cheering interrupted him, and he waited for it to fade away before continuing.

"In fact, I'm pleased to inform you that because of these types of cutbacks we will be able to provide free medical, dental, and vision care for every citizen. That is what I call a step in the right direction."

When the applause faded, he continued in a somber tone. "Now onto a topic that has been near to my heart for many years. Euthanasia. We have long been ending the suffering of animals we cherish by allowing them to be put down humanely when they can't have a life free of pain and suffering anymore. How can we do less for those we dearly love?

"For years, we have forced our loved ones to go through pain and suffering, tests, experiments, and treatments for illnesses that can't be cured. We prolong their suffering with inhumane measures even when they beg us to let them die. No more will we be so cruel as to force this kind of suffering on those who beg us not to. We are forthwith establishing the right for the terminally ill who wish it, to request doctor-assisted resolution of their life."

This statement met with a mixed response. Many applauded the idea, but a few withheld their applause and stared at each other. With that statement, Hayden had ridden roughshod over a very sensitive topic. A topic which has been debated by churches, politicians, philosophers, and probably everyone who ever had the misfortune to see a loved one suffer from terminal illness, for millennia. It had never been resolved.

From the mediocre applause, Hayden knew he better not belabor that point any further and quickly continued to the next topic. "My teams have completed a thorough study on jobs available nationwide, and I am happy to report that there are plenty of jobs available, and soon no man will be without work. Every man in this nation *will* be able to support his family.

"We are cracking down on all illegal immigrants; they have been stealing our jobs for far too long. It ends now. We have expanded our border patrol to prevent entry or re-entry, and we have launched a major initiative to round up all illegals and drop them on the other side of the border."

Cheers and whistles erupted from about seventy percent of the audience, and he waited. He was a bit hesitant about the next announcement.

"Cleaning up our country is going to require more manpower. Also, it has to be recognized that John Brideaux and his new world order left the world in chaos. We have to rebuild our military as quickly as humanly possible so that we can deter anyone from attacking us. Peace through deterrence.

"Therefore, we are establishing a mandatory two-year term of service in the military for all men from the day they turn 18. And right now, every man between the ages of 18 and 21 is required to serve two years."

A stunned silence followed this announcement, and then a murmur moved through the crowd. No one was prepared to lead the way and start applauding.

He made a scathing attack on Daniel Rossler and ended by saying. "As for the search for the prisoners and Daniel

Rossler; we are following up on very good information and believe we will have them in hand soon. For security reasons, I cannot say more than that at this time; but we are closing in on them all."

He started for the door, giving his two-thumb salute, but media representatives began flinging questions at him. He stopped and held up his hand to silence them. "I'm sorry. I cannot add any additional information at this time. Unfortunately, I can't take any questions as I have just been told that my attention is urgently required elsewhere," He lied. He wanted to get out of there as quickly as possible because he realized he had screwed up by making the compulsory military service announcement at the end.

He should have ended with the spending cuts and jobs announcements—the promises which always got everyone wildly excited.

"Damn speechwriter blew it," he growled at Rod Barrett, his Chief of Staff as he walked out the door.

Chapter Sixty-Nine

THE STINGS

About three hours after Hayden's address to the media, Lucas Nguyen walked distractedly down the hallway toward the West Wing parking exit. His friend's behavior lately was odd, and that display of rage in the Cabinet room was frightening, to say the least. He was shaking his head when he felt a slight sting on his neck. Instinctively he brought up his hand, but it never reached his neck—it was the last thing he remembered for quite a while.

Mouse quietly caught Nguyen before he fell, slung him over his shoulder and headed quickly down the stairs toward the access tunnel to the Blair House.

Kerinski, keeping a lookout, brought up the rear and secured the secret entrance behind them.

Once in the tunnel, Mouse placed the General in a wheelchair for the quick trip to the Blair House and onto the monorail. He checked the man's vitals and was relieved to note that his breathing and pulse remained normal and steady.

Upon arrival at Raven Rock, Rebecca checked him

over, pronouncing him to be 'just fine' before he was placed on his bed in his cell and left to sleep it off.

When the cell door clanged shut, Mouse and Kerinski gave each other a high-five in celebration of a job well done. The plan had worked like clockwork.

Back at the White House, Hayden, fearful of entering the Oval Office again, was looking for his friend Lucas to help him understand what might be going on. He didn't believe in ghosts, but what was this? He needed someone whom he trusted to confide in.

After fruitlessly hunting through various rooms he began asking staff members if they'd seen him. All replies were negative, and he sent someone to check the West Wing parking lot where Lucas always parked. His vehicle was still there.

Hayden had his cell phone called a number of times, but there was no answer. He finally had messages sent to the other Cabinet members but received assurances back that Lucas did not leave with one of them.

His car was here, he didn't leave with anyone else, but *he* wasn't here. *Maybe he walked to a nearby club and left from there with a friend.* Hayden smiled. *Yes, that's it. He'd found some friendly female companion for the night.*

Satisfied that he'd solved the mystery, Hayden headed to his room, then realized Carrie wouldn't be there. *Well, she was good, but there are others out there. As President, I'll probably get anyone I want,* he thought smugly to himself.

Just after 4 a.m., Hayden woke to a soft female voice calling his name.

"*Tom! Tom!*"

His eyes still closed, he smiled and spoke, "what is it dear?" He started to turn over, expecting to see the luscious body of Carrie next to him.

"Thomas Hayden! You shouldn't have killed me," the voice whispered again.

"What!" he screamed bolting upright and looking around the room for the speaker.

"I'm going to haunt you from the grave, Tom. Wherever you go, I'll be there, and whatever you do I'll know. Look out for me Tom. I'm everywhere." The voice said, fading away.

Hayden's heart was beating in his throat; his chest felt as if someone parked a truck on it, he was sweating, shivering and panting as he dressed and ran out of his bedroom. Rushing past the guards, he shouted to them to bring him coffee in the Oval Office.

Upon arrival outside the door, his last visit to the office still vivid in his mind, he hesitated before going in. To his relief, Laurie Campbell was not sitting at his desk this time. *I probably just imagined the whole thing.* He thought, shaking his head at his crazy notion.

"Where's Nguyen?" He demanded from his aid.

"We don't know sir. We can't find him."

"Start turning over beds in Washington and find Lucas Nguyen!" He yelled.

"Yes, sir."

"And when you do find him, tell him to get his ass over here yesterday; he's now officially at the top of my shit list!"

"Yes, General!" The aid squeaked as he scrambled for the door.

At Raven Rock, they had been watching Hayden's every move. Roy adjusted some settings on the panel and as soon as the aid left, Laurie Campbell appeared in the office with Hayden.

"Now what are you going to do, Tom? Your Secretary of Defense and most trusted advisor is missing. Maybe he has abandoned you, Tom."

Forgetting for a moment that he was seeing a ghost, he yelled, "What did you do with the prisoners, bitch? Where are they?"

"I'll never tell you, and you'll never find them." She faded from view just as two of his guards ran into the room.

They stopped short when they saw Hayden was alone.

"What are you doing here?" he growled.

"Sorry sir," one of them answered. "We heard you yell and thought something might be wrong."

"Do you see anyone else in here?" Hayden asked, brusquely.

"No, sir," they both answered looking at each other inquisitively.

"Did you see anyone else when you came in?"

"No, sir."

"Then you two better get your hearing checked. Get the hell out of here!" he jumped from his seat, rushed at them and shoved them bodily toward the door.

The two guards looked at each other in confusion. *What the hell was that all about?* But neither of them said a word.

He slammed the door behind them muttering, "am I going mad? Have I lost my mind? She's dead. I know she's dead. She can't possibly be here having conversations with me. And how does she know about Lucas?"

"Because I know everything now that I'm dead," her voice whispered. *"I am now in a timeless realm, Tom. I can see the present, the past, and the future. And I know how it's all going to end for you, Tom. Believe me; it's going to be bad. Very bad."*

He spun around, expecting to see her again, but the room was empty. He clasped his hands over his ears to shut out all sound.

Lieutenant General Kurt Frayser had just reached the exit to the parking lot when he heard someone call to him.

"Hey, Kurt! Can you come downstairs and give me a hand for a minute?"

It sounded like Nguyen, so he hurried down the stairs thinking that perhaps the man had fallen and injured himself yesterday and was unable to get up.

As his foot left the last step, he felt a sting on his neck.

Chapter Seventy

A BIRD'S-EYE VIEW OF THE WORLD

Since his arrival at Raven Rock Daniel had got a taste of the enormity of the task and the demands being President of the United States was going to place on him. Nigel has been mentoring and preparing Daniel as much as he could. Yet, no amount of training and schooling could ever replace real experience and Daniel was getting it in droves.

He started his days with an intelligence briefing from Salome and her Intelligence Committee. This was followed by the daily planning and preparation sessions, with the members of his shadow cabinet who were located at various safe houses across the country where they and their families were kept in safety by Tectus members, all of it conducted via the secured video links set up by Raj. Afterwards followed the mentoring session with Nigel, Sam, Luke and the elders at the Rabbit Hole including Sarah. This usually started with an appraisal of the preceding meeting with the shadow cabinet, followed by Nigel and others imparting more wisdom and advice to their young understudy.

Daniel also had a demand on his time from Cabinet

members for one-on-one meetings to discuss department specific ideas, issues and plans. In between it all he had to deal with the Trepang crisis and participate in the Rosslerites leadership group led by Sam to plan and execute Operation Winnow. The name they had chosen for the operation to overthrow Hayden was a reference to blowing air through grain in order to remove the chaff. "Getting rid of the worthless," Roy had quipped.

Despite the mounting pressure and responsibilities, the fact that he was still recovering from his shoulder wound, and didn't have his family with him, Daniel never complained. He always looked energized and enthusiastic, a true inspiration for everyone around him. Nigel quietly took notice—he was impressed and he was proud, "He is going to be a fine president," he had often remarked to his fellow Musketeers before he had relocated from the Rabbit Hole to Raven Rock in anticipation of the attack on the White House.

It was Nigel's knocking on the office door frame that got Daniel to look up from his computer screen.

"Nigel, come on in!" he invited.

"By my calculations, it's past lunch time, and you've been at that desk since dark o'clock from what I hear," Nigel stated.

"Nigel, we're underground... it's always dark in here," Daniel smirked.

"You know what I mean, don't avoid the subject. None of us wants to face Sarah's wrath for not making sure you take care of yourself! When's the last time you ate?"

"Dinner last night."

"Son, that was nearly 20 hours ago; come on, let's go to the cafeteria and get something to eat."

Daniel noticed the little tablet computer in his hand. Nigel was very seldom seen using computers and gadgets. In fact, Daniel couldn't recall ever seeing the former President ever using a tablet computer; having one in his hand now had some significance. Daniel had to ask, "what do you have there?"

"I'll tell you over lunch, now come on!" Nigel turned away clearly expecting Daniel to follow him without altercation.

Daniel muttered to himself but got up and set out to catch up with Nigel.

They selected a table away from other diners for a measure of privacy and settled in to eat.

"How are our guests?" Daniel asked, referring to Hayden's cabinet members that had been captured and were holding in cells at the underground headquarters. It was part of Nigel's tasks to talk to the captives and persuade them, in gentle ways, about the wrongness of their ways and their enormous disservice to the American people.

"They seem to have accepted the situation, I've got Frayser listening and talking to me. Nguyen is probably going to play hardball. But he is also the one who is probably in the most trouble for killing George Miller, Secretary of Treasury and I suspect some others. I'll keep on working on them; we might just need something from them when the time comes."

"Hmmm. I guess you will fill me in when the time comes?" Daniel smiled.

"Indeed."

"So, what do you have on that tablet?"

"This," Nigel said, "contains a birds-eye view of the

international political status of the world. Salome and the Intelligence Committee have been collecting and analyzing data and have put together a full report for you. It's all on here."

Daniel's eyebrows raised, "Excellent! Let's see it!"

"There's quite a bit of information to sort through in there. Shall I give you the highlights and then you can study the details later?"

"Sounds good. Let's hear it!"

Nigel took a sip off his coffee and started. "Russia is basically in chaos. By nature, it's an inhospitable country that has, in modern times, relied pretty much only on gas and oil to drive their economy. Several decades ago, gas and oil prices began to drop as the Middle East started pumping more oil and also more and more countries started developing their own non-fossil-fuel energy solutions.

"Russia was in the economic doldrums long before Brideaux came to power, his reign only exacerbated their situation.

"The Russian people are hungry and desperate—famine and barbaric scenes of civil unrest have become commonplace. Worse than our own.

"In the past when the Russian people and economy were suffering, their government would launch an offensive outside their borders to draw attention away from their domestic issues. It looks like they are preparing to do the same now, only this time it's not just to hide their domestic issues, it's to get their hands on the food supplies of their neighbors.

"They have also been making some noises about the extradition of Brideaux and his cronies."

"Well, they'll have to join the queue with everyone else," Daniel said.

Nigel nodded and continued.

"China. Before Brideaux's power grab, China was usually careful to avoid all-out war with anyone. However, now they're also feeling the economic pinch and their overpopulation doesn't help.

"In order for them to survive as a nation with what they have now, given the state of the world economy and food production, they would either have to reduce their population by half or get more territory. I probably don't have to tell you what they've decided?"

Daniel shook his head, "So, they're looking at the breadbaskets and land of their neighbors, which means they've changed their policy about war."

"You've got it," Nigel said.

"The nearby Asian countries and countries a bit further away like Australia and New Zealand are becoming anxious now that they feel the eyes of one and a half billion Chinese staring at them."

Daniel frowned. "Okay, that means we'll have to keep an eye on what Russia and China are doing.

Nigel agreed and continued. "The Middle East. The people of the Middle East have pretty much been living in appalling conditions for hundreds of years, except for their crooked politicians and oil sheiks. Right now, that area is a disaster of Biblical proportions.

"Although strife and turmoil have always been part of their daily existence, it has become much worse since Brideaux and is deteriorating by the day.

"As you know, the population of the region was drastically reduced by the Ninth Cycle virus, which wiped out nearly fifty percent of the people of Middle Eastern countries a few years ago; they are still recovering from that. The only positive out of their bleak situation is that they are so busy fighting each other they don't have the time and resources to be training terrorists to attack the rest of the world and convert us all to their faith.

"But having said that, the exception is, as always, Israel. Despite their differences, they are united in their hatred of the Jews, which has continued unabated since the days of Abraham. The issue is that lately their hatred has become stronger than ever. By their reasoning, since Israel seems to have come through most of Brideaux's destructive actions unscathed, Israel must have been in cahoots with Brideaux."

"Now where do you start to argue with foolishness like that?" Daniel noted, shaking his head.

"Well here is some advice for you; never argue with a fool. He will pull you down to his level and beat you with experience."

Daniel grinned. "Great piece of wisdom. I'll remember that."

Nigel continued. "Not much has changed for South America and Africa—in broad terms their lot has been more or less the same before, during, and after Brideaux's time. There are no imminent threats from them. Their situation remains dreadful but there will be nothing the United States, can do to help them until we are back on our feet."

"Heartbreaking, but I guess the reality of 'charity begins at home' rings true now," Daniel said.

"The countries of Western Europe are better off than most," Nigel said. "In spite of the rough times the European Union had a few years ago, which almost led to its complete demise, it did survive the bad patch, which has turned out to be a blessing in disguise for them. All its members have been able to share food, shelter, resources, etcetera.

"They don't have much, but what they have, they're sharing. Their close location to each other, small country size, and excellent infrastructure is helping them to move supplies around quickly, providing relief in places where it is needed most.

"Although they are better off with their food and supplies, they have not been spared the civil unrest that the other countries are experiencing. However, it is not as bad as in the other countries."

Daniel was shaking his head by the end of it, "And that was just the high-level view, the tip of the iceberg so to speak, the part that we can see. Only God knows what dangers are lurking below the surface."

Nigel nodded.

Daniel would only later realize how true his words about the lurking dangers were.

The two men fell quiet while sipping their coffee and finishing their lunch, reevaluating the information.

Nigel spoke first. "The Intelligence Committee believes that the United States, because of our democracy, brainpower, infrastructure, technological advances, and our industrious nature, will be the country that is probably in the best position to get out of this turmoil before everyone else. That'll make us the world leader again."

Daniel interjected. "Why do I get the impression you have some reservations about being the world leader? Isn't it true that most of the world thinks it's best to have America as the guardian of the free world—to be the deterring power to Russia, China, and any other countries with notions of expansionism?"

"No reservations, it's probably best that we are the world leader. The thing is that to a certain extent the playing fields around the globe have been leveled. The military and security forces of every country have been decimated, military arsenals have been destroyed, so has each and every nuclear weapon, even nuclear power stations."

"Oh, my God! We're looking at a new arms race, the Cold War all over again!"

"That's about the size of it." Nigel replied somberly. "We can see only one way that tide could be stemmed - the technological advances available in the Tenth Cycle Library. People like Roy and Raj and their teams can get us to the front and keep us there."

Daniel looked pensive when he spoke. "I sincerely hope you're not suggesting that the library be turned over to the government and used to establish the United States as the World Leader.

"Sarah and I have always said we want to keep the Library out of the hands of any government, we have always been of the opinion that the information was left there by the people of the Tenth Cycle for the benefit *all* of humanity, not just one government.

"But as soon as we started delving into the information we realized that we couldn't open it up to everyone. Our civilization has not reached the level of maturity which the Tenth Cycle had when they left the Library for us. There is just too much technological information, which could be used for malevolent purposes. Many times, Sarah and I have wondered if there was a way we could somehow 'undiscover' and undo what we have done because we as a civilization are obviously not advanced enough to use the information responsibly."

"Are you saying..." Nigel started, but Daniel held his hand up.

"Let me finish. What I was about to say was; in the light of what we are dealing with now, we might have to reconsider our stance. And as far as I am concerned, and I am sure Sarah will support me, the decision is not just ours to make alone. That burden now falls on the shoulders of the leadership of the Rossler Foundation. I would even go as far as to say that it probably should be debated by everyone living in the Rabbit Hole."

Nigel slowly nodded. "Yes, I agree. However, I don't think there is an immediate urgency to make a decision about it. As long as it is in the hands of the Rossler Foundation, as it is now we know the United States will get the benefit. But, to get to the front of the pack of countries who would be jockeying to be the new world power, we'll have to put in a lot more effort and resources to get everything out of the Library and use it to our advantage. And for that it might be necessary to allow the government in as a type of partner."

"Yes, I can see that. I'll talk to Sarah about it. If she agrees, we can float the idea at the leadership meeting tomorrow and get everyone to put their thinking caps on," Daniel said.

"We should keep in mind that as long as we have that library, whether it's in possession of the Foundation or the government, there will be those who would want to get their hands on it, with no regard for costs, money, effort, and lives."

Nigel agreed and then changed the topic. "Daniel, as you know, I've pledged you my support, and I'll always, as long as I'm physically and mentally able, be available to assist you in any way possible."

"Why so melodramatic all of sudden Nigel?" Daniel smiled.

"Maybe because I know that when you're taking your place in the White House you will have to pull this country out of the deepest sewer it has ever been in. It's going to require the leadership of someone who has the ability to unite the people, assemble the best, most qualified and experienced people in a bipartisan coalition to work on resolving the issues.

"It's going to take a leader who will not hesitate to ask for help, a person who is honest and open—never covering up anything, who exhibits openness and true transparency—someone who will tell it like it is and do whatever it takes."

"Sobering thoughts Nigel, sobering indeed," Daniel whispered.

I'm telling you that because I believe you have what it takes, and so does the entire Rossler Foundation leadership group, and every Rosslerite I have spoken to."

"Thank you, Nigel, it's truly humbling and inspiring to know."

Their meal and meeting complete, Nigel handed Daniel the tablet before they went their separate ways.

Chapter Seventy-One

PSYOPS PHASE TWO

Daniel had the team gathered in the situation rooms at Raven Rock and the Rabbit Hole. "Alright," he said, calling them to order. "What's our status?"

"Roy and Raj have provided us with additional spyders and spyflies and they are being deployed as we speak," Jack started.

"I have Kerinski and Mouse setting some of them loose in the offices of each of the four remaining Cabinet members, and Eric has some of the other Tectus members doing the same at their houses.

"Salome and her team are ready for PsyOps Phase two.

"What are you planning?" Daniel asked.

Salome had an evil grin, "We're going to show them that you can't trust spyders because they spread rumors…"

"…And start a divide-and-conquer campaign," Rebecca finished wickedly.

Daniel raised his eyebrows, "This sounds like fun! Do tell!"

"Well, the spyders will be whispering things into

Hayden's remaining Cabinet Members ears, sowing distrust and discord among them and against Hayden.

"We will continue to use Laurie to drive Hayden crazy, and a few other interesting people will start visiting the other Cabinet members as well."

"Yeah, we've already got Hayden completely paranoid," Jack laughed.

"He's been muttering to himself about getting help, and my guess is that he will turn to his friend Potter very shortly. He's already headed toward his office a couple of times, but turned around before he got there.

"I think Potter should be the next target we remove; shake Hayden up some more by removing those he wants to turn to for help. It will drive him crazy!" Salome said.

"Crazier, you mean!" Roy laughed.

"We plan on taking Neeley after that. He is too resourceful and slick; he could disappear on us quickly," Sam explained. "We must take him before he has a chance to hide."

"Alright," Daniel said, "let's grab Neeley next instead, but don't wait too long to get Potter."

Roy butted in, "Howard Baum just entered his office, let's see what we can do here."

They all watched as Baum sat down at his desk and began sorting through the stacks of reports. He didn't notice the figure appear in the chair opposite his desk.

The man waited patiently for a few minutes then said, *"are you having problems Howard?"*

Baum started violently, jumped up, nearly tipping his chair over, and pressed into the bookcase behind him, yelping as he recognized George Miller, recently deceased Secretary of Treasury, sitting before him. He was speechless.

"Cat got your tongue, Howard?" George asked calmly.

"Wh – wh – a – wha – what are you doing here? How…"

"Well, Howard, I've been watching what's been going on around here … you know it's easy for a dead person to do that. Right? Anyhow, I've taken a liking to you; you seem to be a decent person."

Baum had no color left to drain out of him, "oh no, what are you going to do to me?"

"Relax Howard; I'm not here to hurt you; as I've said, I like you, and I'm here to help you! I want to see you get out of this mess alive, unlike me, so I've come to warn you about Hayden."

"Warn me?"

"Sit down before you fall down, Howard."

Baum stepped back to his desk gingerly and melted into his chair.

"Hayden has gone mad," George said, circling his right index finger around his right ear without actually touching it, *"completely off his rocker. You know Frayser and Nguyen are missing, right?"*

Baum nodded.

"Well, Frayser was secretly working for the Rosslers and Hayden found out about it. He had Nguyen and Potter 'take care of him' … if you know what I mean."

Baum was wide-eyed and tongue-tied.

"Potter was supposed to apply some drugs and mild torture techniques so that Nguyen could question Frayser and find out where the Rosslers are, but Potter used too much of one of the drugs and killed Frayser before Nguyen could get the information. Nguyen and Potter had a horrific argument about what they were going to tell Hayden and who was going to take the blame."

"What happened?" Baum whispered.

"Why, Potter had to kill Nguyen to keep him quiet of course. He's told Hayden that the drugs are taking time to take effect and that Nguyen is with Frayser, tormenting and questioning him for the information.

"Actually, Potter has come back only to get a few things before he goes into hiding to avoid Hayden's wrath."

"What does all this have to do with me?"

"Well, like I said, Hayden has lost his mind, and very shortly he will have no one to depend on. That's where you come in. You need to become Hayden's best friend. Do whatever he tells you to do, support him no matter what he says.

"He will rely on you, and that will protect you. He'll come to think you're the only friend he has, the only person he can trust. No matter what he says, just act like you believe him and go along with him."

"You're sure this will work?"

"Absolutely! I'm dead, aren't I? I've already seen it!"

"How will this all end?"

"It's not time for you to know all that yet, but I can assure you that there will be peace."

Baum's breathing and heart rate had just about returned to normal by now.

Getting to his feet, George said, *"I would recommend you tell no one about this conversation. They might think you are the crazy one."*

And with that, he vanished. Baum's heart pounded in his chest as if it were going to explode.

The situation room at Raven Rock rang with laughter.

Hayden had taken refuge in the Lincoln Bedroom in hopes of getting away from the bewildering and terrifying visits from Laurie Campbell. He sighed deeply as he stepped into the room named after his boyhood hero and laid down on the bed.

"I've got to get control of this country," he spoke aloud to the empty room as if he was expecting Abraham Lincoln to respond. "Got to rein them in some more and make them tow-the-line."

A voice from the chair across the room startled him and he sat up quickly to see none other than Abraham Lincoln sitting there calmly, speaking to him.

"I'm disappointed in you Thomas ... killing people to get your way ... you're not the man I thought you'd be."

"What!"

"What happened to you; to your ideals and principles, your dreams, your vision? Your actions aren't those of a West Point graduate not to mention the President of this great country."

"I have experience; I know what's best for this country. She needs to return to her roots."

"As I've always said, 'this country belongs to the people who inhabit it, and whenever they grow weary of the existing government, they can exercise their constitutional right of amending it, or exercise their revolutionary right to overthrow it.'"

"But these people are running this country into the ground!"

"Are they? Or are you?"

"Come on, you know as well as I do, the country has become immoral and violent, the government deceitful and untrustworthy, and everything is spiraling out of control."

"And why do you think this is happening?"

"Are you kidding? Where have you been lately? We had a madman try to take control of the world; a woman try to take over the country, and now that psycho, Rossler, is on the loose opposing my presidency."

"Have you looked in the mirror lately, Thomas? Have you done some introspection? Can you look at yourself and honestly say to yourself, 'I've done the right thing? Just think of all your actions the last few weeks, Thomas, then you answer that."

"What the hell is that supposed to mean?"

"I may be dead, but I see what is happening. Remember what I always said; 'No man is good enough to govern another man without the other's consent'."

Lincoln vanished in what looked like a puff of smoke.

Hayden yelped and exited the room hastily, muttering to himself.

Grabbing the guard at the end of the hall by the arm he said, "get maintenance in here immediately and have them board up the Lincoln Bedroom."

"Sir?"

Hayden started yelling, "I don't want anything getting out …" he caught himself. "Don't question me! I don't want anyone going into that room. Get it boarded up, and I mean NOW!"

"Yes sir, Mr. President!"

As Hayden strode away, a voice whispered to him, *"you can't get away from us Thomas, we're always going to be here. Right next to you, in your ear and in your mind."*

The guard watched an agitated Hayden walking briskly down the hall waving his hands around his head, shouting, "get away from me, leave me alone!"

Deciding Hayden obviously needed some sort of assistance, the guard turned and went in search of General Potter. He would notify maintenance to board up the room later.

The Rowen

Colonel Stillwater was about to enter the dining area, to pick up his usual lunch when he thought he heard his name and stopped just outside the door to listen for a moment.

A woman's voice said *"are you sure you heard correctly? I can't imagine The President would be killing any of his top advisors."*

"I'm sure," a male voice said. *"I don't know the two guys he was talking to; never seen them before ... but he told them he was sure that Potter is responsible for the disappearance of Nguyen and Frayser. Hayden thinks Potter killed them and now he wants him dead."*

"It sounds to me like Hayden has gone completely batty if you ask me." The female voice said.

"Maybe, but he told me that he's going to bring Frank in to replace Stillwater. He thinks Stillwater is incompetent... I have to say I agree with that."

The voices faded away and the Colonel peaked around the door to see who had been talking, but just caught a glimpse of the two people leaving through the other door.

If I didn't know she was dead, I would have sworn that was Laurie Campbell talking ... sure sounded like her.

Forgetting that he had come down for lunch, he turned and headed for Potter's office, knocking firmly on the door when he arrived.

After being invited in, he reported what he had overheard. "So, I'd be careful if I were you, Joe. I don't know if it's true, but Hayden *has* been acting a little strange lately, I'm sure you have also noticed it."

General Joe Potter paled and stared at Stillwater in astonishment for a moment. "I haven't killed anyone! Nguyen killed George Miller, but that's the only one I know of."

The groups at Raven Rock and the Rabbit Hole were awestruck by the effectiveness of Salome's PsyOps tactics. In less than twenty-four hours she managed to sow so much discord and suspicion it would be a miracle if Hayden's advisors weren't at each other throats within the next day or two.

"Who's next?" Aaron asked with enthusiasm.

"Neeley," Roy replied setting a phone and some equipment on the table. "Ready Sam?"

Sam nodded.

"Everyone be very quiet now," Roy said as he dialed the phone. Sam held a microphone near his mouth.

Roy muted the display and the view switched to a view of Neeley sitting alone in his office.

They could all hear the ringing of the phone on his desk and watched Neeley pick it up.

"Neeley," he said.

Sam spoke urgently and quietly, *"Stephen, this is Lucas ..."*

"Lucas! Where the hell have you been? Hayden has been looking all over for you!"

"Shhh! I know ... but he's not looking for me for the reasons you think he is. I've gone to ground, Stephen. Hayden tried to have me killed, but I escaped. He's gone completely mad. He plans to eliminate all six of us and declare himself the sovereign leader."

"What!?"

"I know, I couldn't believe it either, but I saw his goons murder Frayser. You have to get out of the White House and away from Hayden as quickly as you can!"

"How? Where am I supposed to go?"

"I have a friend that can help you get away and get to where I'm hiding. Meet him in the bar at the hotel on 12th and H streets this

evening at seven o'clock. He'll be wearing a Steelers T-Shirt and baseball cap, white running shoes, and black jeans. He goes by 'Fred.'"

"But ..."

"I have to go. Stephen, I don't want to see you killed, man. If you want to live, be there."

Sam ended the call. The others looked at him in astonishment. He shrugged his shoulders.

"Max will meet and drug him, Kerinski and Mouse will be waiting in the basement to take him to Raven Rock."

"But he thought he was talking to Nguyen!"

"Oh, that. Yes, well, Nigel has spent some time talking with Nguyen and recorded his voice. He gave me the tapes, Raj and Roy did the rest with their voice-imitation software and voila, my voice sounds just like Nguyen's."

Daniel just shook his head, "Once again everyone, I'm forever grateful that you are on *our* side! You certainly *are* a scary bunch to have as an enemy."

Chapter Seventy-Two

THE ONLY HOPE WE HAVE

Viktor dressed slowly, watching Telestra in the mirror behind him. After all the years of marriage, he still did not trust her not to turn on him. He knew she had only agreed to be his wife because he threatened to kill her son Deszik if she didn't.

Deszik was her weakness and the only hold he had on her. She also knew he had given standing orders that if he ever died under suspicious circumstances, Deszik was to be tortured and killed in front of her.

"The time has come for the Re'an to mobilize and make our presence known," he told her.

"You will never conquer this world, Viktor. These people will fight you. You might think they are savages, and in some ways, they are, but many of them love their freedom. They will fight you and destroy you."

"They don't stand a chance against us. With our superior weapons and technology, they might as well throw stones at us. And as soon as we have control of our old headquarters at the Canyon and the rest of the technology from our Cycle that is stored there, it will be all over for them. The entire world will bow to the Re'an."

"You're deluding yourself, Viktor. Why can't you leave things as they are now? We have lived well for all this time. Why do you have to control the world? Leave them; they are different than us. It's their Cycle, their time; there's a sixty-two-thousand-year gap between us."

He ignored her and changed the subject. "I've been impressed with Deszik's performance lately and have decided to send him with the team to take over the Canyon site."

Telestra was dismayed but knew better than to object; it would only give Viktor pleasure to know he was succeeding in tormenting her. "I'm sure he will serve with honor."

"You hate that I'm sending him," he snarled when she denied him his pleasure of emotional abuse.

She refused to engage in an argument and remained quiet, frustrating him even more, "you will never be free of me Telestra, accept it. We are Re'an and will live forever."

She turned and left the room; she needed to have a word with Dekka.

His snide laughter rang in her ears as she made her way down the corridor toward the lab and Dekka's reassuring presence.

The once nearly empty corridors throughout the facility had changed drastically over the years as Viktor had forced Dekka and his team to create more and more Re'ans, building up his forces for the day when he would take over the world.

When Viktor had taken Deszik under his wing and trained him to become a soldier in the Re'an army, Telestra and Dekka had decided it was time to start planning Viktor's end.

Because they knew Viktor enjoyed nothing better than harassing and controlling Telestra through the hold he had on her son, they knew Viktor would see to it that Deszik was the most highly trained soldier he could produce.

Viktor had forced Dekka to adjust the boy's chip so that he would call Viktor 'father;' an adjustment that had nearly cost him his life. Telestra had been wild with fury the first time she heard Deszik call him 'father' and had attacked him. Viktor had underestimated her strength at the height of her fury and found himself with a severe stab wound in his shoulder before he knocked her unconscious.

When she awoke, she was restrained and gagged; it was then he had issued the standing order that Deszik be tortured and executed in Telestra's presence if he should die by her hand, of a mysterious illness or other unexplained death.

It was days before Telestra accepted that she could not change anything through anger and violence and she forced herself to calm down so that Viktor would order her release. She became withdrawn and isolated herself.

Several weeks had passed after this incident when Dekka one day enticed her to join him for lunch promising he had a way to help Deszik.

What had unfolded from that meeting was a series of slight and almost unnoticeable adjustments to Deszik's chip at every opportunity Dekka got.

Gradually, so that Viktor would not detect it and Deszik could adjust, they introduced the information to him through his implant. They fed him the story of the B'ran, the L'gundo, the end of the Eighth Cycle and Viktor's plan for the Re'an.

The boy had responded exactly as they had hoped—he embraced the truth and hid his knowledge rather than informing Viktor. One day, Deszik was going to be the downfall of Viktor.

With the knowledge gained from Viktor about his plans, Telestra knew that the day of Viktor's downfall, for which they had been preparing Deszik so carefully all these years, was fast approaching.

"Dekka," she said quietly as she approached the lab station where he worked. "Viktor is about to send a team to the Canyon, and he's sending Deszik with them."

He looked gravely at her. They both knew that this meant Deszik might never return. "Are you ready for that?" he asked gently.

She gazed into his soft brown eyes, the love between them had grown over the years and, had things been different, they could have been a family. Dekka loved Deszik as though he were his own son. "I have to be. Deszik is the only hope we have to get rid of that evil man."

Dekka nodded and took her hands in his. There was nothing else that could be said with words.

A young man, one of the original B'ran soldiers, entered the room, excitement clearly on his face. "Sir! We have detected some minor activity at the canyon location in the United States!"

"What? Are you sure?"

"Yes sir," he pointed at the shiny, metal panel on the wall with a little device in his hand.

Some data, graphs, and text appeared on the panel.

"This could change everything, make it easier," Viktor

said. "We may have access to our erstwhile comrades, and they might be able to join us. How many of them could there be?

"I don't know. But I will keep monitoring them and let you know," the man said and left.

Chapter Seventy-Three

AND THEN THERE WERE THREE

Stephen Neeley looked quickly around his office, got up and began hurriedly shoving things into his briefcase.

A gentle knock sounded on his door, and his secretary stepped into the room. "General, President Hayden has called a meeting in the Oval Office in an hour."

Stephen froze. "Fine, fine," he said as he shoved a few more files in the briefcase. "I have a short meeting in a few minutes, but it won't last long. I'll be back in plenty of time."

"Yes, sir. I'll let him know."

"Thank you, Carol, but don't bother him – I'll be back in less than thirty minutes!" he said as he picked up his suit jacket and headed for the door.

Now I have to disappear until seven o'clock tonight. What the hell am I going to do for four hours?

Leaving his car in the parking lot, he exited through the East Wing and headed for the pub frequented by many Senators and Congressmen.

Taking a seat near the back-door exit, he ordered a

drink and tried to relax. About twenty minutes later, he quietly exited through the back door and hailed a cab.

"Where to?" the driver asked.

"Drive North," he responded.

"I need an address mister."

"I don't have a destination yet, just drive."

"Ok mister, it's your money."

Hayden pounded on the closed door, "Potter! I wanna talk to you NOW!"

Inside the office, General Joe Potter froze. *Was Cameron right? Has Hayden come to kill me?*

"Potter!" yelled Hayden again as he pushed open the door without an invitation to enter.

"Mr. President!" Potter greeted nervously, "What can I do for you?"

Hayden shut the door and composed himself. "I need your help, and this has to be kept quiet, between you and me only, understand?"

"Certainly, Mr. President."

Hayden looked nervously around the room. "Laurie Campbell has been paying me visits, telling me things … she's driving me to desperation."

Potter's brow creased and his mouth tightened in a slight frown. "But… but… she's dead, Mr. President."

"I already know that you moron," Hayden shouted. "Do you think I'd come to you for help in dealing with a live person? I can take care of them myself.

"She's coming to me in dreams and such. Can you help me get rid of that? Is there some kind of drug?"

"Uh, sure. Umm the best one would probably be Haldol."

"How soon can you get me some?"

"I'll have my aide get the prescription filled right away, sir." Potter came around his desk to stand before Hayden," it will be here after the meeting this afternoon."

"Ok, thanks," Hayden said, "See you at the meeting."

As the door closed behind Hayden, a voice spoke to Potter, *"you know you are the only one called to that meeting, don't you?"*

Potter swung around to see Laurie Campbell sitting in his chair. His heart vaulted, and he gasped for air from the sudden pain in his chest.

"H ... how can you be here? You're dead."

"Hayden plans to kill you, you know."

"Yes, so I've been told. Why are *you* telling me?"

"Because I'm mad as hell at all of you, and I'm using Hayden to seek my revenge and destroy him at the same time."

"You're a ghost with no physical form or ability. You can't actually do anything to any of us except try to manipulate us with words."

Laurie rose from the chair, *"Are you sure?"*

Before Potter could reply, he felt a stabbing pain in his butt where one of Roy's spyders delivered a dose of Propofol. "Ouch! Bloody hell. What was that?"

Roy and Raj, still monitoring things back at Raven Rock gave each other a high-five and nearly rolled on the floor laughing when a silly, relaxed grin started spreading over Potter's face as the Propofol took effect.

"Now Potter," Laurie said, *"you are going to go to the parking lot exit of the West Wing and take the stairs to the ground floor. You are not to go anywhere else, and you are not to speak to anyone. Do you understand?"*

"Yes ma'am," he replied, meek as a lamb.

"Good boy. On your way then."

Potter turned without saying another word and left the room.

Laurie smiled as she vanished from sight.

Within minutes Kerinski and Mouse had Potter seated comfortably in a wheel chair, now fully unconscious, moving him smoothly toward the Blair house, destined for a cell at Raven Rock.

An hour later Hayden paced the Oval Office furiously, "Where the hell are they?" he yelled at the two colonels."

Baum and Stillwater looked at one another in dismay. "I'm sure they'll be here momentarily, sir," Baum tried to speak soothingly.

"I don't want them here in a moment; I told them to be here NOW! Find them. Both of you!" The two men scrambled out of the Oval Office.

"What's got in to him?" Stillwater asked after they had put a safe distance between themselves and the raging president.

Baum looked around quickly and grabbed Stillwater by the arm, dragging him into a nearby office.

"This is just between you and me because I'm not sure how true it is, ok?"

"Yeah, sure," Stillwater agreed.

"Again, I'm not sure how true it is, but I heard that Frayser was secretly working for the Rosslers and Hayden found out. He had Nguyen and Potter interrogate him and Potter accidently killed Frayser and then murdered Nguyen to cover it up."

"Holy shit! How the hell did you find *that* out?"

"Let's just say I have my sources. I'm guessing that Potter has gone into hiding."

"Well, that makes sense with what I ah … heard."

"What did you hear?"

"That Hayden wants Potter dead."

"Wow! I wonder if Potter knows?"

Deciding that his involvement would probably best go unknown, Stillwater replied, "if he does, it would explain why he is not here."

"Well, let's see what we can find out."

But when the two of them went their separate ways, it was not in search of the missing cabinet members; it was to find a quiet place to sit down and consider their own situations.

"Hayden, your stupidity amazes me. Those two are going to conspire against you; you shouldn't have let them leave together."

Hayden spun around to see Laurie once again seated at his desk in the Oval Office. "Get out of here and leave me the hell alone!" he yelled. He picked up a small statue sitting on the mantel of the fireplace and hurled it at her. It passed harmlessly through her and she laughed, *"Looks like you've missed me!"*

He launched himself at her, and just as he reached for her, she disappeared from the chair reappearing before the fireplace.

"Give it up, Thomas. You can't lay a hand on me anymore. You can't touch me, you can't make me shut up, and you can't make me go away."

Hayden started screamed in a mad rage, overturning his desk and kicking out a window.

His Secret Service agents rushed into the room, guns drawn.

Hayden reddened. "Get out of here! All of you get busy and find my advisors ... all six of them! And if you don't find them, don't bother coming back!" he yelled as they scurried out of the way of flying objects he hurled at them.

A man's voice laughed at him from the couch, and he looked up to see Abraham Lincoln sitting next to Laurie.

"You're losing it, Tom. This is not the behavior of a leader. You're acting like a two-year-old, Tom," Lincoln said. *"I'm deeply disappointed in you."*

"Noooo," Hayden whimpered as he sunk to the floor and started sobbing.

"Aw look, Abe, you made him cry."

"Yeah. Pathetic isn't he."

"Please go away and leave me alone," Hayden sniffled.

"Not on your life," Laurie spoke vehemently. *"My dad taught me never to start a fight, but he also taught me that if I'm drawn into a fight, how to fight and win. You started this Tom; I will finish it."*

After pub hopping around the distant areas of the city for several hours, Neeley hailed another cab.

"Take me to the Bibiana," he instructed as he settled himself in the back seat. It was an Italian restaurant near the hotel where Nguyen had instructed him to meet with 'Fred.'

The taxi dropped him off and he went inside where he waited a few moments before making his way quickly to the hotel and into the bar. He was still early, so he settled himself in the darkest corner he could find and still see the room, and ordered a drink.

Half an hour later he saw a man matching Nguyen's description of 'Fred' enter the bar and find a table. Neeley watched him and the rest of the room for several minutes. Deciding it wasn't a trap Neeley got up and approached the table and took a seat.

'Fred' nodded at him. "Glad to see you made it … your friend is concerned."

Neeley inclined his head in acknowledgment.

Looking around the room cautiously 'Fred' lowered his voice, "finish your drink quickly and let's get out of here."

Neeley complied, and they got up to leave.

'Fred' led him down a hallway and into the housekeeping area. They paused briefly to be sure the room was empty. "This way, quickly," 'Fred' said. They crossed the room and descended a flight of stairs.

"Where does this go?"

"Basement exit where you won't be seen leaving if someone followed you."

As Neeley's foot planted on the landing, he felt a sting on his neck and knew no more.

Mouse caught him as Kerinski maneuvered the wheelchair into position. They were on the monorail train to Raven Rock in less than a minute.

Chapter Seventy-Four

YES. I DID

Brideaux picked himself up off the floor, "What the hell...?"

In the dim and flickering light, he saw his guard slowly picking himself up and noted that the Captain was also stirring. "What the hell happened, Captain?"

"I'd say we've gotten as close to the surface as we're going to get."

"Did we make it?" Brideaux demanded.

"I'll need to check the photonics to tell," he said, pointing toward another station at the back of the control room. "But I'm pretty sure we didn't."

"Help him over there," Brideaux ordered his guard.

Locklin groaned in pain as he was assisted into the seat. He studied the screens, worked some switches, and watched the readouts for a minute and then stated, "Just as I thought, the ice is too thick. We weren't able to break through it."

"What? I ordered you to surface this ship."

"I'd be happy to let you dig the rest of the way out if you like," Locklin replied sardonically.

"Why the hell didn't it work? I've seen pictures of subs with their towers sticking up through the ice."

"You idiot, Brideaux," the Captain snapped. "The ice those subs surfaced through was on the outer edges and only two or three feet thick at the most. The ice here is more than twenty feet thick.

"You're just damn lucky we're still here to talk about it. Now, I need my crew in here, and I mean right now."

"Why?"

"Dammit Brideaux, I need a report from every compartment on this boat. For all I know we could be taking on water as we speak." Locklin knew this was stretching the truth a bit because they did have warning systems that would tell them if they were, but Brideaux didn't have to know that.

Brideaux bit back an angry retort and considered the Captain's words. "Very well, Captain, but essential crew only," he waggled the gun at Locklin, "essential crew only," he repeated.

"Fine," Locklin said and listed the names of the crew to cover the pilot, co-pilot, and two sonar positions. "I also need you to send two of my men to make a visual check on the boat ... one forward and one aft, send them with as many guards as you think they need, but I have to send them."

Nodding to his guard Brideaux sent him to fetch the men Locklin requested.

Within minutes they reported for duty and quickly began going through the information that was flowing into their stations.

A screeching, groaning metal sound rolled through the boat.

"What's that?" Brideaux asked anxiously.

"Ice movement," the Captain answered, and issued the order, "Take us down and clear of the ice."

"Taking us down, aye sir," the helm answered.

"What are you doing!" Brideaux squealed.

"Getting us away from the ice before we suffer more damage."

"Iceberg dead ahead," one of the sonar technicians yelled.

"Hard to port, down 30 degrees," Locklin ordered

"Hard to port, down 30 degrees, aye, sir" parroted the pilot.

"Down 30 degrees, aye, sir" the co-pilot echoed.

"Too late, sir! Brace for impact!" the sonar technician shouted as he grabbed for handholds.

"All stop! Sound collision!"

"All stop, aye, sir!"

For the second time in less than an hour the klaxon blared. Locklin shouted over it, "Full reverse!"

"Full reverse, aye, sir!"

A deep churning sensation vibrated through the floor as the engines pulled the sub against its forward momentum. Groaning metal accompanied a hard impact and the sound of scraping followed along the side of the sub.

The scraping decreased as the sub dove deeper, pulling away from the iceberg.

"We're clear sir!"

"Why didn't it stop? Why did we still run into that iceberg?" Brideaux demanded.

"Because of inertia; a boat still glides with its momentum; it doesn't stop like a car does."

"All stop," Locklin ordered.

"All stop, aye, sir."

"What's our depth now?"

"200 feet, sir."

"Damage report."

"Sonar sphere is down, chin sonar array still functional. Starboard number one array is also down. All the other side arrays are working. Sail array appears to have taken some damage but is still functioning at the moment; I wouldn't trust it's readings though."

"Sir? I have a malfunction in both bow planes."

"Can they be retracted?"

"Negative sir."

"Shit," Locklin glared at Brideaux. "If it weren't for my orders, I'd kill you myself Brideaux."

Pointing his gun at the Captain, Brideaux responded, "Watch your mouth Captain and remember who is really in control of this sub."

"Captain Locklin of course," said a voice from behind him.

Brideaux whirled around to see Rafael Martinez with a gun pointed right at him. Before his mind could fully process what he was seeing, Martinez pulled the trigger, and Brideaux slammed to the floor as if he'd been hit in his stomach by a twenty-pound hammer.

"That one is from me," Martinez whispered. He adjusted his aim and fired again. "That's for the young Ensign you tortured."

Captain Locklin just watched as Brideaux writhed on the floor screaming and clutching his shattered knee. He was not going to interfere in this personal vendetta.

"You son-of-a-bitch, I'll kill you for this!" Brideaux screamed.

"I think not," Martinez replied and calmly fired a bullet into John Brideaux's head. "And that is for my friend Ruben Weinstein," he whispered.

He turned to Captain Locklin and handed him the gun —butt first. "Captain, the ship is yours. Your men are already free and ready to serve. My fellow Council members have been secured back in their quarters as before." Motioning to the Council member serving as Brideaux's guard he added, "We'll go and join them now."

Brideaux's guard stood frozen in shock while the crewman nearest him relieved him of his weapon. He looked up at Martinez, "You killed him," he said with impressed astonishment.

"Yes. I did," he said as he turned to leave the control center, "and my only regret is I didn't kill the bastard that night in Brussels."

Chapter Seventy-Five

THEY WERE FORCED TOGETHER

Tawndo's mouth went dry and he struggled to swallow as he deciphered the latest data he had syphoned from the Re'an data center at Tunguska.

"We can't waste any more time arguing if it's going to work or not." Tawndo said, as he walked into the lab and heard Siasha and Linkola arguing.

They were startled at his discontented tone.

"They are mobilizing for an attack on us," he whispered.

"But… we're not ready…" Linkola protested.

"I have an idea," Tawndo interjected.

"Let's hear it then," Linkola said cautiously.

"A computer codes and stores files in a server or disc somewhere for later retrieval and the brain is like a biological computer. Why can't we just access his memories and download them into my chip?"

Linkola smiled, "that would seem to be the simple answer, wouldn't it? Unfortunately, the brain doesn't work quite like that. It is a highly complex biological computer, as you put it, and it interacts with itself on many levels to create memory, thought, movement, emotions, senses, et cetera."

"Yes, but his memories are all in a computer now and can be put on a chip and planted back into a brain."

"That is true, but the part you are missing is that the chip is also a medical program that rebuilds the parts of the structure of the host brain to match the original brain."

"Well, then rip those out, shut off the medical part of the chip and just transfer the memories."

"No. The chip doesn't work that way."

"Why not?"

Linkola paused for a moment. "Think of it like this; it would be like setting a computer on a desk and expecting it to work itself."

"Huh?"

"If you just set a computer on a desk, it will not work. It must be connected to power, and, even though it contains all the necessary files, it requires someone to tell it what to do. Turning off the medical part of the chip, even if it were possible, which it isn't, would make the chip useless... there would be no connections and no control.

"Besides, it would mean destroying Robert."

"What? Now I'm really lost; he's already dead."

"Is he?" Linkola gestured toward Tawndo, "his body lives; his mind is stored and available. Is he really dead? If we could separate his memories from the chip, re-animation would no longer be possible and we would have destroyed him."

Korda, who had wandered into the lab during the discourse quipped, "too bad we can't wake him up and ask him what he wants to do."

Siasha looked at Korda sharply. "What did you say?"

Korda eyed her with puzzlement, "that it is too bad we can't wake him up and ask him."

"We are trying to make a decision we have no right to make," she said.

Tawndo and Linkola look at her, "what?" they asked, nearly in unison.

"Robert is the only one who should be making this decision, not us."

"But..." began Linkola.

"No, listen. His body *is* still alive, and his memory *is* stored and available... this is *his* decision, not ours."

"And just how do you suggest we contact him and ask him?"

"I... don't... know," she said, deep in thought. "Linkola, have you scanned the brain since we awakened Tawndo?"

"No, I haven't. I didn't see the need."

"I'd like to see a scan now."

"Why?"

"I don't know. Something you said about the structure of the brain. It could mean something, but I don't know what yet. I need to see the scan."

"Tawndo?" Linkola looked over at him. "Are you willing to undergo a scan of the brain?"

"I don't see why not," he replied. "Let's do it! We *have* to get a solution and *now* might not even be soon enough as far as I am concerned."

Linkola assisted Tawndo onto the diagnostic table and prepared the glucose injection while the clear glass-like panels slid up from beneath the table to cover his body.

After injecting the glucose and activating the low frequency EMP waves, the three watched in silence as the scanner created the digitized display of Tawndo's brain.

Siasha made several adjustments to the knobs and

switches on the control panel and then used the computer to pull up the scan of the brain in the state it was before the re-animation.

"Look at that," she said, pointing to a series of spider-web-like images on the screen.

"What?" Korda asked.

"Yes, I see," Linkola replied looking between the two screens.

"What?" Korda asked again.

"Let's look at the scans from the first two experiments."

"I'll get them," Linkola offered.

"What are you two looking at?" Korda asked again, this time a bit more irritated.

Siasha replied, "The synapse structure in the brain."

"It's pretty," he responded, "but what about it?"

"They are the brain's internal communications network, in other words, how the brain communicates with itself… sort of like a spider web connecting different parts of the brain."

Linkola returned with the requested scans. Siasha connected the data chip to the computer and brought up Linkola's original report, which he produced after the failed merger experiment.

"They are in Appendix 'A'," he told her.

She pulled up the images and studied them carefully, then she sat down, clearly disturbed.

"What is it?" Linkola asked staring at the images anxiously. "What do you see?"

"Look at the synapses."

"I am looking at them," he said studying the scans from the first two experiments. He gasped, "they're… they're…" he looked at all four scans carefully, "they're… oh no!"

"Yes," she said softly.

"What is it? What do you see?" Korda asked.

"Let me out of this thing if you're done with me," Tawndo said. "I want to see what you're looking at."

Siasha nodded for Korda to release him and waited for him to join them.

"Okay, so what am I looking at and what does it mean?" Tawndo demanded.

"Look at the scan Linkola did of your brain before the re-animation." Tawndo looked as Siasha continued. "There is one distinct synaptic pattern in the brain. Now look at the one we just did... see the new pattern? That's you...

"Notice how the original pattern is fading? That's called Apoptosis.... programmed cell death. It's what happens in the brain when certain established pathways are no longer used. The pathways gradually die out.

"As you can see, in the second scan the original pattern has far fewer pathways than it did in the first scan."

Tawndo frowned. "Okay, I'm with you, but what does it mean?"

"Now look at the scans from both of the experiments and tell me what you see."

Studying them closely for several minutes, Tawndo's frown deepened. "It looks to me like there are three distinct patterns, and they are all fairly clear."

"Correct."

"So, what does that mean?"

"It means that the body was very recently killed when the experiment took place. The synapses hadn't had a chance to start dying off. It also means that Linkola's experiment attempted to place two men into the body at the same time and merge them. Essentially, they were merging three people. Although the body of the host was dead, the mind hadn't been removed and the synapse connections were still there.

"Now look down here," she said indicating a lump near the right kidney. This is the adrenal gland, and here is the other," she said pointing to the left kidney.

"It looks like they exploded."

"That's exactly what happened," Linkola said. "But what would cause that?"

"These glands were forced to produce too much adrenaline all at once." Siasha said.

"O ... kay," Tawndo drew the word out, folding his arms across his chest. "I'm sorry, I still don't understand what all this means."

"It means several things," Siasha answered.

"For one," Linkola said bitterly, "it means that the bodies in the two experiments had most likely been killed immediately before the experiment. And that meant that their brains were not given enough time to die off—stop functioning."

"Well, isn't that to be expected?" Tawndo puzzled. "The bodies are only good for a short period after death."

"No. That's not what I mean," Linkola replied tightly. "Those bodies were killed solely for the purpose of using them in the experiment. The lack of degradation in the synaptic pattern indicates there were only minutes between death and the attempted merge. It was done too soon—way too soon."

Tawndo looked at Siasha, horrified. She read the question in his face.

"It's true," she confirmed, "and the fact that all three patterns are so clear indicates that the implantation and activation of the two chips occurred at the same time.

"The destruction of the adrenal glands was caused by a

massive buildup up of adrenaline because it couldn't be released into the body quick enough, and yet the amount of adrenaline in the blood at the time of death is off the charts."

Tawndo looked from Siasha to Linkola who continued the summary.

"The three men in the experiments were all frightened, and were fighting for their lives when they were killed. The body already had a build-up of adrenaline at death. The synapses of the two men that they tried to merge were sending signals to the adrenal gland to produce adrenaline in response to their fear.

"The two men they tried to merge were not prepared, they had no idea what was coming. They were simply forced together at a point when the body was in a state of absolute terror.

"The rapid development of so many new synapses over the existing, probably drove them insane, and the super doses of adrenaline gave them the physical strength to literally tear their bodies apart without feeling what they were doing to it."

Tawndo had grown pale and sat down. "That is the most despicable thing I have ever heard."

"I think we all need some rest," Korda suggested, and everyone nodded in silence.

Chapter Seventy-Six

MEET AT THE SAIL

Captain Locklin, resting in his quarters at the insistence of the Doc, reviewed the report before him. After the Trepang had been hovering at two-hundred feet for nearly a day to allow them to repair damage to internal circuits and systems, they were under way again. The damage to the retractable bow planes made controlling the sub a nightmare. One had been sheared off entirely, and the other one was damaged to the point it could not be retracted and was stuck in the 'dive' position. This was causing the nose of the sub to want to descend deeper into the ocean.

By partially filling the forward ballast tanks with air they were able to keep the nose up enough to prevent the sub from going any deeper, but their forward speed was dismal, and the ride was shaky, to say the least.

An odd note in the report by the sonar officer puzzled him; a brief sonar contact, not long enough to fully identify as a vessel, had shown up and disappeared on two different occasions.

The Russians may have spotted us from the noise of the impact with the ice when Brideaux tried to surface.

Great, just what we need when we're hamstrung. We each know the other is down here, so if we all just play nice, maybe we'll get through this in one piece.

At least they don't know we have the prisoners.

He noted they had left the Makarov Basin behind and were starting their pass over the area between the Mendeleyev Plain and the Canada Basin. Because of the damage to the boat and the inability to rise to make external repairs, the trip to the Chukchi Sea that should have taken hours would now take days.

If Brideaux weren't dead already, I'd be tempted to kill him myself. Shit, maybe I'll still go to the storage room and pump a few more bullets in him—just for the satisfaction.

His vengeful thoughts were interrupted by the sound of a knock on his cabin door, "Captain?"

"Enter."

The door opened, and the chief chef stuck his head in. "I've brought you some food, Captain. Are you hungry?"

Locklin smiled and motioned him in, "I sure am!"

The chef's face beamed as he set the tray of food before his Captain. "Enjoy, sir!"

Captain Locklin grinned as he picked up the knife and fork and began to cut into the steak, "Thank you, Sam!"

Sam gave a salute and left the Captain to enjoy his first decent meal since that lunatic hijacked his boat.

The giant submarine limped slowly through the water, gradually ascending toward the surface. It had taken three days, but she was finally out from under the Arctic ice and over the continental shelf in the Chukchi Sea.

"Bring us to 50 feet," ordered the Captain.

"Coming to 50 feet, aye sir."

Several minutes passed before the helmsman announced, "we're at 50 feet, sir."

"All stop," he commanded.

"All stop, aye sir."

Locklin changed a dial setting on the communication panel to 'Trunk' and thumbed the mic switch in his hand. "Are Larson and Hunter in the trunk and ready to go?"

"Aye, sir," came the response.

"Very well; proceed."

In the special nine-man airlock chamber behind the sail of the sub, Lieutenant Gary Larson and Ensign Marc Hunter were running through the final checks on each other's gear when they saw the thumbs up. Larson indicated they needed another moment and assisted Hunter in securing a pony bottle in the pocket of his buoyancy compensation vest. He would need it if the cold water caused his regulator to go into free-flow.

They both wore neoprene dry suits with a wicking layer against their skin and a thick thermal layer on top of that to stay comfortable in the cold water. They double-checked each other's weight belts and tanks to be sure everything was secure. Finally, they donned the dry gloves that would keep their hands warm and gave the return 'thumbs up' sign indicating they were now ready. Then they helped secure the hatch before water began to pour into the small room.

Within minutes they were entirely submerged in cold water and opened the hatch to exit the sub. As instructed,

Larson made his way to the bow on the starboard side; Hunter did the same on the port side.

Instead of seeing the smooth rounded nose of the sub, Larson was dismayed to see the entire top of the bow crinkled and flattened, pieces of it missing entirely, and part of the sonar sphere exposed. The entire bow compartment was filled with water.

Larson whistled inside his helmet. "You see that Hunter?"

"Yeah, I see it. It's a good thing we weren't traveling at full speed. Sure was smart of the Captain to cut power to the engines as we ascended or we'd all be tinned fish food now."

"Yep. How's the bow plane on your side?"

"Damn, the whole thing has been ripped off; it's completely gone! What about your side?"

"It's still attached, but as the Captain suspected, it's been bent and is stuck at a down angle."

"Geez, can it be fixed?"

Larson, swimming around the plane examining it closely replied, "I doubt it. We'll probably have to remove it. Let's keep moving."

Moving down the sleek sides of the sub, both men examined the surface for signs of hull penetration. When they met at the propulsion duct behind the rudder, Hunter's report was more encouraging than Larson's.

"My side looks alright. I didn't see any signs of damage other than the bow."

"Wish I could say the same. The number one sonar array is history, and there's a gouge starting at the middle of it and angling up the side clear to the reactor room. I didn't see any signs of actual penetration, but I sure wouldn't want to have to trust it at any great depth."

Larson could see Hunter's eyes widen at the news, "Holy shit," he heard him whisper.

"Come on, let's get this done. You take topside, and I'll check the belly of the beast. Meet at the sail and help me check the masts."

"You got it!"

Larson was pleased to find that the 'belly of the beast' as he called it was completely intact and the 'chin' sonar array was undamaged. Hunter reported the topside to be intact as well except for some slight denting to the surface door of the vertical launch tubes, "The row closest to the nose has been flattened slightly, and we may have trouble opening and closing them."

The sail was also intact except for damage to the sonar array, but the masts were another story; every one of them was sheared off. Some were missing altogether while a few hung by their cabling.

"Alright, let's get back inside and get going on repair plans," Larson said.

"Yeah, and get warm," Hunter agreed.

Locklin listened with concern as Lieutenant Larson gave the damage report. Water in the nose of the boat without bow planes would make the sub almost uncontrollable and difficult to surface - if it could even be done.

They were off course, behind schedule, in trouble, and too far below the surface for radio contact. The very low and extremely low frequency radios, VLF and ELF respectively, wouldn't do them any good either, since both were receive-only communications and their masts had been sheared off.

Yet, he needed to let Admiral Johnson know that they were alive and in trouble. Looking at the clock, he made his decision. It was risking detection, but he had to try something.

"Sonar, this is the Captain."

"Sonar, aye," came the response.

"Give me a single ping."

"One ping, aye."

One ping went out at one minute before the scheduled ping. He waited while the time for the scheduled ping passed. At one minute after the time of scheduled ping, he contacted sonar again and had them send a second, single ping.

That's the best I can do right now Admiral; I hope you get the message.

Chapter Seventy-Seven

AND THEN THERE WAS ONE

Thomas Hayden was pacing around in the Oval Office. He was at wit's end; his nerves were shot. The last few days, he had been on the receiving end of several of Murphy's Laws, first was the one that states; if anything *can* go wrong, it *will,* to which someone later added; at the worst possible moment. The second was the one known as Murphy's Law of Thermodynamics which stated; things get worse under pressure.

Civil unrest was spreading like wildfire across the country, violence and crime levels were reaching new record levels every day. People were starving, the promised food distribution was not happening; despair and dissatisfaction were driving people into rebellion and crime. Law enforcement agencies were incapable of maintaining law and order and had become the target of the people's wrath. Brideaux's new world order had laid waste to all security and law enforcement agencies across the globe, including America. These agencies were understaffed and now also under threat of being overrun and killed by the very populace they were supposed to protect.

The cherry on the cake was the rumors that people were planning to hold a protest march in D.C., which would end at the White House.

"Lucas Nguyen, you spineless coward! You couldn't tell me to my face that you didn't have the guts to execute my orders, so you went AWOL instead. You, my most trusted confidant and friend since childhood, we graduated from West Point together and we always looked out for each other. How could you, of all people, do this to me Lucas?

"How the hell am I supposed to run this country without a cabinet," He whined. There was no one in the office with him, but his voice was raised as if there was.

Hayden was furious about the disappearance of his four most senior cabinet members over the past forty-eight-hours, cursing them in frenzied outbursts of rage, the Secret Service agents outside just glanced at each other and shook their heads. Nothing had to be said—the new President was coming apart at the seams.

A few hours later, Colonels Cameron Stillwater and Howard Baum stood silently before Hayden, waiting for his rage to erupt.

"You're telling me that between the two of you and the entire Secret Service, *no one* can find a trace of Generals Frayser, Nguyen, Potter, or Neeley?"

"That's correct, sir," Stillwater answered timidly. "No one has seen or heard from Frayser or Nguyen since their last meeting. As far as we can tell, Neeley went to dinner at an Italian restaurant and disappeared. He was seen leaving, but no one knows where he went. And you were the last one to see Potter."

This can't be happening! Hayden's face was red; his eyes

were bloodshot from lack of sleep, his hair was disheveled, his movements were stuttered—he looked deranged.

"I want every person who reported to each of those men in here with a status report in two hours. They *must* know where their superiors are. I want my protection doubled. Is that clear?"

"Yes sir," they replied.

"Good, add yourselves to the Secret Service protection detail and make sure you *both* make it to that meeting in two hours."

They nodded and left the Oval Office knowing that there were no Secret Service agents left to assign to Hayden's protection detail let alone assigning some of them to their own protection.

As the two of them left the Oval Office, Hayden punched a button summoning his aide. "Dean, get Frank Sterling over here on the double."

Dean recognized the name of the Army psychiatrist immediately. "Yes, sir, right away."

When Dean was gone, that dreaded voice spoke again, *"what's the matter, Tommy? Having a few psychological problems?"*

Hayden looked up to see George Miller standing next to Laurie.

"Oh God, not another one!" Hayden exclaimed. "Just get out of here and leave me alone!"

"A psychiatrist isn't going to be able to help you Tommy," Laurie said. *"You can take all the drugs and psychotherapy you want, it won't help. We aren't imaginary voices in your head, Tom. We're real and you can't make us go away."*

"You really shouldn't have killed us, Tom," George said. *"You're never going to get rid of us."*

"We'll see about that," Hayden shivered as he covered his ears and lay his forehead against the desk. "We'll see."

The Rowen

Daniel and his leadership team were watching. He looked at Sam. "Time for the final stage?

Sam nodded. "Yes, Jack and I believe we have to make the move soon."

Jack nodded.

"Good, let every team finalize their part of the plan and let's meet in three hours to put it all together." Daniel said.

Baum caught Stillwater's eye as the two of them exited the Oval Office, he winked and asked, "Coffee?"

Stillwater nodded and followed.

They got themselves a takeaway coffee from the kitchen staff and found a secluded room in the basement which they were sure was not monitored. Of course, they had no way of knowing that Roy had attached a spyder to each of them earlier.

"Cameron, I... I..." Baum started with a stutter, "I don't know how to say this..."

"Howard, we've known each other for a long time, just spit it out and let's take it from there."

Baum nodded slowly. "The thing is, Cameron, I'm not sure what is going on in this place lately. It's as if everything has started going to hell in a handbasket the last few days.

"Hayden has gone off his rocker; he's hearing voices and seeing things—dead people. He's talking to himself, not just talking, screaming and shouting. And now the generals have disappeared—absconded if you ask me."

"Yes, I've noticed. Stillwater replied hesitantly. "I've noticed all of it, and I'm as concerned as you are."

"I take it you know he had George Miller killed so that

he could be the next in line for the presidency?" Baum asked.

Stillwater nodded.

"And to crown it all," Baum sighed, "I have it on good authority that the people out there are planning a protest march to the White House. I don't have to tell you how that's going to end, do I?"

"Nope you don't; I know, it's going to end in chaos and bloodshed. And I don't blame the people, we are to blame. We've not delivered on our promises. Robert Falcon Scott said, *Hunger and fear are the only realities in dog life: an empty stomach makes a fierce dog.*"

Baum nodded. "You're right about that. People become ungovernable when they're hungry, they will only stoke violence. And, Hayden has made it clear, he wants to shoot his way out of it. I don't know about you Cameron, but I want no part of that."

"Neither do I," Stillwater interjected.

The two men stopped talking and stared at each other for a long while. As if to ask, *what now?*

Baum spoke first. "I'm not going back to my office. From here, I'm going straight to my car. I'm going to pick up my family and I'm going to disappear. Maybe he will find me and court martial me, that's okay. I'll face that if and when it happens but for now I'm getting my family and getting out of harm's way."

Stillwater was staring into blank space when Baum stopped talking. His voice was croaky when he spoke softly, "I... well... I haven't thought that far yet... but... I think there is no other option for me either. Whatever we do it's going to end badly for all of us. If Hayden gets hold of us we're dead, if the mobs get hold of us it will be the same."

Daniel looked at Sam on the screen against the wall and

then at Jack across the table from him. "What do you want to do? Grab them or let them go?"

Before Sam or Jack could answer, Nigel said, "Daniel, I apologize for interrupting, I know you haven't asked me, but if it is possible we must try to keep them alive… and their families. If we abduct them Hayden might go after their families."

"I agree, let's hear what Jack and Sam think. Up till now Hayden has not harassed the generals' families, but he might just get it in his sick head to start doing so. My only proviso is that we don't jeopardize the operation. Jack, Sam?"

"I can get Tectus to pick them all up and take them to different safe houses. It should be quick. None of their families have protection details." Jack replied.

"You agree with that Sam?" Daniel asked.

"Yes, as long as Jack can make sure that it's done quickly and efficiently and that our main operation is not compromised."

"Good, gentlemen, make it happen. See you in a few hours," Daniel ended the connection and turned to Jack. "You sure about this Jack?"

"There are a lot of variables here, six different families in as many locations; it will require a bit of coordination. But I am confident Tectus can pull it off. I'll let them run it as an independent operation as they see fit. That way we stay out of it and whether they pull it off or not won't have any impact on what we are planning."

"Excellent. Please keep me posted."

Hayden was throwing the mother of all tantrums when no one turned up for the meeting he had ordered Baum and Stillwater to arrange. He yelled at the Chief of Staff, the Secret Service agents and anyone else in sight, but all to no avail; none of them had seen Baum and Stillwater since they left the Oval Office earlier, and none of the staffers working for the vanished generals had any knowledge of a meeting they were supposed to attend.

Half an hour later someone checked the videos recorded by the security cameras and saw that both Baum and Stillwater had left in their cars not long after their earlier meeting with Hayden. This last bit of news drove Hayden to edge of insanity as he realized that he was the only one left.

Chapter Seventy-Eight

REDUCE THE TRANSFER RATE

Siasha and Tawndo were in their room silently cuddled in each other's arms. When they had left the lab, they had all agreed to meet back there in six hours. The idea was everyone would rest, but Siasha couldn't. She'd sat at the table in their room going over the original experiment data several more times before she settled into the comfort of Tawndo's arms.

She was quiet for a few minutes before she started talking. "Tawndo, I've got something to say, and I want you to hear me out before you comment. Agreed?"

He looked at her cautiously, "Do I have a choice?" When she just smiled at him, he said, "Very well, agreed."

"I've gone over the original experiment documents several times. I think a merge between Tawndo and Robert is possible." She explained to him in the simplest possible terms what it meant and what risks he would take if he agreed.

After hearing her out, Tawndo simply said, "I'm ready. Talk to Linkola and get him to help you do it."

"Tawndo, if you do this, there is a chance your feelings for me will change when Robert is activated," she started to cry softly, "I don't want to lose you again."

He tightened his arms around her and kissed her gently, "I will always love you, Siasha. My body may change, and the mind that merges with mine may change things, but as long as there is a bit, however small it may be, of Tawndo left in me after this, I will always carry the love I have for you with me.

"I hope you are wrong and that I will still be in control, but if something should happen, know that I love you and with your help, I will fight as hard as I can to bring that to the front so that we can be together as we have always been."

She snuggled closer to his side, tucking her head under his chin and clung to him while she listened to his heartbeat.

He caressed her cheek gently and willed her to feel his strength and his love.

They drifted into an uneasy sleep, lost in their hopes and fears, holding tightly to the love they shared.

Linkola started to object, but she stopped him, "You agreed to hear me out." Siasha said. "Tawndo's body does not have an elevated level of adrenaline in it, and he is not in fear for his life.

"Robert's synapse patterns have faded quite a bit, but many of them are still there and will still work for him. Tawndo's are dominant and will likely allow him to maintain the mind during the merge. He is also fully aware of the procedure and what will be happening to him.

"I believe, given all this, if we temporarily suppress the

secretion of Adrenaline and restrain him during the initial merge, it could be done successfully."

Linkola was frozen with anger. "You already know how I feel about this and yet you want to try again!"

"Yes, I do know how you feel. I've again studied your original research and theory about the merge process. They lied to you and forced you to use the information prematurely, and the result was a disaster.

"You believed in this process once, Linkola. You are a good scientist, and your research is solid. The theory is sound. Merging is possible, and you know it.

"Those men took good research and defiled it by using it before the process was ready and in a deplorable manner. Don't let their disregard and abuse of science stop you. Merging Tawndo and Robert could save this world from a terrible fate if they can stop the Re'an.

"I'm begging you to consider what I've said, evaluate it against your original research, and decide if it is valid. Will you at least do that?"

Linkola was silent for so long Siasha thought he was going to refuse to speak to her. At last, he bowed his head and answered her.

"I don't need to evaluate it… your theory is sound. I too was up most of the night reviewing the data and have come to the same conclusion. I am just afraid to try it. Once the process is started, it cannot be stopped."

Siasha considered this for a moment. "What would happen if we sedated Tawndo so that the two of them came to consciousness at the same time?"

"The synapses start forming patterns immediately. It is likely they would wake up equally, and we would have a repeat of the earlier experiments."

"Could you somehow reduce the transfer rate to give Tawndo and Robert time to adjust to one another?"

It was Linkola's turn to ponder the question. "Well, perhaps. There has never been a need to reduce the speed of the transfer, but maybe an adjustment could be made. I'll have to think about that one. Let's take a look at the equipment and see if it could be modified."

Tawndo and Korda entered the lab just as they were opening the Itran unit.

"What are you doing?" Korda inquired.

At Linkola's nod, Siasha recounted their conversation and concluded by saying, "so we are checking to see if the transfer rate of the Itran can be adjusted."

Tawndo offered to work with Linkola, and, knowing his technical capabilities, Siasha was glad to step aside and let them figure it out.

Chapter Seventy-Nine

WE FOUND THEM!

Cliff Willis stepped into the command center at Raven Rock looking for Daniel and located him in a secluded office on the other side of the big room, deep in conversation with Raj and Roy.

"Cliff! Welcome, please join us." Daniel greeted. "I was just about to go looking for you; I have some good news!

"Raj and Roy here," he said nodding toward the two men, "were just telling me that their teams have successfully installed new software on the Skywalker satellites, which should give us the ability to locate the Trepang!"

"What!" Willis exclaimed in astonishment. "That is great news! Will we be able to communicate with them securely too?"

"That will take a little more work and adjusting once we find her," Raj said, "but yes, I believe we will be able to."

Willis grinned. "Well, fella's, I can help you narrow down your search, but it sure would be helpful to be able to talk to them."

Three pairs of eyes stared at him. "What do you have, Cliff?" Daniel asked.

"We have her location, but something seems to be wrong.

As you know, we haven't received any contact from her for the past five days. However, about an hour ago, we received a ping from her on the agreed frequency at exactly one minute before the scheduled time, and again at exactly one minute after the scheduled time. Sending the signals as they did, one minute before and after the scheduled time is the code to let us know they are in some kind of trouble. Maybe it explains why she is also at the wrong depth and nearly a quarter mile off course."

"Was there any other contact?" Daniel wanted to know.

Willis shook his head. "We've tried the prearranged frequencies, but she's not responding."

"I don't like the sound of that," Daniel said. "Guys, how soon can you use the satellite to have a look at her location?"

"Right now," Roy responded moving toward a station a few seats down.

They all gathered behind him as he connected to the satellite and brought up an image of the Earth on the display monitor.

"Where is she?"

"Over the continental shelf in the Chukchi Sea," Willis said and handed Roy a slip of paper, "here are the last known coordinates."

They waited silently while Roy worked the controls. "That's odd" he muttered.

"What?" Daniel asked.

"She's still at the same coordinates; she hasn't moved."

"Can you tell if she has power, or see her through the water? Anything?"

"All we would get now is a dim outline at best. We'll need time to make adjustments to the software to see more detail," Raj replied."

"Okay, let's have a look at what you have now and then you can start work on the adjustments as soon as we're done," Daniel said.

Roy carefully zoomed in on the sub's location. Raj was correct, what they saw was a dark spot in the ocean, oblong and it appeared to be hanging at an odd angle. There were also several small objects moving around it.

"Looks like she's bow heavy," Willis stated.

"How do you know which end it is?" Raj asked.

"The bow is larger and more spherical than the stern and it is now hanging lower than the stern—could be that she took on some water."

"Not the normal position for a sub when stationary, I take it?" Roy commented.

"No, it's supposed to be perfectly horizontal when stationary." Willis replied. "Question is, what can we do to help them?"

"You said Admiral Johnson told you he was overseeing a project that's produced something, which could be able to reach the sub if we could find her." Daniel said.

Willis nodded.

"Well, I think it's time he starts setting that in motion. In the meantime, Raj, Roy, I want you to try and get clearer images and put us in direct communication with that sub… top priority.

Admiral Johnson listened carefully to what Willis had to say while pacing thoughtfully back and forth in the room, his shiny black military shoes silent on the thick carpet. At last he spoke.

"Very well; I will set things in motion for a rescue. However, I think it's imperative that I speak to Captain Locklin on the sub in person. Which means you'll have to take me to the people who located them."

"Hmm," Willis hesitated. He had a bit of a dilemma, Admiral Johnson didn't know anything about the operation in progress at Raven Rock and although he explicitly trusted the Admiral it was not his decision to make whether the Admiral could be taken to the facility or not. "You'll have to give me a few minutes. I have to get authorization for that."

Johnson was a bit taken aback but didn't say anything. He just nodded his understanding.

Willis left the room to make the call to Daniel on his secured mirror satellite phone. It took less than two minutes to explain the situation to Daniel and get the authorization. He was smiling when he returned to the room where Johnson was waiting. "I've been told by President Rossler that you are most welcome, Admiral."

"Excellent. I'll am ready when you are Mr. Secretary."

Less than three hours later they were all gathered around Roy and Raj at one of the desks again. This time with Admiral Johnson in attendance.

They had a long deliberation after Willis and Johnson arrived about the wisdom of contacting the Trepang. The clearer images produced by Raj's and Roy's tweaks to the software didn't reveal anything that they didn't already know.

Their dilemma was that any communication with the Trepang could be intercepted. However, they had to weigh the lives of the people onboard the boat against the potential consequences of being discovered by eavesdroppers with nefarious intent. The former cause won.

"All right, Roy," Daniel said, "let's see if they're listening."

They had agreed that either Admiral Johnson or Secretary Willis should do the talking as the Captain was unlikely to answer if he heard the voice of an unknown person.

Admiral Johnson gave Roy a frequency, waited while he dialed it in, and then spoke into the mic. "Trepang, Trepang, this is Sting Ray. Come in Trepang."

They waited. Thirty seconds passed and the Admiral repeated the call. That was part of the agreed security protocol.

A crackle came over the speaker. *Sting Ray, this is Sea Horse. Please repeat your call.*

Johnson grinned. He didn't repeat the call, instead he said, "that's the correct response. Tune to this frequency," he said pointing to the dial next to Roy's hand.

When Roy had it dialed in, he repeated his call a third time. "Trepang, Trepang, this is Sting Ray. Come in Trepang."

"Sting Ray, this is Trepang. It's good to hear from you, over."

"Trepang it's a big relief to hear from you. What's going on out there?"

In coded language, Locklin quickly gave them a run down on the events of the past five days, describing the takeover of the boat as a 'restructuring of command,' never mentioning Brideaux or any names, neither referring to prisoners, using the word 'trainees' instead. In similar fashion, he explained the failed attempt to surface and took great care not to disclose their location.

"I've got divers in the water making repairs. They just got our mast antenna working again a few minutes ago, good thing you didn't call any sooner."

"How bad is the damage?"

"In short, we won't be going anywhere for a while yet, and it won't be fast when we do."

"What's your best estimate of when you might be moving again?"

"About another eighteen to twenty hours. We still have to remove the remaining bow plane and it's taking longer than we expected to seal up the damage to the upper bow compartment and get the water out of it."

Johnson looked surprised. "That's a water-tight compartment with internal access only; how are you going to do that?"

Locklin laughed. "I'm not sure we are, but my acting executive officer believes if we seal up most of the damage and start pumping more air into the compartment it will force the water out and we can seal the remaining damage before reducing the air pressure."

"I don't know if that's even been tried before. Let's hope it works."

"Well, the only sure way to fail is not to try," Locklin said.

Daniel grinned, *I surely would like to meet this guy as soon as he gets off that boat. A man with such an attitude is worth knowing.*

"All right, Captain. Keep up the good work. I'm sending help your way just in case it turns out you need it."

"I appreciate that Admiral. This boat took a beating, Trepang out."

"God speed, Trepang. Sting Ray out."

Admiral Johnson placed the mic on the table and clapped Roy and Raj on the shoulders. "What you've done today is staggering, thank you both."

His statement was followed by a group sigh of relief as if everyone had been holding their breath, followed by a release of joyous energy.

"Raj, we found them!" Roy exclaimed softly but jubilantly. "We really found them!" They high-fived each other while the others patted them on the back.

Daniel let the mini-celebration continue for a few minutes, then called them all back to the work at hand. "Ok, ok!" he said raising his hand for silence. "Before you award yourself Congressional Medals of Honor, now that you found them, we need to figure out how to help them. Right?"

He looked at Johnson. "Admiral, I hear you've put a rescue plan in motion. What can we do to help?" he asked motioning for everyone to take a seat at a nearby table.

After settling in to his seat, Admiral Johnson folded his hands in front of him on the table and began. "What I'm about to tell you is highly classified and must not be repeated outside this group."

Heads nodded in agreement all around the table.

"For the past two years, I have been working with a team at the Woods Hole Oceanographic Institute to design and build a new type of DSRV, Deep-Submergence Rescue Vehicle.

"In years gone by, we had two, the Mystic and the Avalon, but they were both decommissioned by 2010. "They were capable of rescuing twenty-four people at a time, up to a maximum depth of two-thousand feet. These DSRV's were short range vehicles only but they could be flown to any port in the world within twenty-four hours and then attached to a submarine and taken to the rescue site.

"Since 2010 they have been replaced with various forms of surface launched, remotely operated vehicles called SRDRS, Submarine Rescue Diving Recompression Systems.

"What isn't well known, is that more crews of distressed subs have been lost rather than rescued since the DSRV's were taken out of service because the tethers don't work as well. They take more than two days to be ready to deploy and then they still have to reach the rescue site. They can't dive as deep, and their maximum rescue capacity is limited to twelve people at a time, sometimes less depending on the vehicle in use. Some have even been lost when the umbilical cable became separated from the mother ship," Johnson paused, looking around the table at the intense faces before he continued.

"The Woods Hole team and I have designed and built a new type of DSRV. We believe its capable of much more than any other ever designed.

"It's both a scientific research sub and a rescue vehicle. It has living quarters for a crew of twelve, including scientists, and can briefly hold an additional fifty in rescue situations.

"It moves independently over long ranges, it's fast, it can mate up with another sub even at an angle of sixty degrees, and it's capable of performing rescues at up to two thousand five hundred feet."

"Why all the secrecy?" Raj asked.

"Because almost all submarine rescues are performed by the military on military vehicles. This is a privately financed and owned vehicle and some of its technology has been designed by MIT students and is almost futuristic."

Roy and Raj grinned. "We love futuristic," Raj said on their behalf.

Johnson continued. "I know our fleet gentlemen, and I'm telling you, this is the most advanced underwater vehicle on the planet."

Daniel grinned. "Well, can we use her? Is Woods Hole willing to participate in a rescue operation?"

Johnson leaned back in his chair, a slightly smug look on his face. "She's already on her way." He looked at his watch and grinned. "She put to sea three hours ago."

At the astonished looks on everyone's face Admiral Johnson explained. "Several days ago, I asked Captain Marcus to ready the sub for a deep-sea rescue mission. As soon as I received the coordinates of the Trepang, I met with him and gave him the mission details. The sub was ready to go and the crew on standby; they started arriving before I left."

Relieved smiles glowed on every face as they looked at one another.

"Well that is great news, Admiral!" Daniel exclaimed.

"Yes, it is" Willis agreed, "but we're not out of the woods yet."

"What do you mean?"

The Admiral answered, "The Trepang is damaged, we don't know how bad. We don't know if we will have to rescue the crew and prisoners or not.

"At this point, sending the Itinerant, that's the name of the DSRV, out is a precautionary measure. If it becomes necessary to use her, we will need a surface ship with a large decompression chamber and medical personnel for support. There are over one hundred people on that sub, the Itinerant can't carry them all at the same time."

"Not to mention a secure jail facility with armed guards," Roy muttered.

"Nah," Raj said, "as far as I'm concerned they can go down with the sub."

Daniel frowned at him.

"It was just a thought," Raj said, holding his hands up as if surrendering. "If we have to choose *that* would be my choice."

"Well, however this plays out, we'll to have to try and keep the prisoners alive." Daniel said.

Willis nodded his agreement. "And keep Hayden in the dark about the operation."

"Agreed," Daniel said. "Now, what are we going to do about a surface ship for support if the need arises?"

"I've had a ship on standby since the Trepang left port... that was just in case we needed alternative, secure accommodations for the prisoners. She is already on her way to the area. She's large enough to carry the decompression chamber and provide the support we need."

Satisfied, Daniel said, "Admiral, Mr. Secretary, it sounds like things are well in hand." Thank you for your diligence!"

Chapter Eighty

A TERRIBLE ORDEAL

"I am ready," Tawndo said quietly but with determination.

He was on the diagnostic bed; his arms, legs, and torso restrained and as an extra measure of care, Siasha had just administered a dose of Quatempar, a drug that caused temporary paralysis from the neck down, subdued the adrenal glands, but left the mind, speech, and vision alert.

Linkola approached the bed. "I need to ask you again, Tawndo. You understand the risk you are facing and are in full agreement with the humane termination of your life by lethal injection if this fails?"

That had been the only way that Linkola would agree to attempt the merge; temporary paralysis and immediate termination by lethal injection if the merge failed. While Tawndo didn't want to die, he did appreciate that Linkola did not want him to suffer mentally or physically, so he had agreed to Linkola's terms.

He spoke softly and measuredly, "Yes. I understand and am in full agreement with humane termination if the merge fails."

Linkola nodded.

"Linkola?" Tawndo's voice stopped him as he turned away. "Thank you for agreeing to do this, especially for taking into account my physical and mental well-being."

Saying nothing, Linkola just nodded and walked away.

"We're going to prepare you for surgery now. You will be conscious, but you will feel no pain while we implant Robert's chip," Siasha said, then whispered, "I love you."

Tawndo tried to nod, but couldn't because his head was held motionless by the restraints in preparation for the surgery. He smiled slightly, "and I am eternally devoted to you, Siasha."

She smiled back, squeezed his hand, and moved to the head of the table. Looking at Linkola she said, "As before, I will open and close, you will do the implant."

Linkola nodded. They both glanced at the instrument tray between them, noting the equipment they needed: Eiser, separator, grips, microchip, and both sealers were there. A new item had been added this time—an injection tube filled with a rapid acting lethal substance.

Locating the area of the previous skull penetration, Siasha again opened a small circular section of the skull bone on the top left side of the head. At that point, Linkola took her place and proceeded with the chip implant; gently tucking Robert's chip deep in the Central Sulcus next to Tawndo's and sealed it in place.

Linkola looked up at Siasha, and then toward the ceiling and closed his eyes as if offering a prayer. He sighed deeply and opened his eyes. "Here we go," he said as he pushed the button on the panel to activate the chip.

The panel lights flashed amber and blue. The setup process had begun. "No red lights, the chip is functioning as it should. You may close up," he said to Siasha.

Just as she completed sealing the incision, a bone-chilling scream erupted from Tawndo and alarms began flashing on the health monitor; the chip setup had been completed, and the transfer had begun.

"No! Not again!" shouted Linkola reaching for the syringe with the deadly fluid.

"Wait!" shouted Siasha grabbing Linkola's hand, preventing him from picking it up. "Wait," she said again stepping to Tawndo's side.

Placing her hands on either side of his head she shouted over his screams, "Tawndo! You are safe! You're alright! Look at me!"

Tawndo continued to scream, and the monitor alarms continued to flash. His heart was racing and his blood pressure dangerously high.

"Tawndo!" Siasha shouted again, "look at me!"

Some small part of his brain reacted, and his pain filled eyes looked at Siasha. "Help me! Please kill me! Please!" he screamed.

Linkola grabbed the tubule and moved to his side.

"Wait!" Siasha shouted again.

"Tawndo, focus! You are alright! You are merging with Robert. His last memory is of being shot. You must understand you are safe and unharmed so that he will understand."

"Nooooo!" He screamed.

"Yes! You are safe! You're safe!" she began to cry.

"Please Tawndo, my love, please, believe me!"

Somehow Tawndo managed to close his eyes and concentrated. The screaming immediately diminished and then suddenly it stopped. The heart rate monitor and blood pressure indicators ceased their upward climb.

"Terrified," Tawndo gasped. "Help me!" he begged.

Siasha smoothed her hands gently on his face, looking deep into his eyes. "You are safe, my love. I am right here with you, and you are going to be just fine. You're almost there my brave hero. Almost. Just hang on for a little while longer." She bent over and kissed him lightly on his forehead while she kept on whispering to him.

Time seemed to stand still while Siasha continued to sooth and reassure her terrified lover. After what seemed an eternity, his breathing slowed and the monitor alarms went silent.

Tawndo opened his eyes. "I love you; but ... who are you?"

Siasha smiled sadly. "I am Siasha; who are you?"

"See-osh-ah. You seem familiar to me. I am ... I am ... I ..." fear filled his eyes, "Who am I."

"Relax," she soothed, "it's ok. You're a little confused right now; you've been through a terrible ordeal. It will all come back before long. Know that you are safe and among friends. I love you."

"Oh. Okay," he said weakly as consciousness left him.

Siasha quickly glanced at the monitors and saw that his breathing and heart rate were steady, and the blood pressure indicator was approaching normal. "Linkola?"

"I think the merge overwhelmed him. The brain has a way of protecting itself by shutting down the conscious mind temporarily. Let's give him some time and see what happens."

Chapter Eighty-One

THE HOPE OF TWO WORLDS

Robert awoke slowly, his eyes opening to the dim light of an unfamiliar yet recognizable place. *Where am I?* He looked around the lab and recognized it for what is was and knew it well, yet he was absolutely sure he'd never seen it before. *What is going on....?*

He started to get up and realized he was restrained. Fear settled into the pit of his stomach, and a sour taste began to rise in his throat, "What do you want?" he spoke to the shadows. He was answered only by silence—he tried to relax and think.

Images danced in his mind; battles in unknown places, a secret life working with - who are they? A cold wasteland surrounding a valley of paradise; sharing drinks in a bar with a very tall man... my brother? Faces of women; faces of - friends? Technological information; geological information; *what is all of this? What does it mean?*

For hours Robert lay quietly as the visions and memories washed through his mind and at last they began to form a whole. He knew who he was. He had been merged with another mind, an ancient but technologically advanced mind. He was human, yet part of another culture, a trusted friend and yet a stranger. He was the hope of two worlds, yet known only by one.

He didn't like what had happened to him, but he understood why it had been done. He could hate these people and refuse to help them, but he knew his own world needed his help and he would not refuse. Given a choice, he would not have done this, but then again, given a choice, how could he not? It was a riddle he could not solve. "Get over it son, and get on with it," he said to himself in a language he didn't understand. W*hat? Did I just speak in another language?*

At that moment, the door to the lab opened, and the instant bright illumination made his eyes water.

"You're awake!" breathed Korda.

"Who are you and what did you say?" He said in English, to Korda's consternation. "Ah, now I remember you are Korda."

Korda smiled. He walked to one of the shelves and picked up two translation devices, mumbling, "Just like Linkola said, he might wake up speaking in his mother tongue."

Ever since they were able to start following the media in the world outside the cave, they had trained the translator to be able to translate between their own language and every other language which they could receive on their devices.

He returned to the table with the translator hanging from a lanyard around his neck, fitted one around Robert's neck and said, "Welcome."

"I am glad you got through the procedure. Are you in any pain Tawndo? Shall I get Linkola and Siasha?"

"No, I am not in pain. I am not, Tawndo. I am Robert."

Korda blinked.

"I know what has happened, and I want to help. Please let me out of these restraints. I won't hurt you."

"I'm not supposed to do that until Linkola and Siasha say it's ok."

"Yes, I know. In that case, perhaps you should bring them here."

Korda nodded, but as he turned toward the door, the two of them walked in.

"He's awake! But he speaks only English; I will get you each a translator."

They rushed to join Korda at Robert's side.

Korda handed them each a translator which they hung around their necks.

"Tawndo! How do you feel?" Siasha asked excitedly.

"With my fingers," Robert replied dryly.

Siasha frowned; that wasn't Tawndo.

"Now, let me out of here," he commanded.

THAT was Tawndo, she brightened again and leaned to kiss him, but he turned his face away.

"Tawndo?"

"I am not Tawndo," he replied tightly. "I am Robert Cartwright. Who are you?"

"Oh, I'm sorry," she said and turned away quickly. She had her hand over her mouth, and her shoulders were shaking with telltale grief as she hurried from the room.

The three men watched her leave. "Don't worry Robert; she will be alright. I will check on her later."

Robert nodded, a shadow in his eyes, "See that you do. Now, let me out of these things," he demanded.

There was definitely something of the soldier and commander that once was Tawndo in Robert, but Linkola noted a softening in his eyes and the set of his chin. Upon release from the restraints, his stance and stride were altered as well. Some of him was Tawndo, but most of him was not Tawndo.

"I suppose you have many questions ..." Linkola began.

"No," Robert responded bluntly, "I don't."

Tawndo again.

Speaking in a more relaxed tone he added, "Thanks to your 'Tawndo', I know all about you, this facility," he gestured around him, "the B'ran, Re'an, the L'gundo, Tunguska, The Healer, Viktor, and all the rest.

"I can't say that I'm happy with what you've done to me; you had no right," he added brusquely. The next moment he was calm again and spoke softly, "However, what is done is done; I must accept it and move on."

Linkola and Korda looked at one another. The personality obviously had not stabilized yet. Would it get worse, or better? Which one is going to be the dominant one? They both wondered and worried.

"I would like to examine you ... Robert," Linkola said. "I want to make sure you are healthy, and I'd like to take another brain scan if you'll allow it."

Robert tensed as if to object and then relaxed, "Of course ... the experiments. You need to make sure my brain is stabilizing and not deteriorating. I'll cooperate," he added as he sat down on the diagnostic table.

Linkola sighed with relief and prepared Robert and the equipment for the scan. Korda assisted.

"This won't hurt a bit, Robert."

"I know. Just get on with it," he growled.

The three of them were silent while the scanner ran.

"Well, your body is healthy," reported Linkola. "Heart rate, respiration, blood pressure, and adrenaline levels are all normal."

"What about my brain?"

"I think it is too early to say for certain, but it does appear to be in good working order. I don't see any damage or anything unusual. Your synaptic pattern appears to be redeveloping rapidly."

"And Tawndo?"

"His pattern is there, but not quite as strong as I was expecting. Perhaps, if you don't mind, we can run the scan again tomorrow? It will give me a better idea of what is happening."

Robert nodded. "I believe the reason why you brought me back is to contact my friends at the Rossler Foundation?"

Linkola nodded.

"Well if this merge was a success I think we should get started on that. For some reason, I have the feeling there is some crisis heading our way which is why we did this. Is that correct?"

"Yes, there is a major threat to us," Linkola replied, "that's why you agreed to the merge. It has never been done before. You are a very brave man. And yes, I agree, we should get started as quickly as possible—as soon as we can be sure that the merge has worked. It will take a few days before we will know for sure, but once it's confirmed, who do you think would be the best person to contact at the Rossler Foundation?"

Jumping down from the table, Robert slapped his hands together and rubbed them vigorously. "My old mate JR! I'm going to see my old buddy JR!" he said with an eager laugh and clapped Linkola on the shoulder.

Robert. No doubt.

Chapter Eighty-Two

FINALIZING THE PLAN

The news about the protest march to the White House reached Daniel and his team through their Tectus contacts who were participating in its planning.

Sam, Jack, and a few others made a quick analysis of the most likely scenario that could develop during such a march. The White House Secret Services agents and any other security forces that Hayden could muster would probably be focused on the defense of the White House. In all likelihood, most staff would have been sent home to get them out of the way, which would leave Hayden's personal protection detail at a minimum. It was the ideal time to make their move on the White House.

The strategy they developed, if they couldn't stop the march, was to bring the crowd close enough to the White House to be a threat, but keep them out of effective bullet range of Hayden's forces. It was one of those things that was easier said than done—crowd behavior was unpredictable at best and almost impossible to control without using force. This was not going to be a protest march down Pennsylvania Avenue to make a few inflammatory speeches and hand over a petition—the people's hunger, frustration, and desperation were going to aggravate the situation. It was going to turn violent—there was no doubt about it.

At the same time, Baum and Stillwater decided to disappear, word came in from Tectus that the pressure from the people to start the march immediately was mounting by the hour and that the organizers were not able to put the march off much longer—it was going to happen that night.

Daniel immediately cleared his schedule and asked Sam to gather the operations team for a final briefing before swinging into action.

An hour later everyone was in the meeting, some at Raven Rock, Dennis and Eric had dialed in from their lair, Sam and the rest were in the war room at the Rabbit Hole.

"Okay, everyone let's get going," Sam started. "Eric, do you have a time for when the march will start?"

"Yes, it's scheduled to start at 7pm, at West Potomac Park near the Martin Luther King Junior monument, about two miles from the White House. From there they will march to the West side of the Washington Monument, which they will reach at about 7:30. There they'll make some speeches and rally the crowd for about an hour before marching to the White House. And that is the part that is worrisome."

"You've made the organizers aware of Hayden's orders to use live ammo and his shoot-to-kill instructions?" Sam asked.

"Yes, we did, "Eric sighed, "and we had a lot of arguments about the wisdom of proceeding with the march in light of the dangers. Alas, they are going ahead with the march—the people are desperate. The best Eric and I could do was to convince them to appoint crowd-marshals to try and keep them out of range of the firearms, which Hayden's men would be carrying, and try to stop them from storming the White House.

"Sam, we're deeply worried that innocent people are going to die tonight and there is very little we can do to prevent it."

Sam looked at Roy and nodded.

"I might be able to assist with that," Roy said. "A while ago I equipped a few of our drones with microwave beam generators to be used against crowds if required.

"What I have is not new technology. However, it might be the first time it is mounted on drones. The technology has been around for more than a decade, known by names such as Active Denial System or heat ray. It is non-lethal and will only heat the skin of the people in the crowd stepping over a demarcated line.

"They will feel their skin heating up very quickly. It will be very uncomfortable, but they won't sustain burn wounds, and I can assure you, once they've experienced it, they will toe the line - maybe even lose interest."

Sam grinned. "Eric, Dennis, any problems with Roy's suggestion?"

"Absolutely not! That's a godsend," Eric replied.

"Excellent. You and Roy will just have to figure out where you want to establish those no-trespassing lines and he will see to it that the area between that line and the White House remains no-man's land."

Roy and Eric nodded.

"I'd suggest no closer than the middle of the ellipse … keep them on the South side of it." Eric suggested.

Sam nodded, "Fine, show Roy where you want it," and turned toward Jack.

"Jack you're next. Step us through the plan as it stands now."

Jack explained how he and Dennis McMahon, the ex-Navy SEAL and second in command of Tectus, would each head up a team. Dennis's team consisting of twenty-five former SEALs, Delta Force operators, Army Rangers, and Recon Marines would be responsible for neutralizing the Secret Service Agents and any other security forces on the outside of the White House and prevent them from reentering.

Jack and his team, consisting of JR, Aaron, Mouse, Kerinski, and a few former Secret Service agents, was responsible for neutralizing the people inside of the White House and getting a hold of Hayden.

Daniel and two Secret Service Agents would accompany Jack's group but would be kept in hiding in one of the tunnels until the White House was secured. As was expected, this idea did not come without pushback from Daniel. He wanted to be part of the action.

"So, what are you saying?" He had objected when Jack first introduced that part of the plan a few days ago. "You want me to say something like; 'follow me, I'm right behind you?' Not going to happen, Jack. I'm going in with you and the team."

Jack knew better than to argue with him and had turned the matter over to the full leadership group at the next morning's meeting.

It took half an hour, but in the end, they convinced Daniel, first by pleading with him to be reasonable, and when that didn't work by threatening to lock him up with

Hayden's cabinet and come and get him when it was all over.

Daniel gave up in frustration but got the last word. "It's obvious you jackasses have conspired against me. Be warned; I intend to deal with you on my first day in office." He had smiled wryly.

"Promises, promises. Didn't take you long to learn political speak, did it?" Sinclair quipped as everyone started laughing.

Sam was smiling now as he reflected about that little exchange for a moment before he continued. "Salome, Nigel, you're next. Take us through your part of the plan."

Salome explained that they were still monitoring every move and every conversation taking place between Hayden and his staff. And it was no surprise to hear that Hayden was on the brink of total collapse from exhaustion and insanity.

"It's not going to take much to push him over the edge," she said, Rebecca nodding in agreement. "His condition is deteriorating rapidly; the disappearance of his last cabinet members has all but cracked him."

Rebecca continued. "However, as desirable as it might seem to push him the last bit, we have to be very careful. We have no idea what he might be capable of if he enters into a state of psychosis—he can cause unimaginable damage and destruction, killing many innocent people—much like a suicide bomber."

"Jack, it is imperative that you and your team take him as quickly as humanly possible," Sam commented.

Jack nodded. "Yes, absolutely. Salome has an idea, which might help to get him isolated right from the start."

Everyone was looking at her to explain.

"We'll let Nguyen appear to him within the next few hours to advise him. You'll remember that he is Hayden's most trusted confidant and friend. The man who we suspect was responsible for the killing of George Miller to open the way for Hayden to become president. We also suspect that he had a hand in the killing of the former Secretaries of Agriculture and Energy, Richard Westfield and Hank McMillian as well as the death of Bob Thompson former Secretary of Homeland Security and probably also Carrie Trent."

"But I got the impression when listening to Hayden's mad ravings the other day that he is going to kill Nguyen for abandoning him," Nigel said.

Salome grinned. "Not if Nguyen appears to him from the dead."

"Ah, okay," Nigel chuckled. "I would certainly like to see that meeting when it takes place," Nigel said.

Sam, ran down the checklist to make sure that everyone understood what was expected of him or her and that they had all the equipment they would need. Raj and his team had already set up, configured, and tested the communications systems to make sure they could be in touch with each group throughout the attack.

Roy was busy double-checking that everyone was sure how to operate his gadgets when Salome interrupted.

"Sorry Roy, I just got word that Hayden is having a session with advisors and the Secret Service agents in two hours, to plan their strategy to defend the White House during the march tonight.

"We should get Nguyen in front of Hayden before that meeting."

"Agreed" Sam responded. "Have you got your holographic movie set ready for that?"

"Yep," Salome nodded. "We've just been waiting for the right moment."

"It still beats me how you and the propeller-heads have made that work. But don't bother to explain, can't afford any brain damage until this is over, I need every brain cell in good working order." Sam grinned, the rest of the elders laughed and agreed with him.

Chapter Eighty-Three

TO ADVISE YOU AS BEST I CAN

Forty-Five minutes later, Hayden paced the Oval Office deep in thought, strategizing his defense of the White House during the protest march planned for later in the evening.

He did his best to maintain his macho appearance in front of the staff, but when he was alone he was a nervous wreck, and he knew it.

There wasn't much governing he could do at this point, and his top priority was saving his own skin. He needed the White House protected - he wanted *himself* protected.

His own pacing began to irritate him, so he returned to his desk and sat down to prepare for the meeting.

Studying maps of the streets and buildings around the White House captured his attention, so he didn't notice at first when General Lucas Nguyen appeared near the fireplace out of nowhere. His skin began to itch and then crawl as the feeling of being watched washed over him. He looked up, saw Nguyen, and let out a high-pitched scream.

Nguyen smiled, "Hello, Mr. President!"

"I'll kill you!" Hayden screamed as he stormed toward Nguyen. "Where the hell have you been?" he shrieked. "I'm going to kill you, you son-of-a-bitch," as he reached for Nguyen's throat to strangle him.

To his horror his hands passed right through the man and with a sudden understanding, he realized Nguyen was dead - a ghost. "Oh, my God!" he whispered, withering even as he spoke. "You're dead! When did it happen? *How* did it happen?"

"After our last meeting, I left your office and went out for a couple of drinks. I was kidnapped and held in custody by a group of malcontents that don't like the way you were doing things. They thought I might be a handy piece of merchandise to have at the 'right' time ... whenever that was."

Hayden slumped into his chair and stared at Nguyen while he continued to explain.

"They kept me alive until about an hour ago, when those crazy people who are organizing the march tonight stormed the place where I was being held and killed me."

"So why are you here now?" Hayden asked quietly.

"To offer you help and to advise you as best I can. Now that I'm dead, I'm not bound by time; I can see into the past and the future."

Hayden's confused and troubled mind grabbed at the information like a drowning man. "So, you know exactly how this is going to go down tonight?" he asked as if he were sitting in front of the Oracle of Delphi.

"Not exactly. When it comes to time and how things happen, it's like coming to a fork in a road—where you end up depends on which road you choose to follow. In other words, there is more than one possible outcome."

Back at Raven Rock and the Rabbit Hole, the audience

spent the next thirty minutes following a deep philosophical discussion between Hayden and Nguyen about death and the concept of time, frequently shaking their heads at Salome and Rebecca's fertile imaginations.

"So," Nguyen said, "there are three possible outcomes. In one, you are arrested and Rossler takes over as President. In another, you are killed by the mob and Rossler takes over as President. In the last scenario, the crowd never reaches the White House, they are peacefully dispersed, and you remain in power as President.

Hayden leaned forward in his chair at the mention of the third possibility. "So, tell me, how can I make that third option happen?"

"Yes, I thought you'd like that option best. Well, you will need to …" and Hayden's face turned from despair to triumph as he listened carefully to Nguyen telling him in great detail how that option would play out and exactly what he, Hayden, had to do to make sure it was the option that would prevail.

As Nguyen finished, Hayden sat back in thoughtful silence for a moment. "Do you know what happened to the other cabinet members?"

"Unfortunately, they got cold feet and tried to run away. They were captured by that rebel group who is organizing the march. That group still has them. I expect they will meet with the same fate as I did."

"How in the hell did they know about the cabinet members running away?" Hayden demanded.

"Your Chief of Staff, Rod Barrett, is the man who has been leaking information from this office," Nguyen whispered.

Hayden's blood pressure skyrocketed, and as Nguyen

vanished from the room, he opened the top left drawer of his desk and took out his gun.

It was time for the meeting and as the Secret Service agents arrived, he yelled at them to find Barrett immediately and bring him in. With a sense of satisfaction, he cocked the gun and laid it on the desk before him; he was going to shoot Barrett the moment he walked through the door. But Barrett couldn't be found anywhere.

His new military officers arrived only moments behind the Secret Service agents and Hayden got right down to business with them. Keeping his meeting with the deceased Nguyen to himself, he outlined what needed to happen just as Nguyen told him.

Hayden appeared calm, cool and collected as he delivered his instructions to his advisors, but he had a wild look in his eyes. They were used to his ravings but this calm, cool and collected business simply scared the daylights out of them.

They didn't exactly agree with his plans but didn't dare to disagree—Hayden's wild eyes and seeing the POTUS with a sidearm ready at hand was reason enough for them to shut up and listen.

The people gathered at Raven Rock and the Rabbit Hole sighed in relief when the meeting ended and Hayden's plan, as suggested by Nguyen, was unanimously accepted without any changes.

Chapter Eighty-Four

OPERATION WINNOW

Eric and a few of his Tectus team members moved slowly through the milling and growing crowd at West Potomac Park. The spyders and nearly invisible ear phones and mics he and his team wore, allowed everyone back at the Ops Center at the Rabbit Hole to see what was happening and the entire team to communicate inconspicuously with one another.

The Ops Center had the video screens and secured satellite connections to the mirror phones and all of Roy's toys; they could monitor and respond to situations and needs in real time as they arose and communicate directly and instantly with all key people.

"Sam, don't be misled by the calmness of the crowd, I can feel the tension, you can cut it with a knife." Eric reported nervously, "it isn't going to last."

Eric checked his watch. *Jack and Dennis, and their teams would be moving into position in the tunnels, readying themselves to approach and enter the White House from opposite sides.*

The corners of his mouth twitched in a brief smile as he

thought of Daniel and the fight he'd put up to be part of the invading party. He had to admire the man; he wasn't the type of leader who would lead from the back.

Making a bet with himself that the two Secret Service agents wouldn't be able to keep Daniel hidden in the tunnel until called for, he continued to move slowly and easily toward the front of the crowd.

Sam's voice came through his earpiece with a status update for everyone. "Alright people, standby, this show is about to get on the road.

"Hayden had his surveillance drones launched a few minutes ago; they're now overhead at the park, monitoring the crowd. Roy, are your drones ready?"

"Already on site about three-hundred feet above Hayden's. Telemetry indicates approximately half a million people in attendance," Roy responded.

"Standing by to jam Hayden's drone's signals and get them out of there," Raj added.

"Very good," Sam replied. "According to our little spyfly and spyder friends, Hayden and his advisors have secured themselves in the Situation Room to watch. Most of the armed guards are still inside the White House."

At 7:30 Eric interrupted, "Scout One to base. The march has begun," he reported as the front of the crowd moved down the street with banners and weapons, shouting slogans.

"Away with Hayden! End martial law! Hayden be gone! Hayden lied to us! We are starving! Feed us! No more promises! We want food!" were just a few of the expressions Eric could see and hear.

"We see them," Sam replied. "Alright everyone, here we go. We have time before they head for the White House, but stand ready and be prepared to move at a moment's notice."

"Kingpin, Sandman, Knight One ... you're a go to enter the tunnels. Proceed to your designated holding areas and stand by." The call sign Kingpin was allocated to Jack, Sandman was Dennis, and Knight One was Daniel.

With the assistance of Mouse, Kerinski, and Elize—the young girl who helped Laurie and Daniel escape from the White House when Hayden took over, the team had put together a detailed map of the White House and its tunnels. They knew every room, hallway, closet, and corner better than Hayden or any of his Secret Service agents.

At Sam's order, the teams began to move out. In the basement of the Blair House, Mouse—designated the call sign 'Kingpin Two' opened the door to the tunnel and motioned for Jack and the team to follow. They moved quietly through the tunnel to the base of the stairs outside the secret entrance to the basement office on the North-West corner of the West Wing where they would wait.

At the same time, 'Sandman Two,' Kerinski, was leading Dennis and his team through a nearly invisible opening in the side of the storm drain they were in. "It's so dark in that alcove, no wonder no one's ever found this," Dennis whispered.

"Yes, it's part of the old drainage system from the White House," Kerinski replied.

Daniel paced quietly in the basement of the Blair House under the watchful eyes of his two Secret Service agents.

He hated the idea of not being with one of the teams. He stopped before the door to the tunnel and glared at it, then turned to glower at his agents before resuming his path across the basement and back.

Their job was to protect him, with their lives if necessary, and they had made it clear to him that they would do whatever it took to keep him safe—even from himself. "Just following orders, sir," they told Daniel.

Elize, who had accompanied them and agreed to stay with Daniel, smiled internally at his frustration but gave him a sympathetic look the next time their eyes met.

Sam turned to his team in the Ops Center. "Let's have a report from everyone, starting with the Situation Room."

One by one the people designated to monitor each area reported.

"Hayden and his advisors are watching the march from the situation room through the video feed from his drones. Two guards are outside the door to the room. Four other guards are moving about the area of the West Wing basement."

"We have a dozen guards waiting in the Oval Office, another dozen in the Cabinet Room, and four moving about the main floor of the West Wing. Two additional guards are stationed at the parking lot exit door."

"Sub-basement and Mezzanine levels are clear."

"I counted about one hundred guards in various locations on the ground level of the main house."

"There's about hundred and fifty scattered around the first floor."

"Add about fifty on the second floor with a half dozen out on the balcony."

"And another fifty on the third floor; plus, a dozen divided between the Promenade and the roof."

"The second floor of the East Wing is clear, and there

are about twenty-five guards on the ground floor. Everything below is sealed up. Hayden was furious when he couldn't get in to the Presidential Emergency Operations Center and had the maintenance staff board up all access points to below."

Hayden and his advisers watched the river of people moving toward the Washington Monument.

"There sure are a lot of them aren't there?" Hayden chuckled. "I really ruffled a bunch of feathers, didn't I?"

His advisors looked at him without speaking. His laughing unnerved them. How could he be laughing at a moment like this? Making a mockery of starving people—his countrymen, famished because of his obsession with power rather than care for his people.

Finally, one of them found his tongue and spoke carefully so as not to infuriate the temperamental president, "that's quite a lynch mob alright," he said in as neutral a tone as he could manage.

Hayden laughed hysterically. "Yep! I've created quite an army of enemies!" he said, slapping the advisor next to him on the shoulder nearly sending him sprawling on the floor. "But, I've said from the outset, I'm not here to win a popularity contest, I'm here to restore our country."

Nobody spoke.

"Look at their weapons!" Hayden laughed while pointing at the screen. "Pitchforks, clubs, shovels, and knives! They think they're going to overpower me with those. Ha! The only things missing are knights on horses with swords and lances." He laughed almost hysterically.

As the marchers gathered around the Washington Monument and the speeches began, Hayden's advisors' anxiety grew with each new speaker, for they were powerful orators. Each one seemed to have a gift for touching the people's emotional core, stirring them deeply, passionately.

The shouting and chanting intensified, growing toward a fevered pitch as the speeches progressed.

Hayden noticed the anxiety of his advisors and laughed. "Quit worrying; I'll order protection for you, keep you safe from the pitchforks!"

He called the head of the security detail on the roof. "Get a dozen snipers up there and tell them if they see anyone at the monument with a gun, they are to take those individuals out before the march to the White House begins."

Turning back to his advisors with glee he said, "See? That easy, nothing to worry about."

The speeches became more seditious and inflammatory, driving the crowd into a frenzy. The people were screaming, shouting and chanting slogans, balling their fists and shouting threats and profanities in the direction of the White House.

Sam and the others at the Rabbit Hole watched in alarm as the speakers fanned the emotional flames of the burning crowd.

Eric moved carefully along the outskirts of the degenerate mob. *Thank God, there are no firearms in sight. At least one good thing came from Brideaux's merciless actions to disarm the people across the world.*

He looked again at the assortment of weapons carried

by the protesters: knives, machetes, axes, shovels, pitchforks, clubs, baseball bats, some crossbows, *and even Molotov Cocktails* he thought, spotting the glass bottles with wicks in the end and knowing they were filled, not with refreshment but with gas and motor oil ... *the poor man's grenade.* Deadly, all of them, but useless against Hayden's men armed with automatic weapons and armored vehicles. They were literally taking knives to a gunfight.

Please, Lord. Let them not get close to the White House; he prayed quietly.

Noticing that the last speaker was taking the improvised stage, Eric contacted Sam. "Scout One to base."

"Base, go Scout One."

"This is the last speech; then they are going to move. This crowd is irrepressible as you can probably see."

"Acknowledged; ordering phase two of Operation Winnow."

Before Sam finished giving the order, Raj's fingers hit the keyboard, immediately jamming the signals of Hayden's drones, took control of them and steered them away from the scene at the monument.

Within seconds the video feed to the situation room in the White House blurred, became snowy, and blanked out altogether.

Everyone looked at Hayden expecting a violent outburst.

Much to their surprise, instead of throwing a tantrum, he was grinning like the Cheshire Cat. It was happening exactly as Nguyen said it would.

"Ok, that's the signal; they're now going to storm the

White House," he spoke gleefully. "Let the dogs out," he ordered, referring to the several hundred heavily armed guards he had waiting all over the White House.

"Make sure they all understand that they have to let the crowd come to within two-hundred yards before they open fire. They must mow them down without mercy—this shit ends tonight—this is the day we teach the people of America discipline and respect for the law. Shoot to kill!

"And when those people turn and run, don't stop firing —they must shoot and keep on shooting until they run out of ammo. Then we'll send in the armored vehicles and chase them down.

"I will not be happy, and I won't rest until we have killed at least five-thousand of those renegades, the more, the better—this needs to send a message to everyone in this country.

"Are my orders understood?" Hayden growled.

"But, Sir!" one of the military officers rose to his feet, "that's mass murder of innocent civilians!" he objected.

Hayden drew his gun and pointed it to the officer. "What did you say?"

"I said, it's mass murder of civilians, sir," the officer whispered, as he slowly sat down.

"Are you refusing to execute my orders?"

"No... sir, but... I..." was as far as he got before Hayden interrupted him.

"Good." Hayden looked around at the others and asked, "anyone else want to query my orders?"

The remaining officers nodded in disgusted silence and left the room to instruct their men.

Sam and the people in the Ops Center heard every word and it filled them with nausea—this man was an animal—they all knew it already—nevertheless, it was shocking to hear it again.

Sam thumbed the button on the mic and gave his orders – "Eagle One, he addressed Roy, get those heat rays up and make sure no one gets over that line—turn the heat up if you have to. I'd rather we treat a few burn wounds than bullet wounds or have to bury dead people."

"Badger, base; activate the mosquitos," he ordered, knowing Raj would release the first batch of etorphine mosquitos, and every guard at every station inside the White House would feel a brief sting before blacking out.

"Kingpin, Sandman, you are a go," he directed Jack and Dennis. "Remember, no shooting unless your life is in danger. If we a can get this done without bloodshed it will strengthen Knight One's position.

"And remember we are recording everything on video so that we can show the public afterward. Be careful and be gentle."

In the sub-basement on the Southeast side of the White House, Dennis carefully opened the hidden door and stepped into a storage room. His team of six followed quietly behind him, and they made their way to the hallway.

Although already assured by the team at the Rabbit Hole that the area was clear, Dennis checked the hallway before leading his team into it.

They exited the storage room to the left, and proceeded down the hall several yards before turning to their right and ascending a narrow set of stairs.

As they reached the ground floor, the staircase widened, and they paused to check that the way was clear. Dennis noted several guards laying on the floor or slumped in chairs. *Well done team!*

He nodded to his team to quickly put zip ties on the guards and remove their weapons before continuing the climb to the roof.

The staircase to the third floor narrowed again and they exited into an empty hallway, stepping over a sleeping guard who was immediately zip tied and relieved of his firearm. They entered a North bedroom and one by one climbed through the window, spreading out according to plan. Three moved along the Promenade and three prepared to follow Dennis, who was unpacking a rope ladder, onto the roof.

"Sandman to Badger," Dennis called Raj, "we're in place."

"Roger Sandman, standby," Raj replied, indicating that he was activating the next batch of etorphine mosquitos to take out the guards and snipers on the roof.

Two drones that were circling the White House would release their loads on those guards outside on the White House grounds as soon as the roof was secured.

Dennis watched as the guard nearest him sank to his knees and fell over on his side. "That's it, let's move!" he whispered and moved up onto the roof with his team following and spreading out to their designated stations. Again, they quickly zip tied their targets and removed their firearms before they moved to the roof perimeters to see what was happening below.

The site that greeted them momentarily froze them in their tracks.

The crowd was enraged beyond sanity. Some of them broke ranks and ran toward the White House followed by others. The frontrunners advanced about one hundred or so yards and suddenly stopped in their tracks.

They're obviously feeling the effects of the heat rays. Dennis surmised.

When they stopped, and tried to turn back they were knocked to the ground by those behind them—the swarm had become a stampede!

"Eagle One!" Sam called Roy, "Move the heat rays back, closer to the crowd. We need to stop them from moving, or they're going to trample each other to death!"

"Roger base! Moving rays now," Roy responded steering the drones towards the masses, strafing the wild, stampeding crowd with the invisible microwaves.

People began screaming from the pain of the burning sensation, quickly abandoning the attack on the White House, and turning away from whatever was burning their skin.

As the people started to turn away, Roy and his team maneuvered the drones and the heat rays to segment the crowd into smaller groups and make channels of escape while still blocking them from the White House.

From his vantage point on the roof and the help of Roy's drones circling the White House, Dennis directed his men on the ground to the remaining guards who were not hit by the first wave of mosquitoes.

Some of them quickly became aware something weird was happening when they lost radio contact with their buddies and commanders. They panicked and tried to retreat which brought them out in the open where the mosquitoes got them.

Within ten minutes every one of Hayden's guards was

asleep. *In about four hours' time there's going to be a few hundred soldiers waking up with Mount Rushmore size headaches,* Dennis mused. *I don't envy them.*

He watched as his team moved about the Southern grounds of the White House quickly and efficiently securing the sleeping guards with cable ties and removing their weapons. Once secured, the guards were dragged to the open lawn area in front of the South entrance to the White House and gathered in small bunches for observation in case some of them didn't receive the full four-hour dose of etorphine.

While Dennis' team was securing the outside of the White House, Jack and his team invaded it from the bottom, stepping into the basement room on the Northwest side of the West Wing. From there it was nearly a straight shot to the Situation Room where they knew Hayden was holed-up.

As he expected, Jack noted that the White House was all but deserted—all the staff had been sent home or taken to some other place out of harm's way. Except for a few Secret Service agents and guards, everyone was outside ready to defend the place against the crowd.

Since the etorphine mosquitoes had taken out the few remaining agents and guards, the invasion was pretty much a walk in the park for Jack and his team. They didn't have to use their firearms, in fact they didn't even have to threaten anyone with their firearms. The advantages their little gadgets gave them really took the fun out of the whole operation in Jack's opinion. *Seems almost unfair,* he thought.

Inside the Situation Room, Hayden's mind ground to a halt when one by one the six men around the table with him, went limp in their chairs as if they'd suddenly fallen asleep. Several of them even slid off their chairs onto the floor.

He froze and gawked at the scene before him. Back at Raven Rock and in the Ops Center at the Rabbit Hole, the audience high-fived. The mosquitoes had done their work.

Hayden, still frozen in place, looked up to see the dark monitors that had held the live video feed from his drones and blinked; he looked down at the unconscious bodies around him. Somewhere in his brain an explosion occurred and his hand slowly moved toward the holster holding his sidearm.

In the hallway outside the Situation Room, Jack's team was busy checking the two unconscious guards, securing them with cable ties, and removing their weapons before moving them out of the way.

They were startled when they heard gunfire inside the Situation Room and all dove for cover away from the door. Taking positions against the wall on either side of the door, they rose to stand with their backs against it, listening and preparing to react to whatever came next.

To their astonishment, the next thing they heard was the sound of maniacal laughter alternating with victorious whoops and shouts of 'I got him! I got him!' followed by more gunshots.

Jack signaled to the man on the opposite side of the door to kick it down and move out of the way. When the door flew open Jack dove through, rolled and came up on his knees, his gun pointed at a motionless Hayden.

Confused, Jack slowly got to his feet, his gun still pointed at Hayden's head, ready to fire. Hayden stood at attention before him. His gun was in his hip holster.

Rebecca's urgent voice came through his earpiece. "Be very careful, Jack! Something is seriously wrong."

Jack eyed Hayden who had not said a word. *He's acting like a young recruit before a superior officer.*

Playing a hunch, he paced slowly around Hayden, his weapon at the ready and demanded in his best drill sergeant voice, "Report soldier."

Hayden barked like a new recruit, "Sir! Yes, Sir! I have killed the General, Sir!"

Jacked stopped pacing, "What? Speak up soldier I can't hear you."

"Sir, I have killed the General. He was corrupt; he killed President Campbell and her Secretary of Treasury, George Miller.

"He also killed the Secretaries of Agriculture and Energy, Richard Westfield, and Hank McMillian as well as Bob Thompson former Secretary of Homeland Security and Carrie Trent.

"And he was planning to kill President Rossler. I had no choice, Sir. I had to kill him."

"I see. What is your name and rank soldier?"

"Sir, Cadet Thomas Hayden, West Point Academy, Sir!"

"Jack, stop! Don't question him further!" Rebecca shouted in his earpiece. "He's had a psychotic break. Take his gun away and get him secured immediately. He's unpredictable and could become very dangerous in an instant. Be careful."

Knowing she could see him, thanks to the spyders in the room, he nodded slightly.

"Very good, Cadet Hayden," he praised, "I'll take your sidearm now. These officers will take you back to headquarters for debriefing. You did your country proud today son."

Handing his gun, hand-grip first, to Jack, Hayden smiled, "Yes Sir! Thank you, just doing my duty Sir."

Jack motioned to his men who came forward and took position on either side of the General.

One of them said, "Let's go Cadet Hayden. We don't want to keep our CO waiting, do we?"

Chapter Eighty-Five

I WILL WORK WITH ANYONE

As soon as Daniel heard Sam give Jack and Dennis the go-ahead for stage two of Operation Winnow, he was through the door and into the tunnel, the two Secret Service agents and Elize sprinting to catch up with him.

Catching up with him, the agents held him back at the door until they received confirmation that Hayden was in custody. They passed through the basement office, entered the hallway, and moved toward the Situation Room stepping over and around sleeping, tied-up guards along the way.

They arrived just in time for Daniel to see Hayden being led down the hall between two of Jack's men. He had to fight an almost irrepressible urge to storm after the man, knock him to the floor and choke him with his bare hands. Magnanimously he turned away and continued in the direction of the Situation Room.

Jack met him and said, "we need to get you up to the Oval Office, Eric should be arriving with the press soon."

The Rowen

Daniel nodded and followed.

He'd just finished settling into the seat behind the desk when Eric came through the door followed by about a dozen reporters and television crews who had been following the march. The spacious office suddenly felt small, but it had been agreed that no other place said "President" more than the Oval Office.

Daniel stood, "Welcome ladies and gentlemen. Thank you for joining me. Please find a place where you will be comfortable for the next twenty to thirty minutes. We will begin shortly."

They were all momentarily speechless. Nigel stepped through the door accompanied by a dejected looking Potter under armed guard by two Tectus members.

Nigel and Daniel nodded to one another, several of Jack's team brought in chairs. The reporters shifted their positions, some taking seats and others setting up cameras.

"Are we ready?" Daniel asked.

In his earpiece, Daniel heard Roy, Raj, and Sam confirm. He turned to Potter, "are you ready General?"

Potter straightened and nodded.

Daniel took his seat behind the desk again and folded his hands in front of him. "Let's do it."

TV and Radio stations across America and around the world suddenly went blank, and then Daniel appeared, and his voice could be heard.

"My fellow Americans, I'm here tonight to tell you that the illegal Presidency of General Thomas Hayden has come to an end.

"He, his advisors, and his militia leaders are all in custody where they will remain until they are brought before courts of justice."

"One of his cabinet members, General Joe Potter, is here and wishes to address you."

The focus shifted to Potter. He straightened and cleared his throat.

"On behalf of myself and my fellow officers that served in General Hayden's cabinet, I want to apologize to the American people.

"In the beginning, we did not know that General Hayden intended to set up a military dictatorship, nor did we anticipate to what lengths he would go to obtain the Presidency.

"As time went by we realized our mistake as we began to see incongruences and instability in his actions and behaviors. He began to malign and belittle the American people, insisting that they were dimwitted and had to be dominated or done away with. He began issuing orders, terrible orders, that we could not follow. By the time we realized he was mentally unstable, it was too late to stop him, and we feared for our lives.

"We regret being involved in General Hayden's government and are ashamed of our association with the man who treated the American people in such a degrading manner.

"We herewith admit that we have done a terrible injustice to this country. We are deeply remorseful for our part in this—there is no excuse. We understand and accept without reservation that we will be prosecuted and punished for our misdeeds.

"Finally, we all acknowledge that General Hayden is not the legitimate President of the United States. He killed people that were standing in his way of becoming president, among them President Campbell and her Secretary of Treasury, George Miller.

"In terms of our constitution, the legitimate president is Daniel Rossler and no one else."

Potter lowered his gaze as he ended his speech and the focus returned to Daniel.

Addressing the people again, Daniel began the speech Nigel had helped him craft.

"Civil unrest is running rampant in our country; violence and crime levels are reaching new record levels daily. People are starving and disillusioned, and in their despair, are being driven to rebellion and crime. I have the deepest sympathy for the people's suffering.

"This is not what I want for the people of America ... this is not what the people of America want for themselves.

"Many millions of our fellow countrymen are without food, water, electricity, and other basic needs. They have had no choice but to revert to stealing, looting, and killing— literally being forced to do whatever it takes to survive.

"As this country's situation became increasingly desperate, law enforcement agencies, left understaffed by Brideaux's new world order, were unable to maintain law and order, and have now become the target of the very people they have sworn to protect. Many of them have been killed.

"These are not the actions of true Americans. My fellow Americans, *please*, let us lay down our weapons and stop the fighting immediately.

"The late President Laurie Campbell promised you food, water, shelter, and medical supplies. Americans across the country were working together to meet those promises, and they were being fulfilled until her untimely death at the hand of General Hayden and his militia.

"General Thomas Hayden made those same promises to you, but he did not fulfill them. Instead, he gave you heavy-handed discipline and tighter restrictions. He authorized the use of live ammunition and used the National Guard and the military to turn our cities into nothing better than prison camps full of starving, forsaken citizens that were his duty to provide for and protect.

"Not only did General Thomas Hayden unlawfully and unconstitutionally declare himself President, but he also ordered the killing of people to achieve his goals. He used military force to keep himself in power and to begin removing our freedom. He was not acting for the good of the people—he was a power-hungry man setting himself up as a military dictator with little regard for the needs or the lives of the people.

"Over the course of the next few days, my team will release all the evidence of General Hayden's meetings, plans, and actions, which we were able to collect. You will be able to judge for yourself. Nothing will be withheld.

"America is a country founded on democracy. America is a country that has thrived because of democracy. America will continue as a democracy!

"In terms of our constitution, as Vice-President, I was obligated to assume the Presidency upon the death of our late President, Laurie Campbell. I accepted the possibility of that obligation willingly and knowingly when I accepted the position of Vice-President.

"In spite of the desperate circumstances this country finds itself in right now, let the record show for all of history that I am proud ... very proud, to serve the noble citizens of this honorable and great country.

"We will all come through this difficult time together by supporting and helping one another because this is who we are as Americans! Let's start now, this very moment. Let every one of us reach out to our neighbor, share what you have with those that don't. Share your food, your shelter, your kindness.

"If we do this, we *will* turn the tide of violence and hopelessness. Start now, and tomorrow will be better than today. Remember, this my fellow Americans, this is the low point, from here-on-out we are building a bright new future.

"I leave you with these three points.

"One: martial law will remain in effect for now. It will be released progressively starting in a few days. As soon as my cabinet has been approved, we will evaluate the state of all our cities, rural areas, and other communities. Those that have stabilized will be released immediately, those that have not will be released as they reach a state of stability. From this moment on, the end of Martial Law is in your hands.

"Two: There has been too much secrecy in government. While some circumstances call for secrecy for the sake of National Security, there is no reason why general meetings should preclude American citizens. The website you see displayed at the bottom of your screen has been set up for the public to see and hear what is happening in the Oval Office and in the Cabinet meeting room. This real-time, live feed, will be accessible twenty-four hours a day, seven days a week, three-hundred and sixty days a year. My staff and I will be making arrangements so that in the future several journalists will be allowed to be present at all meetings when National Security is not at risk. They will be able to record and report on every word said in meetings they attend.

"Three: I will work with anyone, and everyone, who is prepared to work with me to rebuild our country and will not let party politics stand in the way of rebuilding this nation. We don't have the luxury of political differences now.

According to the 25th Amendment, it is up to me to choose the next Vice-President. Instead, to show you I am serious about what I just said, I am asking the House Minority to nominate the person who will be the Vice-President. I will accept and work with anyone they nominate.

"Have a good night, may God bless you and may God bless America."

Chapter Eighty-Six

BELIEVE HIM

At times, the personalities of Tawndo and Robert were engaged in fierce battles for supremacy. Tawndo was the one who dearly loved Siasha more than anything, but he was also the warrior, the erstwhile Second-In-Command of the strongest military force on the planet during the Eight Cycle—a strong and fearless disposition, not easily cowed. Robert was the Australian, the geologist, member of the Rossler Foundation, and loyal friend of JR and Daniel Rossler—equally level headed and opinionated. He didn't hate Siasha, in fact, he liked her, but he didn't love her.

However, for his mission to get in touch with the Rosslers, he had to be Robert, Tawndo the warrior and lover had to be restrained. At times, Linkola's ministrations and Siasha's tender loving care was barely enough to help Robert embrace and integrate his belligerent personalities. But with every passing hour, through his strong willpower, the eruptions of rage, followed by spells of utter exhaustion, diminished in frequency and severity. Within two days, he was able to embrace Robert and control Tawndo, allowing Tawndo to emerge only when he was alone with Siasha.

On the third day after the merging of Robert and Tawndo, Korda dashed into the technical lab where Linkola and Siasha were conducting more tests and scans on Robert's brain functions. "They've overthrown Hayden's government! It's on all the news channels across the world."

Robert slowly rose from the floating examination table, "time for me to get hold of my mate JR."

Linkola and Siasha looked at each other both asking the question in silence, *is he ready for it?*

Robert saw their wordless exchange. "I'm ready; I have to be. We don't have much time left. You've seen the data coming from Tunguska, the Re'an are preparing to come here. Not only that, they are busy reanimating soldiers, which they have been stockpiling for many years, there can only be one reason for that—they are mobilizing for a war."

It was the third day after Hayden had been removed from the White House and it seemed as if the entire country was balanced on the edge of a knife. Hayden still had some support left, but it was disappearing like mist before the sun as Salome, and her team on the Rossler Foundation Intelligence Committee started releasing the recordings of his actions while in power.

Daniel and his cabinet, with Nigel's advice and support, worked around the clock to bring relief to the hungry masses. It required near super-human efforts of unselfish effort, not only from government officials and politicians, but also from the citizenry. Daniel's and Nigel's constant requests and pleas started to bear fruit. The tide of violence and desperation slowly receded as everyone started to bury their battle axes and reach out to each other.

Even so, the atmosphere remained fragile, and therefore it was decided not to move the team at Raven Rock out yet and to keep them and the Tectus teams on high alert.

Of the Rosslerites at Raven Rock, it was only Roy and JR who had their spouses with them. Nigel was the one who suggested that the Presidential suite shouldn't go to waste and that the two married couples might as well use it.

"Closest I'll ever come to being President," Roy chuckled when Nigel gave the four of them a tour of the suite, and it was decided they would rotate on a weekly basis.

They flipped a coin, and JR and Rebecca got the first week.

It was JR and Rebecca's first night, and they were getting ready to go to bed when the lights in the room flickered briefly, and the TV went dead.

JR looked up at the lights, then back to the TV ... and saw his old friend Robert standing before him.

"Arrrrrgh!" he yelled, "Shiiiit! What the hell!

Rebecca, just finishing up in the bathroom, heard the commotion and ran into the bedroom to find JR standing before a man who couldn't possibly be there ... Robert Cartwright.

Her breath caught in her throat preventing the scream she felt.

"Roy!" JR shouted in fury and started for the door.

Rebecca placed her hand on JR's arm to stop him from doing something they would all regret.

"I'm going to kick that sore loser's ass!" JR fumed. "He lost the toss fair and square, and he'll get his turn next week..."

"JR, that's not going to solve anything…"

"… And it's not in the least bit funny to haunt me with the image of my best friend who's dead."

Robert grinned and started speaking. "No, my friend, I am not dead, I'm very much alive. I…"

JR yanked his arm away from Rebecca. "I'm going to show him that some things aren't funny and put a stop to this bullshit."

"JR, Roy would never do something like this to you," Rebecca said. "He'd never be so cruel; besides Salome would kill him if he tried."

"So, what the hell is this then? You know as well as I do that Robert is dead. I buried him, I know he's dead."

"Yes, JR. John Brideaux did kill me," Robert tried again. "I was dead, and you did bury me right there under the rocks just as you remember. But I have been reconstructed, resurrected so to speak, and…"

"Do you think I was born under a rock?" JR spoke incredulously.

"JR let him speak," Rebecca said. "I'm sure this is not a ruse from Roy. I'm not sure what's going on, but I have a sense we need to listen to… this… ah…"

"Thing?" JR completed the sentence for her. "Ah well, let's hear what the thing has to say then," he said, flopping down on the bed.

"Hologram, actually," Robert said, "Perhaps I should explain."

Rebecca reached out to touch Robert, and her hand passed through his arm. She realized that this was not the same holographic technology she'd become so familiar with. This was something in a different class—much clearer and more life-like than what they used to spook Hayden and his people with.

Sitting down beside him, Rebecca said, "JR, this holographic technology is different from Roy's, it's more advanced."

"Alright, mister... thing... whatever you are. Let's hear your explanation, and take note my patience is wearing thin."

"I know this is impossible to believe, but please hear me out."

JR and Rebecca nodded slowly, hesitantly.

"As you know the site in the Grand Canyon, which you and I discovered was constructed and occupied by the people of the 8th Cycle. You know everything about it, well, almost everything.

"What you don't know is that when you and I entered the site the first time it triggered an activation sequence in another part of the facility, which we didn't know existed. The activation sequence brought to life three people who were in a cryonic state or as they call it a deep sleep."

"Robert... or whoever you are, don't..."

"Let him finish JR," Rebecca said softly.

Robert waited for a second, and when JR sat back, he continued.

"Those three people are from the 8th Cycle, in other words..."

"Some sixty odd thousand years old!" JR shouted. "Now listen ..."

"Wait JR," Rebecca stopped him again. "The idea of cryonics has been around since the early seventy's, almost fifty years. You know about it. The thing is we have seen so many mind-bogglingly advanced technologies coming out of the Tenth, Ninth, and Eighth Cycles, why would we want to exclude this possibility?"

JR stared at his beautiful wife and realized what she said

was true. He had to admit that they had indeed seen incredible technologies coming from ancient civilizations. Slowly, hesitantly, he turned his eyes to Robert and said. "Okay, keep on talking, I'll try my best not to interrupt again."

"JR, Rebecca is right, fanciful as it may seem, the Eighth Cyclers have perfected the technology to put human beings in a state of deep sleep for up to a hundred thousand years and awake them whenever they want.

"They can also revive a human body as long as it has not been dead for longer than twelve hours - which is what they did with me. I don't understand the technology... all I know is, it works..."

"Hang on there. Are you saying they brought you back to life shortly after we buried you there, outside the facility?

"Yes, they did."

"Then why have you waited for so long, what's it been, two, three years, before contacting us?"

Rebecca nodded in agreement, looking probingly at Robert. JR had a point.

Robert shook his head slightly. "This is going to be much harder than I thought." He paused for a moment thinking of the best way to break the next bit to them. There was a fleeting moment where Tawndo threatened to take over and issue orders, but he managed to stifle him.

"They only used my body... I was implanted with the memory of another man, one who lived during the time of the Eighth Cycle..."

"Oh, I see," JR sneered. "Not only can these geniuses make people come back to life, they can also pick and choose who you'll be? How damn convenient.

"And while I'm on it let me tell you, my friend Robert's brains were blown away by a bullet. There is no one who could fix, mend, restore, call it what you want, that damage."

"Not today, but the Eighth Cyclers could, and that's exactly what they did," Robert replied.

"Bloody hell. You expect us," JR pointed to Rebecca and himself, "to believe this fairytale? Tell me what does Rebecca do? What's her job?"

"She's a medical doctor, JR."

"And despite that knowledge, you're trying to tell us those wunderkinds of yours can perform all those medical wonders?"

"Exactly."

"Okay, I've heard enough… this little charade is over… I'm outta here," and he moved to get up.

To JR's surprise, Rebecca held him back as he got up. "Wait, JR, I'm still intrigued, I've got a few more questions."

JR stared at her and shook his head. "Okay, go for it, might as well hear the whole story, maybe I can use it to write a best-selling sci-fi novel."

"Robert, I have to say I'm starting to agree with JR," Rebecca started, "but I'll give you a little bit more latitude. JR shared the details of a few of your escapades with me over the years. So, what I want you to do now is tell me a few stories about you and JR, stories which only the two of you could know about."

JR smiled. *Now we're going to sort this out quickly.*

To his surprise, Robert also started smiling. "Okay, *you* asked for it." Fixing a steady gaze on JR, he asked, "You sure she should hear all about it, JR?"

"Absolutely," JR smirked. "I don't keep anything secret from my wife."

"Have you ever shown her those pictures I took of you

on the back of that mule on our first expedition to the Eighth Cycle site in the Canyon?" Robert chuckled as he remembered the comic look of JR swaying from side to side with the mule's gait and those long legs sticking out at a crazy angle—a real life Disney cartoon."

"Huh, what..." JR's eyes were wide as he remembered. "N... hmm... no, I didn't.' He stuttered.

He looked at his wife and found her inquisitive gaze fixed on him and shrugged.

"How about our first trip down that scary elevator? You know the one where you thought you'd died and were in heaven and were surprised to see me there." Robert struggled to get the last bit out before he exploded in laughter.

Another inquisitive stare from Rebecca and another shrug from JR.

"Did you tell her about my reaction to the floating, self-adjusting chairs?"

All of a sudden, the wall of doubt came down. "Oh, my God!" JR whispered. "Robert! It really is you, isn't it?"

"Yes, old friend, it really is me."

"Oh, my God, I can't believe ... what the ... but you ... you were dead! I can't believe this, it's ... it's impossible. I saw ... and Max ..."

"I know mate," Robert whispered, "I know it's beyond comprehension, but every word of what I told you is true."

"But, why, how... "JR shook his head. "Okay, I don't know what to believe ... I'm starting to wonder if I'm awake or even alive. I...it's... it's... just so surreal, impossible..."

JR had entered a mild state of shock. Rebecca put her hand on his knee.

"Robert, I want to believe you, but my brain is protesting... we've ..."

Robert held his hand up. "Here's what I suggest; come out to the Canyon site, and I will show you everything. If you don't trust me, bring guards with you. My only request is that you do it quickly, we don't have time."

"What are you talking about Robert? What do mean by, 'we don't have time'?" Rebecca asked.

"The world is in grave danger. I - or rather my body - has been alive since shortly after Brideaux shot me, but my mind was someone else's. It was only a few days ago that my original mind, Robert's mind, was merged with this other person's and I became fully aware of who Robert is.

"The reason why they did it, the merging as they call it, was so that I could contact you and warn you about the impending peril. And for what it's worth, the merging of two people's minds like they did, has never been done before.

"This body was in danger of being permanently destroyed by the procedure. Nevertheless, I took the risk. I've been through hell and back since that procedure." He paused for breath and to subdue Tawndo who was becoming impatient and threatened to take over.

Shaken to his core, JR stared in disbelief. He looked at Rebecca, she was staring at Robert, and then it seemed as if her doubts also disappeared.

"Let's see what we can arrange. Come back in two hours, and we'll let you know," she said.

"Thank you. That's all I can ask for," Robert replied. "See you in two." The hologram disappeared.

Rebecca looked at JR and started, "JR, I... I don't know about you... but I..."

"Believe him, "JR completed for her. "So, do I, Becky, so do I. Don't ask me why; there is no rhyme or reason to this but I believe what we have just seen was really Robert."

"Let's get hold of Sam and Jack tell them we're going to be away for a day or two. I'm sure they'll be okay with it, we're not that irreplaceable." Rebecca said,

"I agree."

"Oh, just one more thing," she started smiling, "I thought there were no secrets between us and tonight I've learned…"

"Becky," JR laughed, those are not secrets, those are embarrassments. Stuff men don't like to talk about—very bad for the ego."

"Hmm, no that won't do it for me. Unfortunately, my curiosity has been stirred, and my curiosity ranks higher than your ego."

"Okay, I know when I've lost. Let's get our trip authorized first then I'll tell you. And if that really was Robert we spoke to, and he is really alive, you can be assured he will fill in any details which I might leave out unintentionally."

Chapter Eighty-Seven

TO GET THE PARTY MOVING AGAIN

JR and Rebecca's request for a few days R&R was met with understanding smiles at first, but that quickly turned to frowns when their intended destination was withheld. The longer they remained vague about their itinerary, the more questions Sam and Jack had.

"We'll have our mirror phones with us all the time. You can recall us at any time, and we'll be back here in a matter of hours," Rebecca grinned slyly.

Sam and Jack remained suspicious, but they knew they wouldn't get any more out of them. Sam looked at Jack and said, "Your call."

Jack was sitting at the same table as JR and Rebecca in one of the meeting rooms at Raven Rock; Sam was on the video link from the Rabbit Hole.

"It seems obvious that we're not going to get any more information out of you two without reverting to torture, but I'm fairly sure you're not planning to collude with the enemy. Okay, as long as you keep those mirror phones with you, fully charged, and on, I agree."

JR and Rebecca thanked them, jumped up and made for their suite. They had to pack, make travel arrangements, and talk to Robert.

"Oh, just one more condition though," Sam's voice stopped them just short of the door. "You'll tell us all about it when you get back. Yes?"

JR grinned mischievously, and put his arm around Rebecca, "Some of it, Sam, not all!"

Sam had the good graces to look slightly embarrassed, "Well yes," he stammered, "of course, that's what I meant."

"We'll do that then! Thanks again and have a good night," JR shouted over his shoulder as he escorted Rebecca out the door.

In the hallway, Rebecca slapped him playfully on the arm. "That was evil, JR."

"I know, but having them think we're on a romantic getaway will ease their minds."

The next morning, before the break of dawn, JR was tapping Peter on the foot. "Hey, wake up!"

"Huh?" Peter said. "What the hell? Go away and come back in the morning. We agreed to go in the morning, not the middle of the night," Peter said rolling over and pulling the pillow over his head.

"Come on, get up lazy ass. We have to go. Rebecca has packed coffee and sandwiches."

"JR," Peter's muffled voice came from under the pillow, "can't this wait a few more hours? I'm tired man."

"No. It can't. Now come. Get up and get dressed. Or should I pour a bucket of ice water over you?"

Peter rolled back over and sat up, yawning and wiping

The Rowen

the sleep from his eyes. He finally got to his feet. "Does anyone else know about this little middle-of-the-night escapade of yours?"

"At the moment, no; and it's going to stay that way for now. Capiche?"

"Are you in some kind of trouble, JR? This is starting to sound serious. And where are we going?"

"I believe we're all in some kind of trouble, my friend, and the sooner the three of us get to our destination the better. You first get us in the air and then I'll tell you where we're going."

"And that's all you're going to tell me?"

"For now," JR nodded.

"I hope you know what you're getting us into JR," he said slinging his bag over his shoulder and heading for the door.

By the time they arrived at the airport, the Eastern horizon signaled that dawn would soon arrive. Peter got the six-passenger Baron 58 ready for take-off while Rebecca handed them coffee and breakfast sandwiches.

They were airborne and fed before Peter broached the subject again.

"Ok JR. We're in the air in case you haven't noticed. Whereto?"

"Page, Arizona."

Peter turned and stared at JR. "Page, Arizona, that place on the edge of the Grand Canyon?"

JR nodded, "that's the one, yes."

Peter felt a cold shiver running down his spine when he realized that JR and Rebecca were going to the Eighth

Cycle site in the Grand Canyon. He was familiar with the discovery made by the Rossler Foundation and had first-hand experience of the immense evil that was released on the world as a result. He put the plane on autopilot and pulled up a map.

"That's about 1600 nautical miles, eight hours flying. We'll need to refuel somewhere."

"Whatever it takes Peter," Rebecca replied. "We have to get there and find out what's going on. We're praying that it is all a big hoax, but both JR and I have an uneasy feeling it's not."

Peter was quiet for a moment. "Would one or both of you care to explain what exactly is going on? What is urging you to go back there? I know the history of your discovery and, as you know, lived through the consequences. Are you saying we're up for more of *that* kind of trouble."

JR and Rebecca recounted the events of the previous night to Peter. To describe Peter's reaction to what they told him as skeptical would have been like calling Mount Everest a hill. There were points during the discussion where he threatened to turn back to D.C. and find a 'special' doctor to treat his passengers.

"Have you two lost your collective minds! How two highly educated adults like you can fall for such a scam, is beyond me!" Peter exploded at one stage.

Rebecca replied. "Peter, you've lived and worked for the Rossler Foundation for some time now. Are you saying that in all this time you have never realized that almost every bit of technology we have used to defeat Brideaux and Hayden originated in pre-historical times? Brideaux took control of the world with fifty-thousand-year-old technology. We took him down with twenty-plus-thousand-year old nanotechnology, communications, and… Shall I continue?"

"Yea well, if you put it like that... I guess..." Peter interjected stutteringly. "But, you have to agree it's befuddling to think of this... reviving people after sixty-thousand years, bringing dead people back to life and..."

"We're not in disagreement Peter. We are as bamboozled as you are. What we're not prepared to do is to chalk it up to lunacy and ignore it. Don't you agree, that in light of what we have learned over the years, it would be madness not to at least investigate?"

"You're right. Apologies for my outbursts. Associating with you Rosslers for the past few years has certainly done my head in," he tittered.

For the rest of the trip to Page, they talked about the trials and tribulations brought over the world and the Rossler Foundation since Daniel and Sarah discovered the Tenth Cycle Library in the Great Pyramid of Giza, Egypt.

They also speculated about what the danger, which Robert had referred to, could be. He didn't want to tell JR and Rebecca the night before, insisting they travel to the canyon site and be shown.

They landed at the Page airfield shortly after 4pm. The owner of a small helicopter tour company was already waiting for them. They hangered the plane and were picked up by the tour operator and transported to one of his helicopters where the pilot was ready to take off.

It was 5pm when the helicopter dropped them off two miles from the Canyon site. They waited until the helicopter disappeared over the horizon before they shouldered their backpacks and fell in behind JR—the only one of them who knew where they were going.

When they approached the entrance to the facility, JR stopped at the spot where they buried Robert. "He *is* indeed gone!" he exclaimed. "These are the stones we piled over Robert's body and to build the cairn."

Peter looked around seeing only scattered stones. "I don't see anything JR. Show me what you're talking about."

JR pointed to an indentation in the ground. "We tried to bury him here but hit rock almost immediately, so we swept the dirt away as deep as we could, and laid his body here. Then we piled these rocks over him instead," he said indicating the rocks that now laid scattered around the area.

Rebecca looked around the canyon and asked, "are you sure this is the right spot; the right canyon JR? It's been a while."

"Yes!" JR said almost angrily, then looked around himself to double check. "I'm positive."

"You're in the right place mate. Said a voice from behind them.

The three of them yelled in shock and spun around to face the owner of the voice.

"Robert!" JR shouted. "Is it really you or are you still a hologram?"

"It's really me this time," Robert replied offering his hand in friendship.

JR paused for a moment and then took a step forward, slowly and cautiously raising his hand to shake Robert's. He paused again and took a deep breath, before finally grasping Robert's hand.

Feeling the warmth of human flesh respond with a firm handshake surprised him, and it showed on his face. At Robert's questioning look he smiled sheepishly, "Guess I was expecting the cold grip of death. You … you're really a … alive buddy!"

"Yes, my friend. As I told you last night, I am alive. Thank you for coming." He hugged first JR and then Rebecca and kissed her on the cheek. Then he introduced himself to a scared and shaky Peter."

"Dear God, how can this be possible?" A pallid Peter whispered. "Are we hallucinating?"

Robert laughed. "No mate, you are awake and sane. This is real."

They couldn't help just staring at him.

Understanding their apprehension, Robert said, "I think we will all be more comfortable if we sit down."

Giving each other a dumbfounded look, they followed Robert to a nearby tree and sat down on the boulders. They felt a bit better once they had settled themselves on the stones and had a drink of water.

Robert smiled at JR, "it is good to see you again, my friend."

JR nodded, not trusting himself to speak.

"Well, where to begin?" he paused. "It's as I told you last night, there is Eighth Cycle technology here that remained hidden from our expeditions.

"At the end of the Eighth Cycle, a few of the inhabitants that weren't killed by the Beast put themselves into what they call the deep sleep."

"Why didn't we see them when we were here?" JR asked suspiciously.

"Because they didn't know who we were, what time they were in, and quite frankly, they didn't trust us. Brideaux's actions almost prevented them from re-animating me. Can you blame them for not wanting to make contact with savages like that?"

JR shook his head. "No, I guess not."

Peter, scanning their surroundings asked, "Where are

they now?"

"They are waiting inside to meet you. They are friendly, I assure you. Will you come inside with me?"

JR stared Robert in the eye for a long moment. "Tell me this isn't a trap."

Holding his gaze steadily Robert replied, "I promise you, this is not a trap of any kind, and none of you are in danger of being harmed in any way. If you want, you can leave now, and we won't bother you again."

"JR, I don't like this. Let's get the hell outta here," Peter said.

Still looking Robert straight in the eye JR paused a moment longer, then, "I believe him. I'm going inside."

"So, do I," Rebecca chimed in. "This man is Robert Cartwright. I trust him."

"JR, Rebecca!"

JR and Rebecca stood and turned to look at Peter. JR said, "we'll understand if you prefer to stay here and wait for us…"

Peter froze, muttered something that sounded like 'live to regret this' and then reluctantly nodded. "I trust the two of you. If you believe him and trust him, then I'll go with you."

"Excellent!" Robert replied. "Siasha and Korda will be delighted. They have prepared a special meal for the occasion!"

Peter and JR looked at each other again as they followed Robert to the entrance of the installation.

Robert opened the door to the lift for them and looked at JR, smiling.

"Hang on Robert," JR said. He pulled Rebecca close to him and put his arms around her. "Becky hold on to me tight. This is the lift I have never told you about... it's one of the scariest experiences I ever had."

Rebecca put her arms around JR, looked up and smiled bravely, "I'm in the safest place possible."

"Peter, buddy," JR said, "hang onto your skivvies."

Despite JR's attempts to prepare them for the ride, none of them, including JR, were prepared as the earth suddenly seemed to have disappeared below their feet. Their earsplitting screams caught up with them only when the lift slowed down and stopped.

"Rebecca, you look like a kangaroo joey in his mother's pouch," Robert said as tears of laughter streamed down his cheeks.

Peter was trying to hold onto the metallic wall but found nothing to hold onto that would keep him upright. He slowly slumped to the floor and let out a sigh.

"I am never going back in that thing. Ever." Peter said emphatically the moment he crawled out of the lift.

"Well, that means you will spend the rest of your life down here then," Robert chuckled.

"Then I will volunteer for reanimation here and now. Kill me, take my body out, and reanimate me. Just don't ever make me ride in that thing again."

"Don't worry, Peter," JR said. "It gets better over time."

"Nah, not for me it won't."

Rebeca was still speechless and shaking.

It took a few minutes to get the party moving again.

Chapter Eighty-Eight

HOW MUCH TIME DO WE HAVE?

It felt weird to know that their hosts Linkola, Korda, and Siasha were more than sixty-thousand years old. But Robert was right, they were nice, friendly and looked every bit as human as Robert and the three of them. At first, both sides experienced some uneasiness, but as their conversation progressed JR, Rebecca, and Peter, as well as their hosts, started relaxing.

The first mindbender for the guests was the translator. Robert supplied each of them with a device and told them to hang it around their necks. They were stunned at how seamless the devices translated back and forth once they started speaking.

Siasha and Korda invited them to have dinner. Robert explained that the food was probably going to taste weird but assured them that it was absolutely safe to eat. "It is made from rations, which were stockpiled in this facility sixty-thousand years ago. There's enough food in storage to feed one hundred people for more than five years."

As if by prior agreement JR, Rebecca, and Peter waited

until they saw each of the hosts dig into their food before they tried it. Their hosts gazed at them inquisitively after they took the first bite.

"Hmm... strange taste," Rebecca said politely.

JR was a bit more direct. "Army rations."

Peter smiled. "What can I say... interesting... sort of... old."

Robert laughed. "You are too modest. All of us here think it tastes horrible, but we have been eating it for so long our taste buds have been numbed."

That little interlude broke the ice and they all started laughing.

After dinner, the three guests were taken on a tour of the facility and to say they were overwhelmed would have been a gross understatement.

Rebecca had to be torn away from the medical lab; there was just too much she wanted to know and understand, questions, questions, and more questions.

"Come on Becky," JR spurred her on, "we have to move on to the Data Center, we need to see what this danger is Robert is talking about."

Linkola and Siasha promised that they were both more than happy to return and answer all Rebecca's questions after the visit to the Data Center.

Peter remained very quiet, asking few questions, and shaking his head in astonishment with the 'deer-in-the-headlight' look most of the time.

The reanimation process, the end of the Eighth Cycle, the L'gundo, the B'ran, their history, the emergence of the Re'an and their plans ... it was overwhelming.

"But, how did you know where to find me?" JR asked the question that had been on his mind since Robert appeared the night before. "How did you do it, Robert? You didn't even know about Raven Rock or its location."

Robert grinned. "We discovered your laser communications system and tapped into it…"

"What!" Both JR and Peter shouted.

"You were able to crack the impenetrable laser system? No way…" JR whispered. His face has turned pale. "If you can do it…"

"No one else can, JR. Relax," Robert interjected. "I can assure you; no one else can, it's still impervious. Our technology here is the only way it can be done. We've been monitoring your system for any breaches. There have been none."

JR was not entirely convinced but decided to let it go for now.

"So, when we decided it was time to contact you, we only had to track down your mirror satellite phone signal and send the hologram image."

"You know that you'll have to explain how you did that to Raj and Roy," JR said.

"Happy to do that," Robert smiled. "I miss those two geeks. Hell, I miss all of you."

They arrived at the Data Center and Robert began the presentation.

JR, Rebecca, and Peter all became aware of the sudden change in Robert's demeanor. It was as if the good-humored Robert had remained outside the room when they entered. The man in front of them was assertive, military like, humorless, and to the point.

Rebecca leaned over and whispered to JR and Peter, "he's Tawndo now."

They stared at her in confusion but then both slowly nodded as they understood that what they were now seeing was the Tawndo part of Robert.

With military precision Tawndo, the general, stepped them through the information which he had gathered since his reanimation... and his presentation petrified them.

"For decades, The Re'an, based at the Tunguska site, have been building an army with the sole purpose of conquering the world.

"So far I've been able to confirm one thousand seven hundred soldiers. They have stored another two-thousand in deep sleep, which they have recently started waking up and training."

"That's only three-thousand-seven-hundred soldiers. They can't achieve much with that. Depleted and ramshackle as the US military are at the moment they will run over them during a tea break," JR stated.

Tawndo paused for a moment. "Before you send out your military, do yourself a favor and consider the following:

"The B'ran scientists have killed, re-animated, and enhanced people, thus creating super soldiers with immensely augmented anatomy, senses, intelligence, strength, endurance, vision, hearing, and much more.

"These are 'Super Soldiers,' equipped with technologically superior weapons. Particle-beam weapons that emit high-energy beams of subatomic particles that damage or destroy targets by disrupting the atomic and molecular structure. Depending on the power setting of the weapon it can vaporize targets in the blink of any eye.

"Their soldiers are all equipped with short-range particle beam weapons which would be effective up to a mile or more. They also have long range versions of these weapons that could take out targets in the air and on land—some of them can destroy targets thousands of miles away.

"Their soldiers are protected with lightweight liquid

body armor that doesn't restrict movement at all but will protect them against projectiles fired by any handgun or rifle in use in the Eleventh Cycle."

"There is much more I can add, but I think you get the idea. Each of these soldiers becomes a one-man army that can easily overcome odds of up to a hundred to one in any battle."

"Oh, my God!" Peter exclaimed. "We're screwed. Again."

JR was staring into blank space, his mind working overtime. Everyone was quiet. Their hosts watched their guests carefully as they absorbed the information they'd just received.

Then Linkola spoke softly, almost whispering. "We can't stop them by ourselves. That's why we made contact. We're hoping that we can work together to stop them. We have the technology, and we understand theirs, you have the people."

"How much time do we have?" JR asked.

"I can't be precise, but I can tell you they are mobilizing. Their first target is this facility. This was the Eighth Cycle Head Quarters. From here they will probably launch their attack, first on your country then the rest of the world." Tawndo replied solemnly.

JR stood, and checked his watch, it was 4am. "We need to get back to D.C. and talk to Daniel."

Despite Peter's protestations, he was bundled back into the lift and told that the safety of the world was more important than his phobia.

Shortly after 5am they were outside the facility again. As they headed for the rendezvous, JR pulled out his satellite phone and contacted the helicopter tour operator asking him to come pick them up.

By 8am Peter had the Baron 58 at full throttle, lifting off from Page en route to D.C.

JR called Sam and gave him their ETA.

Sam was immediately on high alert. "I thought you and Rebecca needed some time alone. Why are you coming back so soon? Trouble in paradise JR?"

"Trouble, yes. But not between Becky and me. Can't tell you more. But can you please arrange a meeting with the Rossler Foundation leadership for immediately after our arrival. Daniel must be present. I don't care what his schedule is; he has to clear it; make sure he's there."

Sam tried to coax more details out of JR, but he refused to say anything more than, "Just make sure Daniel and the rest of the Rossler Leadership are there and no one else."

After the call, he turned to Robert and said, "Okay, now we have about eight hours to prepare how we're going to break the news of this looming Charlie Foxtrot to them… oh, and explain the fact that you're alive."

Next in the Rossler Foundation Mysteries Series

vinci-books.com/termination

The Rossler Foundation must face their darkest hour yet in *Termination*.

As newly-elected Daniel Rossler assumes the presidency, the Russians seize the opportunity to pursue global domination. However, an even greater danger looms on the horizon—the Re'an, remnants of the Eighth Cycle, who have been secretly cultivating a race of superhumans to seize control of the planet. With billions of lives at stake, the Rossler Foundation faces its most formidable adversary yet.

Turn the page for a free preview…

Termination: Chapter One

Onboard the Itinerant en route to the Chukchi Sea

Captain Timothy Marcus was in his cabin aboard the Itinerant—a small, one of a kind, but extremely efficient, rescue submarine, discussing possible scenarios with the Rescue Team Leader Karl Dunlap and his Second-In-Command, Michael Sommers.

Karl, a former Navy Seal, stood just over six feet tall, had dark hair he kept cut to military standards, hazel eyes, a trim, fit body, and a firm-set jaw. He was a straight shooting, no nonsense type guy that could be counted on to get the job done, irrespective of how challenging the circumstances.

Former Coast Guard Rescue Swimmer Michael Sommers was the opposite of Karl in nearly every way. Standing five-eight, his well-muscled body moved with the grace of a dancer, his round, boyish face and twinkling blue eyes made his unruly blond curls an endearment rather than an eyesore, and his outgoing personality meant he knew no strangers and had few enemies.

Though very different, Marcus knew that both men were dedicated professionals who would give everything they had, and then some, to save lives and complete a mission successfully. That was why he included them on this mission, the Itinerant's first.

She was a brand-new, uniquely designed and built research and rescue submarine, developed privately in combination with Woods Hole Oceanographic Institute, Massachusetts Institute of Technology, and Ben Johnson, a Navy Admiral working on this project in his own time.

For this mission, due to the urgency, the Itinerant was not yet fully set up with all the research equipment she would eventually carry. She had, however passed her sea trials and was capable of a rescue mission. What remained to be seen was if she was suitable for *this* mission. However, it was a risk they had to take; there was no other marine rescue vehicle that could even attempt to undertake this mission.

Admiral Johnson met with Marcus the day before, advising that the navy had a sub in trouble and requested help. His thoughts returned to the conversation.

"I'm more than a little surprised you're bringing this to me, Ben. Why isn't the Navy responding to aid one of their own?"

Johnson sighed. "What I'm about to tell you is beyond top-secret. Aside from our late President Campbell, our current President Daniel Rossler, Secretary of Defense Willis, and myself, no one knows about her mission. So, before I go any further, I need your word that this information won't leave this office – need-to-know and face-to-face only."

Marcus whistled quietly and leaned back in his chair. "It must be some mission."

"It is. The lives of everyone on the sub, and anyone who goes after her, are at risk if word of the mission gets out. Are you with me?"

Marcus nodded slowly. "I understand. You have my word that I'll keep it secret, and you've got your rescue sub."

"All right let me bring you up to speed. As you know, Brideaux and his council members disappeared before they could be transferred to the Navy's Joint Regional Correctional Facility in Chesapeake, Virginia where they were to be held pending trial."

"Bloody brilliant!" Marcus interrupted; his British accent thick in his excitement. "They're on that sub!"

Johnson smiled and nodded. There was a reason the man had risen through the ranks of the Royal Navy so quickly. "That's correct. Several hours before the planned move, President Campbell ordered the prisoners secretly transferred to the *USS Trepang*."

Marcus frowned. "Wait, you don't have a sub designated 'Trepang' anymore. There have only been two – a Balao Class during World War Two, and a Sturgeon Class that was decommissioned in 2000."

This guy is sharp. I like it. "Right again. The name is part of the security measures—a decoy. She's actually one of our Virginia class subs under the command of Captain Reese Locklin.

"Captain Locklin's orders were to proceed under the polar ice cap to Bangor Naval Base in Washington State, where the prisoners were to be secretly transferred to the Northwest Joint Regional Correctional Facility near Fort Lewis.

"While she was under the ice cap, we lost contact with her. Earlier today, she made contact, advising there was an incident, and they have sustained some damage."

"Not good," Marcus said with a frown of concern.

"No, it isn't," Johnson replied, placing a map on the desk. "She's here, making repairs," he said, placing his index finger on the coordinates on the map.

"The Chukchi Sea over the continental shelf – any sign of the Russians?" Marcus asked.

"Nothing definite, only a couple of intermittent blips on a damaged sonar is all they've reported so far."

"But you can bet they're out there."

"Definitely."

"Yeah, they're lurking out there somewhere."

Marcus was brought out of his reverie when he realized Michael was waving a hand before his face.

"Knock, knock. Anybody home? Marcus, buddy, you there?"

"Yeah, yeah, I'm here. Sorry, got sidetracked."

"Sonya just reported a contact on the sonar—could be our sub."

"Great! Let's go see!"

Onboard the USS Trepang in the Chukchi Sea

"But Captain, you really should be in bed resting! Your knee is in no shape for you to be moving about."

"Corpsman Gibbs, I am still Captain of this boat, and it is *my* knee, therefore I will move about *my* boat with *my* knee as I see fit—with or without your assistance. Is that clear?"

Captain Reese Locklin was not a man to second guess. He was an outstanding leader, a tough but fair man, respected by his subordinates and superiors alike – and he ran a tight ship. His reputation as the best captain in the fleet was well earned.

"Yes, sir," Gibbs said dejectedly.

"Good. Then do what you have to but get me to the control room."

Gibbs prepared and delivered a morphine injection before assisting the Captain to a seat in the control room and making him as comfortable as possible.

"Thank you, Gibbs!"

Saluting, Gibbs replied, "You're welcome, sir!"

"Sonar, report. Any more of those intermittent blips?"

"Aye, sir. A few minutes ago—off to starboard, and we have a new contact just coming into range from astern."

"Is the stern contact steady?"

"Aye, sir, and moving straight for us."

"Could be the Itinerant. Keep an eye on it for the signal."

"Aye, sir."

Locklin picked up his hand mic, changed the communication dial setting to 'Trunk', and thumbed the mic switch.

"Has Lieutenant Larson come back aboard yet?"

"Aye, sir. We're draining the trunk now."

"Very good. As soon as he is able, have him report to me in the control room."

"Aye, sir!"

Within fifteen minutes, a still damp Lieutenant Gary Larson stood before the Captain.

"The last of the repair crew just came aboard, sir," he reported. "We've done as much as we can. We can be underway as soon as you give the word."

"Can she make it to Bangor?" Locklin asked.

"It won't be a fun trip, but as long as nothing else happens, I believe she can."

"The Bering Strait is fairly shallow. Normally it isn't a problem, but in our current condition, I'm concerned it could still be a bit of a challenge. Do we have enough control to stay shallow?"

"As with getting here, it will take a team effort, but we have the finest helmsmen in the Navy, they'll get us through!" Larson replied.

"Fair enough. As you know, my Executive Officer was killed by Brideaux. I'm promoting you to acting XO for the duration of this mission."

Larson suppressed a grin. "I'm honored, sir, thank you!"

Locklin let his steely gaze scrutinize the man. "Thank me later, Larson. Others will tell you that serving as my XO is no picnic. I'm not the easiest person to get along with, and I hold my XO to a higher standard than the rest of the crew."

Larson knew Captain Locklin was tough as nails, but he also knew the man cared deeply about the men on his crew. Serving Locklin didn't bother him. However, taking on the XO position meant he was the second-in-command. He would be responsible for administration, maintenance, and logistics, freeing Locklin to concentrate on tactical and operational matters. It also meant if Locklin was unable to perform his duties as commander, he would be in command, and he wasn't sure he was ready for that kind of responsibility yet. But his captain was in pain, their boat was in trouble, the crew was in danger, and he was an officer. Captain Locklin had confidence in him. He was not going to disappoint this fine man. Larson swallowed hard and replied, "Yes, sir."

"Captain!" the sonar officer interrupted excitedly. "The stern contact is maneuvering according to the signal pattern as she approaches!"

"It's about time something went right! Send the response ping sequence as required. Stations everyone! Set course for the Bering Strait, best speed."

"Aye, Captain!" came a chorus of excited voices.

Grab your copy...
vinci-books.com/termination

About the Author

JC Ryan is a bestselling author renowned for his intricate espionage, archaeological thrillers, and conspiracy mysteries. With over 30 acclaimed novels, including the popular Rex Dalton K9 Thrillers, Rossler Foundation Mysteries, and Carter Devereux Mystery Thrillers, Ryan has captivated readers around the globe.

Drawing from his diverse professional background—as a military officer, lawyer, and IT manager—Ryan creates compelling narratives that skillfully blend historical accuracy with thrilling adventure. He is celebrated as a master storyteller, known for crafting riveting plots, meticulous historical details, and engaging, multidimensional characters. Ryan's meticulous research lends authenticity and depth to each story, immersing readers in richly constructed worlds filled with intrigue, suspense, and adventure.

Fans of David Baldacci, Lee Child's Jack Reacher, Tom Clancy's Jack Ryan, Nelson DeMille's John Corey, Vince Flynn's Mitch Rapp, Mark Greaney's Gray Man, Gregg Hurwitz's Orphan X, Robert Ludlum's Jason Bourne, Daniel Silva's Gabriel Allon, Brad Taylor's Pike Logan, Brad Thor's Scot Harvath, James Rollins' Sigma Force, Steve Berry's Cotton Malone, and Dan Brown's Robert Langdon will find JC Ryan's novels equally compelling and unforgettable.

When not writing, Ryan enjoys spending time with his college sweetheart, whom he married in 1978. They are proud parents of two daughters, have two sons-in-law, and are grandparents to two grandchildren.

www.ingramcontent.com/pod-product-compliance
Ingram Content Group UK Ltd.
Pitfield, Milton Keynes, MK11 3LW, UK
UKHW020043211025
464173UK00003B/74